BOY, FALLING

JENNY JAECKEL

Black Rose Writing | Texas

©2021 by Jenny Jaeckel
All rights reserved. No part of this book may be reproduced, stored in a retrieval system or transmitted in any form or by any means without the prior written permission of the publishers, except by a reviewer who may quote brief passages in a review to be printed in a newspaper, magazine or journal.

The author grants the final approval for this literary material.

First printing

This is a work of fiction. Names, characters, businesses, places, events, and incidents are either the products of the author's imagination or used in a fictitious manner. Any resemblance to actual persons, living or dead, or actual events is purely coincidental.

ISBN: 978-1-68433-719-4
PUBLISHED BY BLACK ROSE WRITING
www.blackrosewriting.com

Printed in the United States of America
Suggested Retail Price (SRP) $19.95

Boy, Falling is printed in Jensen

*As a planet-friendly publisher, Black Rose Writing does its best to eliminate unnecessary waste to reduce paper usage and energy costs, while never compromising the reading experience. As a result, the final word count vs. page count may not meet common expectations.

Praise for
Boy, Falling

"*Boy, Falling* reads like a river, through time and across geography, sweeping us up in a story whose current is love, and not just romantic love—though there's plenty of that, and heartache, and sorrow—but the life-sustaining love between friends and flowing through generations of family. It's a beautiful novel, brimming with warmth, a pleasure to read."

—Anne Flemming, author of *Anomaly*

"Across three cities and generations, Jaeckel draws a vivid portrayal of family divisions and reunions, caught in the struggle between society's expectations and the transformative calling of art. A deeply moving and perceptive novel of remarkable breadth."

—Vanessa Winn, author of *The Chief Factor's Daughter*

"Captivating! A timeless journey of hardship and perseverance that pulls you in and doesn't let go until the last page. A must read!"

—Kat Flannery, author of *The Branded Trilogy*

"Both lyrical and stirring, *Boy, Falling* is a richly layered narrative that celebrates family, origins, and the beauty of the authentic self. Jaeckel gets to the heart of what it means to be human and reminds the reader that every one of us is worthy of finding true happiness."

—Christina Consolino, author of *Rewrite the Stars*

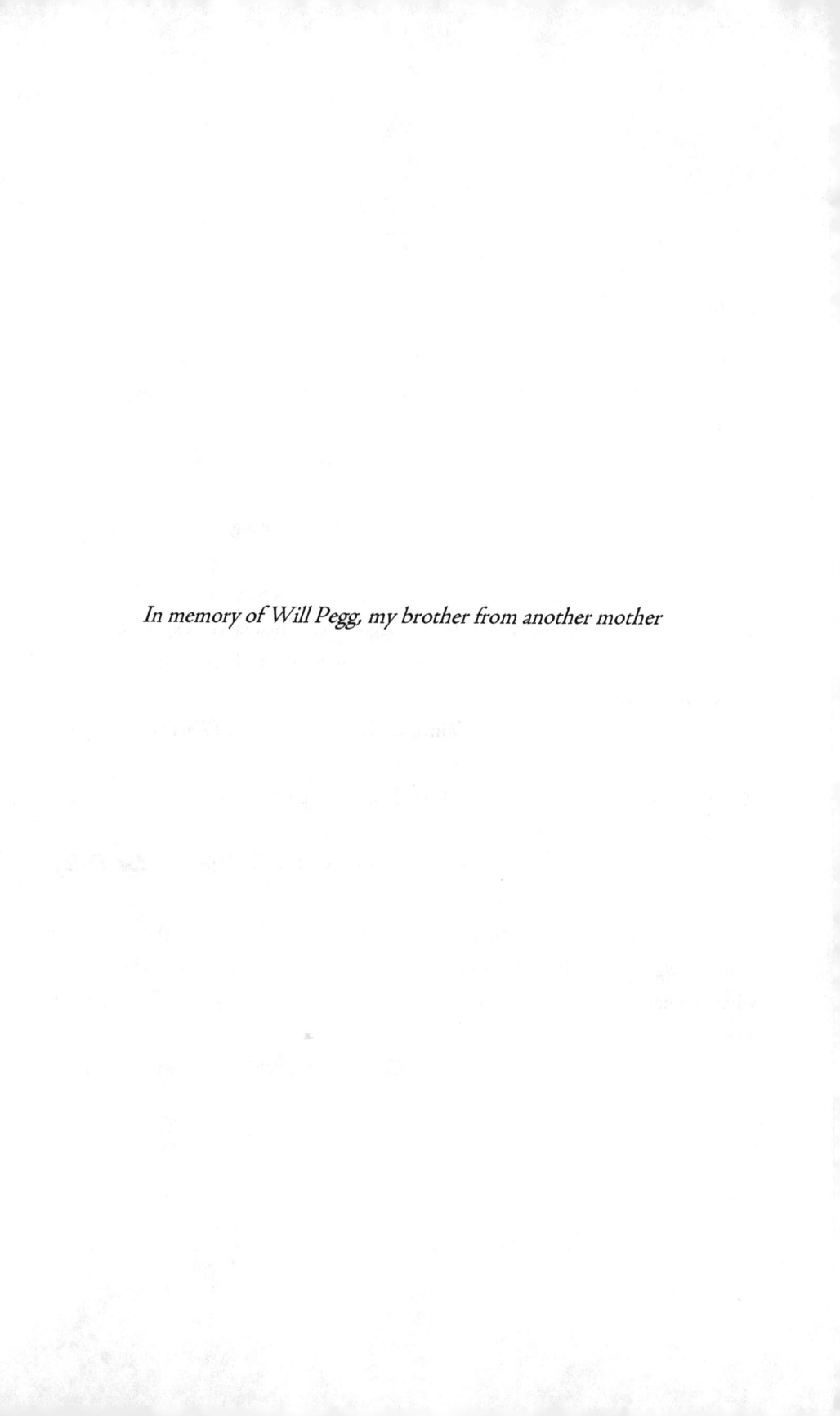

In memory of Will Pegg, my brother from another mother

For Josué + Anastasia,
please forgive any typos in
this copy — it's a first printing.
Very much hope you
enjoy!

♡ Jenny
feb. 2023

BOY, FALLING

Part 1
Gerard

Prologue

He has been falling for a long time. It seems as though he has always been falling, weightless and through the dark, though there is a single, faint shaft of light coming from somewhere, up there.

He sings a little song to himself, a counting song his mother taught him when he was little, before he started school. He holds out his fingers… Here is Mama, here is Papa, here am I, here is Brother, and here is the Fat Man… He always imagined that the Fat Man was a baker, though the song never said so.

He can tell he's falling and not just floating, because he can sense the air moving past his face, tiny fingers of it tickling at his eyelashes, the faintest rush at his ears. Where is Mama? Where is Papa? Where is Brother? Where am I? He is all alone.

He hears a voice.

Son.

Then he feels arms, he has fallen into a pair of strong arms, which hug him to a broad, warm chest. He leans his head against the familiar shoulder, winds his arms around the neck. The falling had been so lonely.

"Who are you?" the boy asks.

"Don't you know me?"

"Grand Papa!"

He can see Grand Papa's face now, because the shaft of light falls on it making shadows of the grooves of time carved deep, and illuminating the pillowy, silver-white sideburns burning bright against the weathered, dark cheeks.

They both look up, to the tiny patch of light, high up and far away. The boy points.

"I came from up there."

"Yes, Son, you did."

Hand in hand they walk.

"I haven't seen you in a long time, Grand Papa," says the boy.

"Did you miss me?"

"Yes."

"It's nice to be together now, isn't it?"

It is very nice. The boy hugs the hand and leans into the arm. He feels Grand Papa's voice resonate in his chest like the low strings on Papa's guitar.

"Where are we going?"

"Oh, places," says Grand Papa. *"We have lots of places to go."*

✦ ✦ ✦ ✦ ✦

Gerard opens his eyes to the blue light of dawn, and swallows against his parched throat. The dream again. He rubs his eyes with the heels of his hands, strips the sheet off his naked body and sits up, remembering. The curtain, sunset-colored voile, flutters at the open window, letting in the tepid air of the Parisian summer dawn, the metallic tang of the Seine, traces of fermenting fruit, the noises of the street coming to life. He reaches for his music composition book where he has left it on the nightstand and grasps his fountain pen with his long brown fingers. The dream lingers in the faint strains of a melody, and he's got to get them down before they're gone.

Montreal, 1895

"Tra-la, tra-la!" Gerard clapped his small hands together and sang. He danced in circles all around the kitchen, "Tra-la, tra-la!"

Mama's footsteps creaked the floorboards behind him as she stood at the stove. He heard the sizzle of oil in a great cauldron high overhead, the plop of dough into it from her spoon and the hiss of the cakes expanding full of air. Papa had thought that vanity cakes were too girlish for a boy's party but Mama waved him off.

"He's barely more than a baby," she said, though Gerard knew it wasn't true. He was a boy, and big, four years old!

"Tra-la! Tra-la! Tra-la!"

Sarai had turned seven on her last birthday and she'd had vanity cakes, and Gerard longed to have everything that she did; she was to him so wise and beautiful, so perfect.

The pile of fried cakes grew, draining oil onto paper on the sideboard—no telling how many of the relatives might stop by—and Mama's heels tapped heavily to and fro. Her apron strings didn't dangle down her back as they used to, but just made a little carnation where they came together. Her belly had grown so big Gerard no longer fit on her lap and had to hug her knee instead when she sat down.

But all of that was yesterday. The party had been grand, so many people bending down to Gerard's height to congratulate him and shake his hand, and he'd eaten so many cakes he was a little ill at bedtime. And though he'd protested when Papa laid him down—he still hadn't mastered the colorful new spinning top with a string he'd been given as a present—he went right off to sleep, even before Papa tucked in the blankets.

Now it was early morning, quiet and cold.

Gerard pressed his nose to the cold glass of the parlor window and made a fog on the pane. There were white patches on the ground outside, and brown ones where the snow had melted. Sarai sat next to him in her nightdress with her hands folded on her lap, hushed and serious because Papa had come into their bedroom to tell them that Mama had given them a new baby sister. She had arrived in the night while the children slept, and Papa left them in the parlor a moment while he went to check on Mama to see if she was ready for the children to come in.

The curtains were drawn closed in their parents' bedroom, but a coal fire was burning on the hearth and it made enough glow to see by. Sarai and Gerard tiptoed to the side of the bed where Mama sat with the new baby, whose name was Elizabeth, after Papa's mother, Grand Mama Rougeaux, who had died a very long time ago. The baby did not look like an Elizabeth. She looked like a tiny, sleeping doll, with eyes sealed shut like a kitten's, breathing through two little flared nostrils. Mama said they would call her Betsy, and Sarai smiled and said Betsy was a pretty name and a good name for a sister, and Gerard nodded, thinking, *Yes, yes! Betsy is the goodest name.*

After a few minutes, Papa took Sarai and Gerard away into the kitchen, gave them their breakfast, and then disappeared back into the bedroom.

"The baby grew inside Mama's belly," said Sarai, spooning up some porridge.

"In Mama's belly?" asked Gerard. This was something new. He looked at the pat of yellow butter, melting into the milk that lay on top of his porridge.

"Babies grow in their mamas' bellies," Sarai said. "Then when they get big enough they come out. Like with Tippet."

Gerard remembered Tippet's puppies from last spring, out in the shed in a crate with an old blanket in it. There were six of them and they squirmed over Tippet's belly looking for milk. In the summer, when the puppies were big and fluffy and romped in the garden, they'd all been given away.

"But we won't give Betsy away," Gerard said.

"No," said Sarai. "She's our sister now." Sarai took another mouthful of porridge, swinging her legs under the table. "I grew in Mama's belly, too," she said. "Mama told me I kicked so much she thought I'd come out running."

"Yeah," said Gerard. Sarai was indeed a fast runner.

"But you didn't grow in Mama's belly," she said.

Gerard looked at her, spoon frozen in the air. "Huh?"

"You didn't grow in Mama's belly," Sarai said again.

"Yes, I did."

"No, sir," said Sarai. "You didn't. A lady brought you from Toronto. A *white* lady."

"You lie!" Gerard burst into tears.

He sobbed so loud Papa came running into the kitchen and scooped him up.

"What's this about?" he demanded, looking sternly at Sarai. She ducked her head and looked up with wide eyes.

"She said I'nt grow in Mama's belly," Gerard hiccupped through his tears.

"The *white* lady brought him," Sarai whispered, and Gerard wailed louder.

"Hush, son," Papa said. "There's nothing to cry over."

Gerard waited for Papa to deny what Sarai had said, and when he didn't, Gerard renewed his wailing. "I want to grow in Mama's belly," he yelled, clinging to Papa's neck.

Papa sat down in the chair, patting him on the back until he quieted down. "Cat's out of the bag now," Papa sighed. "Good Lord…"

He was quiet a long time, then he put Gerard back in his chair and leaned on the table with his big fingers laced together. "Listen," he said to Gerard, "it's as your sister says. A white lady brought you from Toronto when you were a baby because you needed a family. Orphans are children that need families, and you were an orphan." He held up a finger when Gerard started to cry again. "Don't cry anymore now, there's nothing wrong with being an orphan. Your cousin George was an orphan too. You are our baby just as much, Son."

"I'nt a baby," Gerard said, swallowing at the lump in his throat.

"No, you're a big chap now."

"I'm not crying," he said, his face smeared with mucus and tears. Papa dabbed at him with his handkerchief.

"No, not anymore." Papa looked at Sarai. "What do you have to say for yourself?"

"Sorry Papa," said Sarai. She looked at her brother. "Sorry, Gera."

She had done something wrong, had hurt Gerard's feelings. He still felt stung, and a little righteous that Papa had scolded her.

"There's nothing wrong with being an orphan," Papa said again, but Gerard wasn't completely reassured. Rather he was chilled, and as if a pane of glass had appeared between Papa and himself.

All day, all week, and in the months to come, he pondered the mysterious arrival of babies. First there was no Betsy, and then there was Betsy, come to stay forever. Babies could be gotten in two ways, three if you counted the Stork, or four if you got found inside a cabbage. But mostly babies grew inside the mamas' bellies. He knew that now, thanks to his big sister. From time to time other new babies appeared in the homes of relatives or neighbors. If he got a chance, Gerard always asked if they had got it from the White Lady. When he found that the question caused some consternation among the grownups he whispered it to the other children on the sly, but to his disappointment the answer was always no.

The White Lady remained a mysterious phantom, something between Santa Claus and the Bogey Man. As he got older, and understood more, he decided his real parents must be dead, that's what made an orphan. But what if they weren't? What if they were still alive somewhere in Toronto?

Once a family came from Toronto to visit relatives, and they all showed up in church—a mother, a father and three children. The congregation at their church was large and mostly white. Some dozen families like theirs had for years worshipped there, though confined to a small section of pews in the rear of the nave, and without the right to sit on church committees or hold any offices. The Rougeauxes might have filled a much smaller church all on their own. Papa had four brothers and sisters still living in Montreal, his father had had five, and between marriages and children, Gerard had too many cousins to count.

This new family from Toronto was introduced to the Rougeauxes, and others, as the Sawyers. Gerard watched them all throughout the service. Could it be that they were *his* family, come to secretly check on him? He stared so much the mother smiled at him. She was pretty and petite, with a fresh looking face and two plaits pinned like a crown on top of her head. Was that love in her smile? The father, whose woolen collar poked into his black sideburns, winked once in his direction. Then the youngest child, a girl in a red dress with white lace edges, stuck out her tongue at him.

Gerard jumped in his seat, hurriedly fixing his eyes on his own knees and then on Mama's hands as she held her prayer book, with their familiar, warm color. Mama had red tones in her dark complexion, like a garnet that appeared bottle brown until held up to the light, and for this Papa called her his *baccara rose*, an endearment that caused her to glow, even if she refused to smile. Papa himself was a dusky color, like tree bark in the twilight, set off by the starched, white collars he wore every day that bit at the edges of his jaw when he inclined his head over his workbench or the prayer book in church. Gerard's sisters—three of them now, as Betsy had been followed in a few years' time by Amelia—all had something of their mother's baccara rose, but tended toward Papa in color.

Gerard's own skin was lighter, as he was reminded in moments like these, sitting beside Mama and his sisters, trying hard to keep still through the service. It was an unfriendly reminder. That chill that sometimes bothered him now prickled him all over. No, he did not belong there with that family, the Sawyers. He didn't look like those children at all, though neither did he look much like his sisters. He riddled his fingers together and stared at them. "Whole lot of milk in that tea." That's what folks said of colored people whose complexions were light. "A drop" of milk in the tea was maybe said of Gerard, or a whole lot, might constitute a threat of the vilest kind, especially when that person was lighter than his parents. The chill now penetrated the back of his skull along with a brand-new thought—what if the White Lady was his mother?

Was he as light as all that? In truth, no. His difference to that of his family was not greatly marked. But what Gerard wouldn't have given to look more as they did. If only, by some magic, one could take a straw and suck out the single, cold, unwanted drop of milk that had spoilt him before he was even born. Even if the matter of his color, he knew, was hardly the only error contained within his skin.

Eleanor

Gerard could do a lot of things and was proud of it. He could run as fast as the fastest boys, and keep the hoop rolling with his stick far down the street, when they played. He could take Betsy to school, holding her little hand and lifting her over puddles, he could dress Amelia for Mama, help Papa chop wood out back and cut leather in the saddlery shop. Papa had even given him his own leather tool belt on his tenth birthday, though both Papa and Mama wanted Gerard and his sisters to focus their energies on their schooling,

By now Papa had expanded his shop, and these days produced more fine valises than saddles. He had three apprentices working under him, two young colored men and one white, who favored stiff collars similar to Papa's, and spoke his name in deferential voices. Mama, for her part, now had help in the house as well—a tall, serious girl who came weekly to help with the laundry and the garden, and another girl, plump and smiling, who beat the rugs out in the springtime and washed the windows in summer. Mama took care of the fine things herself, not trusting the children or the hired girls with dusting her gold-rimmed teacups or polishing the brasses, and certainly not with her bread baking, which had to be done as only Mama knew how. There was no bread that rivaled Mama's, loaves with crusts like golden shells that split with a ringing *crack* at mealtimes and spongy white insides that lent delicious sour notes to any soup or gravy they sopped up. Her pride was evident when Papa's apprentices, or others, sighed over the eating, even if, as with Papa, she did not smile easily.

The other, and perhaps most treasured source of family pride, lay in the playing of piano, and in this Gerard had always excelled. Though his family kept an upright well-tuned and polished in the front room, Gerard had been sent with

Sarai for three years to the home of their Uncle Albert for after school lessons with his cousins at their clangy old spinet. Uncle Albert had learned from Mémé, his grandmother, who had been Papa's grandmother too, and though many years of grueling hard work with the railroads had stiffened his fingers, he saw to it that his children, and their cousins, also learned. Uncle Albert's children, Elodie and Albert-Ross, suffered most. One hour of practice each per day.

Uncle Albert and Aunt Genevieve had a new baby now, Martine—gotten also without any visitation from the White Lady—whose big eyes grew even bigger when she watched someone playing the piano. Gerard made up a song just for her he called *Teeny Martine... Teeny Martine, no bigger than a bean, got the biggest eyes on her that you have ever seen...* and Uncle Albert nodded in approval when he played it. Learning the piano had always come easily for Gerard. It puzzled him that his cousins struggled with new pieces and sometimes said, when the adults were out of earshot, that they hated to practice, since to Gerard music was as delicious as his favorite blueberry pie. His fingers on the keys felt warm and agile, and while he played warmth pervaded him so fully that the dogged chill was banished completely.

✦ ✦ ✦ ✦ ✦

That summer all the family was in a flutter because Aunt Eleanor, the one who lived in New York City and was a musician, was coming back to Montreal for a visit after having been away for many years. Gerard had never met this mythical aunt, but his parents kept a box of picture postcards from her, sent from all over the world, on a top shelf of the armoire in their bedroom. He had seen it a number of times because Sarai liked to take it and dump the contents onto her bed and arrange the cards to match the squares on her quilt, examining the pictures and the foreign postmarks, and the messages scrawled elegantly in now-faded ink.

Papa's white-haired aunts organized a picnic by the Canal to celebrate Aunt Eleanor's visit, and Mama was nervous preparing to leave the house. She made Gerard change his shirt because of a stain he couldn't even see and sent Sarai to redo her plaits. Even Papa seemed on edge. He checked his tie in the hall mirror three times and reminded all the children to behave, as if they were going to the Easter service at church rather than a picnic with the family.

Gerard saw her from a distance at first, wearing a big mauve hat covered in crepe flowers. She cut a different kind of figure than the other aunts, he saw that right away, especially from up close. Her dress was of a more elegant variety, and though she was not at all stout, like Aunt Genevieve say, there was something weighty about her.

Papa said, "Son, meet your Aunt Eleanor."

"How do you do?" Gerard said.

"Very well, thank you," she said in a low, quiet tone. "It's so very nice to meet you." She didn't smile, didn't bend toward him, certainly didn't squish his face between her palms as Aunt Melody often did, but she looked keenly into his face as if searching for something. It was a curious moment for Gerard, and for a second he wondered if she knew he was an orphan. But just then he noticed a commotion from the cluster of his cousins who were fishing at the edge of the Canal. Someone yelled that Paul had caught a fish and Gerard ran off to join them, leaving the adults to talk among themselves.

✦ ✦ ✦ ✦ ✦

Gerard didn't think much about his new aunt until two days later when Papa came to get Gerard and Sarai from the back garden where Mama had sent them to bury the kitchen scraps.

"Well, you two," Papa said, "you're to have a special piano lesson with your Aunt Eleanor. What do you say to that?"

"Is she here right now?" Sarai asked, wiping her hands on her pinafore.

"No," Papa said, "I'm taking you over to Uncle Albert's."

When they arrived Aunt Genevieve ushered them into the front room where Aunt Eleanor was seated at the piano playing a Chopin nocturne, Gerard's cousins Elodie and Albert-Ross standing on either side of the bench in respectful observation. Uncle Albert, on the sofa on the other side of the small parlor, absently fingered his puffy, silver-white sideburns, watching the ceiling as if the notes of music fell from there.

After the nocturne, Aunt Eleanor had each of the four children sit beside her in turn to play. She listened and nodded, suggesting afterward how to hold their hands, when to emphasize and deemphasize the notes, changes in tempo, and then had them play once more. When it was Gerard's turn it was the same, but after he had played a second time, she picked out a short section and played it over herself.

"Listen to it this way," she said. The variation had a bouncy feeling to it, and it made Gerard feel bouncy too. "Can you try it like that?"

Gerard's fingers hopped like rabbits and almost made him laugh. When he finished he glanced up at her.

"Excellent," she said, with something of Mama's unsmiling glow.

"Gerard, play *Teeny Martine*," Elodie said, and the baby, across the room in Aunt Genvieve's arms, gave a shriek of excitement.

Aunt Eleanor laughed. "Go on, Gerard. I'd like to hear it too."

✦ ✦ ✦ ✦ ✦

In the next few weeks there were several more lessons with Aunt Eleanor and the cousins, with extra time at the end of each just for Gerard. The others were happy enough to stop when they did, though Sarai did ask Papa why Gerard's lesson was longer.

"Your Aunt Eleanor says you have a special aptitude," Papa said to Gerard.

"Haven't I got a special aptitude?" Sarai asked.

Papa sighed. "Perhaps not in just the same way."

And when Sarai frowned, Mama said, "Maybe it's alright if you aren't best at everything."

Special aptitude? It made him wonder. Gerard was sitting with Aunt Eleanor, running through his scales and arpeggios. He wondered again if she knew about his being an orphan, the old longing to know more popping up like a jack-in-the-box.

"Did you know I'm an orphan?" he asked abrubtly, his fingers keeping time on the keys. He glanced up at her face, catching a flicker of alarm. He remembered the puzzlement and unease his questions about the White Lady used to cause, years ago when he was too young to know better. The White Lady was no longer any kind of spirit, and he had disregarded her completely as his possible birth mother. He knew a pair of brothers from school with a colored father and white mother, and his comparison to their loose curls and pale skin gave him a trace of security against that possibility for himself.

But Aunt Eleanor said, "Yes, I did."

"Do you know where I came from?" He kept his eyes on the keyboard this time but saw the foot she'd been tapping on the floor freeze. The notes of the scales rattled against her silence and Gerard guessed that probably she didn't know. "I came from Toronto," he said, casually, showing her that he himself knew and that he wasn't bothered by it. "Papa told me."

She cleared her throat with a small sound. "I see."

"I want to go there one day and see what it's like," he said. He and Sarai had many times, when looking over the picture postcards, discussed the places they'd like to visit one day.

"That's a fine idea." She was keeping time with her foot again.

"I want to see New York too," Gerard said. "Mama told me you went there to study music, and that's how come we never met you before."

"That's right," Aunt Eleanor said, leaning an elbow on the edge of the piano. She rested her face against her hand. "Would you like to study music at school? When you're older?"

"That all depends," Gerard said. "Do they make you eat greens in music school? Because I hate greens."

She laughed. "When I was at music school I ate a lot of potato salad. And beans."

"Okay, then," he said, finishing the last scale. "Yes, I would like to go there."

✦ ✦ ✦ ✦ ✦

Gerard didn't think too long though about music school in the someday, far-off future. If he ever imagined himself grown, it was only vaguely. He'd wear a bowler hat like Papa's and he'd be free from ever again having to choke down Mama's bitter stewed greens—the ones she insisted kept winter pneumonia at bay. But he never lingered long on these things. He had arithmetic homework for school, potatoes to peel for Mama, games with his sisters and cousins, and all manner of chores to help Papa in the saddlery shop. And then there were the new music lessons that Aunt Eleanor paid for, with a series of teachers in a little basement room at the Grand Séminaire, that occupied the whole of his Tuesdays after school.

What free time Gerard had he spent outside with the other boys on the street, the ones Papa called *ruffians* from behind his newspaper, though Gerard heard him smiling. Papa didn't like for Gerard to be indoors too much, saying that a young man shouldn't be overly cloistered with the womenfolk, that he'd become *tainted*. That word made Gerard nothing short of ill, even if he hadn't a clear idea of what Papa meant. It was sinister, that was clear, and to be avoided, and its menace showed up in such unexpected places that Gerard grew to fear it might jump out from anywhere. He keenly remembered the day when he proudly brought Amelia in to breakfast one Sunday, having dressed her himself and made her especially pretty with a pair of Sarai's ribbons. Papa had lowered his newspaper and fixed him with a withering look, eyes bitterly cold, the corners of his mouth drawn down.

"Take your place at the table," he said to Gerard with pure ice in his voice.

Mama, hurrying to settle Amelia in her chair, held her lips pressed together, and Papa said to her, "Tilly, this is the last I'll tolerate."

Mama nodded with lowered eyes, and said to Gerard in a low voice, "Hurry up and eat now."

The porridge tasted like sand and stuck in his throat, and it was all he could do not to cry, sensing that tears would be the last thing needed to convict him fully of his mysterious crime.

But of the ruffians Papa approved, and Gerard was safe playing as they did, for a while, until such time as the confusion returned. One day one of the boys, Lucien from the sixth form—Gerard was in the fifth—said he'd seen an older girl cousin of his washing.

"No, you didn't," scoffed Olin Peters, one of the older boys of their gang. Lucien was known for making up stories.

"I did so," said Lucien, and described the gap between the curtain and the wall, the cousin naked from the waist up, bent over the basin. The *petticoats*. To Gerard's amazement the other boys groaned and laughed, as clearly this was astonishing. Coveted.

Olin gave an exaggerated yawn. "I've seen more than that."

"Like what," Lucien challenged.

"Ta-ta's."

The other boys screamed. Lucien had only seen his cousin from the back. When they demanded details, Olin said he'd seen the Desmond girls changing after swimming at the river the previous summer, when his older brother, for a joke, had shoved him into their tent. This had the boys rolling on the ground, writhing with laughter and pleasure, all except for Gerard, whose bafflement closed like water over his head.

He had always supposed himself to be just the same as these other boys, with the possible exception of the high, fancy piano lessons. But now it was clear they shared a powerful fascination of which, up to now, Gerard had been entirely unaware.

Now Lucien's words from a few weeks ago came back to him, on a day when Gerard had found a stone in the street with two thin white seams running through it forming a cross. He had run to show it to Olin.

"You follow him around like a puppy-dog," Lucien had said with clear disdain.

That had stopped Gerard in his tracks. He looked from Lucien to the stone in his palm and back again, shame spreading from his chest and into his guts.

"I don't," he said, suddenly knowing how true it was. He loved Olin. He had a funny mad craving for his attention and took every opportunity to get it, and now he saw, through Lucien's eyes, that this was just as despicable as dressing Amelia in ribbons.

To prove Lucien wrong he hurled the stone as hard as he could at a nearby house, and when the gesture was answered by the sound of breaking glass, Gerard took off running. All the boys ran.

Now, with the other boys moaning over visions of ta-ta's, Gerard had the equal urge to flee. Stammering an excuse, he ran. His swift feet carried him home through the damp streets and long shadows of the late afternoon, and by the time he'd reached the curb in front of his own house, where he sat hunched and panting, another notion had all but caught him. That he did understand that desire of those boys, but not for the bodies of women. His eyes squeezed shut by themselves, the chill coming over him in a sickening wave.

The only thing to do, once the initial horror had subsided, was to hide it away, under a solid rock of fiction. Gerard began joining in the greed-tinged laughter of his friends when the subject of girls came up, as it did more and more as time wore on. He carved the initials *E.L.* into the bark of a tree with his penknife when the boys lolled by the canal one day in spring, and protested in mock defense when his friends guessed, shouting, that it was Evelyn LeForte, the girl at school with whom he shared a desk. In fact, he liked Evelyn very much, even found her beautiful—with her intricately done-up plaits, curling lashes, and smile flashing white against her ebony skin—but his feelings, as if she were another sister, were nothing like the secret longing he still had for Olin.

But perhaps all that was needed was perseverance. Papa always said if one put his mind to a problem, *and* his effort, that that was the surest way to succeed. Gerard wrote Evelyn's name in cursive over and over in his composition book so that the pages began to resemble the slate board where his classmates wrote out their punishments: *I shall not speak out of turn*, a hundred times. One morning he even picked a bunch of daisies to give her, only to throw them in the gutter before reaching the school. He'd been told to persevere, but he'd also been told not to lie. Needles of truth came up through the surface of his days, stabbing at his fingers the way Sarai complained real needles did when she practiced her embroidery. Under the cloth, over which spread perfect vines and roses, bunches of violets and cherries looking ripe enough to eat, lurked the menacing glitter of sharp metal. Sarai yelped at these moments, startling Gerard from his homework and eliciting an equally biting reprimand from Mama who did not abide such *cavillations*.

Gerard began to fear anything that set him apart as different from his family, his schoolmates. He looked upon with dread any person who seemed to others to be strange. As for the cavillations forbidden by Mama, Gerard did not object when she sent him to the haberdashery several blocks from their home for more thread, or a packet of buttons, hair oil, pins or combs, though he dreaded the sight of the bachelor shopkeeper—a white man with an excessively waxed brick-colored mustache and nervous eyes. The shopkeeper's manner of speech and way of walking were unlike those of most men, and folks called him *funny*. Gerard had seen him steal quick glances at himself with a little mirror he kept in his apron pocket, when he thought no one was looking, which made Gerard wonder if he didn't have other, stranger habits. Surely, this was the kind of tainted person Papa warned of.

✦ ✦ ✦ ✦ ✦

Music, though, was a permissible difference, as his special aptitude was a good thing. But even with this Gerard wasn't always sure. One Sunday at church, after the choir had sung a few hymns to open the service, the choir director announced that they had a special guest. Miss Nancy Drake was a student at the Halifax Conservatory of Music, the director explained, and would bless them with an operatic piece. Never had he heard a human voice like this. It was angels. The sound flooded him, down from the top of his head and through to the soles of his feet. Turning away, he put his face in the crook of his elbow unable to keep tears from leaking from his eyes. Mama, sitting at his right, bent over him whispering.

"Son, what's wrong? Are you ill?"

He couldn't answer. He was thirteen now and practically a man. Shaking his head he willed himself to regain his composure and his breath. The congregation was so appreciative that Miss Drake accepted the director's request to perform once more at the closing of the service. Gerard, having a warning this time, begged Mama to let him go to the water closet when Miss Drake took the stage again. He ran down the aisle as the first notes assaulted him and then dove around the corner into the cloakroom, where he wept unseen among the coats.

He might have been ashamed of his tears, but he was too overcome with the beauty of Miss Drake's singing, the breaking of his heart. As if in answer to an unspoken plea, the very next day a letter arrived from Aunt Eleanor addressed to Papa and Mama. Though her letters arrived with regularity, bearing questions about Gerard's musical progress and the string of teachers, young or wizened, that kept him occupied on Tuesday afternoons in the basement of the Séminaire, this one inquired, for the first time, as to whether his interest in pursuing music in New York was serious.

"If he does choose to dedicate himself to this path," Papa read aloud from the letter in a subdued tone, standing with one elbow propped up beside the lamp on the parlor mantle, "he shall need to focus all the more: lessons twice weekly instead of once, daily practice of no less than two hours, coverage of specific masters and technique, which I myself could supervise via his teachers."

Gerard and Sarai were seated on the horsehair sofa, schoolbooks on their laps, while Betsy and Amelia played jacks near Papa's feet on the hearthstones, where they were allowed when no fire was lit. Gerard heard Mama busy in the kitchen and knew from Papa that she had read the letter already, earlier in the afternoon. He guessed she did not appear just now because she was displeased. Mama didn't like for people to go away.

Papa finished the letter and sighed, eyebrows raised, then fished inside the gray envelope, still elegant despite being battered with postmarks, and withdrew what looked like a newspaper clipping. This he unfolded and handed to Gerard, and Sarai leaned over to see. It was a page from the newsletter of the National Conservatory of Music of America, Aunt Eleanor's alma mater, which, at present, was still one of the few conservatories of music that accepted women, colored students, and even those from whom disease had taken the ability to walk or see. The article from the newsletter described a number of musicians and singers from the previous graduating class, who had secured employment with the Metropolitan Opera.

Opera... The memory of the angelic voice from the day before swelled in his ears, but with it came an anxiety. All that practice, more lessons, would set him apart from his sisters and cousins, friends, in a new way. He'd have less time to help with chores—at the shop, at the house—if his parents would allow it.

And what else would he lose?

His cousin Albert-Ross had been making extra money the last few years, playing piano here and there in the city's dance halls, to which Uncle Albert and Aunt Genevieve had agreed, so long as he promised not to consort in any way with the "low" girls who danced there. What Albert-Ross did bring home, besides pockets full of silver coins, was a growing cache of knowledge of new kinds of music, called *rags* and *habaneras*, that—though less powerfully than this new thing called *opera*—captured Gerard in their glittering snares. Albert-Ross taught these songs to Gerard, so long as Gerard went with him Saturday mornings to deliver cases of Uncle Albert's beer, brewed and bottled at home, to those same dance halls. While Albert-Ross laid the reins across his lap and cleaned his nails with a toothpick, Gerard had to jump down from the wagon and lug the wooden boxes inside, returning with boxes of empty bottles. Gerard had thought that he could do like Albert-Ross, when he got older, and that playing in the dance halls would make a man of him, and that he'd laugh like his cousin did when recounting stories of rough behavior, with his shoulders wide and relaxed, and all his teeth showing.

If Gerard lost all these things that anchored him, it would only be a prelude to the great fact that would dwarf them all: that he would leave Montreal, his home, altogether, and enter an entirely new world alone, a tiny cold fish in a vast, icy sea. He almost didn't want it. And he might have rejected the idea, had not the pull of the currents been so strong. Laid out on the surface it appeared as though he had a choice, a conceit that struck him as funny, quite nearly. He'd have as much luck stopping a river from running its course. Papa and Mama would accept his answer. Yes, he would go.

New York, 1909

The train sat on the tracks, coal-black and hulking, vibrating with a subterranean sound that shook Gerard's limbs inside the new woolen suit Mama had so carefully stitched. His three sisters were crying, half because they loved him and would miss him, he knew, and half because the others were crying. It wouldn't do to permit any tears for himself now, being eighteen, a man about to leave home for the strange land of New York City.

"Respect your Aunt and Uncle," Papa said, sounding as though the wind had been knocked out of him. Gerard nodded, an awful lump in his throat.

Sarai clung a moment to his lapels. "Do get me a Sears catalogue," she said through her tears. "As soon as you can. If I don't make Amelia a dress in time for her birthday she'll break." Sarai had plans to copy the clothing models. She was a wizard with sewing, better than Mama even, and she considered the styles in the Eaton's too archaic.

He laughed, which soothed the lump a little. "You know that's the first thing I'll do."

Gerard picked up the heavy valise Papa had made in his shop, and Mama's dinner basket snagged on the edges of his suit pockets when he shifted it in his arm. Tucked in the valise were two samplers embroidered by his sisters. One was a gift for the Higgins family and one was for him. Sarai had instructed him that he was to hang his beside his bedstead where he could read its message every night and every morning:

Dear Brother,
Though far you may roam,
Remember us here,
In your loving home.

Each of them had stitched her favorite flower below by way of signature: a purple aster for Sarai, a pink wild betony for Betsy, and a yellow tulip for Amelia.

The train whistle cut a cold streak in the air. Mama's face was dry-eyed but pained, her arms folded tight around her middle, even with Papa's arm, reassuring, around her shoulders. When Gerard kissed her goodbye she looked away. He told himself that the first letter he wrote would be to her, he would tell her not to worry about him, and he would sign the letter, *Your Loving Son.*

❖ ❖ ❖ ❖ ❖

Gerard slept for much of the journey, dozing and waking so that the scenery outside the dusty window and the jostling of passengers in the aisles intermingled with shreds of dreaming. In his mind his foreign Aunt Eleanor—called Nora by her husband, Gerard's Uncle Hig—was more his destination than the city. Besides himself, Aunt Nora was the only Rougeaux to leave the fold in Montreal, and she had done so at the same age as he was now, bound for her audition at the Conservatory, but all alone with no relatives to receive her. Of what tougher stuff than him she must have been made.

After her studies, in which she excelled, she and Uncle Hig toured Europe on and off for a decade, with an all-colored company called the Frangipani Orchestra—most of the picture postcards Gerard and Sarai used to play with had come from that time—and now the two ran their own music school, the Higgins Institute for Colored Musicians.

Stepping off the train onto the crowded platform, Gerard wandered in a daze with his valise and dinner basket, moving in the general direction that the other passengers from his train did. Then, just as he passed under the arches of the main hall he saw Aunt Nora striding toward him. She was so much shorter than he recalled—but of course she was!—dressed in indigo crepe, a fierceness about her manner Gerard hadn't quite remembered from before. Uncle Hig was as tall as Gerard was, but broad and gentle and smiling, the coat of his brown suit unbuttoned, revealing a comfortable middle. And then there was their little girl. Gerard didn't see her at first—only when, upon shaking Uncle Hig's hand, he looked down to see a pair of enormous black eyes peering up from the shadow cast by her mother. This was Jeannette, all of five years old and named for Aunt Nora's Conservatory mentor. Gerard crouched down on the concrete and took her little hand. She smiled. He loved her already.

From there it was a bee-line straight to the Higginses' piano.

"Show me what you can do," said Aunt Nora, briskly removing her gloves. Gerard glanced over at Jeannette. How she reminded him of his little cousin Martine with those big eyes... *Teeny Martine, no bigger than a bean...* He had half a mind to play that old song for starters.

"Nora, let the boy rest," said Uncle Hig, down on one knee by the door, helping Jeannette out of her summer coat. But Aunt Nora won out.

"I don't mind," Gerard said to Uncle Hig, seating himself on the green crushed velvet of the piano bench. He wasn't too tired, not after so much napping on the train. Jeannette's wide black eyes were glued to him still and he winked at her with a little smile. She hadn't said a word to him yet, and she threw her arms around her father's neck, burying her face in his upright collar, but not before Gerard thought he caught the trace of another smile back.

Working his hands and fingers to limber them, he lowered his eyes to the gleaming keys. He'd been working on a Beethoven sonata—Number 15 in D-Major—for just this moment and was proud of what he'd been able to do with it, but when he finished the piece Aunt Nora looked at the floor, shaking her head.

"Well, I expected better," she said, and sighed. "We've a lot of work to do."

His heart sank.

Uncle Hig put a hand on his shoulder. "It wasn't as bad as all that," he said. "She's got blasted high standards. But we'll get you up to it, don't worry."

✦ ✦ ✦ ✦ ✦

Aunt Nora turned that summer into army basic training, with herself as drill sergeant and Gerard the lone soldier. But no matter how hard-hitting her approach—quite different from the mild *bien*'s and *très bien*'s of his teachers in Montreal—he didn't resist. If an exercise proved difficult, a determined energy rose within him to meet it. Under Aunt Nora's gaze Gerard's fingers felt electric in a way they never had.

Into this compelling momentum, Jeannette crept stealthily each morning with her dolls, dancing them along the edges of the furniture in their ridiculous little frocks and yellow curls, tapping their patent leather feet on the Anatolian carpet. This day Aunt Nora had him reworking the Beethoven and when his energy flagged he paused to crack his knuckles and watch Jeannette. As soon as Aunt Nora left the room he bent toward his little cousin.

"You ever seen a windmill?" he whispered.

She nodded slightly, eyes growing even bigger, dolls frozen in the air.

Jumping off the bench he scooped her up and swung her in a circle, the dolls falling to the floor and Jeannette letting loose with the prettiest laugh. When he set her back down she hugged his legs, "Again!" And he obliged, until the Sergeant returned carrying a great sheaf of papers from the room they used as the Institute office, calling out instructions to Gerard. Administration for the music school was an unending task—not least, the seeking of patronage from the philanthropic upper classes—but Aunt Nora kept an ear attuned to Gerard's progress while she worked. "Don't *rush* it, for Heaven's sake," she called out on numerous occasions. And, "rushing again!"

Evenings after supper Aunt Nora all but booted Gerard out the door. "Go and see something," she barked, slamming the door in his face. Perhaps she sensed his hesitation. Inwardly he still shrank before the face of the big, hungry city where he knew not one soul outside the Higgins home, but he did find that every time it was easier.

Harlem, he found, was home to a mix of peoples not entirely unfamiliar: Italians leaning out of their shops and apartment windows, yelling at neighbors, Jewish folks in their native tongues doing the same, wafting smells of cooking mixing with that of horse dung from the streets. There were no Québécois of course, hurling their French around every corner, but there were colored people. So many more colored people than he had ever seen, and this was striking, particularly on certain streets, certain blocks, so many more thousands than back home. And when the sun set, the pavements and bricks emanating heat like bakers' ovens, the darkening sky giving back the milky glow of the city lights, that was when Harlem began to come alive with that other kind of music. From the street doors of taverns and dance halls on Lenox Avenue came the strains of piano players beating rags out of their instruments. Open windows on any street might issue guitars and blues harps, lone voices singing, or gangs of children playing hand games on stoops, chanting rhymes in intricate rhythms. The music and the presence of all these people soaked into his skin, and each time he returned home vibrating anew, with possibility, with anticipation.

Other times Aunt Nora sent him out in the middle of day, on an errand for the school or the household, and these were little missions that took him further afield, to other districts on the streetcar, the elevated line, even the subway, which seemed to Gerard the most audacious of all human creation. In and around these other destinations colored folks were few and far between, and simply walking along sidewalks, entering shops, and ringing doorbells—without the obvious signs of labor, such as a broom, shoeshine box, or cook's apron—earned him looks of suspicion. Passing a fashionable couple on a street in Harlem often got him a smile or a wink from the lady, a friendly nod from the man, whereas in other places, under the brims of those same panama hats and parasols came glances of cold hostility. More than once Gerard turned to search behind him for some sudden threat, having read such alarm on a passing white face that he broke out in gooseflesh.

But then Sunday would come, and he'd go to church with the Higginses at St. Luke's African Methodist Episcopal, and all would be reversed. Whereas the congregation in Montreal to which the Rougeauxes belonged was largely white and only tolerated the colored families, here all the congregants were varying tones of brown and black, as well as the deacons, the choir, the organist, the secretary, every single person on every committee, and the minister himself. After the services concluded, it was a good hour at least before they would actually leave the church, what with so much handshaking, cheek kissing, and cries of "Glory!" every time Aunt Nora or Uncle Hig presented Gerard to someone new. All of this would have been wonderful, if a bit overwhelming, had the old pangs of shame not racked him from underneath, especially when folks introduced their daughters a little too insistently. Maybe he hadn't sinned in body, but there was no purging what lurked in his soul.

✦ ✦ ✦ ✦ ✦

One Friday, Aunt Nora returned home in the afternoon, bursting in on Gerard and Jeannette playing marbles in the parlor.

"Cancel your plans for tomorrow," she said to Gerard, flipping through a stack of mail. "I've just been given two tickets to a matinee at the Met. It's *Don Giovanni*, and you need to see it."

"Do what Mama says," Jeannette whispered to him. "I'll get Papa to take me to the zoo."

"Good idea," Gerard whispered back.

Aunt Nora paused in her bustling and looked at them over her shoulder. "That better not be a mutiny you all are planning."

That night, despite retiring in a state of anticipation for attending his first opera the next day, Gerard had a curious dream. He was wading near the bank of a river. It was night, the sky starless, the only sound a rustling of rushes that brushed against his bare legs. All of a sudden, at his feet, floating in the black water lay a sleeping infant, like Moses in the Bible story but without the basket. This baby floated by itself. Gerard reached for the baby, thinking that it should be brought out to dry, but his hands came up empty. He tried again and again but every time the baby floated just a bit further away, worrying Gerard that the baby might stay in too long and become a fish.

When Gerard woke in the morning he remembered the dream. But this faded swiftly, subsumed in the activity of the Higgins household, the hours of practice that Aunt Nora demanded and the various *et ceteras* to be finished before their departure not one dot after two o'clock.

Stepping into the great opera hall Gerard had the sensation that he had crossed the threshold to a world he had long been approaching. A whisper of the previous night's dream came back to him—the floating infant, the black water—before quickly fading again. On the far side of the hall, a massive curtain of gold damask glittered like a portal, a sunburst chandelier like something fallen out of the sky. Rows and rows of expectant plush seats rose up from the stage, submerged from beneath in inky black shadow, gilt molding lit the ceiling with cupids and the faces of lions, shining bronze in the dim light.

Aunt Nora and Gerard's seats were both close enough and high enough to the stage to afford an excellent view, the exceptionally tall feathers on the hat of the lady seated just in front of Gerard notwithstanding. Then the house lights darkened, the music from the orchestra swelled, and the curtains parted. Again, angels. The same otherworldly singing that had so moved Gerard the time he heard Miss Nancy Drake in the church in Montreal. But this time there were numerous singers, each lending a different sound and energy to the drama that began to unfold, as the licentious Don Giovanni made clear his desires and pursuits—women, mostly, with food and drink thrown in. Deceptions and counter deceptions, protestations and conquest, the characters entwined, recoiled, and then reconfigured, bearing masks and then unmasking themselves, revealing faces so vivid with white makeup, rouged cheeks and lips, and black-lined eyes, that Gerard half expected them to shed these identities as well. Absorbed as he was in the spectacle, a prickle of unease disturbed his throat, making him swallow. Fallen masks lay scattered about the stage.

Placid and dignified, Aunt Nora sat beside Gerard with her hands folded, leaning toward him from time to time to whisper in his ear the meaning of a line, the symbol in a gesture, a bit of history that illuminated for Gerard the given scene.

At last, when Don Giovanni found himself in a cemetery with his servant, having escaped yet another entanglement among the mortals he so easily dominated, a statue—a *statue*—came to life and intoned his doom, should he not repent his sinful ways. The servant cowered in fear, but when Don Giovanni merely invited the statue to dinner at his sumptuous palace, Gerard nearly burst out laughing. The *audacity*. How money and power made man think himself equal to the gods, how crushing would be the blow when this illusion was broken, when the statue would come to the Don's door as promised and drag him down to Hell.

The roar from the audience applauding on its feet brought Gerard back to himself, breathless. He rubbed his eyes, swallowed again, felt like laughing again but did not. Aunt Nora took his arm as they bustled outside again with the crowd, stepping back out onto the street. The sunlight dazzled his eyes. Beside him, Aunt Nora was a shadowed silhouette, a dark shape like the fierce bright outline of an eclipse.

Just that morning he'd seen her silhouetted by the light from the window as she sat at her writing desk, as he passed in the hall. But now in his mind's eye he saw something else: Nora, paused in her work, twiddling a pen in her fingers just as he always did when he was thinking. He heard her sharp laugh when surprised. Just like his. Her face like a mirror to his own.

"Gerard, are you alright?" Aunt Nora clutched at her hat in a sudden gust.

He shook his head, struggled to loosen his tie. She hailed a cab, and they climbed into the carriage where he leaned back and closed his eyes, sensing the jostle and the slap of the reins as the horses lurched into motion.

✦ ✦ ✦ ✦ ✦

He was in fact quite ill. Uncle Hig helped him into bed while Aunt Nora rang a doctor. Gerard burrowed down into the blankets, shivering despite the heat, and pulled the pillow over his eyes. He wanted darkness, and he must have slept, because the next thing he knew it was evening. The window was dark and the lamp lit, and a bearded doctor in a black coat and eyeglasses drew up a chair beside the bed for a cursory examination. Nothing to be alarmed about. He left a prescription for chloral hydrate, of which a drop or two was to be added to the drinking water taken by the patient.

For two days he tossed in sweat-soaked sheets. When he woke he drank greedily from the water glass, staring agonizingly at the embroidered sampler made by his sisters, the colored flowers, the stitched words …*loving home*… and prayed for sleep to take him away again. The embroidery twisted and curled as dreams lapped at the shores of his wakefulness, boats sailed over rivers of black water carrying babies and children in danger of going over waterfalls and disappearing forever. Until finally he woke with a clear head and there was nothing to be done but to get up, rub the grit from the eyes, crack the knuckles of his long brown fingers, pad in bare feet down the hall to the parlor, and sit down at the piano.

He played stiffly at first, then fluidly. He played his heart.

"That's it." It was Aunt Nora's voice. He'd thought himself alone in the house at first. She must have been in her office, and Uncle Hig out with Jeannette. "I knew you had it in you." She laid a hand on the side of the fallboard, tenderly, as if on his shoulder. In fact, she had never once touched him, not since the first time he'd met her as a boy when she shook his hand. He understood now that she had been afraid to.

The sight of her hand blurred, it swam in the tears that welled up in his eyes and began spilling over his cheeks onto the keys.

"You're my mother, aren't you. Aunt Nora, aren't you my mother?" His eyes stayed fixed on the piano keys, splinters of white and black.

She remained silent a long moment.

"If you hate me," she said, faintly, "I'll understand."

Gerard shook his head. "No…no." He took a breath and turned to look at her. "Is Uncle Hig my father?" She stepped slowly over to a chair, gripped its arm and lowered herself to sit, bright tracks of tears marking her face. She swept them away with the palm of her hand.

"No. Another man. When I was very young."

He waited.

"A professor at the Conservatory, in fact," she said. "A composer." She looked at him with sorrowful eyes.

"Did you love him?"

"I was too young to know about loving a man."

"Did he love you?"

"No."

"And when you found out that… About me?"

"He ignored it."

It seemed a knot of her pain churned in Gerard's own stomach.

"What was he called?"

"Gerard Batiste."

"You gave me his name," he said, not without wonder.

"Only his Christian name. But yes, I did."

Gerard started to ask another question, but Nora held up her hand. She stood. "Damn it, I need some coffee if we're going to take this any further."

While the coffee was brewing—double the amount of grounds that folks usually used for one pot—Nora went into her office room and came back with a newspaper clipping. An obituary several years old, of Gerard Batiste, from a New Orleans paper. Gerard looked at the speckled photograph, a face he would study again and again, and ran his eyes over the faded type that gave more details: his place of birth, career, accolades, married life.

"We had a brief affair. Very brief," Nora said, "during my first months at the Conservatory. And then I rant back home, and they sent me away to have the child." She cleared her throat. "To have you."

"And then a white lady brought me...?"

"Yes, one of the women I stayed with in Toronto. Everyone wanted to keep you in the family," she said, "but without the shame of my being unmarried." Nora's voice dropped to a whisper. "I hope you can forgive me. Forgive all of us. It seemed the best thing at the time."

Gerard's throat all but closed. "I've had a good life," he whispered. "The best."

Nora pinched the bridge of her nose a long minute, then took a sip from her cup.

"What was my father like?"

"You know, a composer. A professor. Brilliant." She sipped again. "A magnetic sort of person. All the colored students idolized him." She rubbed her temples. "Who knows how many girls he went after. I hate to think it."

"A Don Giovanni," Gerard said.

Her sharp laugh bit the air, her laugh like his. Then a groan. "*Oh*, I hope not."

Gerard gazed into his cup. He hadn't touched the coffee but he smelled how strong it was. The aroma alone was fortifying. "I've always liked coffee this way," he said.

She smiled. "Me too."

Mr. Sanderson

A monrh after Don Giovanni Gerard accompanied the Higginses to a private concert luncheon, a benefit for the Institute held in the home of the wealthy Mrs. Winters, one of the Institute's leading patronesses. Nora and Uncle Hig played several pieces, as did a handful of other artists, including a curious little man with a toasted cinnamon complexion and perfect pencil mustache, who played the piano as if he were a *ballerino* dancing on the keys. The ladies who comprised the audience, all of them white, applauded clutching jeweled fans with gloved hands that muffled the sound but gave the fluttering impression of a flock of unsettled doves. Except for Nora, all of the performing artists were male and colored, striking Gerard a bit strangely, since under other conditions, here in New York, these magpies among the doves would likely be looked upon with antipathy, or fear, or at least condescension. But here, in the Winters' drawing room, the general mood was one of amusement and appreciation, and further, Gerard saw that the little man, Mr. Sanderson, was a great favorite among the patronesses.

In the interval between the performances and the luncheon Mr. Sanderson held court in one corner, bathed in the light of the large bay windows, with Mrs. Winters at his side and a revolving cluster of the other ladies who laughed with delight every time he complimented their elaborate hairstyles or whispered into one of their ears while looking askance at another lady across the room.

Nora and Uncle Hig made the rounds of the room, thanking everyone on behalf of the Institute for coming, for their generous attention, and for their appreciation of the arts. They introduced Gerard to the other artists as their nephew, having decided together to keep the real truth to themselves. Gerard was grateful on this point; the knowledge was still too new, too raw, he hadn't even written about it to his parents much less decided what it meant to him in the privacy of his own mind. Besides, his being the Higginses' nephew was true in its own way. It was the best description for the relationship despite the technicality. No one else need know, at least for the present.

Now they approached the corner enlivened by Mr. Sanderson.

"Sandy," Nora said, gently interrupting the group of ladies, "please meet my nephew, Gerard. From Montreal." She nodded at Mrs. Winters. "He's here to study music," she said. "Though you won't hear him play anytime soon."

Sandy gave Gerard a sidelong up and down, and a little smile that tilted his pencil mustache to one side. "Charmed," he said, offering a prim handshake. "You're a lucky young man to have Miss Nora for your aunt. If anyone's going to whip you into shape it shall be she."

"She's got a good start on me," Gerard said.

"I expect she has," Sandy said.

Nora gave her due to the ladies and led Gerard away.

When it was time to eat, the artists were seated interspersed among the patronesses. The colored staff of one man and two women in uniform came and went from the kitchen with wine and various dishes—a parade of little cakes piled up with salmon and vegetables and creamed cheeses, served with silver tongs. To his relief, Gerard was seated between Nora and Uncle Hig, which spared him too much would-be conversation. The lady seated on Uncle Hig's other side had relatives in Montreal and so gave Gerard an earful about her visits there, but after that he gave himself up to enjoying the cakes.

For much of the meal, Gerard's attention fell on Mr. Sanderson, who kept his side of the table well entertained with a stream of humorous anecdotes.

"And that Charles Beaker said..." Mr. Sanderson was saying just now to Mrs. Winters and the others, "'I haven't heard poetry like that in a *hundred years.*' He turned fifty last spring you know, and I like to tease him about his age. So, I said, 'Well, Charles, I think *you've* been around at least that long,' and he said, 'Sandy, I'm not a day older than *you* are!' And I said, 'Be serious! You know I haven't seen the last of my forties. And he said, 'My dear, what you lack in years you make up for in experience!'"

The ladies laughed gleefully, and Mr. Sanderson, smiling, took a sip of his wine. "But then he said—and this is more—he said, 'Everyone knows that when it comes to the arts, you're a great *uplifter.*'"

Peals of uproarious giggles resounded across the table, shaking the glasses and the cutlery and the crystal chandelier overhead. Gerard laughed too, pressing his napkin over his mouth, despite being unsure of the meaning of the joke. But he dared not let his mind go too far. Something unbearably ticklish was writhing in his belly.

✦ ✦ ✦ ✦ ✦

By three o'clock the last of the guests had said their goodbyes and made their way out to the street. Gerard walked beside Nora while Uncle Hig went up to the corner to see about hailing a cab. Two glasses of wine had gone a touch to his head and he hazarded a jovial comment of his own.

"That Sanderson's a funny one," he said. "I mean, isn't he... *funny?*"

Nora quit walking and fixed him with a ferocious stare. "*Funny?*"

"He's not the usual... sort," said Gerard, uneasy.

"Mr. Sanderson is a great friend of ours," Nora said, unblinking. "He's an artist. A very fine one."

Gerard was silent, duly chastised.

"And he's a tremendous asset to the Institute."

"Yes, Ma'am."

"In that room were some of the wealthiest women in all of New York," Nora went on. "He charms the absolute *hair* off them. Make no mistake." Then her eyes bored into his own, straight to the back of his head. "And as far as you are concerned, there are things better left *unsaid.*" She lifted her skirts then and quickened her step toward Uncle Hig. "Now move. I'm up to my eyes."

When they approached the corner Uncle Hig shook his head. "I don't think we'll have much luck with a cabbie today."

He meant finding a colored one, as no white driver would stop to pick them up. They'd have to walk several blocks to the nearest subway station and then, more than likely, stand for most of the ride if the car was crowded. Nora would remark later that she paid in blisters for the privilege of begging white folks for their money.

Seeing that a cab was now waiting she lifted her skirts and hastened her step. "Hurry up now, for Heaven's sake. Damn it, you've got a lot to learn."

✦ ✦ ✦ ✦ ✦

Gerard would see Mr. Sanderson again soon, indeed many times in the coming years, as he was an essential member of the Higginses' inner circle. One evening late in August, when the heat of summer had sucked half of the Hudson river into the air, they attended another fundraiser hosted by Mr. Sanderson himself at his damask-covered apartment. This was a small benefit for a newly founded organization, the National Association for the Advancement of Colored People, headed, in part, by the eminent Dr. W. E. B. Du Bois, to whom the Higginses had been devoted ever since making his acquaintance on a musical tour in Europe some ten years before.

The audience of this evening, both colored and white, lounged on sofas and folding chairs, or propped themselves up in the three doorframes that edged the large parlor, while a poet introduced as Devar—an attractive colored man of around thirty, dressed in a long, Japanese-style robe—stood beside the piano reading from scrolls of paper that fell to the floor and unrolled across a zebra-skin rug. Mr. Sanderson, seated at the piano, listened with his eyes closed, filling the spaces between poems with flourishes of music.

Gerard stared, incredulous, throughout the performance, first at the poet—who moved his hands gracefully to his words, wide sleeves falling to the elbow when the arms raised, a lustrous V of smooth brown skin showing where the robe dipped down in front—then at Mr. Sanderson, rapt in the music and poetry. When the piece concluded to enthusiastic applause, the two bowed together.

In the mingling that followed, Gerard drifted away from Nora and Uncle Hig toward a corner where Devar stood with a glass of wine, accepting compliments from a cluster of guests.

The poet turned his gaze on him, smiling. "Are you a Higgins, then?"

"A Rougeaux," Gerard stammered, "from Montreal."

"Charmed," Devar offered his hand, palm down, fingers pressed together like a woman would, bringing a flush of heat to Gerard's cheeks and right down to the nether regions, when he took the poet's hand in his own.

Just then Nora appeared at Gerard's side, jerking his arm toward the door. "Thank you for the evening," she said to the poet over her shoulder. "We must be off now."

The next thing Gerard knew they were out on the street, with Uncle Hig behind them. "Nora," he said, "slow down, please."

Half a block from Mr. Sanderson's Nora stopped short. "Art is art," Nora faced Gerard, "but we will not have you associating with certain people."

Gerard's head spun, another trespass, he wouldn't dare defy her. "Yes Ma'am."

Uncle Hig threw an arm around his shoulders. "Now, now. Let's just have a nice walk home. What did you think of the music?"

◆ ◆ ◆ ◆ ◆

Once back at the house, after Gerard bid goodnight to the Higginses, he lay awake a long time. Disturbed as he was by Nora's angry warning and the curdling shame of his blunder, he couldn't help but wonder on the nature of Mr. Sanderson's relationship to the poet, Devar. Might Devar be Mr. Sanderson's… what would one even call it? Not *beau* or his *intended*, certainly. A *consort* maybe?

Gerard laughed at this last thought. A giddy, silent laugh, as tears slid from his eyes and down to the pillow and he stared in wonder at the dark ceiling. Wonder. And relief. That a *funny* man could love someone, and be loved. Perhaps he would not be relegated to scraps of mean reassurance—as were certain people, people like the nervous shopkeeper in the haberdashery back in Montreal—gotten from secret glances into little mirrors kept in apron pockets. Reassurance that he was even still there at all.

Gerard Batiste

In September, when the Higgins Institute reopened its doors at the brownstone on 146th Street, Gerard became an official student, studying each morning, running errands for Nora and Uncle Hig in the afternoons, and often picking up Jeannette from school. A clarinetist named Clifford Mobley caught his arm one day at the end of classes.

"Hey," he said smiling. "I hear you're the nephew from the north."

"That's right," Gerard said. He'd noticed Clifford for his funny laugh that started with a high whoop and then rolled like a tin can down a flight of stairs.

"I'm going to the corner for a sandwich. You want to come along?"

"I'd be glad to," Gerard said. He always had room in his stomach and did long to make friends, though having grown up surrounded by family and others he'd known his whole life left him with little idea on how to do it.

That sandwich, an unusual egg salad made with parsley and bits of ham, became the first of many with Clifford and soon with a handful of others, all of whom auditioned with Gerard the following May for a place at the American Conservatory. Not everyone was accepted, but Gerard and Cliff, both elated, made the cut.

Gerard's sister Sarai married soon after that, and Gerard returned to Montreal for the wedding and to see the family. Several times he thought of confiding in his sisters, or his mother and father, that he'd learned the truth about his parentage. But it seemed too fragile an equilibrium, his visiting for so short a time, and he wanted only to be the son and brother he'd always been. The wedding was a happy occasion, and no telling what upset his new knowledge might cause.

In the fall, he began his studies at the Conservatory with great vigor. He rented a small room in a boarding house that catered to Conservatory students, but took supper with the Higginses every Sunday, always staying long enough for a few games of backgammon or checkers with Jeannette. She was growing into a long-legged, keenly observant older child, whose eyes, though still large, no longer seemed to take up most of her face. She always ran to the door when he arrived and hugged his arm until it was time to sit at the table. Nora and Hig had decided it would be best to tell Jeannette that in actual fact Gerard was her brother, as children usually accepted things more easily than when they were older. After a bit of initial confusion, for Jeannette the new knowledge was a boon, a brother-cousin was far more exciting than just a cousin and only increased her adoration.

"Let your brother have his arm back now, Honey," Uncle Hig would say those Sunday evenings. "The boy's got to eat. Look how skinny he is!" Gerard had gained a few inches in height since landing in New York, but not in width. His shoulders promised a larger future frame, but as of now his shirts still fluttered when the wind blew. Whatever Gerard ate, which was considerable, converted itself directly into music, and the mental energy it took to keep up with his many courses at the Conservatory, all of which launched him through door after door of discovery. His classes in the history of opera and theory of composition were among the most exciting, as were conversations among his classmates on new works not included in the Conservatory curriculum, such as an *avant garde* French composer called Erik Satie. Satie's music was nothing short of startling to Gerard, and at the same time was so spare and intimate that touched him very deeply. It was music that entered his heart like opera did, but through a different door.

By his second year, Gerard was spending more and more time composing. He knew all of Satie's works by heart and made a study of what he considered all of the most crucial elements, incorporating them into his own pieces which he produced for piano, and later for small ensembles. Though he easily immersed himself in all he was learning and creating, not a day passed that he didn't lift his head to stare at his surroundings—the walls, the windows, worn places on stone stairs, students rushing to classes clutching instrument cases and sheet music—and recall that his birth parents met here, taught here, studied here, and, in the case of his father, composed original music. Knowing that his father, Gerard Batiste, was both an admirable composer and a womanizer likely to take advantage of young students such as Nora, was disturbing. The fact that he was a product of this kind of moral lapse found no resting place in his mind, if anything it left the sense that he owed something to Nora, something that might make up for the pain he had caused her by being born.

One Sunday after supper and Gerard's weekly report on his studies, Nora asked him if he'd be interested in seeing the compositions of Gerard Batiste. Nora had brewed her strong coffee, and though she appeared calm on the outside, Gerard guessed that perhaps she'd needed a little extra fortification to broach the subject.

Gerard glanced nervously at Uncle Hig, who looked back at him both intently and with great warmth; it was wholly comforting. Uncle Hig was nothing if not generous. He had known Batiste too after all, and had been deeply upset when he'd learned of the affair years later, believing that Nora had been the victim of a man who had callously abused his power.

"Do you think it's worth it?" asked Gerard, addressing both of them.

"Why wouldn't it be?" Nora said.

When Gerard couldn't find the words, Uncle Hig said, "His immorality?"

Gerard nodded, and Nora said, "Gerard, your father was more than just his mistakes. In truth, I hardly knew him, but I know he was more because that's the case for everyone. Myself included."

"But his action was..." Gerard struggled, "...unforgivable."

Nora fixed him with her trademark stare. "Really?"

"Think of the result," Uncle Hig said gently, "of that error."

"It almost ruined your career," Gerard said to Nora. "Your life."

"No, Son," said Uncle Hig, laying his large hand on Gerard's shoulder. "It gave us *you*."

✦ ✦ ✦ ✦ ✦

A few days later Nora met Gerard in the Conservatory library and led him to the section reserved for work by Conservatory faculty. Moments later he held two leather-bound volumes of sheet music in his hands, *Gerard Batiste, Selected Works*, imprinted on the covers in silver type.

"Play them," Nora said. "Learn about him. Then, if you want, we'll discuss it."

"I will."

"Good," she said, and then surprised him by giving him a furious little kiss on the cheek before hurrying away.

Over the next several weeks Gerard played every one of the pieces, listening to them for clues into the man. There was significant artistry to be sure, but arrogance too, and under that layers of brashness threaded at the edges with a certain insecurity. A few of the pieces Gerard genuinely liked. Perhaps he could derive from these something new and make his own variation. He would title it "Legacy" or "Inheritance" or he wouldn't title it at all. Maybe he'd just let it be nameless.

✦ ✦ ✦ ✦ ✦

When war broke out in Europe, the papers filled with names of foreign places. Canada allied with Britain first and Sarai's letters included the names of young men they knew who had volunteered, many of whom they would never see again. The papers filled with articles on the foreign news, especially after the Black Tom Explosion in New York harbor, and when President Wilson declared war on Germany.

There was much talk in the Higginses' circle about the role of black soldiers. Dr. Du Bois argued that the service of black soldiers in Europe would serve the struggle for equality back at home, and though Nora and Uncle Hig generally shared Dr. Du Bois' ideas, they regarded Gerard's choice in the matter a purely personal one. Gerard dreamt one night of his father and mother standing in the open field by the canal in Montreal, where the family picnicked in the summer, holding out a Browning rifle and saying, "Go and do it." In the dream, as he reached for the gun his sisters appeared, pulling at his sleeves and crying, "There's enough in the kitchen, there's enough in the kitchen," which he understood to mean, however absurdly, that taking up the gun wasn't his role.

In real life, the idea of using a gun was instinctively abhorrent to Gerard, and though the subject of the war naturally came up in his correspondences with his family, none of them ever discussed whether or not Gerard would enlist. Over the radio came the constant repetition of a new song,

> *America, I raised a boy for you*
> *America, you'll find him staunch and true*
> *Place a gun upon his shoulder, he is ready to die or do*
> *America, he is my only one, my hope, my pride and joy*
> *But if I had another, he would march beside his brother*
> *America, here's my boy!*

And flyers pasted to shop windows boasted the accompanying image of a white soldier in uniform with his lace-draped mother standing bravely at his side—an image in which Gerard recognized nothing of his own.

Regardless of his feelings about the weaponry, Gerard couldn't say he knew anything much like patriotism, either for the United States or the Dominion of Canada. With a bitter taste in his mouth, he recalled the acrobatics he and Clifford Mobley had had to undergo just to rent a room in a boarding house in Chelsea near the Conservatory—presenting their letters of acceptance to numerous places before being turned away, until finally Nora arranged a telephone call to one proprietress from a former Conservatory colleague of hers attesting to their respectable characters. None of this had been necessary for their white classmates to do. When at last the landlady in question relented, she did so on the condition that Gerard and Cliff would be "the only two" and ever after, when meeting them on the stairs or dining room, never once returned their polite greetings.

Countless times, as he travelled about on his own business, he was harangued, menaced, threatened, reminded of his race by a world that considered him less than. But these reminders were yet more jarring when they came from people he'd begun to trust, certain professors at the Conservatory, for example, like the one in whose office he beheld—during an early interview—a framed vaudeville poster bearing a cartoonish drawing of three "negroes" in crushed hats and patched trousers, their ghastly pale lips ballooning around corncob pipes. All throughout that meeting, Gerard kept staring at the poster, hovering a few feet behind the professor's shoulder, so that soon the professor followed his gaze back toward the wall.

"Ah," the professor had chuckled. "My old review. I played three summers with that company in my youth. Really takes me back." He turned his benevolent, nostalgic smile back on Gerard, his blue eyes twinkling, and for a second Gerard's vision blurred, the shadowy image on the wall filling all the empty space.

Then there were his future prospects, that was worth considering. Nora and Uncle Hig, despite their formidable talents, their training, and their dedication, were never able to succeed as performing classical musicians, except for the tours in Europe in their all-colored orchestra. To earn their living in New York they had founded the Higgins Institute, opening a place for themselves in the thin margin their country allowed them.

No, if he held any sort of collective allegiance it was in support of his own people. Graduating from the Conservatory in 1914, at the age of twenty-three, Gerard knew he was lucky, one of the few with the means and opportunity to devote themselves to the arts and the life of the mind. If he were to contribute anything of value it would be through his music. Even so, if he were conscripted he didn't know what he'd do. Among his peers there were more than one who declared themselves *conscientious objectors* and against the war, but refusing the draft meant facing a year in prison and who knew what social consequences thereafter. As such, the call never came; Armistice came first.

In the dance halls where Gerard played almost constantly now, earning a decent living in piecemeal fashion, soldiers and Navy men were the loudest and most belligerent of the revelers. He heard the shrill edge of desperation in their voices even when they laughed, or when they wanted a certain song played over and over again and had to be escorted out if they became too insistent. They had a similar presence at a movie house where Gerard played the organ along with the silent films, that too-loud laughter, the catcalls at the screen when the heroines swooned. Gerard recoiled from those swaggering men, and he pitied them, yet he desired them too. But those men and everyone else wanted music. Humanity was thirsty for music, and so he played, and wrote, and studied, and played some more.

Then in 1918 came the Influenza, with the deadliest wave hitting just before the Armistice. A sickly panic descended over the city with the summer heat. Who had ever heard of an influenza in the spring and summer? The hospitals were overrun, especially in October, when the worst of it came. Many of the young people Gerard knew and worked with, performers of all kinds, were felled. People said the soldiers had brought it from overseas. Gerard wrote anxious letters home, fearing bad news. He quit the Sunday dinners with the Higginses for a time in case he himself might bring it into their home and endanger Jeannette, as the young were the most vulnerable.

✦ ✦ ✦ ✦ ✦

But with time the tides turned. The war was over, the influenza finished, and life was returning to the living. Life swelled. When the new decade of the 1920's arrived, so did a burgeoning energy that filled Harlem's streets, bursting into music with artists of all kinds writing, performing, painting, philosophizing, breaking rules, and the whole world clamoring for jazz. Since during the war, throngs of colored people were flooding into the city from the Southern states, rivers of people seeking work in the shipyards and other opportunities unknown in the dusty cotton fields they fled, where Jim Crow cut them down before they could even unbend themselves. And with them they brought *blues*, mouth harps, cigar-box banjos, songs of survival and heartache, and threads of joy clung onto for dear life. Everything was happening in Harlem these days, on the streets, inside clubs, in homes, in bedrooms.

After the long depravity of the war, the current times for Gerard were a kind of rebirth, and he once again felt launched through countless doors of discovery, at least in the arts, but even this didn't soothe the private turmoil he lived with daily. Since the night at Mr. Sanderson's apartment with the poet, Devar, Gerard let himself imagine things. Nightly he closed his eyes and let images of men play out silent films in his mind, relieving the torture of his celibacy alone beneath his sheets. First it was Devar, Devar and himself tumbling together. Then it was certain friends from the Conservatory, or men he saw around town with lovely eyes or smiles, broad shoulders, or curving buttocks that showed their shape when a man put his foot up on a hydrant to get a scuff off his shoe.

Gerard hadn't had the least idea of how any of these things might be made real, how anyone did it without risking their lives in ill-placed overtures, until one unexpected night during the war. Gerard had gone to one of the dance halls where he worked, and soon after midnight a young, red-haired Navy man in a white uniform came to lean an elbow on the piano. He'd been drinking but was neither sloppy nor belligerent, said he was from Maryland and requested "The Lights of My Hometown." When Gerard played it, he sang along in a sweet, husky tenor. His name was Macarden and he had a lovely sad smile.

When the song was over the sailor requested another, then another, and, seeing no problem with it, Gerard obliged. The manager of the place let him do as he liked, so long as people kept dancing and kept drinking. Soon enough a cluster of the young man's shipmates were making their wobbly way to the door.

"Your buddies are leaving," Gerard said.

Macarden waved after them, elbow still resting on the piano's top. "I'll be seeing enough of them. Tomorrow we're shipping out." He looked sorrowfully into the bottom of his empty glass, then turned his bleary eyes on Gerard. "Why don'tcha let me buy you one? You've been so nice to me."

Gerard shook his head. "No thanks."

"Teetotaler?"

"Working."

"Right." The young man wiped a pale wrist at his freckled cheek. "Gotta stay nimble, right? Jack be nimble, Jack be quick and all that?"

"Sure."

They said nothing for a while. Gerard continued playing. He was improvising now, a wistful melody. The young man's sad mood was contagious.

At closing time Macarden was still there, slumped in a chair in the corner, sleeping. Gerard had packed up, collected his pay, and he shook the young man by the shoulder. The sailor reached up and grabbed Gerard by the sleeve without opening his eyes. "Time's up?" he murmured.

"Uh huh." Gerard was sorry for him, a young man alone in the city, shipping out the next day toward a fate uncertain at best. "You got a place to stay?"

Macarden shook his head, eyes still closed. "Park bench, I guess," he said. "Summertime's good for that."

"I can put you up," Gerard said, surprising himself. "I don't live too far." This wasn't like him, in fact he'd never offered to put up a stranger, only occasional friends after parties when they'd had too much. It didn't bother him though, this night, that the young man was a stranger, nor that he was white. In fact he reminded Gerard of a classmate from the Conservatory, a handsome redhead called Pinny by his friends, who occasionally sought out Gerard to compare notes on a performance.

Macarden's pink-rimmed blue eyes focused on Gerard's face and half-smiled. "If it's not a bother."

◆ ◆ ◆ ◆ ◆

Back at his room, Gerard made a pallet for Macarden on the floor under the window. They undressed with their backs turned to each other, the younger man still softly singing "The Lights of My Hometown." Gerard was tired—it was the end of a long day—and though his limbs felt heavy, a nervous tension sent a crackle, like radio static, up and down his spine. It twisted into his belly.

The curtain was drawn over the half-open window, but the glow from a streetlamp cast a ghostly light into the darkened room. Macarden, reflected in the oval mirror Gerard used for shaving, bent to remove his trousers, shoulders wide and pale, with a little pool of shadow that lay at the nape of his neck, beneath the line of his shorn hair.

Macarden quit singing. "Toilet down the hall?"

"That's right."

Gerard got into bed in his shorts, pulled up the sheet and turned to the wall. *No need for this damn erection to make a tent,* he thought, *plain for all to see.* When the young man returned, Gerard feigned sleep. The heaviness he felt crept over his eyes, and he concentrated his attention there, letting his fatigue win the battle over his loins, and soon enough he slept.

Then something moved him.

Gerard's eyes flew open, his heart jumped. Staring at the dark wall, he sensed the bedsprings bend and slope with the weight of another body. Macarden lay down beside him, inches of space between them. Neither moved. And for a long minute it seemed that neither of them breathed. In the short time that he'd slept, Gerard had kicked off the sheet, and now the other man moved again, edging closer. Then a hand caressed his arm, the young man's chest touched his back.

Macarden's lips touched the back of his neck, then his jaw, his ear. Paralyzed, Gerard felt Macarden's hand travel up his thigh, over his stomach, and then slip itself down the front of his shorts. Gerard gasped, the other man's breath heavier now, near his ear, as he pressed himself against Gerard's backside. Heart beating like mad, Gerard's head spun as if drunk. Macarden's hand encircled him, pulling, stroking, his own sex straining at the place where Gerard's thighs came together. Regaining his ability to move, Gerard reached back, running his hand over Macarden's leg, gripping him fiercely, until all at once Gerard shook with spasms.

After a moment or two, when he'd caught his breath, he turned over to face the young man and the two began kissing clumsily. Gerard scarcely knew what to do with his lips and the terrifying notion that he would swallow the other man whole, but then as if to enact this he moved down in the bed and took Macarden in his mouth until the sailor moaned, his hot seed hitting the back of Gerard's throat.

They remained tangled together, breathing, neither of them daring to speak. Gerard never wanted it to end, even as a voice from deep in his mind shrieked at him that he was tainted and would die of syphilis. But Gerard didn't know for sure that he hadn't died already, and that if that was the case then Heaven and Hell were a single mixed-up place.

When Gerard awoke, the bright morning sun trying to burn a hole through the curtain, Macarden was gone. Groggy as hell, he sat up and looked around. The pallet on the floor was neatly folded and he was alone, and if there was a word in his mind now it was *Halleluyah*, because something in him had been freed.

✦ ✦ ✦ ✦ ✦

That first encounter was followed by another a few months later, when a handsome brown-skinned man in a beige linen suit folded a note inside a dollar bill and dropped it in into the tip jar of the old upright he was playing at another dance hall. The note read, *Come by for a drink sometime*, was signed, *Martin P.*, and gave a Harlem address.

It was an affair as exhilarating as it was educational, especially since Martin liked to keep the light on and was clearly experienced, and his affectionate nature drew Gerard in like a retriever puppy. But three or four weeks in, when Gerard knocked on the now familiar green-painted door, Martin opened up but didn't undo the chain. He had on the gold silk robe he favored and he spoke in a low voice, saying that he was sorry but he couldn't let Gerard in because, well, he wasn't alone.

The next instant Gerard was back on the street, head spinning as if reeling from a hard cold slap in the face. By the time he recovered himself he was angry, but not at Martin. What had he expected, after all? A proposal of marriage? He laughed bitterly and a passing couple gave him an odd look. You'd better sharpen up, he told himself. Grow up. Lord. Don't be so goddamn naïve.

And then, on another night, a year after the Armistice, he ran into Devar, the poet, in a little bar on Amsterdam Avenue. He'd gone in alone after a gig because he was restless and didn't yet want to go home, and Devar was at the bar with a shot glass and a teacup, scratching at a napkin with a fountain pen. Gerard didn't recognize him at first, it had been several years after all, and neither did Devar recognize him until they were several minutes into a conversation.

"You're the nephew!" Devar exclaimed. "Miss Nora's! I can't believe it. You've grown up." He pursed his lips in an approving smile.

Gerard attracted more attention these days. He was tall, and by this time his lanky form had filled out and the weight settled him in his body, allowing him to move with more confidence. Whereas the wind once unsettled him, a new ease in his limbs added to the rest of him the grace he'd always had in his hands. That drop of milk in the tea of his complexion, which he now knew to come from his father, mixed with the deep darkness of Nora's—so like the strong coffee she favored—and lent the features of his face a fine definition, especially his eyes—black, luminous, and innocent.

"You look the same," Gerard said, thinking that Devar, with his strong jaw and cheekbones and arched brows, was still very attractive, even more so with a little gray in his hair.

Devar rolled his eyes. "Sweet of you to say."

They began seeing each other often, fell easily into bed and to Gerard's amazement had long conversations afterward, intimate talks in which for the first time Gerard confided in another without keeping any secrets. He didn't know if he was in love with Devar, but they grew very close, through a winter and a spring, until Devar began talking about going away to Paris.

"Why Paris?" Gerard wanted to know. All kinds of exciting things were beginning to happen right there in Harlem.

"It's a new frontier," Devar said, stretching languidly as he often did when lying down. "I want to see what it's like, I've lived here my whole life and I could use a change. People there want to live again and they want artists from here."

"They want poetry?"

"If it comes with music, yes."

When Gerard stayed quiet, Devar guessed his mood. He stroked Gerard's cheek. "You won't be too sad, will you? Without me?"

Gerard didn't know how to answer. Of course he'd be sad, but what kind of claim was a man allowed to have on another?

"What is it you want, Gerard?"

"Love that lasts, I suppose."

Devar smiled, with a note of sadness too that Gerard was relieved to see. "You'll get it, I'm sure." He put his arms around Gerard and tucked his forehead by Gerard's ear. "I'm sure you will."

Langston

In 1922 Gerard was thirty-one, a grown man and well-established as an artist, thanks in part to Mr. James Reese Europe and his Clef Club that organized and promoted all the best black musicians in town. One night, at a private party thrown by the owner of a popular cabaret, Gerard took a few turns at the piano. The fluid playing he'd been noted for at the Conservatory became electric when turned to jazz. He wasn't a fiery player, nor was he known for any outrageous style, but he played music that, as appreciative listeners often said, got down to *business*. At a late hour Gerard finished a piece and took a break, accepting a drink from one guest and a cigarette from another. Elaine Parker, a star dancer from the host's cabaret leaned her elbow on the edge of the keyboard and offered him a light, which he accepted, returning her smile.

"Now that was some nice playing," she said, looking at him slyly. She was a dazzlingly beautiful woman—skin golden as taffy, thick black hair oiled into submission and swept up in an elegant chignon The low-cut gown sparkling with sequins, robust cleavage glowing with the heat of the room, and her perfume, would have easily overwhelmed most men.

"Thank you very much," he said.

She slid onto the bench next to him.

"You're fancy, ain't you?" she said, tapping a red nail against her white teeth. "It's okay," she said, when he was too surprised to answer, "I respect that. I've got lots of fancy friends. It's only disappointing once in a while." She winked.

Fancy. It was a nicer word than funny. It wasn't bad at all.

"Maybe you'll introduce me to your friends," he said, and she laughed.

"I don't think you'll need my help."

"What about you?" he said. "You must have them lining up around the block."

"Oh," she sighed. "They line up but they don't stay."

"Fools."

"Ain't it the truth."

For a few minutes they smoked in silence. Finally, Gerard said, "Why don't I play a song for you?"

"Would you? Just for me?"

"I'd be glad to."

"Do you know 'Nobody'? Bert Williams?"

"Course I do, that's an old one."

She swatted his shoulder. "Don't say *old*."

When he played she sang, low and sweetly,

When life seems full of clouds and rain,
And I am filled with naught but pain,
Who soothes my thumping, bumping brain?
...Nobody...
When winter comes with snow and sleet,
And me with hunger and cold feet,
Who says, 'Here's two bits, go and eat'?
...Nobody...
I ain't never done nothin' to Nobody.
I ain't never got nothin' from Nobody, no time.
And, until I get somethin' from somebody sometime,
I don't intend to do nothin' for Nobody, no time.
and when the song finished she kissed his cheek.

Though Gerard was doing well—he turned down at least as many gigs as he took on—the places that paid best had a whites-only clientele. Harlem was in vogue and visitors from Downtown flocked in nearly every night which, in certain venues, produced a mixing of races and connections that helped support the work of black artists. That was real progress. On the other hand, so many white patrons often left Harlemites feeling gawked at, like zoo animals. Black folks were suited to entertain in the whites-only clubs but could not go in and have a drink. Jim Crow was as bitter as ever. Gerard's desire for more and better grew by the day. His ambition was never simply to entertain, but to compose, to work in opera.

Vibrant as Harlem was, many said, Paris was the place to be if you wanted to be taken seriously as an artist, where you weren't ruled right, left, up, down and sideways by the color bar. Devar had been at the forefront of that wave, and now Gerard was convinced that Paris was it, especially if you were a jazz musician; the French were mad for jazz. You'd get work before you even got off the boat.

In the spring of 1924, Gerard, having diligently put away his savings, applied for a passport and visa and took out stacks of library books to improve his French, of which he already had a fair grasp. He plied Nora and Uncle Hig with questions about Europe, where they had toured in their younger years, before the war. He dreamt of Montmartre, the quarter of Paris most soaked in the history of the avant-garde and artists of every stripe, not least the composer Erik Satie, Gerard's greatest influence, still living in that famed quarter of the city.

Nora and Uncle Hig were in support of his plans for France right from the start, though Uncle Hig said they'd miss him mightily when he told them during a Sunday dinner, and Nora patted Jeannette's hand when tears welled in the girl's eyes and dropped down to the tablecloth.

"Jeannette," she said, in a voice low and stern, "be a grown-up girl. This is a grand opportunity for Gerard."

Jeannette was eighteen now, a young woman with a subtler version of her mother's composure, and a big, soft heart just like her father's.

"I know," she said. "I just hate that France is so damn far."

Gerard laughed, blinking the sting from his eyes, and thinking that, when the time came, he'd miss them mightily too.

✦ ✦ ✦ ✦ ✦

Then, in early November, Gerard attended another benefit party, for the NAACP, with all three Higginses at Happy Rhone's Cabaret. Dr. Du Bois had only risen in prominence, the organization was flourishing, and he wrote at length about the role of colored musicians, writers and other artists who didn't just pursue their art for their own sake. Instead, they constituted what he called the Talented Tenth that would lift up everyone. The arts were to be revered on many levels, and these were ideas that Nora and Uncle Hig lived, breathed, and devoted their lives to with their Institute and many other activities. They had a library full of Dr. Du Bois' books and had urged Gerard to read them all, which he had with great interest.

The benefit party was well seasoned with Harlem celebrities of all kinds, though the star of the evening was a poet, brand new on the scene. Langston Hughes was just twenty-two years old, vibrant, with big, soulful eyes, hailing from

Kansas and Cleveland, mostly, and just back from Europe. In a warm, clear voice he read out his recently published poem, *The Negro Speaks of Rivers*, and captivated the crowd. After the reading one of the party organizers introduced him to the Higginses and Gerard.

"Good to meet you folks," the young man said, shaking hands all around. He dabbed at his hairline with a handkerchief, a beautiful smile animating his face even more. "A little hot in here."

"Son, that was a wonderful poem," Uncle Hig said. "I think you've captured something new and timeless both."

Langston ducked his head, "I thank you very much."

"Yes," Nora said, "Timeless and new, exactly. It was very moving."

Langston gave a little laugh, bowing theatrically at the waist. "You all are extremely kind." He glanced at Gerard, ready to graciously accept any further praise, but Gerard only nodded, suddenly tongue-tied. He had been moved by the poem as well, but more so by the presence of the young man, and nodded again in Langston's wake when the younger man left them to receive more congratulations from the crowd, a turbulence rising up in Gerard's chest.

He was in a daze. All the next day he tried to shake it off, dislodge the image of the young poet that kept hovering behind his eyelids. Words from the poem floated back to him—*muddy bosom, golden, dusky, deep, flow of blood in human veins*—all these brought Langston himself to Gerard's mind, a young man and the rivers he spoke of. At last, with just an hour before he had to get to a club for that night's gig, he sat down at his own piano and played out a few notes. That relieved a little of the pressure. The notes seemed right, and he jotted them down on a new page in his composition book. He took it further, experimenting, and notes fell like rain onto the page. It was a start.

He saw Langston again at another party not two weeks later, but they didn't speak, the crowd was just too thick and Gerard didn't want to risk being tongue-tied. But as it turned out they would be traveling in similar circles, at parties all over Harlem, and occasionally in the Village or Downtown, the highbrow and the lowbrow both. Swanky "at-homes" at 409 Edgecombe, Harlem's most exclusive apartment house, or soirees given by the white writer and photographer Carl Van Vechten, were places where one not only had a good time, but where all colors mingled and where rising black artists would meet publishers and patrons.

At the bottom rungs of the social ladder were the "social-whist" parties, given by regular black folks who had no other choice but to work like dogs every day and once in a while throw a party where refreshments were sold to make the house-rent. One found these parties through smart little cards stuck into elevator grates and on telephone poles, or else through friends, or friends of friends. Here one found good food and terrible gin, and, away from white onlookers, artistry in the music and the dancing that rivaled the best.

In this way, Gerard and Langston crossed paths a handful of times between November and January. The young poet was living down in D.C. but came up to New York as often as he was able. He had many friends, was popular with both men and women, Gerard noticed, but didn't seem to be romantically attached to anyone. When they met, they exchanged friendly greetings—terrible, consternation-causing moments for Gerard—but mostly Gerard watched Langston from afar. The young man was so often surrounded by happier people, while Gerard, aching and unable to get ahold of himself, kept a certain distance.

One night, at the home of A'Lelia Walker, the heiress of Madame Walker's Hair Straightening Process, Gerard found himself elbow to elbow with Langston on a crowded balcony. Heart beating wildly, he steadied his voice with a great pressure of will and held out his silver cigarette case. "Smoke?" It was December, a clear night, and the cold drew the heat off so many bodies packed together.

"Thanks." Langston accepted the cigarette, and a light, with that charming smile. He blew a stream of smoke into the icy air. "Man, if this is a regular thing, I'd hate to see what goes on at Christmas."

Gerard laughed. "Miss Walker always packs them in."

"I'll say."

They both turned to look a moment through the French doors behind them, where Miss Walker's gleaming turban could be seen bobbing and weaving among the guests like a silver cork in a roiling, reveling sea.

Langston's dark eyes fell on Gerard's face. "They tell me you're a jazz musician."

Gerard's steadied heart leapt up anew. Had Langston asked about him? Just as swiftly he dismissed the thought. Everybody talked about everybody, what they did, what stars were on the rise, in what constellations they grouped together. "Yes, sir."

"Where all do you play?"

Gerard listed off a number of clubs and Langston let out a whistle, impressed. "You must be damn good then."

Gerard's face burned, despite a whoosh of cold wind coming up from street below. Car horns echoed. "You'll have to see for yourself."

Langston laughed. "I will." He took a drag from his cigarette. "Ellington's the king though, right?" He winked.

Gerard laughed again. "And Hodges is the prince."

"Who's that?"

"Saxophone."

"Okay."

For fifteen or twenty minutes they talked jazz, Gerard struggling to focus on the subject at hand while overcome with Langston's presence. That smile, those eyes, that laugh, that keen observation. It seemed the young man could turn his gaze on anything and see right into its core. But there was something curious about him too. As he had said of himself in his poem, "...*my soul has grown deep like the rivers.*" Gerard sensed that this was true, that under the affable charm lay secret depths that Langston did not readily show, that the glimmer on the surface served to deflect an outside gaze—even as it sought to attract—playing as if it were all sparkle and dazzle with nothing underneath at all.

Gerard longed to know everything about him, but, damn it, might never get that chance. He was headed to Paris, as soon as his visa came through. That was his plan. Back at his apartment, in the wee hours, he sat at his piano, searching for the notes that would release this pain, forming themselves into a new piece that began to infiltrate his dreams. Weeks passed, and though the image of Langston never left him. He ended each night alone at his piano, playing out what lay in his heart.

Then, after numerous disappointed evenings, they met again. It was one in the morning, at a social whist party, real singing, real dancing, real music, good food and God-awful gin. Gerard had gone with Cliff Mobley and Tom Dre, another friend from the Conservatory, after they had finished their gigs for the night and were looking to relax. Tom and Cliff saw a couple of girls they knew, downed a couple drinks and got right into the crush of dancers.

The hosts of the party were a pair of smiling sisters and their mother, who must have been close to Nora's age, and Gerard could tell from the aromas drifting out of the kitchen that the food would be delicious. They heaped up a plate for him for a quarter and filled a small glass with what he guessed was turpentine.

Gerard hadn't realized how hungry he was. He sat on a chair next to a pair fellows who were enjoying the music sitting down, holding their cigarettes in their lips in order to have their hands free for clapping and then switching the cigarettes to their hands so they could yell. There was a tall, skinny kid killing it on a stand-up base, a girl with a coronet, and an older man burning up the piano and singing.

The front door wasn't far away and refreshing puffs of cold air came in as folks trickled out and new guests arrived. Then the door opened again.

It was Langston, blowing on his hands through pursed lips.

He had on a sailor's pea coat, no overcoat, and looked half-frozen. It was February and bitterly cold, and Langston looked relieved to be inside, full of smiles—that sunny, charming as hell smile—as several people crowded over to shake his hand, slap him on the shoulder, and call out that Poetry had arrived. A rush of gravity glued Gerard to his chair, fusing his hands and plate and gaze to his lap. He hadn't the largesse of many performers, but shyness like this was extremely rare. For a long stretch he sat like that, stock still.

When the musicians took a break, Gerard pried himself off the chair and ambled over to the piano. It was a clangy old upright, probably a hundred years old and still hanging in there. He touched the keys and let a bit of what had built up in his chest out into a tune. He closed his eyes. Sometimes he even played better that way.

"What do you call those blues?" a voice said, when he came to the end. Langston stood there with a smile, those big, soulful eyes looking at him with curiosity, a glass of the turpentine in his hand.

These blues, Langston Hughes, Are the Hughes blues... thought Gerard, but he said, "Oh, nothing much," willing his voice to come out from the depths of where it had just before retreated. He reached over to shake Langston's hand. "I thought you might show up here."

They spoke as they had done at A'Lelia Walker's. Langston said he wished he could sing, and Gerard said that his poetry was as good as any song, even better, and Langston said Gerard was too kind. Langston told Gerard he was looking to further his education, and was saving up to go to college, Howard University.

"I'll be headed to Paris, myself," Gerard offered, no longer sure if it was true.

"That so?" Langston took a sip from his cup and winced. "I've just been there."

"I heard that." Gerard dabbed at his temples with the handkerchief from his breast pocket. "You'll have to tell me what you know." Needles pricked under his arms and he held his breath, but before the younger man could reply, the musicians came back, and some friends of Langston's whisked him away, and Gerard had nothing to do but go see what Tom and Cliff were up to.

Another hour passed by, with Gerard hopelessly elated that he and Langston had spoken but falling slowly into despair that the conversation would not resume. But then George Banks, a mutual friend, approached him, saying that his wife Clarice had the sniffles and that he'd promised Langston a place to stay, but now

Clarice didn't want anyone in the house, and would Gerard mind too much? Langston came up behind George, "Man, don't worry if you can't have me. I don't want to put you out."

"No trouble," Gerard said, feeling as though his heart had stopped beating. "When you're ready to go, say the word."

"The truth is, I'm beat," Langston said. His eyes drooped.

"Let's go then, I'm ready."

Having said their goodbye's, Gerard and Langston walked the several blocks to Gerard's building through the bracing cold. When Gerard asked him about his travels, the younger man said he'd been to Africa and Europe and Mexico, working on ships and any job he could get, adding that he'd had to fend for himself from a very young age. Gerard marveled at how worldly Langston was already, he almost imagined himself as the younger one, his thirty-three sheltered years not matching in grit Langston's hard-won twenty-two. All this only added to his sense of falling, as did each step that brought him closer to being alone in his apartment with Langston. He was glad for the sobering effects of the icy air.

The stairwell was nearly as cold as outside, and their footsteps echoed the five flights of the walk-up. Gerard's apartment was hardly lavish, just one room with the toilet down the hall, but it was both spacious and cozy, with a steam radiator, a small gas range stove, and a couple of electric lights, and altogether more elegant than rooms he had rented in his younger years. Two big windows looked out onto the fire escape, and the slanting ceiling bore a skylight. A claw-foot tub stood behind a screen, and he had a Turkish rug that Nora had given him, a small wardrobe, pictures of flowers painted by Jeannette, and his own spinet piano. And he had the sofa, where more than once he'd put up other artists who needed a place to sleep for the night.

Gerard took their coats and Langston looked around.

"How'd you ever get a piano up here?"

It had taken two years for Gerard to save the funds for his banged-up little spinet, and then the better part of three hours getting it up all the stairs, with the help of four friends.

"She's a workhorse," Gerard said, running his hand over the worn varnish, "but I love her."

Langston spotted the tub.

"You've got a real bathtub," he said, marveling. "What I wouldn't give for a bath."

"You'll get it," Gerard said, blowing out some air. One way or another the young man would be getting naked in his proximity. He didn't dare to hope, but he almost laughed, lighting the range under a big pot to get the water heating. "But it will just take a little while. Tell me more about Paris."

"Where to start," Langston yawned. "You've got to see it for yourself. There's nothing like the lights along the Seine at night. Makes you feel rich when you're dirt poor." He yawned again, a gesture that saddened Gerard almost immeasurably. He detected no tension in the younger man's manner that might have signaled a mutuality of the attraction.

But Langston said, "What about you?" changing the tone. "Jazz and blues, you've got it. But there's something different about your playing."

"How so?"

"Like you're holding something back. Like it's not your true love."

"My true love," Gerard said.

"Yeah, what is it you truly love?"

Lord above. Why was this man, this young man vibrant like no other, asking him this very thing right now? With all his heart Gerard wanted to say that he was pretty sure what he truly loved was the man he was looking at right now. Instead he said, "I'm a composer." Even to his own ears this rang a bit false, though it was true enough.

"I knew it," Langston clapped his hands. "What kind of music?"

"Neoclassical," Gerard said.

"Sounds highbrow, what is it?"

"It's a different approach to the music," Gerard said, reaching for scraps of the academic words that seemed so distant at that moment. "Clarity, order, economy… Saying more with less."

Langston nodded, "I see."

"And I love opera," Gerard said, swallowing. Langston might think him old-fashioned. But he'd asked for the truth, and this was the closest Gerard could get.

"There's nothing like the human voice," Langston said, with reverence.

The bath was ready, and Langston undressed behind the screen, while Gerard paced helplessly to and fro, picking up discarded items—shirts, papers—and setting them down in other equally useless places. He heard a light splash of water as Langston got into the tub, letting out a deep sigh. Gerard lowered himself into the armchair. It was futile to resist the pain.

A minute later Langston's voice broke the silence. "Let me hear something of yours."

Of mine, Gerard thought. He struggled up, his limbs weak with a new rush of nerves, and crossed the small expanse of floor to the piano bench. He spread his fingers over the keys, finding the notes of the piece that he'd been writing about Langston. There was no other choice. Countless times Gerard had imagined of playing it for him but hadn't ever believed he would. He played with his eyes closed, the young man of his dreams a few feet away, naked and untouchable.

"That's awful pretty," Langston said, when Gerard finished. "Won't you play it once more?"

If you only knew…

When Gerard finished, the silence lingered long. Then he heard a faint snore. He peeked around the screen. The young poet was asleep. Gerard stepped closer, Langston's lithe body lay half under the water, his arms draped over the edges of the tub. Reflections from the water and the streetlight outside played over his beautiful face. Gerard's heart sank further, but resigned, down into his entrails.

"Langston," Gerard touched his shoulder. "Wake up, you'll drown in there."

The young man opened his eyes.

"I was dreaming," he said, still half asleep. "I thought I was in Paris again."

Gerard stepped to the other side of the screen and sat on the edge of the bed. "Towel's right there," he said.

"I'm still tipsy, I guess," Langston said. Water gurgled in the drain and a moment later Langston emerged, wrapped in the towel.

"Thanks a lot for that bath," he said. "And your music. I mean it."

• • • • •

Gerard didn't sleep much that night, though Langston seemed at perfect peace, snoring softly, unaware of Gerard's quiet agony. He spent the long hours watching ghostly squares of light slide furtively over the ceiling, thrown by the headlights of passing cars, a persistent hope fighting with a damning resignation.

In the morning, or what was left of it, Langston insisted on buying Gerard a coffee and doughnut down the street, saying Gerard looked like his hangover was killing him. Gerard chewed the pastry tasting nothing but cardboard. He sipped the coffee, sensing its heat but not its flavor, and he heard Langston's words without registering their meaning, only that the young man was heading back to Philadelphia, writing out his address on a scrap of paper with a pencil.

"Look me up sometime, won't you?" he said, handing Gerard the paper.

"I will," said Gerard, fumbling the scrap into his wallet. "I have an uncle down there, and cousins."

"Then I'll be seeing you," Langston said, smiling his gorgeous, summery smile and standing up, tossing a crumpled napkin onto the table. They shook hands on the street and parted ways.

By the next day, Gerard had resolved to go down to Philly the following week. Surely it wouldn't hurt to visit. Who was it that said a slowly kindled fire burns brightest? *Perhaps... perhaps...* But then the mail arrived, and with it a letter from the US State Department, informing him that his visa to visit France had been approved, providing that he travel within thirty days.

Gerard laid the letter on his writing desk. Next to it the paper with Langston's address, one edge held down by an inkpot, fluttered like a trapped butterfly in the breeze from the open window. For half an hour he teetered on the edge of tossing in one dream for the hope of another, but reason, landing heavy on his heart, won.

Within four weeks Gerard had wrapped up his affairs in New York, bid a difficult goodbye to the Higginses, had gone to Montreal to see the family, and left for Paris. There had been no time for an extra trip south.

Paris, 1925

The first letter he wrote from abroad was to Langston. That was on the deck of the Danish steamer taking him from Quebec City to the French port of Le Havre. He wrote,

> *Dear Langston,*
>
> *I hope very much it's not an unpleasant surprise to hear from me. I'm bound for Paris, looking out at the sea and thinking of your fine words, your poetry, which will surely bring you much success. No doubt you have many admirers, and you can count me as one of them.*
>
> *I know very much that you* know *what it is to pursue the artistic dream. That's what takes me to Paris, but it's not without regrets. I'm not so young as you are. I've had my chance at an education—as I know you are hungry for—and, outside of formal school, I think there's no better place to be educated than in Harlem, in today's day. I guess for me Harlem is a safe haven, a nest, and now I aim to spread my wings in bigger skies. (I'm no poet, as you can see!) But, as I say, I don't leave without regrets, one in particular.*
>
> *Langston, you've made such a deep impression on me. If this admiration is unwanted, I understand. But if it's a connection you also sense, please write and tell me so. Perhaps we can get to know each other further through writing, and perhaps, in another year or two, will see each other again.*
>
> *Sincerely yours,*
> *Gerard Rougeaux*

Gerard read the letter over several times, tapping the end of his fountain pen against his lips, and then put the pen away in the breast pocket of his suit. He folded the letter, got up from the deck chair where he'd been sitting and leaned his elbows on the ship's rail. The early spring air was cold but windless, smelling of salt from the Atlantic that stretched to the horizon in every direction. He read the letter once more, and then with quick, deliberate movements tore it up and tossed the pieces out into the sea, where they were lost in the ship's churning white wake.

During the subsequent days of his journey, Gerard managed to banish any thoughts of the young poet, but each night they crept back in, through an unguarded back door in his mind, suggesting that Langston might return to Paris—why not?—and that they might meet again. In his heart, though, he knew. He'd left America behind.

✦ ✦ ✦ ✦ ✦

Gerard had not always been a faithful letter writer. His letters from New York back to Montreal, to his parents and his sisters, were sincere but sparse. More often than not he managed to record the antics of certain animals in the city, for the entertainment of his nieces and nephews—all his sisters were married now—which he wrote on the backs of picture postcards. Like the time a neighbor's chow dog ran off with a loaf of sliced bread and left a trail all over the stairs, he'd written about that, or how the red-colored dog down the street tried to play guitar with his back leg, strumming his ribs as fast as could be. And there was a pair of tom cats that battled for control of the fire escape outside his apartment, only pausing in their fighting to listen to the howl of a little white dog with short legs and spots one floor down who sang better opera than what you got on the wireless.

Now, arriving in a new city, country, continent, at the age of thirty-four, he began what became for him the sacred ritual of writing letters daily. He was more reflective now than he had been in his younger years, when life was so engrossing, so immediate. Even with everything new again, he spent many moments in thoughtful quiet. He bought sheaves of onionskin paper at a stationers, and set down for his parents, his sisters, the Higginses and close friends the important details of his days—the garret room he rented in a *pension* in Montmartre, with its single arched window; his petite landlady who kept her unnaturally blond hair pinned up with Chinese combs; the various cafés where he wrote his letters; his meetings with the managers and owners of nightclubs where he sought work, or other musicians whose names he'd been given by friends in New York; the wonder of being in Paris itself, not only its grand avenues and monuments, but the small streets of the city, the cobblestones and winding staircases, the secluded doorways, balconies, alleyways, and courtyards full of flowers, the ornate drinking fountains. He loved it all, and writing letters allowed him the intimacy to share this new experience with his people back home.

Montmartre (he wrote to Sarai) *is built on a hill. The grand Basilica (Basilique) Sacré-Coeur sits on the very top like an enormous white cake. You climb hundreds of stairs up to the top and see the whole of the city below you. The millions of rooftops with their red chimneys. At sunset, there is nothing like it. And there are so many colored folks! It's another Harlem, but entirely different at the same time.*

Often times he wrote out a page or two of sheet music for a piece he was currently working on, to include in the letters, asking Nora and Uncle Hig especially for their critique.

His first news from Paris, though, was that Monsieur Erik Satie had died, just weeks after his arrival.

I had so hoped to meet the old man (Gerard wrote to the Higginses) *I had wanted desperately to be able to pay my respects. They say he was a misanthrope and had such an eccentric fondness for umbrellas, among other things, that he kept one under his coat to keep it dry when it rained! Anyhow, meeting one's heroes can be hazardous, disappointing if the artist in the flesh doesn't live up to one's adoration of their art. As it is, my dream is forever preserved. So perhaps it's better this way.*

Oh, dreams... He sat back in the wrought iron chair of the café where he was writing, thinking of Langston again. Then, to distract himself bent over the onionskin paper again and described for Jeannette—whom he still thought of as a child despite her twenty years—the pair of doves that were building a nest on the sill outside his window at home. They were a devoted married couple, but seemed to argue a lot, particularly about how to decorate their parlor. One month later when he received a letter from Jeannette, clearly charmed by his description of the doves, she wrote that he should write a comic opera about them.

This letter was followed soon after by one from Sarai, describing in detail the wedding of their cousin Martine to Leo LeForte, a younger brother of his old school friend Evelyn, the one he'd once pretended to be sweet on. Gerard shook his head, marveling at how time had passed. *Teeny Martine, no bigger than a bean...* now a young woman married. *She was so happy,* wrote Sarai of the bride, *her face lit up like a sunbeam. The only one happier was the groom.*

The next big news in town came a few months after that, when everyone was talking about the *Revue Nègre* with Josephine Baker, that funny little colored girl from St. Louis, who was about to become the biggest star in all of France. The possibilities for negro artists did seem unlimited here... In his letters the fanfare in town danced a two-step with the smaller stories of Gerard's first forays that led to fruitful connections, or led nowhere. But soon Gerard was playing nearly every night at clubs and music halls, and had, a few heartbeats later, auditioned his compositions with three different theater companies.

Every day was an adventure. Though Harlem had been a place of unparalleled creativity, Paris blew off the roof. Devar was no longer in Paris, Gerard was disappointed to find out, as he'd moved back to the States, but what a parade of characters there was here. Montmartre was full not only of Harlemites, but of colored artists and entrepreneurs from all over America and beyond. Add to this, European artists and writers of every type, packing the cafés by day and the clubs by night, joined by Mexican painters, musicians from all over the Caribbean, Jewish intellectuals. As for the color bar, what Gerard had heard was right. He could eat anywhere, ride in any train car, sleep in any hotel, so long as he could pay, and the French—a generous, passionate, opinionated people—identified him first and foremost as a musician, a person not only deserving of respect, but of reverence.

Gerard kept the scrap of paper with Langston's address—growing smudged and yellowed—in his billfold, a sort of talisman. He bought every issue of *The Crisis* at a nearby bookshop, Dr. Du Bois's magazine which published many of Langston's poems, and pored over them alone in his room. He knew he could write to Langston via the magazine, if the address in his billfold was no longer good. But he never did.

Anna Paraibel

Dearest Nora, Uncle Hig, and Jeannette, (Gerard wrote) *you will be glad to know that of my new connections in Paris there are many colorful people, and a few even promise to become true friends. One of these is a tall, eccentric singer from Martinique named Anna Paraibel...*

On an evening during his third week in the city, Gerard found a notice, handwritten in pencil and stuck into the grill of the first-floor window of a little club called *l'Abbaye*, declaring that a piano player was needed *tout de suite*. Pulling the notice from the grille, Gerard entered the club and gave it to the man at the door with his card, then ordered a gin with lemon and honey from the bar, preparing to wait until the manager had a moment to speak with him.

On the little stage at the back, a black woman in a pink taffeta dressing gown, marcelled platinum hair and matching eyeshadow sang a sad, campy love song in a trilling, high-pitched voice. *Il m'a quitté, je ne sais pas pourquoi, et je ne sais pas où il est,* she crooned. The audience laughed, calling out mock sympathies, in step with the ironic mien of the performer, until, with a turn and a flourish, the singer pulled off the platinum wig and dropped the robe, revealing a full tuxedo. Without missing a beat she picked up the part of the runaway lover, singing in a low, throaty voice, *Ma cherie est partie, je l'ai quitté et ça fait deux de nous qui ne savons pas pourquoi je l'ai fait.*

In the course of a single show, as Gerard would soon learn, Anna belted out blues like Bessie Smith or delivered those forlorn little songs with an ironic innocence that nevertheless made you cry. Visually she was extremely versatile too, performing in glamorous evening gowns, colorful garments from her island home that shone against the deep hue of her skin, or in the tuxedos she favored, with her hair slicked back and oversized bowler hats. French audiences, who relished a modicum of shock and confusion, loved her.

Gerard began accompanying Anna on piano one or two nights a week, finding they had an excellent chemistry, even if in her company he grew markedly unsettled. If she decided that anyone working at *l'Abbaye* displayed a sign of pretense she was quick with a cutting statement, her searing Caribbean French as equally penetrating as her gaze. "Do shave that rat off your face immediately, Marius," she said once of the manager's new goatee. "It doesn't suit you at all." She turned her attention back to the purple lacquer she was just then applying to her nails at a table below the stage. "I'm an artist," she said, to no one in particular, "but I despise artifice."

How a woman came to be both so different and so self-possessed he had no idea, and at first he took pains to avoid being alone with her, thinking a person such as himself would not bear up under her scrutiny. But one night, between performances, he chanced upon one of the waiters—a long-limbed young Dane who spoke French as if his tongue were on stilts—standing outside Anna's basement dressing room.

"Ah, Monsieur Rougeaux," the waiter said. "Can you deliver this?" He thrust the small, round tray he was holding toward Gerard. "Marius wants me upstairs." Before Gerard could even protest, the young man had run off, his feet clanging on the iron staircase, leaving Gerard staring at the little glass of sherry perched in the center of the tray.

He knocked on the door and was answered by Anna's deep voice. "Come in, young Hamlet."

Pushing the door open he found Anna reclined on a little couch with a sleeping mask over her eyes. Gerard blinked, searching for a place to set down her drink. Tins of makeup and hair oil crammed the edges of her dressing table, amid vases of flowers, both fresh and wilted. He cleared his throat.

Anna lifted the bottom edge of her mask. "Oh, dear," she said. "I thought you were Biergh. I'll take that." She unfurled a hand in his direction.

It was Gerard's turn to speak, he knew, but the cat had gotten his tongue and for a split second he thought it might be lost for good.

"Won't you sit?" Anna took her sherry and waved at the dressing table chair. "Do close the door though, there's a terrible draft."

"I'll just stay a minute," he said, finding his voice again and setting the tray on his knees. "Blanchard's put me on at the beginning this time."

"Mm." Anna sipped her drink. "Tell me, how are you liking Paris?"

"Very much." Damn, he was sweating.

She laughed. "You look as though I've trapped you in a jar. Like a butterfly."

He laughed too, pulling at the knot in his tie to loosen it. "Do I? Please forgive me."

"If you forgive me too."

"What for?"

"If I'm too forward, I suppose." She tossed back the last of the sherry and stretched her arms up over her head. "It's just that I feel you and I are going to be friends."

She had hit the mark calling him a butterfly, Gerard thought later. Though perhaps a more apt comparison would be a moth, one drawn—despite himself—irresistibly, even suicidally to her flame. His little wings would catch fire in her presence, and when the ashes fell, what would he find left in their place?

Another day, during a break in rehearsals, two of the other musicians began debating which styles of singing and dancing were better suited to men versus women, and when this extended to playing instruments, Anna cut them off.

"Men *this* and women *that*," she said, waving her hands around her ears. "I don't see what all the fuss is about. I may be a woman on the outside, but on the inside I feel I am just as much a man. I am both, to be sure." She was unperturbed by the silence that followed and took a slow drag on her cigarette. "Oh, Vadim," she said, "close your mouth before a fly goes in."

Gerard burst out laughing.

"I wish I were half the man that you are, Anna," he said to her later, when he walked her to her flat.

"Don't you think you are a little bit woman inside?" she asked.

"How would I know if I were?"

"It's just a notion," she said. She looked him up and down a moment. "Why don't you come up for a drink. I've a piano up there, you can play me one of your originals."

Anna's flat was as colorful and varied as herself—a proper kitchen with every white surface edged in blue tiles, a bathroom done in reds and emeralds and purple enamel, a bedroom hung with costumes and large windows draped in brown velvet to keep out the daylight when sleep was needed. The strangely windowless sitting room was most colorful of all, hung from floor to ceiling with paintings of all kinds, many of them done by Anna herself, others by artists she knew, such as the cadre of painters from Mexico who considered her one of their own, affectionately calling her *La Veracruzana*. And she had a piano, a little spinet tucked in among the rest of the furniture.

"What a wonderful place," Gerard breathed, as Anna took his coat.

"Thank you, *Cher*," she said, smiling. "I do love it. It's my sanctuary." She poured them each a glass of wine in the sitting room and arranged her long limbs on the divan. "When you're ready," she said. Gerard sat at the piano and inwardly chose a piece. When he finished, he looked over to see Anna stretched out languidly, eyes closed, and thought for a moment she had fallen asleep, but she took a sip of wine and said, "Do continue." Gerard would learn that this was how Anna listened best, with her *whole body*, as she said.

He played another, and one more, and then played the piece he'd written for Langston. When he finished the last one he folded his hands and they sat a few moments in silence.

Anna sat up. "You are Satie's child," she said. Gerard had told her of his influence. "But you are a rebel son. One who would have angered the father because he dared to take his own road."

Anna's words struck such a place in Gerard's heart that his throat closed and his eyes stung.

"I've never heard such music," she went on, unfazed by his sudden emotion. "It makes me feel as if I am sailing alone on a forgotten sea, yet I know exactly where I am going." She shifted onto her back and looked up at the ceiling. "I won't be the only one who realizes it," she said. "No one composes like you."

Cartier

"Think it over," the man said, handing Gerard his card, creamy gilded paper thick enough to stand up on its own. It was Jean-León Riskin, owner of *La Méditerranée*, a club that had a reputation for producing innovative music, and he'd just offered Gerard a job for double what he usually made.

It was April of 1927, Gerard had been in Paris for two years and was gaining notoriety—he'd even just been commissioned by a small company, the *Théâtre Vivarium*, to compose an operetta—though playing clubs and dance halls still provided most of his living.

"I'd better go before Blanchard finds out I was here," Riskin said, glancing around. Louis Blanchard was the owner of the music hall where Gerard had just finished a set, Riskin's arch rival.

"He's not in Thursday nights," Gerard said, tucking Riskin's card into his breast pocket.

"I know," Riskin said, still looking this way and that. "But he has his proxies." He nodded to Gerard and hastily left the hall.

One week later, Monsieur Riskin led Gerard backstage to a practice room in the basement of *La Méditerranée*, where four white musicians were finishing an energetic piece. The guitarist hopped off his stool and came to shake Gerard's hand.

"Claude Cartier," he said. He whipped a shock of black hair out of his face and took a drag from a cigarette that had been resting on a music stand. "American?"

"Canadian," Gerard said, unsure why he said so, having been so long in New York.

"Is there a difference?" One of the other musicians laughed and Cartier spun around. "I've got to get the lay of the land, you know," he said, gesturing widely. He looked back to Gerard with interest.

"Perhaps our French is better," said Gerard, and everyone laughed this time.

"I'm in charge of these ruffians," Claude Cartier said. "But Jean-Léon is the real top dog." He introduced the rest of the band, Henri, Yves, Marcel.

"He's the stage director," said Henri, the drummer, pointing at Cartier with one of his sticks, "and an actor."

"That's right," said Yves, the bass player. "He acts like he loves you and then he ignores you for good." More laughter.

"Hey," Cartier said, "knock it off or he won't like me at all."

"Inevitable!" said Henri.

"Ok, *Canadien*," Cartier said, turning his back on the drummer and gesturing toward the empty piano bench. "Won't you join us?"

✦ ✦ ✦ ✦ ✦

"You're fitting in well," Cartier told Gerard one afternoon during a rehearsal break. Yves had gone out to a café down the street and brought back ham sandwiches and beer the café owner brewed himself.

"I appreciate that." Gerard said, wiping mustard from his lips with a napkin. He had cultivated an adaptable style that served him well, what with playing with so many different musicians over the years. "You fellows are a great bunch, I'm enjoying it."

"I'd like you to show us something new though, something from New York. I get the idea you're holding back on us."

"I'd be glad to," Gerard said.

"What's your dream, ah?" Cartier was looking at him more pointedly, his dark eyes glittering. "What brought you to Paris? I have a feeling it was more than jazz."

The comment struck a chord, reminding him of the time two years before when Langston had asked him a similar question. He told Cartier he considered himself a neoclassical composer, that his dream was to work in opera.

"Ah, high culture." Cartier took a swig of beer and polished off the last bite of his baguette. "That's why you seem so sophisticated." He winked at Gerard. "I play the violin you know. My mother is Jewish, it was compulsory."

"Why don't you tell him your dream?" Henri chimed in.

"It's scandalous," Yves said. "He wants to go to Berlin."

"What's in Berlin?" asked Gerard.

"The real nightlife," Cartier said. "I have friends there. Cabarets with true artistic freedom, satire that makes you sweat. Nothing is sacred and all convention is fair game."

"So you're an iconoclast," Gerard said, impressed by Cartier's passionate energy.

"Oh, I am," Cartier said. "All the way down to the gutter. I love it. High culture for you, my friend, the gutter for me."

"That does sound scandalous," Gerard said, laughing. "I hope you get your chance."

◆ ◆ ◆ ◆ ◆

A few weeks in, Cartier asked Gerard if he would meet with him once in a while to work on arrangements. Cartier was eager to learn what was current in American jazz and to incorporate more improvisation, and in the next month they met several times. When Gerard refused to take payment Cartier insisted afterward on at least buying the sandwiches and beer.

"How is your Monsieur Daudet?" Gerard asked Cartier one day during a break. This was one topic, lately, sure to get Cartier going. Léon Daudet was a writer and royalist leader who had recently escaped from prison.

"It's the farce of the century," Cartier said, laughing bitterly. He slapped a hand on the issue of *L'Humanité*—one of the few newspapers in France, he said, that contained anything close to the truth—that lay beside them on the table. "Daudet is typical of monarchists the world over. Obtuse and loud, a puppet of the aristocracy who uses what cunning he has to persecute society's most vulnerable citizens." Cartier ran a hand through his hair and shook his head. "Vile, all of it."

"It's good material," Gerard said, eyeing the notebook Cartier kept full of scribbles he used in his theatrical satire.

Cartier smiled, a wolfish grin if Gerard ever saw one. "It's excellent material."

"We've got plenty of those types in America," Gerard said, smiling too.

"Yes, I'm sure you have."

◆ ◆ ◆ ◆ ◆

Gerard began to look forward to their meetings with an anticipation that surprised him. Claude Cartier was attractive, yes, but though he wore no wedding ring, he often mentioned a woman he called Miri. Henri or Marcel, for example, would ask Cartier where he was taking Miri the next day, and Cartier would say the *Parc Monceau* or the *Bois de Vicennes*, adding, "You know how she loves her flowers."

Still, his time with Cartier left Gerard enlivened, and unsettled in a different way than he felt in Anna Paraibel's company. Cartier brought an unusually sharp focus to the music, working at variations with a relentless precision that one might have called mathematical, if not for that passionate energy that punctuated everything he did. He laughed, he moaned, he pulled at his hair when the solution to a problem evaded him.

But as serious as Cartier was about his music, he was just as relentlessly playful, joking with band members, jumping over chairs or up on tables at any moment. Gerard had never met anyone like him. He wondered what kind of woman this Miri was, what kind of woman would inspire this Claude Cartier's evident devotion. She must be beautiful, intelligent, talented. She must be very special.

A little sad to think about it, if he admitted the truth. But more than once, returning home for the night after one of their meetings, or after work, playing into the wee hours to the exuberant crowds at *La Méditerranée*, Gerard recalled Cartier's face, his eyes, black and flashing, meeting his own here and there, lingering perhaps for a second longer than necessary before turning away. Gerard twisted and turned in his bed, chiding himself for imagining things.

✦ ✦ ✦ ✦ ✦

One Saturday night after their show the fellows were more jovial than usual, Yves in particular kept swatting Henri on the ass.

"It's his birthday, is all," Marcel said. "We tend to beat each other up on such occasions."

"I can see that," Gerard said, rolling his eyes. And then to Henri, "*Bon anniversaire.*"

"*Merci beaucoup, Monsieur Rougeaux.*" said Henri, bowing low, giving Yves yet another opportunity to strike.

Out on the street Gerard turned away from the knot of them, intending to head home. Cartier had his arms around Henri's and Marcel's shoulders, but looked around for Gerard, already a few yards away. "What, aren't you coming?"

"Where?"

"Nadine Maria's. She's throwing Henri a party. You won't believe her place."

"I don't know," Gerard said. He was tired; before their show he'd played a long matinee at *l'Abbaye*.

"Rougeaux, be serious," Marcel shouted. "You're coming with us. Don't break Henri's heart."

Gerard laughed. "Alright, why not."

Nadine Maria's apartment was indeed stunning, a penthouse with sky-high ceilings, huge windows and an excellent view of the Seine, lit up now in all its glory, just as Langston had once described it. And so many people packed inside, they could barely get in the door.

"All this for Henri?" Gerard asked, shouting above the noise.

"Not at all," Cartier shouted back. "Nadine loves any excuse to throw a party. She's filthy rich."

"No doubt."

Deep in the center of the throng a jazz band was playing and nearly everyone was dancing. Cartier pulled at Gerard's elbow. "You dance, don't you?"

"Yes, but I need a drink first."

"Let's get one, then."

In the heady atmosphere and crush of dancers Gerard quickly lost sight of his group, except for Cartier, who never seemed to be more than a few feet away—dancing, leaning in to shout in someone's ear, taking a drink or a cigarette, laughing. Gleaming black hair and eyes set off by his white shirt, damp patches under his arms and between his shoulder blades, sleeves rolled above his elbows showing the muscles of his forearms made intricate from countless hours of guitar, graceful hands, Claude Cartier was the most vivid thing in the room. Gerard couldn't take his eyes off Cartier's cheeks, flushed pink and boyish, shadowed blue below with a day's growth of beard.

Cartier danced with both men and women, as many of the other guests were doing, as did Gerard too, who, under the right circumstances, adored dancing. Deep in the sway of so many bodies, Gerard wondered if the mysterious Miri might appear, or what she would make of her man's carousing. But quite suddenly he was in Cartier's arms.

"What's a big, strong, handsome man like you doing in a place like this?" Cartier said in mock coquetry. They were both quite drunk by then.

Gerard laughed. "I'm dancing with the most beautiful girl at the party."

"I'll slap you if you get fresh with me, *Monsieur*."

"Oh, your honor is safe with me, *Mademoiselle*."

"Ah! A damn shame!"

The next thing Gerard knew, partners had switched again, and he was doubly intoxicated, Cartier's scent lingering in all his senses.

✦ ✦ ✦ ✦ ✦

They met next a few days later, "first thing in the morning"—noon—on a Tuesday, to work on an arrangement for Thursday night's new show, but before long Cartier threw his pencil down on the little table where he was making his notes and rubbed his eyes. "I need to take a walk outside. I feel like a damned mole."

"Excellent idea." Gerard stretched his arms over his head. On a summer day such as that one the basement of the *La Méditerranée* was getting to him too. "Let's go."

They walked three quarters of an hour in the park below the *Basilique Sacré-Coeur* and then sat in the amphitheater in the *Jardin des Arènes*.

"Paris is beautiful in July," Gerard sighed, enjoying the sunshine and light, balmy breeze. "Like May in New York. New York is terrible this time of year, you—"

"I can't go to bed with you," Cartier said abruptly.

Gerard's mouth hung open.

"We work together." Cartier said. "I'm very strict on that point."

Gerard was still too shocked to answer. Lord, had he been that obvious? Leave it to Claude Cartier to say whatever was on his mind.

Finally, Gerard said, "Maybe I should quit." He was only half-joking.

"Oh no," Cartier shook his head. "You're brilliant with us."

"Then I suppose you'll have to go."

Cartier laughed.

"Anyway," Gerard said, leaning back on the bench, "I don't think Miri would be too pleased if we did." He cleared his throat. "Go to bed."

Cartier turned to him sharply, eyes wide. "What's my mother got to do with it?"

"Your—" Gerard burst out laughing. He slapped his knees. "Your mother? All this time I thought—"

Cartier was laughing now too. "My God, my mother—"

"I thought she was your girlfriend, or your wife." Gerard was still laughing.

Cartier was too. "Obviously!"

Gerard sighed and wiped his eyes with his sleeve. He took a breath. "All the same." He held a hand out. "Just friends, then?"

Cartier shook his hand, lingering with a squeeze perhaps one second longer than necessary. "For life."

"Damn shame," Gerard said, which set them both laughing again.

At last they stood. "Back to work?"

"Yes. Back to work."

✦ ✦ ✦ ✦

Gerard was with Anna, having a glass of wine in her gallery sitting room and listening to her new recording of "Blue Skies," a gift from an admirer. When the record ended, they sat in silence a few minutes, but Gerard's mind wasn't on the music; he was thinking of his conversation with Cartier the week before in the *Arènes* amphitheater.

Anna changed the record on the phonograph and instead of returning to her divan, perched on the chair opposite Gerard's. "What's troubling you, *Cher?*"

"Just a little preoccupied, I guess."

"With?"

Gerard sighed. "Claude Cartier."

"From *La Méditerranée?*"

"*Oui.*"

"Well?"

Something about being with Anna always broke down the reticence he usually had with others. He gave her the state of affairs.

"You like him, then?"

"Very much."

"Then, Gerard, you must woo him."

Gerard half-laughed, shook his head. "But he's told me, Anna. He doesn't want it."

"I think he's told you what he *does* want."

Gerard shook his head again. "No, his rules—"

Anna leaned forward and caught his face in her hands.

"You *idiot*. His rules! What makes you think he won't break them?"

✦ ✦ ✦ ✦

And because of that talk with Anna, despite the voice in his head that warned him he should be content with friendship and not ruin it, he took the risk. In the days that followed, he wrote a new piece of music. As he had with the piece for Langston, he wrote from his heart, setting down the notes in the pages of his composition book, scratching out what wasn't right and trying again until he was satisfied he'd captured just what he'd wanted to. When he finished, he copied out the piece on fresh paper, placed it in an envelope, wrote only *Claude* on the front, walked the distance to the building where Cartier lived, and dropped it in his mailbox.

And then he waited.

It would be three days until he saw Cartier again, at *La Méditerranée*, three days in which he had two shows at *l'Abbaye* and time to work on his operetta. To his surprise, rather than being anxious about how Cartier would respond, or if he would respond at all, Gerard was strangely calm. It was not so unlike his student days at the Conservatory after a particularly difficult performance exam when he'd prepared well and done his best and was awaiting his results, he was free. He had a taste of that freedom now, but perhaps more than that it was the act of giving his feelings expression without restraint. That in itself was liberating.

When Gerard finally saw him again, Cartier said nothing about the piece. Rehearsal, performing, everything was as usual. Cartier was band leader, professional, nothing more, and Gerard began to sense the edges of his bit of freedom crumbling away until, at last, he wondered if he'd made a mistake after all. The voice in his mind that had given him warning now reappeared to say *I told you so*. He hoped that at least things at work wouldn't change, and that personally no harm had been done. He valued Cartier's friendship, truly, and thought perhaps he should apologize.

But the next night, at home in his garret room after a show at another club, preparing to go to bed, he heard a faint knock at the door. It would be the concierge, he thought, who kept odd hours, wanting to know if he'd seen her cat when he'd come in, or if the repaired leak in one of his windows was holding up in this spate of summer rain. But when he opened up, it was Claude, leaning one elbow high up in the doorframe, as if weary from a long journey.

"I'm not bothering you, am I?" He smelled faintly of alcohol, and his eyes looked especially dark.

Gerard stepped back. "Of course not. Come in."

Cartier cast a glance or two around the room. "Nice place."

"Coffee?"

"*Non, merci.*"

Awkwardly they both sat, Gerard on the bed, Cartier on the only chair, a comfortable Louis XVI that had come with the room.

Claude leaned his head in his hands. "Look, I just wanted to thank you," he said, "for your music."

Gerard waited, unsure as to whether Cartier meant the piece he'd written or his work at *La Méditerranée*. Perhaps he was being let go after all, for overstepping.

Cartier twisted in the chair. He pressed his eyes with his hands. "It's beautiful." He pinched the bridge of his nose. "It's damn beautiful." Gerard began to speak but Cartier cut him off. "What are you trying to do to me, ah? Make me fall in love with you?" There was anger in his voice.

"No, I—"

Cartier cut him off again. "Because it's working, goddamnit."

He got up and in two steps crossed the distance to Gerard and stood over him, as if he might strike him, but Gerard didn't flinch. His heart stayed open before the storm that was Cartier. Gerard seized his wrists and for a second Cartier struggled against him. But in the next moment they were kissing, falling together onto the bed.

Hurriedly they pulled at their clothes, shirts off, trousers, underclothes, until everything was off and their embrace was at last unimpeded. They rolled, devouring each other with kisses long and deep, Claude's hands around the back of Gerard's neck, his own running the length of Claude's spine, over his magnificent bare shoulders and down to his narrow hips. Claude was so light in Gerard's arms, and the concentrated energy of his touch seemed to intensify Gerard's own senses. When Claude took him in his mouth, the pleasure that shot through him was almost unbearable. Then Claude turned and moved back against him so that they could unite completely, and they rocked together until waves of heat broke over them both.

✦ ✦ ✦ ✦ ✦

For two days, they barely left Gerard's room. A heady vortex of bedclothes, tobacco smoke and, of course, music, sucked down to the very bottom of a turbulent sea Gerard never wanted to leave. But when finally they broke the surface again, for Gerard the world was changed. The leaves of the trees unfurled their green vapors into the humid August air and floated them across the Seine.

Ethers of baking bread and brewing coffee rose through Gerard's windows and touched his cheeks with gentle hands. A new face greeted him in the mirror. He laughed at himself, because it was all perfectly ridiculous, but he didn't care in the slightest.

"What do you miss about your home, Gerard? Now that you're here in Paris?" Claude was sitting up in bed, tangled sheets over his legs, smoking a cigarette with his arms folded. Gerard had been standing at the window, gazing down at the street where Claude lived, watching little parades of worshippers streaming out of the *Basilique* after the service. It was a Sunday.

"How do you know I miss it?" Gerard said, coming to sit on the bed and pulling closed the robe he was wearing, one of Claude's.

"Don't you?"

Gerard lay down, sighing. "At times I miss everything. My parents' house, for example."

"What in particular?"

"The old maple tree in the back garden," Gerard said, its image suddenly vivid in his mind. He hadn't thought of it in years. "It had a large hollow in its middle, burned out in a fire before I was born. My sisters and I used to play in it when we were little."

"Ah, an enchanted place."

"It was that."

Gerard saw himself there now as a small boy, Sarai helping him climb down inside the old trunk, earthen floor smelling of damp, ants and other tiny insects marching up and down the interior grooves in the wood still blackened from the ancient fire. How he had imagined himself a big, benevolent giant guarding over them.

"I remember my grandmother's attic," Claude said, crushing the end of his cigarette on the blue glass saucer he used for an ashtray. "My father's mother. It was also an enchanted place."

"Trunks of old clothes you dressed up in? Big, dusty mirrors?"

Claude laughed. "That was it, exactly. My first theater."

"Did you imagine yourself famous?"

"Of course." Claude slid down beside him, pulled the robe off his shoulder and kissed him there. "It's lovely, the thought of you playing, as a child. Out in the wilds of Canada."

Gerard laughed now too. "Montreal is hardly the wilds."

But Claude didn't seem to be listening anymore; he was busy pulling the robe open further and pressing his lips to Gerard's warm skin. Gerard ran his fingers in Claude's thick hair, over the pale skin at the nape of his neck. He sank willingly into the enchantment of the moment, home neither near nor far away.

✦ ✦ ✦ ✦ ✦

Langston's first book, *The Weary Blues*, was published that year. Gerard found a copy at the bookshop on the Rue Pigalle, where he bought his copies of *The Crisis*, and read it straight through that night. It was beautiful, moving, thoughtful, everything he might have expected, though he would have purchased it for the cover alone, given the portrait of the poet on the back. Gerard had long since let go of his feelings for Langston, but a wisp of them remained, curled like a seashell in one of his heart's corners.

Claude, spending the next night with Gerard, picked up the volume from the floor where it lay beside the bed and read a few pages. He studied the picture on the back. "Is he a friend of yours?"

"Of a sort," Gerard said.

"A lover?"

"No."

"You fell for him though."

How did Claude always know these things?

"I did once," Gerard said.

Claude handed him the book. "Read me something, won't you? Pick a short piece. You know my English isn't good." He lay down, listening with his arm over his eyes, and when Gerard had finished Claude gave a short, quiet laugh. "*Mon dieu*," he said. "I'm jealous." He sat up and shook his head. "What's wrong with me?"

"What?" A little current ran the length of Gerard's spine.

"Yes, I'm jealous of this man." He took the book again from Gerard's hands and studied Langston's face. "Because you loved him."

Claude Cartier had to be the most forthright person Gerard had ever met. He was ashamed of nothing, it seemed, not even when he surprised himself.

"I don't mind," Gerard said.

Claude laughed, cuddling up to Gerard. "No, why should you?"

"I'll take it as a compliment."

A few minutes later Claude spoke again. "What would they say about us in New York?" Claude thumbing again through the issue of *The Crisis*. "A black and a white together?"

"Most folks wouldn't take well to it, but two men of any color—"

"Such a fuss they make," Claude cut in, "over a bit of pigmentation."

"They?" Gerard felt a tension rising.

"The Americans."

"It's a hell of a lot more than a fuss," said Gerard, his throat suddenly tight. "My people are persecuted over there, exploited, murdered."

"Gerard," Claude's voice was low, "I didn't mean it like that."

"What does it mean to *you*, anyway? A black man as a lover?"

Claude was quiet a while, then he said, "Perhaps that's what I wondered about, really. Your feelings. About me in that respect. A Frenchman. A Jew."

How did Gerard feel? Maybe a bit disloyal at times, if he admitted the truth. Disloyal to his family. To the Cause. But what was he really supposed to do? Marry a good black woman and raise a brood of children?

"It's a complicated question," he said at last.

Claude stroked his cheek. "Yes, of course."

✦ ✦ ✦ ✦ ✦

If Gerard was troubled at times with such questions, or Claude's intention to go away to Berlin and make a life there, passion stretched his heart open with hope. Who knew what was possible, after all? Hadn't life surprised him a thousand times? At other moments, doubt made its unwelcome appearance, causing him to worry about risks recklessly taken, cautioning him to pull back and slow down. And there were other moments, strange ones, such as the night when Henri caught his arm in the stairwell leading up to the stage at the club. The others already on the other side of the stage door.

"Gerard, be careful."

"What?"

"Claude is something of a saboteur."

Gerard stopped in his tracks. "What do you mean?"

But just then Riskin burst through the basement door. "Hurry up, *les gars*, for God's sake," he said, shooing them up the stairs like geese. "I've got guests at the front tables who are positively wetting themselves."

Miri

"I'm going to Miri's for supper tonight," Claude said, tucking under his arm the issue of *L'Humanité* he'd just purchased at the kiosk near his place. They were on the street, about to go their separate ways, Claude to buy a few sets of new guitar strings and Gerard to a meeting with the director of the company, *Théâtre Vivarium*, that had commissioned his operetta.

"Ah yes, the Sabbath," Gerard said, noting that it was Friday. "Is she religious?" Most of the Jews he knew were entirely secular, as Claude seemed to be—politics and art and discourse were their gods. But that was the younger generation, perhaps the older was more traditional.

"Oh, very," Claude said. "She's a Jungian."

"Psychoanalysis?" Gerard knew of it, had even heard it called the "Jewish science."

"That's it." Claude lit a cigarette and blew a stream of white smoke into the frosty air. It was December, and the streets and the rooftops were dusted with a light layer of powdery snow. "She took it up after my father died. It's interesting. Symbols, dream interpretation, that sort of thing. She has many devoted patients."

"I imagine."

Gerard had a great aunt back in Montreal, who'd been a big believer in the importance of dreams. Much of the time his own dreams were a vague and irrelevant mash of things he supposed were the flotsam and jetsam of living, if he remembered them at all. The previous night, for example, he'd been trying to hang his hat on a lamp post. Then again there were those that lingered in his mind in his waking hours, with clear images and such real emotions that it did make him wonder if they carried a message. He still remembered his dream of the baby floating in a river from so many years before.

"Why don't you come with me?" Claude said. "To dinner. You'll like her."

"I'd be honored, *Monsieur*."

Claude laughed. "She'll like you too."

✦ ✦ ✦ ✦ ✦

Miriam Hazan Cartier met them at her door, a petite woman with bobbed silver curls and the same smiling dark eyes as her son. She wore a simple dark blue dress, draped over by a bright purple scarf with red flowers.

"You must be Gerard," she said, holding out a delicate hand. "Claude rang me from the theater."

The apartment was modest but elegant, tastefully furnished with eclectic things—vases of blown glass, little birds done in black pottery, a cubist painting of a man at a desk piled with books, a small African bust carved in polished mahogany.

"My husband," Miri said, when Gerard admired the painting.

"Papa wasn't really green," Claude said, helpfully. "But it does capture him."

"This is marvelous," Gerard said, bending to get a closer to the African carving.

"Isn't she beautiful?" Miri asked.

"She looks like a queen."

"That's what I call her, my Queen."

"What about this?" Gerard said, turning his gaze to a small earthenware pot beside the carving, its black surface gleaming with golden veins. "Was it broken?"

"Yes," Miri said, "it's a *kintsugi*, from Japan. Broken pottery repaired with lacquer and gold dust."

"Papa was a great admirer of anything from the East," Claude said.

"It's a tradition," Miri said, "that embraces the flawed, the imperfect."

"How you've always dealt with me, I suppose," Claude laughed.

Miri reached up and squeezed his cheeks. "Don't you know it." She winked at Gerard.

They sat together at a dining table covered in a lace cloth. Miri lit two candles—eschewing the traditional head covering and prayers but observing a moment of reverent silence—and served a chicken roasted with generously seasoned potatoes and vegetables. Claude delivered all the news from the clubs and theaters around town. The gossip was that the young American pilot Charles Lindbergh, made instantly famous by his solo flight to Paris from New York, was spotted in the audience at the *Folies-Bergère*, gone to see Josephine Baker in her banana skirt.

"I would think *La Bakair* would be too risqué for American tastes," Miri said.

"Surely the prospect of seeing her," Gerard said, "was what drove him to make his flight."

Miri laughed. "The *Bronze Venus* is ravishing, to be sure."

When Claude mentioned Gerard's operetta Miri lit up with questions. What was the music like, she wanted to know. Where had he trained? Who were the composers he most admired? Her favorite was Verdi, and Gerard said that *Falstaff* was his favorite comic opera.

All too soon it was time to go, Friday night being a big one at *La Méditerranée*, and there was still much to prepare. Claude drained his wine glass and stood up, kissing his mother on both cheeks. "Thank you, *Maman*," he said. "It was delicious, as usual."

"Wait a moment," she said, putting her light hand on Gerard's shoulder. "I want to show you something." She disappeared down the hall and promptly returned with a photograph in a silver frame.

"*Maman*, no!" Claude protested. "Gerard, you don't want to see this."

Miri ignored him. "We had this taken after his first recital."

Claude groaned. "Oh, it's all over now."

Gerard laughed. "Look at him." He took the photo from Miri's hands to study it closely. Young Claude Cartier, seven or eight years old in a suit with short pants, stood solemnly, holding a violin on his shoulder with one hand, and a bow at his side with the other. His big dark eyes, fringed with lashes, belied the hint of a smile.

"I'm sure you were very proud," Gerard said to Miri.

"Of course."

"Was he talented from the start?"

"Terribly."

"Terribly lazy," Claude laughed. "*Maman* had to chase me down to practice."

Miri laughed too. "I suppose it's true." Then she glanced at the clock on the wall near them, the brass pendulum swinging back and forth. Almost eight. "Well, you boys had better be going." She squeezed Gerard's hand. "Please come again."

Back outside the air had grown colder and a new light snow was falling, collecting on the bare limbs of trees and steps leading to doorways.

"Your mother is lovely," Gerard said.

"Didn't I say you'd like her?"

"I've met another side of you."

"And how do you like it?"

"Better than any opera."

♦ ♦ ♦ ♦ ♦

The next time Gerard joined Claude for supper at Miri's he brought a bouquet of red zinnias. "They reminded me of your scarf," he said.

"What would we do without hothouses in winter?" she exclaimed, bringing the flowers to her face to smell them. "They are too beautiful." She went to the kitchen for a vase.

This time Miri wanted to know all about Montreal, Gerard's family, New York, and how it was he had decided to come to Paris. She had such a kind interest that he let slip the fact that he was born out of wedlock and adopted by his uncle and aunt. His face flashed with heat, but Miri was unperturbed.

"You never told me that," Claude said.

"No," Gerard said. "I suppose there aren't many good opportunities to mention such things."

"Well," Claude said, tilting his head toward his mother, "she's used to people telling her everything. She inspires confidence."

"That she does."

"You're both sweet," Miri smiled. "You might be surprised at what goes on under the surface for people. Every person is a whole world of secrets. I've learned that in my work."

Gerard suddenly recalled the dream he'd had the night before Don Giovanni, of the infant floating in a river at night, the haunting image, how he'd been worried it would turn into a fish if he didn't bring it out to dry.

"Claude told me you interpret dreams for your clients," Gerard said. "I still remember one I had many years ago. It's funny how it has stayed with me."

"Tell us," Claude said.

"There wasn't too much to it I suppose," Gerard said. "I was walking in a river at night and came upon a baby asleep and floating in the water. I thought he'd become a fish if I didn't get him out and dry him off." Gerard smiled. "I know it sounds silly, but the emotion was very strong."

"How so?" Miri asked, eyes intent on his face.

"It's hard to put into words. Just that there was a sense that all of it was important. The night, the river, the baby who needed tending to…"

Miri sat back in her chair, thoughtful. "The symbols in dreams can mean many things, she said. "A river often speaks to the flow of life, and nighttime the deep subconscious. The baby is the most potent symbol in your dream. It may speak to a vital quality of yours left behind in childhood that craves a revival. It may mean your soul, or rebirth, the possibility of new life ahead."

"And the fish?"

"The fish, in Jungian terms, is often symbolic of a deep level of the unconscious, since it swims below the surface, and that combined with the nighttime atmosphere of your dream, may mean you fear if you don't act, that forgotten quality, so vital to yourself, will be lost completely."

"Amazing," Gerard breathed. "All of that from a few images."

"The mind, particularly the subconscious mind," Miri said, "is so much wiser, so much more powerful than we know."

"I suppose Herr Freud would have it be all about sex and desire. Repressed desire in particular," Claude said, taking a mouthful of Miri's cooking. Chewing and swallowing he smiled at Gerard. "Of course, he's right. That it's all about sex."

Gerard felt the blood drain from his face. *In front of Claude's mother for God's sake?* He had supposed that Claude had told her he was a friend, not more, but how much did she know? Never in his life would he have dared with either of his own parents. And which was worse, now that all his secrets were out on the table—being a bastard or a degenerate? But when he raised his eyes to glance at Miri she only appeared amused, still the picture of calm, sipping her wine with a thoughtful expression. He was a fool. Of course, she knew.

"Well, not *every*thing, Claude," she said. "And when you grow up one day you may learn that."

◆ ◆ ◆ ◆ ◆

When they left for *La Méditerranée*, the winter air was almost unbearably fresh. Gerard felt it rush into his lungs. Was it being in the presence of a parent, a mother, who *knew*? His nostrils tingled and tears started in his eyes. He rubbed them away and laughed, making Claude glance at him sideways. Their footsteps on the paving stones echoed in the corridor of buildings still edged in little whorls of snow.

"Your mother is a remarkable person," Gerard said.

"True. I'm disgustingly fortunate."

It was still the dinner hour and for the moment the street was empty. Gerard grabbed Claude's hand, breaking his stride, and pulled him in for a kiss.

"Take me home tonight," Claude said after.

"If you play something nice for me."

"I will."

Spring, 1928

It was April again, fresh green leaves announcing their tiny debuts; everything that had been sleeping in winter was waking up anew. At times Gerard regretted having to work indoors, but new prospects were budding for him too. His operetta was going into production, his involvement with *Vivarium* was proving enlivening, and everyone said that work with small companies often led to work with the grand ones, not least the *Académie Royale de Musique*.

It's grand to read of your expanding prospects, and about all your fascinating new friends (Jeannette wrote to him.) *Mama has told me of our forbearer from the island of Martinique, the island of your friend Miss Paraibel and of her adventure there when she and Papa travelled with their orchestra to the Caribbean many years ago. I have so enjoyed hearing about your artistic partnerships, not least with your Mr. Cartier. I love my work with the little students at my school, but it's nothing so glamorous as your life in Paris. What a happy time it must be for you!*

Gerard read this last line with a wince. He'd been reading Jeannette's letter after returning home alone from *La Méditerranée*. It would have been a particularly happy time to be sure, but things had taken a turn with Claude.

For over a month now Claude had been becoming more and more frustrated with the program at *La Méditerranée*, his conversations with Jean-Léon Riskin—the club's owner who had poached Gerard from his rival the year before—were growing more tense. The satirist, the actor in Claude, the one who longed for the cabaret life in Berlin, wanted to bring acts of this kind to *La Méditerranée* but Riskin had no interest and dismissed Claude's ideas out of hand. Apart from work, Gerard found Claude more quick-tempered than usual. If he approached Claude, standing at the open window of his garret room smoking a cigarette and lost in thought, to put his hands on his shoulders, Claude stepped away. Rather than linger in bed together in the morning, Claude was now likely to rise and dress before Gerard even awoke, and then bid him a quick, preoccupied goodbye. But much as the growing distance pained him, Gerard kept quiet. If he went unwanted, he told himself, at least he'd preserve his dignity.

One evening, working on an arrangement at the club, Claude threw down his pencil and dug his fingers into his hair, mumbling something Gerard didn't quite hear.

"What's that?"

"I said," Claude said in a flat voice, "I'm wasting my life here."

That stung. But he also understood. He might have felt the same if he'd had to stay in New York. "Why don't you go, then?" he said.

"I haven't got the money," Claude snapped. "You know that. I need ten thousand francs at least to start over in Berlin."

Gerard stood up, closing his composition book with a slap. There was still an hour before the start of the show. "I need some air," he said. "I think I've had enough of your tantrums." He turned to climb the stairs and Claude said nothing.

✦ ✦ ✦ ✦ ✦

Several days later, as the band was setting up on the stage, Riskin appeared with a guest—a man in a gleaming, cream-colored suit and straw boater, and the bearing of one conscious of his irresistible good looks. Claude hopped down to the floor when Riskin waved him over, shook hands with the other man, and in a few minutes returned to the stage.

Claude's face was flushed. "I think the boss is trying to make peace with me," he said to the band, as Riskin and his guest made their way out. "That fellow, Renaud Dutertre—"

"I've heard of him," Yves said. "Big man."

"Right, well he's setting up a cabaret in Marseille and needs a consultant, so I'm recommended." He looked at Henri. "You want to go? I'll need a percussionist."

"When? How long?"

It would be a few days only, in May.

Claude looked at Gerard and shrugged. "It's money."

A raw quiet anger rose up in Gerard's throat. He turned away and sat down at the piano, massaging his hands to warm them.

✦ ✦ ✦ ✦ ✦

Apart from what was necessary at work, they didn't speak again until Claude and Henri returned from Marseille. The low-grade anger had remained with Gerard, but it somersaulted like a circus clown, mocking him with different guises. At first, he was angry with Claude, fed up with his being so absorbed in his frustration and treating him as a mere afterthought. Soon enough, though, he was angry with himself. Hadn't Claude told him he intended to go to Berlin from the start? Hadn't Claude said, in light of their attraction, that he didn't think things should go further? These thoughts dogged him anytime his mind wasn't on his music, most often when he struggled to sleep at night alone in his bed. Why had he ever listened to Anna and her romantic notions? But when, finally, the anger gave way, all that remained was sadness.

He recalled a distant night back in Harlem, the beautiful singer who'd called him fancy and the melancholy moment they'd shared about lovers who'd left.

They line up, but they don't stay.

Gerard's feelings changed once more, the night before Claude was to return. Between them they had never used the word "love," but hadn't they something significant together? Something real? A hopeful challenge rose in his heart. It was good before; couldn't it be made good again? He punched the pillow, resolving to talk things through with Claude. He would begin with love and without accusations. They would be two adults, talking and behaving as adults must do.

But in the end, it didn't go like that.

Gerard had left Claude a note in his mailbox, asking him to ring when he was back in town, and then went to meet Claude at his apartment, a small bouquet of peach-colored tulips over his arm. At the door, Claude did not embrace him, but eyed the flowers with a reluctant expression.

"A romantic gesture," he said. "I hardly deserve it."

Gerard laid them on Claude's writing desk. They both sat.

"How was Marseille?"

"I don't know. Hot."

Claude stood again, ran a hand through his hair and faced the window, away from Gerard, shoulders tense.

"Tell me about the cabaret," Gerard said. "How did you advise the big man?"

Claude shrugged, patted his pockets for his cigarette's and lit one. "It's got a nice view of the sea," he said, blowing smoke. "I told him to knock out a couple of walls, met a few of the musicians."

"Surely that wasn't all."

"No."

"You're nervous," Gerard said.

"I'm not. I am. Shit…"

All at once, all the words Gerard had prepared left him and a dreadful cold invaded his insides. He knew from the way Claude was standing that something had happened.

Claude turned around, face haggard and fearful. "Dutertre—"

"The big man."

Claude half-laughed. "Yes, the big man."

"What about him?"

Claude didn't answer for a long minute. He turned again to face the window, shook his head. "You shouldn't have brought me any damn flowers."

"What do you mean?"

"Don't make me say it."

"You—?"

"Yes."

"You went to bed with him?"

"Yes!" Claude smashed his fist against the window frame.

Gerard gripped the arms of his chair and stared at him. "But this is crazy."

Claude stayed quiet.

"Why? Why did you do it?"

"Obviously, I wanted to."

"What, did he pay you for it?"

"I'm not a prostitute."

"I don't know what you are."

Claude stayed quiet again. Gerard paced the room.

"You're trying to hurt me. Deliberately."

"No." Claude shook his head. "No."

"What have I ever done to you?"

"Nothing!" Claude crouched on his heels, head in his hands. "Nothing. You're so good. You've never done anything. Don't you see?"

"See? See what? What the hell are you talking about?"

"That I'll never leave here. If I'm too attached to you, I'll never leave. I'll never go to Berlin."

Gerard couldn't move, couldn't breathe. Finally, he lowered himself back into the chair. "So, this is your way of doing it. Going to bed with some wealthy man on the bloody Riviera."

"Apparently."

"What kind of sickness is this?"

"I don't know."

La Vol

"You must come up soon and see the new painting in my gallery," Anna said with her mouth full. "Rosario Cabrera made it for me as a parting gift. It's magnificent."

They were at the restaurant near *l'Abbaye* but Gerard wasn't eating much. He'd ordered a bowl of *crème de laitue* that was growing cold in front of him.

Anna ladled another spoonful of lamb with mushrooms and peas into her mouth. "When I told her how distraught I was that she was leaving, and after such a short time, she said I should visit her in Mexico City. I'm sure I shall one day. I'm dying to see it."

"Were you more than friends, then?" Gerard asked, reluctantly dipping his spoon in the soup.

"Sadly, no. She's married, poor thing. And hopelessly loyal."

Gerard leaned back into the plush purple of his seat. The restaurant was more known for its décor than its food, but both appealed. "What are your views on fidelity?"

"Fidelity? Personally, I don't much see the point. But it depends on the pair, don't you think? Their agreement, their temperament."

"I'm sure it must."

Anna, sopping up gravy with a chunk of soft bread, noticed his tone. "Not convinced?"

"I'm not convinced of anything," Gerard said, his voice lightly breaking. He hadn't wanted to bother Anna with his troubles yet again, but there they were, leaking out.

She took his hand across the table and scrutinized his face. "What is it, Gerard?"

"Anna, I'm losing him."

She waited.

"It's happened so suddenly, I hardly understand it. I mean, I don't understand it at all."

When he'd told her everything, she said, "He's fighting a battle."

"Against what?"

"Himself."

"Yet I'm the casualty."

"Yes." They sat in silence a few minutes, Anna slowly finishing the last of her lamb stew. She dabbed her mouth with her napkin and leaned back, looking at the ceiling. "It's dreadful, I know. A lover of mine once left like that. Without warning."

"Here in Paris?"

"Belgium, actually."

"What did you do?"

"Nothing at first. Nursed my wounds. Then I came here."

Gerard gave his cold soup a little stir. "It matters less to me that he slept with that man, than to think of what he might do next. Because that could be anything at all."

"You're wise to think so."

"Am I?"

Yes, *Cher*." She took his hand again. "You'll have to let him go. For now, at least."

"It's killing me."

"I know. I'm sorry." All of a sudden her eyes widened and she straightened up. "Gerard!" she said. "Let's go to the seaside. Silvio will lend us his car. Can you take a few days?"

"I suppose I could."

"There's nothing like salt air for a broken heart, I promise you."

Less than a week later Gerard spoke with Jean-Léon Riskin and took his leave from *La Méditerranée*. He needed the time anyway, for the *Vivarium* and the things he'd been putting off, such as finishing a new portfolio to submit to the *Théâtre National de l'Opéra* and the *Opéra-Comique*. Claude wasn't the only one going after an artistic dream. Now was the time, he told himself, to get serious once and for all.

In June, he found a letter from Claude in his mailbox. They hadn't spoken for weeks, not since his return from Marseille.

Dear Gerard,

I'm in sad shape and I don't imagine you want to hear from me. I won't ask you to forgive me, but I would like you to know that I'm sorry. Everyone regrets your leaving La Méditerranée, as do I, but I think we both know it's for the best. I hope your work is going well and I wish you every success. Marcel told me your operetta opens next month, and I'll go to see it, if you don't mind. I'll take Miri with me. Gerard, I mean it that I'm sorry. Please don't think, by my actions, that my feelings for you were anything but sincere. You've had an effect on me that no one else everhas, and this makes me doubly unworthy of you. My life depends on going to Berlin, though I admit at times I doubt it myself. All I know is that I need to go and find out. If there is any way for us to remain friends, or, rather, be friends in the future, I would be very grateful.

Yours,
Claude

When he finished reading, Gerard folded the letter and placed it in the lacquered box where he kept all his letters from home. It really was finished, and this realization stabbed his heart like a dagger, bringing a fresh rush of tears to his eyes. Images of their love affair flooded his mind, one after another—the fiery beginning of the story, the middle tender and passionate, and then the end, sudden, confusing, excruciating. He would answer the letter or not, it didn't much matter now, and just yet he didn't know what to do. For now, he would work on his compositions, letting the music carry the conversation that his innermost feelings needed to have, conveying everything that words couldn't say.

But words did have their vital place. Gerard revived his daily communion with his loved ones back home by writing letters, a practice that had grown less frequent in the last year. With the letters, he began to send the little artifacts of his life in music—the program for his operetta, new sheet music, leaflets for the shows of his artist friends, even a few of Anna's cast off drawings. She sketched madly on paper before creating a painting, or when she designed a new costume that she then sent to her tailor, a little rotund Frenchman with a bulbous nose and oversized white mustache and goatee. Gerard had no hand for drawing whatsoever, but he could paint a portrait with words, and these elicited, to his great relief, longer and more frequent letters from home. He said once to Anna that he felt like a three-legged stool. One foot in Paris, one in New York, and one in Montreal. His sisters especially, Jeannette included, wrote most often, keeping

Gerard up to date on their doings as well as those things Nora and Hig might not want to discuss, such as their health.

Thankfully, his parents in Montreal were still doing well. Gerard sent them an particularly long letter packed with leaflets for performances drawn in the Art Nouveau style of which Mama was particularly fond. Papa had written him to say that Mama had a thick album of these that she kept with Gerard's letters. Enclosed in the letter was a picture of Gerard's cousin Martine with her new baby son in one arm, and her other child, a toddler, clutching her leg. Martine's husband Leo, Papa wrote, was terribly proud of his family, but even prouder of the new camera he'd purchased, and gave out snapshots like a one-man ticker tape parade. *Martine and her little ones*, he'd written in pencil on the back of the photograph, *Gus and Marc-Pierre. M.P. is the baby.* Gerard placed the snapshot on his music stand, smiling at Papa's words each time he looked at it, until over time it became buried under sheets of music.

Nora was also strong and in good health, but what was very concerning was Uncle Hig. Jeannette wrote to say that her big, strong father, was beginning to weaken from an illness of the kidneys. They were to give him pills twice a day and told by the doctor not to put salt in his food, but that otherwise there was no known treatment. Gerard worried for Jeannette, still so young, for her sensitive soul. He was reassured thinking of Nora's strength, like the bones of their family, keeping everyone upright and protected. But if Nora was the bones, it was Uncle Hig who was the heart. He didn't dare think what they would do without him.

Jeannette was twenty-four years old now, she'd attended a teachers college after high school and now taught music at a school for colored children on West 112th Street, on Harlem's south side. Though her parents had seen to a rigorous musical education, Jeannette had never had any aspirations toward a professional career in music. Rather, she enjoyed teaching, enjoyed the children. *I love seeing their minds ignite*, she wrote once, *watching their little passions play out when they sit in a circle around me during percussion time, with our collection of drums and shakers and triangles.*

Gerard was seated at an outdoor table at one of the cafés he favored near his apartment, writing a letter to Jeannette, the light of the early September afternoon slanting and golden, signaling the coming of fall. A breeze disturbed the paper and he set his cup on the edge. *I have just seen a set of Spanish castanets in a shop,* he wrote. *Shall I send some for your students? They are black but painted with bright flowers, just what children would love, I think.* In fact, he had already purchased them, and they lay in a box, wrapped in tissue paper on his writing desk. The painted flowers reminded him of Jeannette as a young girl, for the times they had walked together in Central Park in the springtime and the paintings she had once made him that hung for years in his apartment in New York.

"A letter home?" came a voice, breaking through his thoughts. Gerard looked up. It was Claude. Small as Montmartre was, Gerard hadn't seen him since their break, nor had he answered Claude's letter. He hadn't meant to let it go unanswered, but the right words didn't come and time had passed.

Gerard nodded. "Yes, a letter to my sister."

"You look well," Claude said. He was thinner than when Gerard had seen him last, four months ago, and the shadows under his eyes had deepened, but he was the same man.

Gerard gestured at the chair opposite. "Would you like to sit?"

"You don't mind? I'm not disturbing you?"

"Not at all."

Gerard's hands were clumsy folding up the letter paper and tucking it away in his coat pocket with his fountain pen. For a few minutes neither spoke.

"Listen," Claude said finally, "I went to see *La vol.*" *La vol de la mouette* was the name of Gerard's operetta. Claude half-laughed. "I saw it three times, in fact."

"Thank you, I appreciate that." Gerard took a sip of his coffee, wanting to warm the tightness in his throat. Claude had always said he needed to hear a piece of music three times, if he cared about it, to be able to take it in properly.

"The strings were a little overpowering at times," he was lighting a cigarette and shook out the match, "but it was wonderful. From start to finish. Miri thought so too."

Whereas before Gerard would have been eager to hash out the work with Claude, note by note, he preferred now not to linger on the subject. "How is Miri?"

"She's well, thanks. But not too happy with me since—" he shifted restlessly in the chair, tapped a clump of ash into the tray in the middle of the table. "I know she'd like to see you again. If she hasn't invited you for coffee or anything it's only because she doesn't want to seem to be meddling in my affairs."

"I trust she wouldn't," Gerard said, beginning to feel terribly sad.

"Gerard, I'd like to see you too. Now and then, if you're willing. As friends. I know it's my own fault, but I've missed you a lot."

The sadness in Gerard's chest grew turbulent. He wanted to answer no, or that he'd think it over, or that Claude had no right… But he couldn't push him away. "I'm here most afternoons," he said. "Writing letters. Here or at the café by the kiosk."

"I'll look for you then."

"Alright."

Gerard stood when Claude did, to shake hands goodbye. Then Claude leaned over, swiftly kissed Gerard on the cheek and turned to go, leaving Gerard's heart beating rapidly long after Claude had disappeared from view.

Friendship, 1929

Another year and a half had passed. Gerard and Claude met with an uneven regularity at the café, took walks in the city, a few times took Miri to a concert or the cinema, twice attended gallery shows of paintings by Anna and her friends. It was a kind of friendship new to Gerard and he was relieved to find that it was possible at all. His heart and mind were in the right place, in relation to Claude, even if at times his body hadn't quite fallen in line, jumping to life when Claude casually touched him during greetings and partings, leaned a hand on his shoulder when viewing a painting or whispered in his ear during a film because the actress on the screen fainted before her cue. But he entertained no hopes of more, and placed those threads of longing or sadness aside when they arose.

Claude still spoke of his plans for Berlin. He had put away his ten thousand francs, but was waiting for the right opportunity, which, it turned out, arrived the next year. Kuno, his close friend there, constantly kept his eye out and the two communicated frequently in letters. The full nature of their relationship, begun years ago when Claude has visited Berlin, was unknown to Gerard, but that sort of thing was no longer his business.

In the middle of all this came two events that punctuated, for Gerard, two points of great contrast. The first was that months after submitting his portfolio to the *Théâtre National de l'Opéra* he was offered a residency at the *Palais Garnier*. It was the chance of a lifetime, the kind that Gerard had been working toward ever since as a boy he'd heard Miss Nancy Drake singing the music of angels in his church in Montreal. Gerard spent an ecstatic few days touring the *Palais*, meeting with the directors and rereading the history of the *Théâtre National* in the *Bibliothèque-musée*. But then, at the end of his fourth day, he received a telegram from New York, from Jeannette, telling him that her dear father had passed away.

Holding the slip of yellow paper bearing the awful words, Gerard found himself crouched on the tiled floor of his building's foyer, tremendous weight bearing down on his shoulders. As soon as he could move he ran to the nearest telegraph office and sent a return message: *Most grieved* stop *sincerest condolences* stop *message to follow.*

Samuel Higgins, Nora's husband, Jeannette's father, his Uncle Hig, was no longer with them. It seemed incredible—big hearted, gentle Uncle Hig, his second father—gone. In the next days Gerard ran from place to place, calculating the time and funds needed to make a trip back to New York. As he traveled the distances between the offices of the telegraph and the ticket agent, his bank and home again, memories of Uncle Hig came. Little, ordinary, wrenching things: Uncle Hig with Jeannette as a small child on his lap, helping her buckle her shoes; walking arm in arm with Nora after church services; eating his roasted potatoes with a knife during Sunday dinners; his warm, comforting hand on Gerard's shoulder.

Back in his room, bankbook, calendars, steamer and train schedules spread out on the bed, nothing was adding up. Though his operetta had been a success, it had paid very little, and had absorbed countless hours he would otherwise have spent earning money playing the clubs. Overland travel and liner passage would be terribly expensive, but worse was the time returning to New York would take, a good month round-trip, and in that he would lose his residency at the *Théâtre National*. He would have to forfeit this chance that, competitive as such rare positions were, would surely never come again.

For twenty-four hours he remained in his room, pacing, recalculating all the numbers, sleeping fitfully and dreaming of lost tickets and missed trains. He awoke in the night, bathed in sweat, still dressed and surrounded by all the loose papers. Pain pounded his heart, thinking of Nora and Jeannette and the numbers he couldn't reconcile. Though overcome with shame, deep down he knew he couldn't go. He couldn't pay the price that it would mean. Sitting up in the bed, he switched on the electric lamp, gathered pen and paper, and began a letter home.

The street was dark and quiet when he ventured out to drop the letter in the postbox, the first light of morning touching a cool hand to the sky where a single star showed itself, burning dimly. He made his way to Anna's apartment and when she let him in, he apologized for waking her, for always coming to her with his troubles, for not being able to stop his tears.

"Shhh, *Cher*," she said. "You are a brother to me. I'm glad you've come."

"This is how I repay them," he said of the Higginses, "after everything they did for me."

"Yes, by keeping alive what they dreamed for you."

He shook his head. "I've abandoned everyone I've ever cared for, my entire family."

"I don't know about that."

"Don't you?"

"Ah, Gerard." She placed a hand on her own cheek, closing her eyes. "I left many behind as well. My island, my Martinique, is never far from my mind and heart, but it doesn't want me there. I was born to leave it."

"But if I can't go back…"

"Only for now. We don't know about the future."

"How could I forgive…how could they…" his words fell helplessly apart.

"You can't take away their pain anyway. And you can't stop yours."

"It's unbearable."

"Yes. But you're still here." She wiped a tear from her own cheek. "We are both still here."

1931 - 1933

Gerard looked up from his writing paper to see Claude coming in the door of the café. A dusting of snow covered the shoulders of his wool coat and felt brim of his hat, his cheeks rosy with the cold. "May I sit?"

"Of course." Gerard moved his own coat from the chair opposite.

Claude signaled the waiter for a coffee. "How is Jeannette?" He guessed correctly that the letter was to her. For the last several months every other of Gerard's letters were to her.

"She's just gotten married." Gerard smiled and shook his head, disbelieving.

Claude sipped his coffee and sighed. "That's wonderful. Please tell her congratulations for me."

"I will."

Claude took another sip of the coffee. "I also have news."

"Oh?"

The music hall in Berlin where Claude's friend Kuno worked had just gone out of business. Claude's eyes glowed with excitement as he spoke. The owner had taken out a big loan, quite a risk in the dire times that had plagued Germany since the war, and the place was now in foreclosure. This by itself wasn't so unusual. The effects of the market crash in America were being felt all over the world and were only straining the German economy further. Kuno had written to say that he and a new partner could take the theater over and make it a cabaret, if Claude would be the third investor and stage director. Full artistic freedom. It was exactly the opportunity Claude had been waiting for.

"When will you go?" asked Gerard, his heart falling despite everything.

"Next month."

"I'm happy for you."

They were quiet a few minutes, then Claude said, "Will you write to me?"

"You couldn't stop me."

Claude laughed. "I'm grateful to you." Then he said, "Will you do something else for me? Will you keep an eye on Miri?"

"With pleasure. And I'll save all my pocket money for flowers for her."

Claude said again, "I'm grateful. Truly."

✦ ✦ ✦ ✦

The night before Claude left for Berlin he came to Gerard's room to say goodbye. He sat in the Louis XVI chair and Gerard in his desk chair, and they spoke of Claude's travel plans, Gerard's work at the *Palais Garnier*, the climate in Germany, both temporal and political. Finally, Claude rose. "I should go," he said. "Early train."

Gerard walked him to the door, a grave sadness weighing on his heart. "Goodbye," he said, eyes wet. Claude put his hands on his shoulders and kissed him on both cheeks, and then, to Gerard's great surprise, on the mouth. Claude's warm lips against his own, and then his tongue, and as he reached his arms around Claude's waist the sadness gave way to a dazzling heat. Pulling at their clothes they stumbled back toward the bed.

✦ ✦ ✦ ✦

Claude's first letter, a month after his arrival in Berlin, was bursting with energy. At last he had found an environment with the intensity he longed for.

> *The arts are truly alive here* (he wrote.) *German politics, the economy, it's a bloody mess, but that's what makes art so vital. People are desperate for release, and clarity, and we don't just entertain, we have something to say. You can sense a tremendous pressure building here, on the streets, in the public places, as if the country is about to wake up. What better time to help stir the pot of dissent? Gerard, if ever you desire a change, think about coming here and joining us.*

Gratifying as it was to read these words, the more Gerard read in Claude's letters and in the papers, the more uneasy he became. Though things in Paris weren't going as well as before due to the economic downslide, he could not seriously consider relocating there. Still, Claude's letters remained optimistic, always full of the new ideas he was trying out, the performers and the colorful patrons of the cabaret, the collaborations and negotiations with his two partners that constituted its own little three-ring circus.

Gerard's letters to Claude were decidedly less glamorous. As tourists disappeared, audiences dwindled and theaters closed. For Gerard, commissions to compose dried up, and the grand prospects that usually followed a residency at the *Théâtre National* never materialized. At the same time, letters from his sisters in Montreal and from Jeannette in New York described harder times than Gerard had ever remembered. By the summer of 1932 he was taking what work he could get and even began teaching for the first time, a few hours a week at two different music schools, and a few private lessons for those who still could afford to pay. What extra money he had he sent home to Montreal or New York, or bought flowers for Miri, as he had promised Claude he would do.

By now, with the Nazi party gaining strength in Germany, his unease in regard to Claude grew into a quiet dread that sickened his stomach. But when he wrote of his concern for Claude's safety, Claude wrote back that he wasn't worried, that the foreign press made more of the German crackdown on subversive activities than was accurate. He cited as proof the devotion the German people showed for the American opera singer Marian Anderson when she made her debut that year in Berlin. *You see?* he wrote. *A black woman, an artist, worshipped here as a queen, as an angel descended from heaven. Her color makes no difference here, just as in the rest of Europe.*

Claude wrote that the Nazis were barely more than a fringe element, and that their leader, who proclaimed the coming of a new German empire, one to last a thousand years, was nothing more than a raving lunatic. *He won't last until his next birthday.*

Then, when in 1933 the raving lunatic was appointed Chancellor of Germany by President Hindenburg, Claude wrote that the Nazi's flew their disgusting banner all over the city while stars of David, scrawled by local thugs, decorated the broken windows of Jewish homes and businesses. Newspapers reported constant arrests, beatings, even killings, and bonfires of books that had been deemed forbidden. Gerard begged Claude to reconsider his place in Berlin, fearing he would end up in prison, or worse.

It's madness, (Claude wrote to Gerard) *but the Communist Party is still the larger. They'll keep the Nazis in check. And you should see the crowds we're getting. The cabaret is packed every night. People are desperate for a dose of sanity, to hear the truth as only good satire tells it. They want hilarity, and a chance to enjoy themselves. Our work here is more important than ever now.*

Dreams, 1934

It was the boy, falling head over heels in the darkness so slowly that Gerard didn't know if it was peace or torment. He must be sleeping, this little black boy, whose untucked shirt tails tangled in the gray suspenders clipped to his short pants, soles of his bare feet showing pale as he tumbled. Who was this child? Gerard was desperate to know.

Now there was another figure, a man, an older man with silver sideburns that shone like white clouds against his dark skin. The man reached up a hand, gnarled and brown as an old oak, and touched the boy's heel, caught his ankle and drew him into a safe embrace. The cloud-like sideburns touched the child's cheek, a voice hummed, like the low strings of a guitar.

Gerard awoke, the pale light of dawn at the window, orange voile curtains fluttering in the metallic breeze off the Seine. He rubbed his eyes and struggled to recall the dream—the boy unknown, but the man, the silver-white sideburns and the deep voice, so familiar. Low notes. He reached for his composition book and his fountain pen, to write a fragment of music, another piece of flotsam and jetsam from these dreams that had begun to accumulate on his waking shore.

He visited Miri on a Tuesday evening, bringing a bouquet of flowers—purple asters, because they were in season and not so expensive, as funds were short—and because they reminded him of Sarai. The ancient embroidered sampler his sisters had made for him when he left Montreal for New York still hung beside his bed, the colors faded and the white cloth yellowed. A pink wild betony for Betsy, a yellow tulip for Amelia, a purple aster for Sarai, who, at the age of forty-six was now already a grandmother. How long it had been since he'd seen her, though they still kept a fragile closeness through letters and the rare photograph.

He would tell Miri all about her, and also about the dreams that had lately been haunting him.

That evening Miri had prepared a light and fragrant meal with wild rice and mushrooms, the asters on the table in her blue vase. They spoke of current affairs, troubling news from Miri's cousins in Frankfurt, about Sarai's new grandson, which lightened their mood, and, of course, about Claude. At last, Gerard asked her if she would give him her professional opinion on something.

"A recurring dream," he said.

Miri laid her napkin beside her plate. "Let's go into the study."

The small study, where Miri still saw her patients, was lined with bookshelves and little mirrors in ornate frames her late husband had collected, that gave the effect of tiny, jeweled windows into alternate rooms. Miri took up her reading glasses and a writing tablet and sat in a leather-covered chair beside a chaise with an angled backrest.

"Will you be comfortable here?" she asked, indicating the couch.

"Yes, of course."

"Gerard, have you always had recurring dreams in your life? Or dreams that seem significant to you? Visions even?"

"Not at all." Gerard chuckled softly, leaning against the backrest of the chaise. "I'm hopelessly ordinary in that respect. Although..." he rubbed the back of his head, "there was the dream I told you about, the first night I met you. With Claude."

"Yes, of course. The baby in the water, wasn't that it?"

"You've a wonderful memory. Better than mine." He sighed. "But that's all, I think."

"We'll just explore then," Miri said. "An open book."

"Alright."

"Let yourself be at ease," she said, in a soothing voice. "Take your time, and when you're ready, tell me about your dreams."

Gerard closed his eyes, letting himself relax into the couch. Images from the dreams came to him swiftly and vividly—the falling boy, the familiar old man with silver sideburns—and these he described for Miri as best he could.

"It's funny," Gerard said, "but I realize now that the old man must be my Uncle Albert. I don't know why I didn't place those sideburns sooner."

"Tell me about him, your uncle."

"I didn't know him terribly well, he was a bit stern. But I learned to play piano at his house. All of us, all the cousins, learned to play at his house. He wasn't much of a musician himself, he worked for the railroads and later became a brewer, but he saw to it that we all learned."

"Remarkable."

"I never thought of it, but I suppose it was because of him that I discovered music, my knack for it." Gerard thought of his cousin Martine, Uncle Albert's second daughter, with the big eyes that he later recognized in Jeannette. With a laugh, he remembered the song he'd written for her. "I even composed my first piece in his home." He remembered placing the photograph of Martine and her two children—the one that Papa had sent—on his music stand.

"Your first ever composition."

"*Teeny Martine*," Gerard sang, laughing again. "*No bigger than a bean...*"

"What about the boy in your dream, is he familiar too?"

"Not exactly." He thought a moment, the image of the boy floating up behind his closed lids, replacing the vision of his baby cousin. "He's familiar in a way, but I can't place him."

"How would you describe him, his emotions?"

"Lonely at first...asleep...weightless...lost..."

"Does that change?"

"Yes. When the old man embraces him, carries him, there's a sense of warmth, and comfort. The two join together, he's supported."

"And you say this is a recurring dream?"

"Yes, but it hasn't always been the same. At first the boy was alone. Only the last time the old man was there." Gerard rubbed his eyes but kept them closed. "And the first one or two times," he remembered now, "the boy entered a house. An empty house. Abandoned perhaps."

"Anything else."

"No. No I think that's all of it. All of it that I can put into words."

They remained quiet a few minutes.

Gerard opened his eyes. "Shall I sit up now?"

"Yes," Miri smiled, "we'll just chat about what it might mean." She flipped through the notes in her tablet. He waited.

"First, I must say that dreams can mean different things simultaneously," Miri said. "See what rings true for you as we speak about it."

"Alright."

"If we look at it in a linear sense, first we have the boy entering a house. The house is the symbol that most represents the self. Really, everything in a dream will represent aspects of the self, but a house can be a special totality."

"I see."

"But this house, rather than being alive, lived in, full of light and people as a house might be, is dark and abandoned. So, the boy, your child self perhaps, enters it, seeking to explore it, perhaps to find a home, perhaps to return to it, perhaps something else." Miri shifted in her chair and turned a page in her notebook. "This may warrant more exploration, to be sure.

"And then we see him falling," she continued. "Not fearful, not exhilarated, but with a sense of being alone and lost. Falling, in dreams can represent a time of transition, the transition of middle age for example, where the younger self transforms into the older self, from a period in life where one has a great deal of focus on the future, to a time when one reflects, often too much, on the past."

"That would be fitting," Gerard said.

"But falling may also indicate a time when one's former touchstones have, for one reason or another, gone away. When the hallmarks of one's identity have been lost or left behind, and one may experience a groundlessness, a loss of gravity."

Gerard let out a breath, tapping his hands on his lap where they lay. "Also fitting."

"And then we have the older man, a father figure—"

"Or grandfather!" Gerard said. "I just remembered the boy calling him *Grand Papa* in one of the dreams. How strange."

"Father, grandfather, and uncle too."

"Yes, that seems to be right."

"And he receives the boy with love, and the boy is held, comforted. The older, wiser aspect of the self supports the one that is small, young, insecure. This would indicate that an inner force, a wise and loving one, may now support the whole."

Gerard's throat ached. "Miri, this is quite something."

She smiled. "There is always so much more to us than we guess."

"Is it always aspects of the self, then? The things that appear in dreams?"

"That's what Dr. Jung has taught us. And I believe so." She closed her notebook. "But the real mystery, I think, is what the *self* is in the first place."

They sat in silence again. Gerard sensed his mind revolving, as if awash in thoughts rearranging themselves without alighting on anything in particular. "What comes next?" he said after a few moments. "What do I do with all this?"

"It helps a great deal to give form to the energy and emotion that arises. Giving it a place to expand can be a relief, a catalyst, and can also help us to understand it further."

Gerard thought instantly of the fragments of music he'd written down in his composition book.

"I've been writing music, actually," he said.

"Perfect." She leaned forward and squeezed his hand. "Do keep writing. It will take you where you need to go."

✦ ✦ ✦ ✦ ✦

On a morning in August refreshed after a quiet morning with his composition book, Gerard stopped at his usual kiosk to buy a copy of *L'Humanité*. Before he took two steps away from the kiosk an article at the bottom of the front page caught his eye, reporting that the German president, Hindenburg, had died and Adolph Hitler had assumed absolute power. Gerard stopped walking, staring at the newsprint, a sickening dread overtaking his senses. After a moment, he recovered himself and hurried to the nearest office of *La Poste*, purchased an aerogram, and wrote a brief letter to Claude begging him to return to France.

He received a short reply from Claude less than two weeks later, telling him not to worry, that he and his partners were being careful, and that he would write again soon. But that was the last Gerard heard from him.

✦ ✦ ✦ ✦ ✦

Claude's words did not allay his fears. In the next weeks, Gerard went about his business as if under a heavy weight. One night he dreamt again of the falling child, but this time the boy turned so that Gerard saw the crisscross of the gray suspenders against the white shirt—that crisscross between the shoulder blades. The boy was no longer a boy, but Claude. Gerard reached toward him with his hands, his skin black against the white cloth, and when his fingertips touched Claude's shoulders seams of gold appeared along the ridges of his veins. Gold lines spread from the backs of his hands to the insides of his wrists, burning with heat. He awoke, fretfully rubbing his hands and his arms, as if the gold seams were still there and he could rub them out.

And then, one morning in September, when Gerard was walking along the Boulevard Voltaire on his way to teach a piano lesson, a voice call his name. Turning around, he was surprised to see Henri from *La Méditerranée*, running to catch up with him.

"I've been looking for you everywhere," Henri said, out of breath. "Yves remembered you were teaching out this way today, what luck."

"What is it?" Gerard said, trying to make out Henri's queer expression.

"It's Claude."

A sound like radio static closed in over Gerard's ears, blotting out the noises of the street and most of what Henri was saying.

Madame Cartier had called the theater…

Cabaret…

Raid…

Hospital…

Gerard blinked, frozen for a second to the pavement, then he ran like lightning to Miri's apartment. He was drenched in sweat when he arrived at her door, knocking loudly and calling her name. When she opened the door, she was strangely calm and extremely pale.

"Gerard. Good. Come in."

He followed her into her bedroom. A valise lay open on the bed and she sat down beside it, searching a pocket of her dress, then held out a piece of paper that bore the name and address of a hospital in Berlin.

"He's there." She'd gotten a call at dawn from Kuno, she explained, Claude's cabaret partner. A gang of twenty or more Brown Shirts had raided the place just before midnight. "They…beat everyone," she pressed a knuckle to her mouth, "and Kuno made it out through a window, into the back alley. He says they destroyed everything. Stole the money from the strong box. He said they—" here she stifled a sob. Gerard gripped her arms, kneeling in front of her on the floor. "—killed two people and left them in the street."

"And Claude?"

"Kuno found him unconscious behind the bar. What was left of it. Got him to the hospital in a taxi. He's gone into hiding now—Kuno. Planning to leave the country." Gerard searched her face. "And now I'll go to Berlin and get my son. I'll get Claude," Miri said in a thin voice, "and I'll bring him back here."

"Miri, no—" Gerard took her both her hands. "It's impossible. You'd risk your life."

She sobbed once and he took her in his arms, the bones of her shoulders as small as a bird's. "I'll go."

For a moment she clung to him. Then she drew back.

"You?"

"Yes, of course."

She nodded. "We must prepare you a bag then." She had already made a parcel of sandwiches and a thermos of coffee and had been to the bank where she had withdrawn a quantity of bills in *Reichsmarks*. She had also been to the chemist and purchased a vial of laudanum and a bottle of iodine. How she had managed the presence of mind to do all of this Gerard could not imagine.

With everything in Miri's valise, they went together by taxi to Gerard's apartment for his passport and a few items of clothing, then directly to the *Gare du Nord* station.

When they said goodbye Miri kissed Gerard's cheek and said in a choking whisper, "*Merci*, Gerard. *Bonne chance.*"

"I'll bring him," Gerard said, not knowing what the truth would be. "Don't worry."

Berlin

Night was falling by the time the train crossed the Belgian border into Germany. Three German officers with swastika armbands entered the car to check papers.

"*Deutsche Passkontrolle.* All passports please."

An elderly couple and a young man were ordered off the train for questioning, and a few others had their luggage searched. Gerard saw two of the officers look in his direction and say something about *der Schwartze.* He was the only black person on the train, or in that car at least, a detail that caused a cold sweat to prick his skin.

Now the head officer stood over him, flipping through Gerard's passport with black-gloved fingers.

"What is your business in Germany?"

"Musician," Gerard said in German, forcing a smile. "Piano. Hotel."

"How long is your stay?"

"Three days," Gerard said, hoping it wouldn't be that long, invisible needles attacking him in the armpits and under his collar.

The officer fixed him with a cold stare, was about to spit out another question but then loud voices from the front of the car made him turn around. Another officer was attempting to remove a small leather bag from a woman's clutching hands. The head officer threw Gerard's passport at him, striding up the aisle to aid his subordinate by dragging the woman out of her seat and to the exit. When the train once again lurched into motion, neither she nor the other three passengers had returned to the car.

The strangeness and fear of the moment, Gerard's own and that of the collective atmosphere on the train pushed Gerard's mind to a giddy edge so that, bizarrely, he almost laughed. And then, in almost the next moment, he was hit by an overwhelming fatigue. He slept much of the journey through the darkened German countryside, waking every time the train screeched into a station, and then dozing again with his arms over Miri's valise.

The train arrived at the *Hauptbahnhof* in Berlin near dawn, the hands of the great clock in the station approaching five o'clock and the sky dark with rain. Gerard pulled his hat brim low over his forehead and hailed a taxi, showing the driver, a young man in a tweed cap, the paper with the name and address of the hospital. The driver nodded and Gerard climbed into the back of the car, reaching for the pack of cigarettes in his coat pocket—anything to steady his nerves—then held the pack over the back of the front seat.

"*Zigarette?*"

"*Danke.*" The driver took one and accepted a light from Gerard when they stopped at a traffic signal.

The streets were still mostly deserted at that hour. Along the *Kurfürstendamm* the rain made pale halos around the streetlamps and glittered in the branches of the plane trees that lined the boulevard. The tall facades of buildings loomed behind, bearing the twisted cross of the Nazi banner. By the time the taxi drew up to the imposing stone walls of the hospital the sky had changed from black to dark gray. Gerard paid the driver and, on impulse, tossed the cigarette package onto the front seat.

"*Danke*," the young man said again, this time with a smile that for a second showed a couple of missing teeth.

Heart beating hard, Gerard stepped through the heavy wooden doors of the hospital and found his way down an echoing stone corridor to an enclave where a nurse in a starched cap and apron sat reading a stack of charts. She shook her head when Gerard asked if she spoke English or French, but held up a finger for him to wait and walked swiftly around a corner. Several minutes later she returned with another nurse who, to Gerard's great relief, addressed him in French.

"Can I help you?"

"I'm here to see about a friend."

She looked at him askance. "Visiting hours aren't until this afternoon, one o'clock."

"I'm afraid it's urgent," Gerard said.

The nurse looked at him a moment without speaking. She was young, but violet shadows under her eyes belied fatigue. A strand of dark hair had escaped her cap and hung over her forehead. Gerard held her gaze as steadily as he could.

What he would be asking would be unorthodox at best and dubious to anyone with authority.

"Come with me please."

He followed her brisk step down the corridor to an empty hallway.

"What is the urgency?" she asked in a low voice.

"He's a Frenchman," Gerard said, explaining nothing. "I wish to take him back to Paris so his mother can care for him."

"Is he a Jew?"

Gerard hesitated. As an injured man brought by taxi to the hospital by another who had fled, as Kuno had done, Claude would be suspect as a subversive or some other sort of criminal. As to whether or not he was known to be Jewish would put him in a worse position, Gerard had no idea. Claude had said in his letters that there were many Germans who did not subscribe to the Nazi vitriol, but the wrong answer now could cost Claude his life.

"Yes," Gerard whispered.

"The name?"

"Cartier."

She led him to a large ward with two long rows of beds, where two other nurses were tending to patients. Most everyone was sleeping, or, Gerard guessed, in varying states of unconsciousness. Gerard followed behind the nurse, heart in his throat, searching each crumpled form for anything that resembled Claude. At the end of the second row, the nurse bent beside a patient with his face toward the wall. The light was especially dim at that side of the ward and Gerard saw little more than the outline of a rough blanket. Retrieving the chart from the foot of the bedframe, the nurse waved Gerard back out into the corridor with her.

"Head injury," she said in a low voice, looking at the chart. "Broken ribs, contusions. No apparent internal bleeding."

"Are you certain that's him?" Gerard asked. Kuno might not have even given the hospital Claude's real name.

"It's him," she said.

"Is he well enough to travel?"

"Not at all," said the nurse in a whisper. "But if you expect the police he'll be better off going with you. If they get ahold of him he'll be dead before the day is through."

Gerard stepped back into the ward and knelt between the bed and the wall, looking into the swollen face, at the dark hair plastered down with bandages and dried blood. It was indeed Claude. He put a hand on the wrist that lay uncovered alongside his body.

"Claude," he whispered, gently squeezing. The skin was cold. "Claude..."

Claude opened his eyes and looked confusedly at Gerard.

"Do you know me?" asked Gerard. Despite the head injury the chart had stated, *lucid*.

"Gerard?" Claude mumbled in a whisper. "You... What are you doing here?"

Gerard nearly fainted with relief. "I'm taking you back to Paris."

Claude swallowed, wincing in pain. "Am I in that much of a mess?"

Gerard nodded.

"Alright, then."

The nurse told Gerard to wait in a recessed doorway in the corridor until she returned with a wheelchair. "Those two," she said, meaning the other nurses, "are going out in a moment to make their notes." She was tense but composed, a glimmer of sweat just perceptible on her upper lip. *She's done this before*, he thought.

When the two others had left, the nurse took Gerard back into the ward and together they helped Claude into the wheelchair. "There are no discharges until after the doctors make their morning rounds," the nurse whispered. "And the shift change is in half an hour so we'll need to hurry." Gerard didn't ask any questions. He and Claude were now at the mercy of this unknown woman, a person who had no reason to risk her own safety for theirs. For all Gerard knew she might only be pretending to help them.

Covering Claude with a blanket, the nurse wheeled him out into the corridor, where, unexpectedly, one of the other two nurses reappeared, posture stiff, eyes darting between Gerard and Claude. She asked a question voiced in shrill German. A drop of icy sweat trickled down Gerard's spine.

The first nurse answered curtly, and after a long, tense moment, the second one nodded, letting them pass.

"I've told her the patient has a fever and a rash," the nurse whispered to Gerard. "And that I'm taking him to quarantine."

Gerard exhaled. "Good Lord."

They dressed Claude in a supply room, in clothes from the valise, an ordeal as he was in terrible pain, and then hurried to a rear exit where the nurse asked them to wait. She returned minutes later with a folded paper. "You'll need this at the border," she said. "Leave the chair out front and I'll get it once you've gone."

"Thank you," Gerard said. "I can't—"

"Do not come back," she said, turning on her heel. In a matter of seconds she had disappeared from view.

"It's quite the escape," Claude said hoarsely, as Gerard struggled to get him over a stair. Gerard pushed the creaking chair around the great building and back toward the street, breathing heavily. "I certainly hope so."

The same taxi was still out front, the driver slumped against the door with his cap pulled down over his eyes, sleeping. Gerard knocked on the window.

Once in the taxi Gerard unfolded the paper the nurse had given them. It was a discharge form, *Verkehsunfall* handwritten in ink, as well as what appeared to be a doctor's signature the nurse must have written herself. *God bless her.*

"*Verkehsunfall*," Gerard said to Claude, showing him the paper. "What's that?"

"The cause of my injuries," said Claude, squinting at the form. "Traffic accident."

✦ ✦ ✦ ✦ ✦

From the hospital, they drove first to Claude's building where Gerard woke the landlady. Coming out to the street in her robe, she ducked her head into the taxi's open window, spoke a moment with Claude, then led Gerard up to Claude's room. Claude had told Gerard where to find his passport, in a pressed-tin box with his important papers. Gerard found the box in the wardrobe and grabbed an overcoat from the hook behind the door. Everything else they would have to leave, though there wasn't much. Claude's guitars and music had been at the cabaret anyway.

Five minutes later they were heading to the station.

Claude leaned heavily on Gerard as they made their way to the platform. A train for Paris was leaving in thirty minutes and there were just enough of Miri's *Reichsmarks* to purchase tickets that afforded them their own compartment. Gerard arranged the coats and valise on the bench seat so that Claude could recline, and he gave him a dose of the laudanum. It would have to do. When the conductor appeared, Gerard showed him the discharge form from the hospital and their passports, along with the tickets.

The conductor eyed them with a blank expression, another cold look that Gerard took for suspicion, sweat prickling his scalp. They were hardly out of the woods yet. But then the conductor signaled to a porter who, moments later, brought a wool blanket and a flask of water.

"*Danke schoen*," Gerard said, voice almost breaking. He took the water and blanket in his hands, hope and gratitude burgeoning up under the weight of his anxiety.

When the train finally jolted into motion and gained speed Gerard looked out the window at the gray sky, the buildings blurring and the rain slashing razors at the glass, and began to breathe normally for the first time since the previous afternoon when he'd seen Henri on the street. A lifetime ago. But all of a sudden Claude was shaking violently, as if having a seizure. Gerard knelt on the floor embracing him, fearing he would fall off the seat. Claude's breath came in ragged gasps, eyes squeezed shut, groaning in pain as he shook.

"I thought I was a dead man," Claude managed to say, and then the gasps turned into silent sobs.

Gerard held him, pressing his lips to the side of Claude's face. "It's alright now," he whispered again and again. "It's alright."

At last Claude quieted. Gerard found a handkerchief, and as gently as he could dried Claude's face.

"How is Miri?" Claude asked.

"She's very strong."

"I know."

"She'll be very happy to see you."

"What about the others from the cabaret?" Claude's voice choked.

"Kuno is the one that got you to the hospital and called your mother," Gerard said. "But I don't know anything else."

They were silent a while, and then Gerard helped Claude take a sip of water from the flask.

"I might close my eyes a little," Claude said.

"Good."

Mercifully, Claude slept. Gerard remained on the floor to make sure he didn't fall, from shaking again or from a sudden movement of the train. Exhausted, he leaned his back against the seat, listening to Claude's breathing.

✦ ✦ ✦ ✦ ✦

Gerard must have slept too, because all at once the train was pulling into another station, Magdeburg. A rush of adrenaline brought him to an immediate, heightened alert, as it would at every station, every time he had to show their papers, though by an immense force of will he managed to appear composed. Even as time put distance between them and Berlin, Claude's injuries would likely raise alarms, especially when they reached the Belgian border. And what if his condition worsened, putting him in further danger before the journey's end?

With the help of the laudanum Claude drifted in and out of sleep for hours. When they were passing through the countryside on the outskirts of Dusseldorf, fields of ripening rye and oats undulated in rolling hills of green and muted gold, he tried to sit up. Patches of blue sky had here and there opened up through the rain.

"Tell me some of your opera," he whispered.

"My opera?" It took a moment for Gerard to recall his project, and that he had told Claude about it in his letters, the music and images derived from his dreams. He sighed. "Where to begin?"

"Why not at the beginning?"

Gerard closed his eyes and leaned his head back, next to Claude's.

"The footlights," he said, "on the curtain, change color as the orchestra begins tuning and then goes quiet. Sunset colors. Yellow, orange, red, purple, and then black. The curtain opens and the stage is completely dark. Now we hear the voice of a single clarinet."

A thin ray of sun penetrated the clouds outside and entered the compartment, fluttered over them and then faded. Gerard softly sang the notes of the melody, the ones that his voice could reach. He had a husky singing voice not in the least like a clarinet and he'd never had much of a range, but he spoke the notes he couldn't reach knowing that Claude would be able to imagine it, as if he were reading sheet music.

"Great start," Claude murmured, barely audible over the low rumble of the train.

Gerard described the figure of a dancer, suspended high in the air at stage left, coming into view as a shaft of light emerged from above. The figure would spin, ever so slowly, head over heels, and then vanish as the light disappeared. A moment later the dancer would reappear, but in a lower position at center stage, vanish again in darkness, and finally reappear, lying on the floor at stage right. As Gerard sang the next section of the melody, rain once again slashed at the compartment windows.

✦ ✦ ✦ ✦ ✦

They crossed the Belgian border without incident, and had nothing but raised eyebrows to contend with upon entering France. Either the discharge paper from the hospital, along with the passports, was sufficient, or the officials, mercifully, played along. By ten o'clock at night they were headed to Miri's in a taxi. It seemed the rain had followed them from Berlin and was now falling cold and heavy over the streets. The windshield wipers cut only a small swath of clarity and the going was agonizingly slow. Claude was in dreadful pain now and no longer so lucid as before. Gerard thought to ask the driver to take them directly to the hospital, but by then they were only a few blocks away from Miri's apartment.

Miri came to the door before Gerard even knocked.

"Gerard," she said. "Thank God. Where is he?"

"Down in the taxi," Gerard said. "Miri, I think he'd better go right to the hospital."

"Of course." Miri grabbed her coat and bag and began to lock the door.

"You'll need shoes," Gerard said, noting the bedroom slippers on her feet.

"So, I do," she said, looking down. "Claude will get a laugh out of this tomorrow."

"He will," Gerard said, desperately hoping that she was right.

Moments later they were headed to the *Hôpital Saint-Louis*. Miri rode in the back seat with Claude, holding his hand and murmuring in his ear. Gerard, up front with the driver, heard Claude say, "I'm sorry, *Maman*," and Miri's anguished voice reply, "No, no, *mon cher fils*. You're here now, it's alright. It's alright."

In another two hours Claude had been admitted, seen by a doctor and tended to by a pair of nurses. They had given him a dose of morphine and now that he was asleep they said Miri could stay with him. Miri and Gerard spoke in the corridor before Miri went in to keep her vigil at Claude's bedside. She told Gerard to go home and sleep, and that she would keep him informed.

"Thank you, Gerard, with all my heart, for bringing my boy home," she said, gripping his arms. "Our Claude is home now."

Gerard hugged her and kissed the top of her head.

"I'll see you tomorrow."

✦ ✦ ✦ ✦ ✦

Three days later, with Gerard's help, Miri brought Claude to her apartment. The bandages had all come off and he was clean and combed, but very thin and very pale. Miri made a bedroom of her study and set up one of Claude's old guitars on a stand by the bed. A nurse came once a day, and the doctor twice a week. Claude had undergone a series of x-rays and there was a concern about a bruised spleen and kidney. He'd been passing blood.

Miri kept great pots of beef bones boiling all day in the kitchen, making broth to build Claude's strength. He still slept much of the time, said he couldn't focus enough to read, and playing the guitar was still too much for the pain in his ribs. Gerard came often and, at Claude's request, related more of his opera. It was a disjointed telling, because Claude often fell asleep or had trouble remembering parts, but Gerard found it didn't much matter, the scenes might be rearranged in any number of ways and still work. He hadn't realized that in the writing. In fact, in the course of telling it to Claude, he devised a way of ordering the opera so that the direction was not only circular, but flowed forward and backward with certain scenes repeating in reverse order. An ending still eluded him, but the progress brought him a measure of satisfaction.

The whole telling took a few weeks, and when Gerard finally finished he said, "That's it. Most of it. All I've got, I mean."

Claude had his eyes closed and Gerard thought perhaps he was asleep again, but Claude said, "Bravo," and smiled faintly. He opened his eyes, eyes that looked bigger and darker than ever, and gazed at Gerard from where he was stretched out on the chaise. "It's magnificent," Claude said. "Truly."

1934 - 1935

Claude was recovering. By the winter holidays, when the streets of Paris were alive with strings of lights and ice skaters in the *patinoires*, he could move around the apartment with a cane, and stand long enough to prepare coffee. He spent much less time in bed, and many daylight hours in an armchair instead, reading bits of the newspaper until the letters jumped around too much. "The damned things won't stay still," he said to Gerard. Regarding the loss of his cabaret and his friends, Claude remained silent. Only when they got word from Kuno, from the home of relatives in England, that he and their third partner were safe, Claude said, "At least there's that. That's the main thing."

When he came to visit, Gerard often found Claude sitting in the front room, by the window that looked out onto the street, listening to records on Miri's gramophone. At times the nurse was there, checking his pulse or temperature, or another friend from *La Méditerranée*. Miri was more at ease now, and regularly left Claude while she shopped for groceries or attended to other business. She shared with Gerard whatever new thing the doctor had said, and had also given him a key to the apartment. She was concerned about Claude being disturbed by the bell when she was out, because he still slept at odd times throughout the day, and besides that she said it made her feel safer knowing Gerard had a key. "You are my anchor," she said.

One day early in the spring, Claude told Gerard he wanted to take a walk outside and buy a pack of cigarettes. He was still using a cane during the brief times he did walk outside, and gripped the railing on the staircase to steady himself, as the stairs, up or down, were a laborious feat of balance. Gerard had asked Miri privately what the doctor had to say about Claude's mobility. Was there any reason to worry that he wasn't recovering faster? It had been several months since the raid on the cabaret. Lots of people suffered beatings or accidents and were better in days, or weeks. Miri said the doctor had assured her that recoveries took their own time, and that she should be patient. Claude's injuries were "complex."

There was a kiosk at the edge of a little square where Claude liked to go, because of the large chestnut trees and the iron benches where one could stop and rest. The roots of one of the old trees had grown around the legs of one of the benches, so that the iron bars were submerged in the wood, and Claude said it was like a pair of long-time friends, two old men who argued over which had gotten there first. "You can see that every day it's the same argument," he said. "Day in and day out, closer than a married couple."

Sitting on the bench, Claude tore open the pack, put a cigarette between his lips but didn't light it. He asked Gerard how his opera was coming along, if he'd discovered the way to end it, and Gerard said no, that part remained a mystery.

"Endings can indeed be evasive," Claude said. "And shy. Even in comedy."

"That's the truth."

A light rain was falling. The bare tree branches didn't provide much cover, and the mist made a net of white beads on Claude's hair. He'd taken off his hat because, he said, he wanted to feel the rain on his face.

"We ought to go back," Gerard said. "I don't want you catching a cold."

"A minute more."

They sat in silence, Claude with his eyes closed, the cigarette still unlit. At last, Gerard reached up, took it from Claude's lips and put it in his coat pocket.

"Let's go."

He helped Claude to his feet and kept ahold of his arm as they walked back to the apartment and settled him in the front room armchair, a wool blanket across his lap and his feet up on the ottoman. He got a towel from the bathroom and dried Claude's hair.

Gerard looked at his watch, he had a lesson to get to and said so regretfully. Miri would be home in an hour. He bent to kiss Claude on the cheek, but Claude cupped Gerard's face and kissed him on mouth.

"*Je t'aime*, Gerard," Claude said.

"*Je t'aime, aussi*, Claude. *Beaucoup.*"

✦ ✦ ✦ ✦ ✦

It happened very quickly. Late that night Miri rang Gerard to say she was taking Claude to the hospital, because he had a fever and was having trouble breathing. Gerard told her he would meet them there and within the hour he found Miri standing at the end of a corridor, outside a pair of double doors.

"They've taken him in there," she said, fluttering a hand around her forehead to brush away stray hairs that weren't there. "They won't let me go in."

There was nothing to do but wait, and they found a bench within sight of the doors.

"Surely he's getting oxygen now," Gerard said. "The nurses are probably getting him to sleep."

Somehow Gerard dozed off, leaning against the wall, Miri with her head on his shoulder. He slipped into a dream. He was swimming, summertime, the Saint Laurence River back in Montreal. His parents were on the shore, tiny figures waving. *I'm out too far*, Gerard thought, beginning to panic. The current was carrying him away…

But then he sensed someone shaking his shoulder.

A doctor knelt before them, two nurses stood behind him a few paces away. "*Madame*," the doctor said. "*Monsieur*. I beg your pardon."

Gerard saw it in his face before he said more.

Pneumonia. Oxygen. Epinephrine. Cardiac arrest.

Everything they could.

Very sorry.

Miri fell forward, her body limp, and the two nurses rushed forward to support her. He saw their mouths move but heard no sound. Darkness busy with pinpricks of light crowded the periphery of his vision until all he saw were the nurses' hands under Miri's elbows. When sound returned to the room he heard her sobbing. She was crumpled on the floor and he put his arms around her, tears streaming down his face.

After a time Miri grew quiet, her breathing ragged.

"We'll take you to him, Madam," one of the nurses said, pushing wads of tissues into Miri's hands. "Are you ready?"

She nodded, clutching Gerard's arm. "*Cher* Gerard, help me."

Together they stood, with the nurse on Miri's other side and followed the doctor down the glaring white corridor, through the double doors and finally into a darkened room toward a bed covered in an oxygen tent. The sides of the tent were drawn up, and there under a sheet lay Claude.

Miri threw her arms over her son, her sobs muffled this time in the pillow, and Gerard knelt down, laying his cheek against Claude's hair.

✦ ✦ ✦ ✦ ✦

It was morning and Miri was quiet. A nurse appeared with two attendants. The body would have to be taken away, and Miri was to sign a set of papers.

"Where are you taking him?" Miri asked, as the attendants transferred Claude's body, covered completely in a sheet, to a gurney.

"Downstairs," the nurse said, meaning the morgue.

"What now?" Miri asked.

"Best to go home," the nurse said. "Make your notifications. And try to get some rest."

Gerard held Miri's hand in the taxi back to her apartment. Neither could think of sleeping so Gerard brewed a pot of coffee in the kitchen and helped Miri think through the phone calls she would have to make, and then he helped her make them.

Nothing Gerard had ever done was so terrible. Every time he uttered the words he felt as though he were killing Claude himself and brutalizing those on the other end of the line. At least there weren't so many calls to make. Each person on Miri's list would notify a handful of others, and that would suffice.

Two of Miri's women friends, Frieda and Hélène, came within the hour to help with arrangements, and to make sure Miri had a bath and something to eat, and they sent Gerard home, telling him to do the same. Hélène hooked a maternal arm in his and led him to the door. He should go to bed early, she said, and come back in the morning. He promised he would, grateful to be told what to do.

Gerard let himself into his room, feeling as though it were an alien place. This room where he had lived for nearly ten years, and in which he'd spent countless hours with Claude. He sat down on the bed with the brass key in his hand, and his coat still on. He put the key in his pocket and his fingers touched something unfamiliar. He drew it out.

It was Claude's cigarette, lying blurred and white on his palm.

❖ ❖ ❖ ❖ ❖

After the funeral, attended by innumerable black-clad mourners, Miri sat *shiva*, staying at home for seven days, with all the mirrors in the apartment covered in black cloth and a large candle burning in the foyer. Friends and relatives came, bringing food, condolences, and prayers. Henri, Yves, and Marcel came with flowers, kissed Miri's cheeks and embraced Gerard like brothers.

The first two days Gerard stayed well into the evening, sunken into the sofa and feeling bruised all over, listening to visitors remember Claude in his boyhood, his student days, from *La Méditerranée* and elsewhere. There was a funny story about little Claude and a box of kittens, crying because he couldn't decide which was his favorite, and another about a philosophical argument he'd had with a professor, so fierce he'd almost been expelled.

Anna Paraibel came the second afternoon. She held Gerard's hand for an hour and made him eat a dish of the spicy fish stew she brought in a heavy cast iron pot, saying it was her grandmother's recipe and would fortify him. Even Miri, who had hardly been eating, accepted a plate of it, thanking Anna sincerely.

Gerard left that evening with Anna, walking her to her flat and then on alone for miles along the Seine. Here were the bridges, the boats, the cafés, the lights. At last he crossed the *Pont Neuf*, pausing to gaze from the railing down at the water—deep, wide, black, gleaming reflections dancing over its surface—and then made his way home.

His legs were particularly heavy climbing the stairs, assuring him that he would sleep. The light was dim in the corridor and fitting his key into the lock Gerard almost missed the letter that was lying on the mat in front of his door. Picking it up, he recognized the familiar pen strokes of Sarai's handwriting. He stared a moment at the return address in Montreal. What a comfort it would be having a letter from her this night. Inside, he hung up his coat and hat, put a kettle on for tea and sat down to read.

There was general news from the family, reports on the work of the adults, the schooling of the children, a scandal or two in the community, and then there were Sarai's funny little rhapsodies about Nicolas, her first grandchild, who was two years old now and the prince of her world. Gerard turned the pages smiling, until, toward the middle of the sheaf of pages, the tone of the letter took a sudden turn. *I am very sorry to say now that I have bad news, sad, tragic news...* Gerard sat forward in the chair, a clenching in his chest. He drew a hand over his forehead thinking, *No more, not now.* But after a moment he braced himself and read on.

...a terrible loss for our cousin Martine. It seems her little boy, Gus, had gotten into an abandoned house, exploring with some other boys. He fell through a rotted floor into the cellar...

...died instantly...

...only seven years old...

The words swam before his eyes, and behind them rose up the image of his dream. The boy, falling. He closed his eyes tight, a terrible pressure taking over deep in his chest, his heart a cracking clay vessel. Perhaps he was dying too, because all at once he was unraveling, backward in time on a spool of thread, across the ocean to a version of himself that did not yet know Claude, across miles of earth to another that hadn't yet set foot in New York. Pulled further by some kind of umbilicus that connected him by blood to his cousin and her dead child as yet unborn, and hurled further into a vast black nothingness, where there was no sound other than that of a heart beating. And if there was any other thing it was the sense of an arching black sky, etched in gold with the vague lines of a face. Nora's.

1935 - 1938

Gerard slept and woke, the sun rose and set, and it was still 1935. He chewed bread and drank coffee. He lathered and shaved his face in the mirror above his washstand. He returned to his work, to his music, but he put his opera away, stacking it quietly in the bottom of a suitcase with his other papers. He went to see Miri every few days, and they took walks or attended concerts or to visited the cemetery, though they never lingered there too long.

Most often they walked in the *Marche aux Fleurs*, where the stalls overflowed with life and color, delicate and bold. Gerard always bought her a small bouquet, despite her protests, until she gave up and smiled, her big sad eyes so like Claude's. The youthful Miri was gone now, as if she had aged overnight. Her hair was whiter and had thinned, like her frame, her natural vibrance diminished, but among the flowers Gerard sometimes caught a glimpse of the Miri he'd known before.

✦ ✦ ✦ ✦ ✦

One day in late summer Gerard accompanied Anna up to the terrace of the *Basilique Sacre-Coeur,* where she set up her paint box and easel. These days she was painting more and performing less. Gerard sat nearby on a bench in the shade of a Ginkgo tree, picking out notes on Claude's old guitar. Miri had given it to him after the *shiva,* and it had since stood in the corner of his room beside the bed until very recently when he asked another musician friend for an informal lesson. Anna hummed along as she moved her paintbrush between pallet and canvas, improvising a tune in her deep voice to the chords of the guitar.

"I feel like a cowboy, strumming like this," Gerard said after a while, setting the guitar aside.

Anna glanced at him over her shoulder. "You don't much look like one, *Cher*, sorry to say."

"And here I had gone and gotten my hopes up."

Anna laughed. "Such reckless dreams."

Gerard smiled, then sighed. All dreams were reckless.

"How is your Spanish coming along?" Gerard asked, changing the subject. They were both learning something new. In fact, Anna had been picking up the language from her Mexican friends for years but had lately gotten serious and hired a tutor.

"*Muy bien!*" Anna stretched her arms up, then folded them and studied her painting. "Hugo says my accent is very good, except for the R's, they remain too French."

"I have faith in you."

"Well, *muchas gracias.*" Anna turned to wink and him, and then looked out at the vista—all the red rooftops of Montmartre, the blue Seine reflecting the sky, a white haze over the city beyond like a veil of silk tulle. A breeze rustled the leaves of the Ginkgo tree over Gerard's head. There was peace in it.

✦ ✦ ✦ ✦ ✦

Autumn came and Gerard and Miri went to see the leaves turning colors in the *Parc Bagatelle*, scarves round their necks, wool coats buttoned. Miri's red beret matched the flowers on her purple scarf and the crisp air brought a touch of pink to her cheeks. Later that day, alone in his room, Gerard picked up the guitar, its fall colors amber and brown like the leaves collecting on the ground outside. His fingers were no longer so clumsy on the strings and the music came more easily. He plucked the low strings, resonant and soothing, and the higher ones that reminded him more of Claude that were sometimes harder to bear.

In early December a few inches of snow fell, a quiet blanket of white over the streets and the bare branches of trees. Gerard visited Miri on a Thursday afternoon, and since she said she was tired they sat with cups of tea watching the snow from the window as it piled up on the rails of the balcony.

Just three days later, he received a call from Miri's friend Hélène, gravely regretting to inform him that she and Frieda had found Miri that morning in her bed, having passed away during the night. The doctor they had called had said it was most likely her heart that had given out, and that by every sign it appeared that she had gone peacefully. She had survived her son less than one year.

✦ ✦ ✦ ✦ ✦

After the funeral Gerard returned home and covered his single mirror with a black cloth. Miri's closest relatives held a *shiva* at her apartment, and when Gerard arrived the next day Hélène greeted him at the door. Hélène, scarcely bigger than Miri had been, wrapped an arm around his waist and took him to greet the relatives he'd met just after Claude had died. Then, alone, he wandered down the hallway toward the study, pausing outside Miri's bedroom door, which was ajar.

The room still smelled of her perfume. The bed was empty and made. Not every man was lucky enough to have three mothers who loved him, each in her own way. Perhaps it was a bitter price that one day he'd have to lose them all, yet he was inexpressibly grateful. He sat down on the *maïs éclaté* coverlet and picked up one of the framed photographs that stood on the bedside table. There were Miri and Claude together, an artistic photograph rather than a formal one they'd had taken for her birthday several years ago. Claude had his arm around Miri, leaning his head toward hers, while she looked back over her shoulder toward him. Their smiles were radiant. Beside this one was the one of Claude as a boy with his violin, and behind that was another of Miri and Claude's father in their wedding clothes. So young.

Three wooden hooks on the back of the door were still draped with Miri's scarves and shawls, including the purple one with red flowers. Gently he took it down and folded it, placing the cloth between the two photographs of Claude and Miri, and Claude as a boy, and took them to the kitchen where he found Rainier Hazan, Miri's first cousin and closest relative. He asked Rainier very simply if he might let him have these things.

"Of course, you may," Rainier said, wiry gray eyebrows frowning over his kind eyes. "She would certainly have wanted you to have them."

Gerard put out his hand, but Rainier pulled him into a brief embrace. He asked Gerard to please keep in touch, and Gerard nodded, unable to speak.

For Gerard, the streets of Paris that had once seemed so lively and full of possibility now echoed like a mausoleum. Where once there were friends on every corner, now the cafés were peopled with lingering ghosts. Reports in the newspapers of violence in Germany and elsewhere, raising the specter of war, horrified and depressed him. Vividly he recalled the devastating images from Europe during the Great War, from the newsreels shown in the movie houses where he'd played the scores for silent films, and photographs in the daily papers, with lists of the names of the dead spooling out beneath. Now and again a searing anger threatened to rise in him, but each time he clamped it down. He couldn't let it take him over; there'd be nothing left.

The one place in Paris Gerard still felt at home was at Anna's, where the figures in her sitting room gallery kept them company on many an evening, along with glasses of wine and the records she set spinning on her gilt-edged phonograph. The lamplight and the mauve color of the walls that showed in the little avenues between the paintings added to the comforting, cloistered feel of the room. Anna would raise her glass as if to make a toast. "Let's pretend that everything is perfect right now," she would say. "In the whole world, all is well."

More than once he fell asleep on her divan, only to awaken there the next morning covered in a duvet. Anna would be asleep in her bedroom and he would quietly go, leaving a note on the stand where she kept her gloves and keys, to thank her, and to tell her again that she was saving his soul.

✦ ✦ ✦ ✦

"Do you see we have reached our middle age and not married?" Anna said, one autumn night in her gallery. She was sketching a little drawing of him with a piece of charcoal, a pad of paper propped on her knees.

Gerard looked at her askance and laughed. "I didn't realize our trousseaus were ready yet."

"I'm serious, Gerard," she said, waving the piece of charcoal in the air a second. "Haven't you ever thought about it?"

"Marriage? So as to rejoin normal society, you mean? A wife to bring home to my family?" Decades ago he had toyed with that idea a few times, before painfully admitting to himself that it was preposterous. When members of his family ever asked him, in their letters or during the few times he'd visited Montreal since leaving, if he'd yet found a girl to marry, he'd said no, or avoided answering entirely. Better that than to invent an outright lie.

"No, I don't mean like that. Of course not." Anna studied her sketch. "I simply mean love and devotion with another, like Armand and Maxime for example."

"I believe they have an arrangement," Gerard said, meaning that though the pair had lived together for years, they both had other lovers at times.

"All the better!"

"Do you see yourself like that one day?"

"I hope I *will* see myself like that one day. And I hope I will see you like that too. I would indeed like to grow old with someone so dear."

Gerard took a sip from his wineglass, an ache in his chest.

"Did you ever think about Claude that way?" Anna asked, gently. "If he had he lived?"

"Anna, please."

"Well?"

"Why ask me that now?"

"It doesn't hurt to imagine what might have been."

"Doesn't it?"

"I don't mean to linger too long on it." Anna put the pad and charcoal aside, wiping her blackened fingertips on a smudging cloth. "The point is to consider what you want to have. In life. Going forward."

"Yes, perhaps."

"Be open, *Cher*."

"Perhaps one day."

✦ ✦ ✦ ✦ ✦

One morning, after waking up on Anna's divan and walking the quiet, early streets toward his building, the thought crossed his mind that perhaps, after all, it was time to return to America. A letter had come from Jeannette a few days before. Nora was ailing, indeed had not been well since they lost Uncle Hig, and though her grandchildren, Jeannette's two girls, cheered her, she was no longer the force she once had been. Jeannette feared she might not make it through another winter.

I wish we could see you again (Jeannette wrote.) *You would be pleased to see how the girls' piano playing is coming along. Esther has even said she wants to be an opera singer.*

At last, I will see you soon, (wrote Gerard.) *I think that Paris has finally finished with me. If New York will have me back again, I will see if she can once again be my home. Being near to you and yours will be a blessing.*

He was no longer young. It was time to take stock of what mattered most and what he had left, and, except for Anna, these things waited for him across the Atlantic. He began to move through the city viewing it through the bittersweet lens of anticipated departure. The proprietress in the kiosk where he bought his newspapers and cigarettes, the side doors of theatres where he had rehearsed and performed, the old women in black who swept the *Place du Tertre*, his neighbors, trees with starlings in their branches and iron grates around their bases and initials carved into their bark by overwrought youths. To all these things he imagined little farewells.

When he next saw Anna at her flat and told her of his decision, she said, "Of course you are going, *Cher*. I'm surprised it wasn't sooner."

"I would never have survived without you," he said, his voice wavering. "And I'm not at all sure how I'll do without you when I go."

"Well, don't *weep* for me," she said, with a dismissing wave. "You might see me in New York, you never know. And anyway, I believe I'm bound for Mexico before long."

"Anna, I must tell you something else." He hadn't planned to say this thing, but it came upon him suddenly, gargantuan and magnificent, like a whale breaching the glittering surface of the sea. "Anna, just knowing you has changed me. You've not only been the best of friends, you've made me a friend to myself. All my life I was a fickle friend to myself, and at times no friend at all, but not anymore. I learned that from you. I can't tell you what that means to me."

She stared at him a long moment, then raised the tips of her long fingers to her eyes. "Grandiose," she said, and went to cry in the bathroom. When she came back ten minutes later she said that she was famished and that Gerard had better take her right out to dinner.

"We will speak of nothing but happy memories," she said, dabbing her eyes with her handkerchief. "Of all the good things that have happened since we met all those years ago."

✦ ✦ ✦ ✦ ✦

And so, Gerard prepared to leave Paris. In his last weeks, having tied up most of his affairs, he visited all of his favorite places, not to burn them into his memory but to speak with them, silently. *Thank you*, he said, internally, *Thank you for being here for me. I won't forget you.*

He saw everyone in the city he cared about, as there were still many. He spent a whole afternoon at the café called *Les Pénières*, across from the building where Claude had lived before going to Berlin, just to be near those old stones, and another afternoon at the cemetery, where he took flowers.

Anna refused to cry anymore on his account, but they saw each other as much as possible. One afternoon she met him at a café near *l'Abbaye* they had used to frequent, dressed as a man in an ecru suit with a yellow silk cravat and a gray fedora that hid her hair. She smiled when Gerard complimented her unrivaled sense of style, and when the waiter addressed her as *Monsieur*.

"I do believe I will see you again, *cher* Gerard," she said, stirring cream into her coffee with a *madeleine* biscuit. "Perhaps soon."

"I will gladly believe so."

"We both."

At last he packed up what was left of his things in two large suitcases, stowing the photographs of Claude and Miri carefully within a thick envelope of letters in Claude's pressed-tin box. His composition books, the books by Langston he'd collected, the drawings Anna had given him, and several colorful leaflets from favorite performances he packed securely against the essential stacks of folded clothing—all the things he needed to wrap his body and his soul so that he might move through the world and into the unimaginable future. It was May of 1938. Gerard was forty-seven years old. The past was fleeting and gone, and he was about to start all over again.

Jeannette

Gerard spent much of his six days at sea writing letters home to Montreal, and a handful of short notes to folks in New York that he hoped he would soon see in person. Paris already seemed far away, a dream almost, but one that made him a stranger to himself. Writing the letters strengthened his feeling that the roots he sought were out there, and that he was connected to them still.

He also played Claude's amber-colored guitar, finding a new and growing kinship with it, like a piano he could hold in his arms, a remnant of the man he had loved. He played Satie. He played jazz. He played melodies from parts of his opera. He found himself making up a tune to play for his Jeannette and her children when he saw them, because she had invited him to stay when he arrived from Europe.

Those plans were made through letters back in March, the ones exchanged in the first months after Jeannette's telegram that proved she'd been right in fearing that Nora would not survive another winter. Pneumonia had taken her, just as it had Claude. That illness that preyed upon the weak. The passing of the woman who had given him life, who had been his greatest mentor, was not something he could begin to assimilate when saying his goodbyes in Paris, he hadn't the strength for it. He'd had to pack it away like another of his possessions, to be taken out later and reopened on new ground.

The last day of the voyage Gerard woke early to a cold, clear morning with a few stars still visible. He stood by the rail, breathing in the wind. The planet Venus shone most brightly, the one his father had always called the Waking Star. How many times had he pointed it out to Gerard when he was a boy? When rising early to fetch wood in the dark, to see to the horses, short journeys to go fishing in the summer. Papa would crouch down so that his shoulder touched Gerard's, and Gerard would follow his father's big arm, past his pointing finger and into the sky.

The first traces of the harbor came into view as the sky paled. Lights from tugboats, edges of islands, and eventually the towers of industry, rising up over the water. Soon enough he would disembark, find his way through the familiar and the strange, the streets he knew, to the address in Harlem where his sister would be waiting.

✦ ✦ ✦ ✦ ✦

His first sight of her out on the street, just after he'd paid his cab driver, took his breath away. She was at once the child he'd always known and the mature woman he'd not yet seen, running up to him in her apron and housedress, shoes slipped on hurriedly with no stockings. When they embraced he felt her arms around his neck exactly as he had when they'd parted at the harbor all those years before. Glancing up he saw two little faces behind a window pane and his heart leapt again, and then he blinked and the faces were gone.

"I can't believe it's true," Jeannette said, drawing back.

"That's both of us then," Gerard said, smiling.

She led him through the apartment's narrow hallway to the room she called the nursery, and had him set his two suitcases down beside a closet door. It was a little nook of a room, with a bedstead squeezed under a window that looked out onto the brick walls of an airshaft. The ceiling of varnished brown boards sloped on either side of the window, and six or seven rag dolls lay tucked in neatly under a pink and white coverlet on the bed.

"Oh my," Jeannette said of the dolls, "looks like we forgot these." She gathered them up and hurried across the hall to the main bedroom. The low tones of her voice sounded through the wall, and the higher ones of one of the children answering, then Jeannette reappeared. "The girls are hiding out just now," she said. "They're shy."

"I don't blame them," Gerard said, still adjusting to speaking English again. "A stranger taking over their room, and all."

"No, no, don't think it. They sleep with me most of the time anyway since their daddy is away working." Jeannette pressed her hands to her cheeks, as if to contain a rising emotion. "The girls miss him, but we're glad he has work."

"When will he be home next?" Gerard asked, sitting down on the bed. He was wobbly, remembering that after almost a week at sea it took a day or two for the body to get used to being on land.

"Maybe a month or two," Jeannette said, sitting down on a little chair with a round plush seat, the only piece of other furniture in the room. She looked intently at Gerard. "I'm getting used to how you look now." She laughed at herself for saying so. "I expect I look a lot different to you too."

Gerard ran a hand over his high forehead, his thinning hair threaded now with silver. Jeannette, who'd been rail-thin as a girl, had a fuller form now, a presence that reminded him of Nora, but warmer, gentler, more like her father. Her thick black hair was pinned back in soft twists and she patted them with a graceful hand. She was beautiful to look at, but he saw in her face that losing her parents—with her husband away and times hard as they were—had exacted a toll on her youth. He wanted to scoop her up, just like he used to, twirl her around and say, *I've got you now.*

The bedroom door was half-open and a rustling noise came from behind it. Jeannette went to look and came back with her two girls in tow. She had Esther, the older one, by the hand, and the little one, Maudie, came with her face buried in her mother's skirts.

"Say hello to your uncle, Babies," Jeannette said.

Esther looked up at him with the same enormous eyes Jeannette had had as a child. "Hello, Unka," she said, just above a whisper.

Gerard eased himself down to the floor and sat on a woven rug that lay over the floorboards.

"Goodness," he said. "How big you are." He looked up at Jeannette. "Has the Tooth Fairy been here lately?" Esther broke into a smile, revealing three gaps in her front teeth, and nodded. "Did she bring you a present?" Esther nodded again and raced out of the room, returning with one of the dolls that Gerard guessed had been made with some of the same rags as the rug.

Maudie, curious about the commotion, peeked out from the folds of her mother's skirts and then ran off as well to retrieve another doll. A moment later the four of them and two dolls, were seated on the rug.

"The Tooth Fairy came three times," Esther said, holding up as many fingers. "But she won't ever come if you don't settle down and go to sleep at your bedtime."

Gerard laughed. "Yes, that's right."

"When *I* get big," Maudie piped up, "I'm gon' lose a toof too." She pointed to the one she had in mind and leaned toward Gerard so he could see. With him sitting on the floor, and Maudie standing in her stocking feet, the *toof* in question was exactly at eye-level.

"It's a beauty," Gerard said. They were all of them such beauties.

New York, 1939

It is September first and unusually gray and cold. Gerard walks the esplanade of Battery Park in hat and overcoat, carrying his worn leather attaché case. The harbor is teeming with boats and barges, smokestacks and gulls, though the dark wind-blown mist obscures his view of it.

Gerard has spent the past year renewing connections and seeking work, and he's just come from a meeting with one Mr. Abner Milton, introduced to Gerard by his old friend Clifford Mobley. Milton is a businessman with an office in a Financial District high rise, who wants to make a name for himself as an innovator in music and might prove interested in Gerard's work.

The meeting had been pleasant enough, if inconclusive, but Gerard is making do in New York, can't complain, and if this lead doesn't go anywhere there will be something else. But for some reason he's uneasy. He's left a portfolio of sheet music with Milton, though at the last moment had decided to remove the folder that contained the pages of his unfinished opera, which he carries now in his attaché along with his wallet and a few other small items. The last time he looked at his opera was before Claude died, four years ago now, this sheaf of papers that represents his countless hours, sleeping and waking, with the most intimate music he's ever composed.

On the esplanade, the choppy gray water to his right and the park's spit of greenery on his left, Gerard is nearing Castle Clinton, a pink sandstone building that now houses an aquarium, and thinking that he'll bring Jeannette's girls here one day soon. *How delighted they'll be*, he tells himself, fighting his growing sense of disquiet, *to look at strange creatures from the sea*. But as he gets closer he notices a commotion out front, a small crowd of people are milling about and he can hear voices over the wind. A newsboy darts from the crowd and runs toward him, hefting a sack full of papers and waving one above his head. Other newsboys are running toward other people on the esplanade. Something has happened.

The newsboy reaches him, his cap is falling off and the knee of his short trousers is torn. "Hitler's invaded Poland!" he says, panting. "You want a paper, Sir? A nickel!"

Gerard stops. An especially icy wind has just hit his face.

Yes, he wants a paper. He unlatches the attaché to get his wallet, but the wind catches it and the pages of his opera spill out onto the ground. He scrambles to collect them and the boy helps, handing them back to Gerard and fixing his cap, then holding out his palm for the nickel. Gerard places two coins in the boy's hand, one for the paper and one for his help, turning his attention to the headlines. The boy races off. Everyone will be buying papers today.

Leaning on the sea rail, Gerard struggles to take in the words of the article, sensing heavily what this will mean for Europe and for much of the world. Of their own accord, his fingers curl around the newsprint and the disordered sheets of his opera he has clutched underneath, bending and crumpling the edges of the paper, an unbearable anger shaking him like an earthquake, this thing locked away for years is breaking from its hold.

A scream rises in his throat, a wordless curse that in the next second is snatched away by an enormous gust of wind. He flings the papers in his hand over the rail. All of them. The white sheets scatter into the air over the cold edge of the seawater, fluttering, twirling, further away, growing smaller, until they are lost completely in the mist and cloud.

He crouches down to the ground, struggling to breathe, pulling his overcoat tightly around him and staring at his empty hands. His opera is gone, taking its final act spread across the sky.

Eyes shut tight, he blocks the whole world out. At least for a minute, because it hurts too much. *Endings can be evasive*, Claude had said. *And shy.*

At last a noise rouses him—a factory whistle from across the harbor—and he opens his eyes. The whistle sounds again. Noon. He's still there, the cold pavement of the esplanade beneath him, the wind shushing at his ears.

I'm here and you're gone, he thinks.

A seagull's cry pierces the air and Gerard looks up, watching the bird wheel away toward another of its kind.

Finally he stands, collects his things. Buttons his coat. He turns his back to the water and sets his feet to walking, returning him to the heart of the city.

Part 2
Jeannette

New York, 1919 - 1928

Before meeting Macon Halvorsen, Jeannette had really only had one beau. That was when she was fifteen years old, a student at The Wadleigh High School for Girls on West 114th Street, serious about her studies, a little bit shy, with a love for music and a romantic heart. Jeannette had a willowy frame that had not yet settled into grace and she was buxom like her mother, which threw things off a bit more, and a lovely face with what folks called "doe's eyes," that added to her air of innocence.

Most of the boys she knew were ones she'd known all her life, from church and elementary school, and Jeannette thought it funny how they were, on average, different from the girls. Back in the elementary school, for example, in the minutes before the first bell rang, all the girls would be grouped together in little chattering clumps, while the boys tended to wander about alone, each in his free-floating individual world. Now when she saw boys her age, at the park near St. Luke's where young people congregated on weekends, for example, it was somewhat the same, but the boys often grouped together too, shouting and laughing and pushing each other and doing little stunts, like hopping up on the little brick pillar of the water fountain and leaping off. Whether that was to impress each other or the girls, Jeannette couldn't say, but the girls spent a whole lot of time watching them from the corners of their eyes.

Carrell was a boy who existed outside this melee. Jeannette had met him at Hammond's grocery store where he worked stocking shelves and sweeping the floors and bringing in deliveries from trucks that came up the back alley. He had a lovely shy smile that revealed a single, enchanting dimple in his right cheek, which she first glimpsed one day when he set down a crate of eggs near to where she was selecting a package of baking soda from a stand by the front counter. Since

Jeannette's family lived just down the street from the grocery, and since she often sat out on the stoop, Carrell began stopping by in the late afternoons to pass the time of day. His soft voice, as they chatted, made an appealing contrast with his wiry frame.

Mama didn't exactly approve. "That boy is as country as they come," she said once, after Carrell had offered to "tote" their groceries home for them. And another time, after he'd given Jeannette a little bag of plums, Mama remarked that the plums were just as black as he was. It was true that Carrell was from country people, as his family had come up from Mississippi to work in the war plants. Jeannette's best school friend, Dolly, came from country people too, though not so recently. Her mother was also from Mississippi, her father from Alabama, and Mama didn't much approve of them either, because the Higginses were of a higher class, educated and cultured colored professionals who kept company with the same. Still, Mama never prevented Jeannette's associations, perhaps in part because Papa always wrapped an arm around her shoulders and said, "Let her be, Nora. Jeannette's got to make her own choices." Mama calmed under Papa's arm like that, Jeannette knew, because the crook of her father's arm was the safest place in the world.

For her part, Jeannette saw very plainly the differences between her family and Dolly's. She loved the way Dolly grabbed her arm and hung on when they crossed the schoolyard or traipsed down the street together, and Dolly's laugh, so free and easy, showing all her teeth (and tonsils too, Mama might say.) Visiting at Dolly's home was great fun, where her brothers and sisters made such a noise and commotion that her mother, Mrs. James, had to chase them out with her broom to get her work done.

Jeannette was aware that she got to do things Dolly didn't, like go to concerts and literary evenings and fancy parties full of glamorous people, but between these times, afternoons at home when her parents were at work at their institute could be a little lonely. When she paused in her piano practice or homework the only sound--beside a passing car or voice from outside--was the ticking of the grandfather clock in the hallway, and she envied Dolly her big family. Jeannette did have one brother, of course, Gerard, but he was grown and lived elsewhere in the city, and they only saw him once or twice in a week. She understood that she and Gerard shared a mother but not a father, that Gerard's father was another man that long ago Mama had known before Papa.

How well she remembered the brilliant day when she was just five years old, that her parents and Gerard had sat down with her in the parlor and told her that he was not her cousin, as she had thought, but in actuality her brother. It was better than Christmas. She had jumped up shouting, "Yippee! Yippee!" and Gerard and Papa both burst out laughing and she could have sworn she touched the ceiling. But then she'd looked at Mama and didn't know if she was laughing or crying or about to sneeze; she was making a funny wheezing noise that sounded like a combination of all three. And then Mama pressed a handkerchief over her face and hurried to the water closet with Papa striding after her, but Jeannette scarcely noticed because her very own brother, great big Gerard, was twirling her around through the air, with a smile that radiated all the way down to her toes.

So, Papa had been the first man in her life, the crook of his arm the safest place in the world, and then there was her brother Gerard, like Christmas, and then, briefly, there was Carrell, like a sweet spring day. They spent hours on the stoop talking and even sometimes holding hands, until the sad evening in July when he told her he was bound for Chicago with his sister, who had gotten them good jobs at a hotel there. Jeannette bit her lip to keep from crying, then suggested that they might write letters, but Carrell admitted that he hadn't had barely any schooling, and from the way he said it Jeannette guessed that in fact he couldn't read or write, and that was the saddest thing of all. But she gave him her address anyway, and hoped for a word from him, a postcard maybe, that in the end didn't come.

◆ ◆ ◆ ◆ ◆

Three years later, Jeannette and Dolly graduated from Wadleigh, and while Dolly began working where her mother did, at a busy lunch counter near the shipyards, Jeannette enrolled at a teachers college. Her grades were excellent, and she'd written in her application essay about her volunteer work with the literacy program at her church, which she'd done in memory of Carrell, sitting with men and women as old as her parents as they practiced reading aloud and writing on tablets with pencils, large shaky letters like children would. What moved her most was how proud the students were when they finished the program, how they walked taller, no longer bearing the shame of being unlettered. They pressed Jeannette's hands with tears in their eyes and said God would bless her, because the world had opened up for them and she had helped them get there.

Though she still spent much of her free time with Dolly, Jeannette made new friends among the small group of colored students at the college, including a young man named Percy who aimed to specialize in mathematics—Jeannette would specialize in music education—and who was the first to catch her special interest since Carrell. But Percy was engaged, and though he seemed to like Jeannette too, walking to classes and to the library together, their friendship would only go so far.

Macon

By 1928, Jeannette was twenty-four years old, no longer so young, working as a music teacher at the Harriet Gaines School for Colored Children. It was joyful work, the younger children excited for the chance to play the little drums and triangles, the older ones serious when they had their turns with the handful of violins and clarinets owned by the school. At holiday times she organized concerts for the parents who pressed her hands afterward, much as had the folks at St. Luke's she had helped learn to read.

Gerard had gone to live in Paris, and though she missed him dearly, she now had three years' worth of picture postcards pinned to her bedroom wall. Weekends she often visited with Dolly who had married the same year that Gerard left and now had two little girls. Gone were the days when Dolly and Jeannette and Dolly's older sister Martha practiced tap dance routines on the James' kitchen linoleum, Martha and Dolly saying that they would join a vaudeville troupe just as soon as they could and that Jeannette would play the piano for their solos. Dolly was now Dolly Sutherfield, and Martha had gone to live in Buffalo.

At home things had also changed. Jeannette was proud to be another working adult in the household, one with an independent life in many ways, though it was natural that she still lived with her parents. But not all the changes felt natural or happy. Knowing her parents would not choose to write about it to Gerard, Jeannette took it upon herself to pass along certain information to her brother in Paris.

Papa has been troubled by back pain (she wrote in a letter to Gerard) *for the last several months, and he's tired like I've never seen him. Mama makes him lie* down in the early evenings and lately on the weekends too, during the day, except for church. Dr. Kalman says it's a problem with his kidneys and that there isn't much to be done besides take his pills twice a day. We're not to put salt in his food, which makes everything so bland. But you know Papa, he doesn't complain, and he shushes our worries with his good humor. We are still hopeful that things may yet turn around.

I'm grieved to receive news of your father's illness (Gerard wrote back) *and I canonly imagine your distress. No doubt you and Nora are his biggest comfort in life. I regret being so far away and wish there were something I could do. My affairs here are complicated, what with attempting to build my career. I've got some scaffolding in place, but it's rickety as the dickens. All my time I spend running from place to place, tightening screws and laying down loose boards for platforms. Well, such are my silly metaphors!*

Despite the best efforts of the doctor and everyone in the family, Papa continued to decline. Finally, in December of 1927, the Higgins Institute for Colored Musicians, which Jeannette's parents had run for over twenty glorious years, had to close its doors, so that Papa could rest and Mama could devote herself to his care. Their savings, liquidated assets, and Jeannette's modest teacher's salary sustained them, as did the loving care and casseroles of their community. Mama was an efficient nurse, or tried to be. Caring for an ailing husband was a different business from professional music. It was wrenching for Jeannette to see her father, always so strong, have to reach for the wall to steady himself when shuffling from one room to the next, wincing with the burning pains that seized his middle. And to see her composed, exacting, commanding mother falter before a pile of cutlery needing to be put away, or a bundle of just-delivered clean laundry, not knowing where to put the socks, confused as if suddenly living in an upside-down world.

Jeannette strove to be a grown woman both her parents could lean on—organizing schedules and pills and housekeeping and finances and friends who offered help—even as she felt more like a lost child herself every day.

Though now she was tired returning to work on Mondays, seeing the faces of the children always refreshed her, and turning them into knowers and players of music was magical in a way she couldn't quite describe. The little domain of her classroom, where most of the time everything was happy, fortified her, and the children loved her too—hugging her around the waist, eager to show her they had practiced, bringing her little gifts from home.

Then came Macon Halvorsen. He was a young, colored salesman who came to the school the first Wednesday of each month after classes finished, each time with a new item in his case—wood oil, scented soap, black board erasers, neat boxes of pencils. But after spotting her in the Director's office one day, where she'd gone to hand in an envelope of coins the children had helped raise for a set of new music stands, he began to drop by more often.

"Miss Higgins," he'd say, finding her straightening up in the music room, "I believe I've got something you'll like to look at." He had things in his case a young woman might want—hairbrushes and pins with beads, little coral brooches in the shapes of flowers. One day he gave her a pair of cherry wood combs.

"For your pretty hair. A gift," he said, sitting down at one of the desks, with an arm set akimbo on his knee. "Won't you let me see you try them on?"

Macon's gaze was steady, his strong jaw well-shaven, his suit coat fit cleanly over his shoulders with nary a wrinkle anywhere, and Jeannette was flattered by his attentions if a little unnerved.

"I'm afraid I can't do my hair right without a mirror," she said, noticing the pressed creases of his tan suit. He wore no ring on his finger and she wondered who did his pressing.

"Won't you try? For me?" He winked and smiled.

"Alright, I guess." She tucked the combs into her hair, one over each ear.

"There now," he said, smiling wider. "Just so."

✦ ✦ ✦ ✦ ✦

The following Wednesday Macon asked to walk her home, and she accepted. It was twelve blocks between the school and her house, and Macon spent the time telling her that he wasn't just a salesman, but an entrepreneur.

"I've got two fellows working under me," he told her with evident pride. "And I'm planning to expand."

"You seem a confident man, Mr. Halvorsen," she said. "I expect you'll do well."

His smile broadened, making his somewhat slanted eyes narrower, his ochre coloring setting off his thick black eyebrows. He held himself straight as a poker, making the most of his moderate height. Up close he smelled of sweat and cologne, a scent that was disquieting, as it came from under his clothing.

It was early March and winter was struggling to hold on a little longer, sending down bits of snow and ice that rapidly melted in the warming winds. Jeannette felt lighter with this change after such a hard, heavy winter, and she began to look forward to Wednesdays when Macon would come with his case and ask to walk her home. By April he came on Fridays too, offered his arm, and she hooked her elbow over his, letting a little of her weight rest there.

One day he lingered longer after their goodbye. "When will I meet your people, Miss Jeannette? You do want to introduce me, don't you?" His tone was slightly teasing, as if he meant to soften the demand.

"I would like to do that sometime soon," she said, glancing uncertainly at the curtained parlor window. "But as I've told you, Papa is ill. I'll have to find the right time."

Jeannette didn't want to disturb her parents, it was true, but she also wanted more time to decide how she felt about Macon. On the one hand, he was strong and solid, and clearly liked her very much. She liked the feel of his arm in hers, and his charming smile, and everyone said ambition was a good thing in a man. On the other hand, there were things about him were unsettling. Though he enjoyed telling her about his business dealings, he was evasive about his origins, at times saying that he was reared in Carolina, other times Virginia. When Jeannette inquired about his folks, he simply said, "Dead and gone," and looked into the distance with a certain studied wistfulness.

✦ ✦ ✦ ✦ ✦

"Ain't he taken you out to eat yet?" Dolly asked, a few diaper pins clamped in her lips on one side, her hands busy changing the baby. May, the older girl, played on the floor. "A picture?"

"He did ask me if I wanted to see the new Charles Chaplin at the Lafayette, but I said I couldn't go. I had to help Mama."

"You had to, or you *said* you had to?"

"I'm just not sure yet. If I want to be alone with him. For that long."

Dolly finished dressing the baby and swung her onto her hip. "He tried to kiss you yet?"

"On the cheek, a few times." Jeannette giggled, remembering Macon's mustache tickling her face.

"Oh!" Dolly laughed. "Look out. You'll be diapering babies just like me before you know it."

"I don't know—"

"You're just scared of it," Dolly said, the tail end of her laugh still lingering in her throat.

"Scared of what?"

"*It*, the big *it*. Girl, I know all you ever did with a boy was hold hands."

"I've been dancing," Jeannette said. It was true, she and Dolly had been to lots of dances together before Dolly was married.

"Mm hmm."

"What do you think I should do, go to the pictures with him?"

"Why not? He ain't going to eat you."

Jeannette laughed. "I guess you're right."

✦ ✦ ✦ ✦ ✦

When June rolled around, just before the summer holidays, Jeannette and Macon had been meeting regularly for close to four months, often taking routes longer than necessary between the school and Jeannette's house. They'd been to the pictures a few times, and Macon had held her hand or put an arm around her shoulders but had otherwise stayed proper. One evening, when the breeze was fresh and the sky still bright, they passed by several shops with big windows. Macon stopped in front of one with a pair of mannequins dressed in fine lace gowns and straw garden hats with big matching bows.

"When we're married," he said, gazing at the window and pursing his lips, "I'll buy you a set just like that."

Jeannette didn't know how to answer. She'd thought he might broach the subject of marriage at some point, but she still wasn't sure of her feelings. It seemed to her that Macon had done everything right up till now and she didn't see how she could fault him. The truth was she wasn't dreaming about any wedding day, she was too terrified about what was happening at home. Papa slept more and more of each day and required more medication for his pain. Mama sat beside him for hours in stupor, as if a sinister spell had come over the house, and neither was Jeannette immune to it, because it made a part of her go to sleep as well. She became forgetful, letting the coffee boil over on the stove or leaving the milk bottles outside until the afternoon and they spoiled. She watched her hands reach out to remedy her mistakes as if they belonged to another. It was hardly a time for romance.

She did remember what it was like to be with Carrell, and Percy from the college too, how her heart fluttered, how she recalled those moments for a long time after, as if savoring a sweet. When lovers clasped each other in the pictures, or in the novels she read, she sometimes felt a sort of swoon herself, a heat spreading from her belly down between her legs, and up to her heart, making it beat harder. But she couldn't much locate that feeling in herself now, not with Macon, though she there was a reassurance in his presence. With her students and with Dolly she felt buoyed, light. But it was a fragile lightness in the face of Papa's illness.

Papa

Though Jeannette didn't bother her parents with too much detail, they were aware she'd been keeping company with a young man. Papa roused himself enough each evening when Jeannette arrived home for a short conference, and while Mama went to prepare supper, he took her hand and asked, "So, tell me. What's the news of the day?"

Jeannette knew it was a great effort for him to make himself alert for their conversation and that it pained him not to be the father he'd always been, so she did her best to pick out the most pleasant bits and recount them with frequent smiles—the antics of her most mischievous students, a hat she'd seen in a shop window she thought she might try to duplicate on her own, how Dolly's younger child, toddling now, had sat down in a pan of water left out for the cat. Papa smiled and chuckled and hung onto her hand, and said things like, "Ain't that something," or, "I know you'll make it beautiful," or, "Oh, children," until his eyes drooped and his grip loosened, and Jeannette said that he had better rest before supper was ready.

On one of these evenings, Papa said to Jeannette, "Honey, bring Mr. Halvorsen over to the house on Sunday. It's far past time we met him."

She squeezed his hand. "I'll ask him."

◆ ◆ ◆ ◆ ◆

It was a brief meeting, as Papa couldn't sit up for long. Macon sat erect on the edge of the parlor sofa with his hat on his lap, and, to Jeannette's relief, conducted himself with the utmost respect. Papa and Mama asked Macon about his family and his business and his interests, and all the while Jeannette kept staring at his hat, thinking she should have hung it up for him on the rack by the door, but that now it was too late, or that she shouldn't have hung it up anyway because he should go before Papa grew too fatigued. It was almost hateful, that hat, because the more she looked at it, the less she knew what to do.

The next time Macon walked Jeannette home from work they walked a roundabout way and passed by a row of red brick townhouses. Stopping to gaze at them, he said, "How would you like a house like that? When we're married."

"They look nice," Jeannette answered, and stayed quiet the rest of the way home, determining to speak to her parents that very night and ask their advice. But as it happened, she did not get that chance.

Nearing her house, Jeannette saw that, strangely, no light glowed through the parlor curtains. "Papa must have gone to sleep in the front room," she said to Macon. "Let's say goodnight here."

"I'll be seeing you soon then," he said, kissing her cheek, and went off whistling, back in the direction they'd come from.

Walking the last yards on the pavement and up the stairs to the door, Jeannette was gripped with an unease that made her movements so slow it was like moving through mud. But before she was able to fit her key into the lock, she heard someone calling her name.

Turning, she saw it was the next-door neighbor, Mrs. Doolin, rushing toward her, long skirts gathered in one hand while the other waved in the air. "Jeannette," she said, panting, "your father's gone in an ambulance to Harlem Hospital, God bless him. Your mother's there too." She grasped Jeannette's hands—hands that looked, more than they ever had, as if they belonged to someone else—and spoke words whose sound arrived long after the mouth moved.

"Mr. Doolin will take you in the Ford. Right away."

✦ ✦ ✦ ✦ ✦

The jaws of that dark night bit a brutal cold into Jeannette's heart. Her father, the most gentle and solid presence in her and Mama's life, left them. In the empty white corridor outside the room where Mama lay with her arm still crossing Papa's chest, Jeannette rang Mr. Harris and Mr. Joop, his oldest friends, two men who had been like uncles to her, to tell them that Papa had gone, and that she and Mama needed them to come. Wrapped in their strong arms, Jeannette and Mama were shepherded home, where soon the many others closest to them gathered in to grieve, to comfort, to assist in all ways necessary.

After a few days, Macon came to the house. He'd been to the school and the director had told him Jeannette was absent, because, sadly, there had been a death in the family. They stood alone in the parlor, Mama was resting in her bedroom, and when she hid her face in her hands he held her until her shoulders stopped shaking. Then he dried her face with his handkerchief, and whispered, "I'm sorry."

Mama always said that the day of Papa's funeral they'd have to block off the street, and that was nearly true. All those people created a great press of love and grief, concentric circles with Mama and Jeannette and the casket as its center. In the receiving line, one face after another swam before Jeannette's, so many offered hands and embraces and heartfelt words it became difficult to distinguish one from another, even though so many were familiar and so many were dear. But at the end of it all Macon was still there, holding his hat and waiting for her.

Dolly was there, with her husband and children. Mama's brother Dax came up from Philadelphia with his wife and their two young daughters, pretty as anything. Jeannette's Aunt Melody, whom she had met several times, came from Montreal—an ethereal figure wrapped in lisle and crepe, so unlike Mama in speech and manner it was still hard to believe they were sisters. A telegram came from Paris from Gerard sending his sincerest condolences, with the promise of a letter to follow. Others had come from out of town too, friends, colleagues, and countless former students, and so a long, long line of people followed the hearse to the burying place at the cemetery.

Alma

The older folks of the community took charge that first week, bearing up Jeannette and her mother, and within days Jeannette's Auntie Alma, not a blood relative but her mother's closest friend, arrived from Chicago with a trunk so large it scarcely fit through the door. With Auntie Alma's help especially, they survived those first terrible weeks. Uncle Jack, Alma's husband, sent his regrets that he would not be with them too, a recent gallbladder operation prevented him from traveling, and he was home under the care of their grown daughter, Althea.

Petite, silver-haired Auntie Alma, though she'd lived in the North since her youth and had traveled the world as a singer, cooked like she'd never left her native Kansas City. Jeannette and her mother had little appetite, but Alma plied them with glazed ribs, sweet potatoes and pots of savory stewed greens, the leftovers of which got fed to visitors. One sweltering evening in July, when heartache and the heat made supper impossible, Alma spent two hours making vanilla ice cream that she served with cold raspberries. Alma herself consumed a man-sized bowl and then returned to the kitchen for a stack of turkey sandwiches. Mama watched Alma in amazement.

"You always could eat," she said. "Lord knows where it all goes."

"Well now," Alma said, with her mouth full, winking at Jeannette, "that's a marital secret."

It was the first time they laughed since Papa died.

When they'd finished eating, Alma wiped the table clean and brought out albums of photographs from the room downstairs that had long been the office of the Higgins Institute. They pored over these and the two Alma had brought from Chicago in a trunk, with her and Mama telling old stories, many of which Jeannette had never heard.

❖ ❖ ❖ ❖

The whole month of August while Jeannette was engaged at the school, cleaning the music room and organizing supplies with the other teachers, Auntie Alma took Mama on walks in the Park, or bathing at the west 60th Street pool. Mama was reluctant every time, but Alma insisted they go, as well as insisting on making plans for the future. As Papa's illness had drained their savings, Alma thought it would be a good idea for Jeannette and Mama to move into one of the three bedrooms in the house and rent out the other two to boarders. If they took the big bedroom there would be space enough for shelves and the big writing desk that had served as the administrative helm of the Higgins Institute. With all her contacts, between artists and patrons, Mama could still organize private concerts, and that would be another way to supplement their income.

In late September, as Auntie Alma prepared to return to Chicago, Jeannette was grateful to begin classes with her little pupils. Their enjoyment of the music and their passionate little dramas of excitement and frustration gave her a much-needed focus away from missing Papa and worrying about Mama, and of course Macon, who was eager for them to be married, and would not wait on her forever.

"Well, Miss Jeannette," he'd said, the Sunday after classes resumed, "I think it's time we made it official. Next month we'll take ourselves to the Justice of the Peace. Can you make a dress by then?"

A flicker of anger stung the back of her throat. She hadn't accepted his proposal, not that he'd exactly made one. He hadn't even asked her what kind of wedding she wanted. But just as swiftly the emotion was extinguished by doubt. Hadn't Macon stood by her all this time? Hadn't he been patient with her in her grief? Maybe she owed it to him.

At last she said, faltering, "I haven't money for material."

"I'll take care of that detail," he said, smiling broadly. He drew his billfold from his coat pocket, handing her a generous stack of notes, and she took them, unable to look him in the eye.

The next night, after washing the supper dishes and saying goodnight to Mama, Jeannette found Auntie Alma in her bedroom folding clothes into her great trunk.

"Hey, Baby," Auntie Alma said, "come in here. I want to see if this fits you." She'd been fixing a seam on one of Jeannette's dresses.

"Auntie," Jeannette said, sitting on the bed, "did you love Uncle Jack from the start?"

Alma lowered the dress and fixed a look at her. "Has Macon asked you to marry him?"

"He thinks we ought to get married next month," Jeannette said, gnawing her thumbnail.

"Have you talked to Mama about it?" Alma took a seat beside her on the bed.

"I don't want to bother—" Jeannette broke off speaking, tears were coming up fast.

Alma put her arms around her. "Don't underestimate your mother," she said. "She's always been strong." Jeannette nodded, wiping at her eyes. "But how do you feel? About Macon? Do you love him?"

"Maybe," Jeannette said, when she was able to speak again.

Alma snorted. "Maybe not." She smoothed a few stray hairs off Jeannette's forehead, a tender gesture that made the tears come faster. Mama was never one for many tender gestures. "Honey, please don't rush into anything," Alma said. "Will you promise me to take your time?"

Jeannette nodded, wiping her tears with her sleeve. She would wait.

But after Alma left, things were less clear than ever. By October Jeannette and Mama had moved their things into the downstairs room and gotten three women boarders for the upstairs, a pair of sisters in her parents' old bedroom and another woman, who worked as a church secretary, in the room that had been Jeannette's. It was strange to have the others living there, but Jeannette was glad to have more people around so that Mama was less alone while she was teaching at her school. Mama took care of the cooking, though it was utilitarian in style and consisted of one large pot of something that simmered all day on the stove. She hadn't made any move toward organizing the private concerts that Alma had suggested, though Jeannette urged her to, and when friends came by to take her for walks, such as the lively as ever Mr. Sanderson, she said that the pain in her knees and hips, even with using a cane, was too severe for it.

In the evenings after Mama went to bed Jeannette often stayed up writing letters, to Auntie Alma and to Gerard, anxious to have witnesses to the little struggles of life, and the bigger ones, especially when she was alone.

The pleasant news of the day that Jeannette had brought back to the house to cheer her father, she now culled out from everywhere—her students, the other teachers, the newspapers, neighbors—with a desperation that made her voice shrill when she meant it to be cheerful. Mama responded to her conversation with few words, not much more than, "Is that so?" or, "I see," or, "Mm hmm," until it was pointless to try anymore.

The day to day is manageable (Jeannette wrote to Gerard,) *but it gets awfully quiet around here when it's just the two of us, and at times it is hard to bear. Mama has always been strong, as you know, and reserved, but she's never lacked for a word until now. With Papa gone it's like half her soul has disappeared with him.*

How grown you sound in your letters (Gerard wrote back) *I shouldn't think of you as a child anymore. That image in my mind is far outdated, to be sure, as you will know better than I. It is comforting to think that Nora has you as her support, but I wonder if you are holding up alright. Have you your good friends around you? How is Dolly James? Or rather, Dolly Sutherfield, you did tell me she married not so long ago.*

In fact, Jeannette was not sure at all how she was holding up. It took all her energies to take care of what Mama wasn't able to, make sure she was eating, and to teach school. When Macon asked her how her wedding dress was coming along, she said that what with her mother and everything she hadn't had time to get started. Jeannette also hadn't spoken to Mama about him again, as Alma had said she ought to. The moment was never right.

The month of October progressed, the leaves of the maple trees on their street turned color and fell, soaked with rain. But then, during the last week of the month, everyone was suddenly talking about what was happening on Wall Street—stocks and bankers and finance, some kind of crash. It had an ominous ring, the way folks were talking, the way the announcers read out the news on the wireless in the evenings, but Jeannette didn't pay it all that much attention until the day in mid-November that the school director called her into his office.

Mr. Graves, a white man with a ruddy complexion and yellow eyebrows, a color combination that had always struck Jeannette as unnatural, sat at his wide desk shuffling a stack of papers. Though the children at the school were colored, most of the staff was white, as was all of the administration.

"Please have a seat, Miss Higgins," he said. "And please close the door behind you." When she had done as he asked, he removed his glasses and laced his fingers together on the desktop. "Miss Higgins, we've always been very happy with your work here at the school…"

Jeannette's face grew hot and then cold, and then a faint dizziness took hold of the top of her head, as if a string attached to it were being pulled in a little circle. Mr. Graves explained that the Board had had to make some difficult decisions. That the school was in danger of closing because of the market crash, it had had much of its assets invested in stocks and now that was why the school was in such a dire position. Everything that could be done had to be done to keep its doors open, surely she could understand that the students depended on the school remaining open.

"And so, Miss Higgins, I regret that that is why today we must let you go. Miss Dixon will be taking over in the music department."

Jeannette's confusion deepened. Miss Dixon was the white assistant music teacher, she was younger than Jeannette, and, Jeannette knew, had neither attended a teachers college nor had she much music education. "Mr. Graves," Jeannette cleared her throat. "Miss Dixon is much less experienced than I am, much less educated."

Mr. Graves' ruddy face turned a deeper shade of red, making his yellow eyebrows stand out like Jeannette had never seen them. "Miss Higgins, that may be the case, but the Board has taken a decision. I'm afraid there is nothing I can do."

"I don't mean to argue," Jeannette said, "but you said you've been happy with my work and I don't believe Miss Dixon handles the children as well as I do—" In fact, Jeannette knew Miss Dixon to be a nervous girl who often confused the children with her mixed-up instructions.

"The Board has taken its *decision*." Mr. Graves said, anger edging his voice. It dawned now on Jeannette that she'd lost well before this meeting. When Jeannette didn't speak again, he said, "Miss Dixon will begin her new position tomorrow. Please don't tell the children you are leaving, we don't want to upset them."

"Yes, sir," she said, finally.

"You may go back to class now. Please close the door behind you."

Jeannette returned to her classroom in a state of shock. She finished the day, many of the children hugged her around the waist as they always did, then she collected her things and left. Out on the street, her shock began to crumble. For over three years she'd held this job that she adored. She'd thought, after Papa, that her heart was as broken as it could get, but she'd been wrong. The tears came and there was no stopping them, but then she heard her name.

"Jeannette! Jeannette, wait!" It was Viola Harper, the second-grade teacher, a tall, angular, colored woman with a streak of white hair over her imposing forehead. She'd been Jeannette's first friend at the school, and was, as Jeannette saw now, furious.

"Jeannette, they let you go?" Viola struggled to catch her breath, having run the half-block in her high heels. She looked fiercely into Jeannette's face. "They did, didn't they." She clutched at her coat and rolled her head up to the sky. "Goddamn them. Me too."

"You too?" It was unbelievable, Viola was one of the senior teachers.

"Goddammit, all of us, they sacked all of us."

"All the colored teachers?"

"That's right."

"It's criminal."

"No, it ain't. But it should be."

Jeannette put her hands on Viola's, where they gripped her lapels. "What will you do?" Viola had three children, with no father in the house.

"No earthly idea."

✦ ✦ ✦ ✦ ✦

When Jeannette returned home, Mama was resting in their room, a folded newspaper beside her on the bed. She leaned in the doorway, "Mama?"

Mama opened her eyes. "I'm awake."

"You eat yet?"

"No." With effort, she sat up, leaning against the headboard.

It was five-thirty, not too early for supper. Jeannette went in the kitchen and fixed a tray with two bowls of the stew Mama had made and a plate of sliced bread, and returned to the bedroom, sitting on the edge of Mama's bed. After they'd eaten, Jeannette broke the news, which Mama took in perfect silence, staring out the window for the longest time. At last, she patted Jeannette's hand. "We'll get along," she said. "We'll get along somehow." She closed her eyes. "I think I'll just rest a little more."

It did not seem to Jeannette that it was certain they'd get along. There on the bed with Mama, who soon began to lightly snore, she felt more alone and groundless than she ever had in her entire life, more so than she even thought was possible. In all that vast, cold vacuum, there was now but one stable thing left, or so it appeared, and that was Macon.

Dolly

Jeannette and Macon were married at the Harlem Courthouse, a building Macon said was as pretty as any church, on the last Thursday before Christmas, a cold, gray day threatening snow. Jeannette wore the dress Dolly had helped her make of light blue wool that went well with her bouquet of white carnations, and a matching hat with a little veil of white tulle. Macon wore his best suit, with one of the carnations pinned to the lapel. The fellow that still worked for Macon, J.P., came as his witness, and Jeannette was attended by Dolly, since at the last minute they had decided that Mama wouldn't come, what with her pains and all the ice on the sidewalks.

Helping her dress that morning, Mama said, "You look beautiful." She tried to smile, but Jeannette heard the break in her voice. Suddenly, she said, "I know I've failed you."

"Mama—"

"Since Papa passed. I know I'm not what I used to be."

"Mama, don't. Please." For both their sakes, Jeannette was desperate to remain level ground.

"I'm glad you have someone to take care of you now. That's all I'll say." She reached for her cane and made a move toward the hall. "I'm off to the kitchen. A proper wedding lunch isn't going to fix itself."

The ceremony was over before Jeannette knew it, Macon's bristly mustache kiss leaving her lips buzzing. J.P. wanted to buy Macon a celebratory drink before heading back to the Higgins house where Mama was preparing the party, and so Jeannette and Dolly braved the cold without the men. A wind had kicked up and they ran in their heels to catch the streetcar, clutching their hats and handbags, and then each other, laughing like they used to. Jeannette thanked Heaven that Dolly was there, so warm and bright and lively, excited that she and Jeannette would finally both be married ladies. Her jubilance was catching.

Getting off the streetcar they walked a long circle past the building where Dolly's family lived, Hammond's grocery, their old school building, and other places from their girlhood.

"Don't be scared tonight," Dolly said, hugging Jeannette's arm closer. "It only hurts for a second, and then it's a sweet ride."

"Dolly!" Jeanneatte's face burned.

"Are you shocked I said so?"

"I am scared, I guess. Everything's going to change."

✦ ✦ ✦ ✦ ✦

Lunch was wonderful, with the help of several women friends from church Mama outdid herself with all of Jeannette's favorites, including piles of crispy fried bass, mixed greens rich with fatback and onions, and savory, golden hushpuppies. Friends and neighbors arrived bearing more plates of food, bottles of Hell Gate beer, and gifts for the newlyweds. Mr. Sanderson, one of the Higginses' oldest friends, took charge of the piano, directed other guests who had arrived with instruments, and brought the house down with music. Jeannette hadn't realized how much she'd missed music, and how absent it had been at home for most of the past year. Folks danced, and she danced with Macon, then many of the guests, and Macon again.

At ten o'clock the revelry was still going strong, but Macon announced it was time for the two of them to go. Jeannette acquiesced, glad that Mama—who had been smiling and laughing the whole evening—would have lots of company still. While Macon carried Jeannette's suitcase and hailed a cab, the crowd spilled out onto the street cheering their departure. Everyone blew kisses and waved.

They were quiet on the short ride to the new apartment, Jeannette's ears ringing from the noise of the party. Macon threw his arm around her shoulders and told the driver it was their wedding day.

"Congratulations, y'all," the driver said, smiling into the rearview mirror, and when they pulled up the curb of a brick building, Macon gave him a big tip.

The door was around the back, up two flights of wooden stairs that also served as a fire escape and opened into the kitchen. Macon flicked on the electric light, a bare bulb that hung from the middle of the ceiling. Ducking through the low doorframe, Jeannette saw that the place was furnished with a bedstead, a table and chairs, and not much more. A radiator hissed in the corner. Someone had hammered two nails in the wall beside it, and they hung their coats up there.

While Macon took the suitcase into the bedroom, Jeannette opened a kitchen cabinet, finding a set of cream colored dishes with flowers painted in the centers and four green drinking glasses. In between the kitchen and the bedroom a small sitting room lay empty, with one window covered in a temporary muslin cloth.

"What do you think of your new home?" Macon said. "I know it's not pretty yet. I want you to decorate it to your taste."

"It's good and clean," Jeannette said. "That's a start." It would be fun to fix the place up, make it homey, she'd get Dolly to help her, and while she was musing Macon came up behind her and put his arms around her waist. His moustache grazed her ear.

"Come on to bed now," he said.

She shivered.

In the darkened bedroom, a spear of streetlamp light coming through the muslin over the window, Jeannette fumbled with the suitcase searching for her nightgown. On the other side of the bed Macon was undressing before the room's small wardrobe. The bedsprings creaked as he got under the covers, and she slipped the flannel nightgown over her head before she removed her dress and underthings.

"The waiting is sweet," Macon said in his teasing tone, "but not so sweet as what awaits."

"I'm coming," she said. "Patience is a virtue, you know." She heard him chuckle in the darkness.

When at last she had nothing on but her nightgown, Jeannette slid nervously under the cold sheets. Macon moved toward her, and she realized with a start that he hadn't anything on at all. She felt his hard thighs against hers as he kissed her, and a chill as he lifted up her nightgown and straddled her with his arms, getting the weight of his body between her legs. He moved briefly over her, up and down, so that his hardened sex trailed over her belly, and his face across her bare breasts. And then, pressing his hips against hers, he entered her. A brief sharp pain made her gasp as Macon pushed himself quickly in and out two or three times and then moaned by her ear, letting his full weight down on her.

A moment later he rolled off her. She lay stunned, catching her breath, and then inched the nightgown, from bunched around her neck, back down over her knees, and clutched the blanket to her chin. They lay in silence a few minutes,

Jeannette thought perhaps Macon had gone to sleep, but then she sensed the bed vibrating. He was doing something under his side of the blanket, making the bed shake and breathing in rapid, shallow breaths. Then he embraced her again, moving her legs apart and pushing himself into her over and over, so that without warning her body responded and she clung to him, high little noises escaping from her throat.

When it was over he withdrew from her, picked up a robe from a chair on his side of the bed and went to the water closet. She heard the tap running. She was damp everywhere, and wished she had another nightgown to change into. Macon returned and got back into bed with a long exhale, and Jeannette went to the water closet herself, an intense throbbing between her legs, and a stinging when she urinated. She thought of Dolly's words, *a sweet ride*. More of a rough ride. But if Dolly liked it, maybe she would also, after a while.

Macon was already snoring when she got back in bed, and she lay awake for a long while, shock colliding with an intimacy she wasn't used to. There were no tender words from her sleeping husband, as she now wished there might have been. She felt as if he'd flung her up onto a foreign shore and then left her there alone, which was a sensation that lingered, being Mrs. Macon Halvorsen and not much like herself anymore.

✦ ✦ ✦ ✦ ✦

The first few weeks Jeannette busied herself with fixing up the apartment. Macon had given her a sum of money for it, and between that and the wedding gifts and several items from Mama she soon had what she needed to make a home of it. Dolly came with her girls, several times, and she and Jeannette talked fabrics and colors and rugs while May and Iona banged wooden spoons on the pots Jeannette had given them.

Macon went straight back to work, saying that sales wouldn't wait, and in the evenings he surveyed her progress with a satisfied nod. He ate the meals she cooked, bent over the plate with his knife and fork, with the same air of things being as they should. Her special touches—fine needle work on the new curtains, bay leaves and fried onions in the stew—were not things he noticed as much as she would have liked, since the details of his workday most occupied his mind.

Each night, after their couplings, he pulled himself off of her without a word and went to wash in the water closet, and after taking her turn, because it seemed the thing to do to follow suit, he was always asleep. At breakfast time, Jeannette asked him where he planned to go that day, what he planned to sell, and sometimes it pleased him to talk about it. But one morning, when sales had been poor the day before, Macon said, "A woman shouldn't bother her man with too many questions, now. It might make him tired of her."

Jeannette stood as if stung, turned her back and busied herself at the sink, and when Macon left he didn't kiss her goodbye. When the door banged closed and the sound of Macon's footsteps faded on the stairs Jeannette couldn't stand the apartment's silence and emptiness a moment longer, so she went out, first to Dolly's and then to see Mama. She'd do the grocery shopping on her way home.

✦ ✦ ✦ ✦ ✦

One evening in February Jeannette heard voices on the stairs outside, and then a clatter, as Macon and J.P. burst through the kitchen door in a gust of frozen wind, carrying a shining wooden baby's crib.

"What's all this?" Jeannette asked. She wasn't expecting, and Macon had been complaining about money being tight, since sales had continued to drop.

"I reckon we'll be having a son soon," he said, more to J.P. than to her. "A little Macon Junior."

"We'll just set it up for you, Miss Jeannette," J.P. said, rubbing his hand up under the brim of his hat and smiling.

"It can go in this corner, I guess," she said, bending to move a stack of boxes that contained of Macon's wares. "Where'd you get it from?"

"House sale," Macon said.

And J.P. said, "He got a real good price for it, too."

"It does look nice," Jeannette said, when they'd set it down. She put a hand on her heart, sensing it flutter at the thought of a someday baby. "J.P. will you be staying for dinner?"

"Yes, he will," Macon said, "and I hope you've made something good so's he can see I've done well in choosing a wife."

J.P. laughed, took off his hat and held it to his chest. "That's plain to see," he said, with a shy smile at Jeannette. "I don't know that you deserve all your good luck."

Jeannette, flushed with the compliment, took their coats to hang over the radiator. "We'll be glad to have you."

✦ ✦ ✦ ✦ ✦

Saturday nights Macon sometimes took Jeannette to a little club near their home and seemed pleased to introduce her as his wife to folks he knew. He held her close when they took a turn on the dance floor, never drank too much, nor did he look at other women, and Jeannette told herself that these were things to be grateful for. J.P. often came along with his girl, Winnie, and his easy laughter, not unlike Dolly's, always livened things up. He'd endeared himself to her at more than one supper, always telling her the meal was delicious, especially if Macon had said the potatoes were too dry and needed gravy or that there was too much pepper in the meat.

"Miss Jeannette," J.P. said, one of these Saturday nights at the club when Macon had gone to the gents, "don't pay too much attention to his hard ways."

Jeannette took in J.P.'s and Winnie's kind expressions. "I don't know," she said. "Sometimes I think I'm not what he wanted in a wife after all."

"That can't be," Winne put a hand on hers. "You're the sweetest thing. And good at everything too. And so smart."

Jeannette laughed, "Oh Winnie, you don't know."

"She does know," J.P. said. "Because it shows so well. I mean it. Just don't take Macon too hard. He's a better man than he lets on. I can't tell you how many times he's looked out for me. And he's crazy about you. More than crazy."

"Men can be like that," Winnie said. "They don't let you see what all goes on inside, their tender feelings. It's not because of you."

But then Macon returned and took his seat beside J.P. "Did y'all keep Jeannette entertained?" He leaned close to J.P.'s ear. "A wife is a liability," Jeannette heard him say. "You'll realize it when you marry up yourself."

Jeannette tried to take what J.P. and Winnie had said to heart, but Macon's "hard ways" were getting more difficult to ignore. As winter gave way to spring, harder times were falling on most everyone. Folks had less money to spend and Macon's business continued to suffer. He was often in such a bad temper when he arrived home in the evenings it seemed everything and its dog annoyed him. Why hadn't she scrubbed the kitchen floor? he'd demand, even though she had, he could see those stains a mile away. Why had she spent all the grocery money already? Didn't she realize it had to last the whole week? The soup was too salty. He had a damn sore throat.

Jeannette suggested that she look for some kind of work, teaching music again maybe, to help with expenses. Though she didn't say so to Macon, she missed teaching dearly and missed earning her own money. But Macon wouldn't hear of it.

"No wife of mine will work outside our home," he said. "They'll have to shoot me first. If a man can't provide for his wife, he's nothing. *Nothing.*" He stood up from the kitchen table and paced the room. "And a wife has got to have faith in her man."

The weak sunlight of early morning glinted off the varnish of the table and it gave Jeannette a queer sensation in her stomach. She leaned her forehead in her hand.

"What's wrong?" Macon had turned to face her, hands on his hips.

"Nothing," Jeannette said. "Just maybe the fish from last night was off."

After Macon had gone, Jeannette had a soft-boiled egg and a cup of coffee, but when she stood to clear the dishes her stomach lurched, and the next thing she knew she was throwing it all up in the sink. Something shiny caught the corner of her eye, a ray of sun had found the polished crib in the corner. Its gleam made her dizzy.

The nausea continued, and when her menses were late she told Macon, worried that he would be displeased, angry even, and say that a baby would be yet another "liability." But to her relief he smiled, embraced her and kissed her forehead. "Didn't I tell you?" he said. "Didn't I say we'd have a son soon?" He lifted her up and they both laughed, and that day he left for work in a good mood.

As the weeks passed, Jeannette's nausea continued and she was dogged by a heavy fatigue. She'd heard of morning sickness of course, but this was relentless. Just about every food turned her stomach, and every smell, including the smell of things she had never noticed before. The drain in the kitchen sink, it seemed, billowed forth with a foul odor. The breath of a neighbor saying good morning, a little too close by, nearly knocked her off her feet. "It's sure to be a boy," Macon said, unconcerned whenever she ran for the toilet. "The sicker the momma, the stronger the babe. My Grandma Halvorsen used to say that." He declared they'd call the baby Macon Charles, after himself and his father.

Business picked up a little with the spring and Macon said they should look for a bigger apartment, but by June it had dropped off again and his dark moods returned. As Jeannette had feared, he did at times add to his complaints the fact that now she was having a baby, as if he didn't have enough on his mind already. As if it had been her doing alone. When she dropped by Dolly's house, as she did more often now that the weather was better and her fatigue had lifted, Dolly told her what J.P. had said, not to take her husband's comments too much to heart.

"Times are getting harder and that puts more pressure on everybody," Dolly said, loading stacks of cloth diapers into Jeannette's arms. "I'm so glad I don't need these anymore. But you never know. I might have to ask you for them back."

"You know I'll bring them," Jeannette said, stuffing them into a large sack she'd brought.

Dolly put her hands on her hips and studied Jeannette. "What are you hoping to have, a boy or a girl?"

"It might go easier with Macon if it's a boy," Jeannette said. "That's what he wants."

"What about you?"

Jeannette smiled. "Just a baby."

✦ ✦ ✦ ✦ ✦

The first day of July was a Tuesday and Jeannette brought home a broken highchair someone had put out on the curb. J.P. was handy with woodworking and she thought he might be able to fix it for her. She got it up the stairs, sweating in the sun, cleaned it up with rags in the kitchen, and then sat at the table and looking at it, imagining a baby, her own baby, sitting there eating soft foods. Noodles, maybe, bananas if they could afford them, with chubby little fists. The thought was sweet enough to bring tears to her eyes.

That night when she and Macon went to bed she sat up a while, fanning herself by the open window until Macon said she was disturbing him. He had to be up earlier than ever because he traveled further afield now to make his sales. Jeannette lay awake a long time, still hot but trying her best not to toss and turn and wake her husband. When at last she did sleep, she was caught in agitated dreams of burning houses. A house was burning and she had to get to the fire escape, but a fireman had trapped her with a pair of strange long pliers that squeezed her middle. Each squeeze caused a pain sharper than the one before. And then she woke, in a pool of blood.

✦ ✦ ✦ ✦ ✦

"I never saw a man so scared in my life," Dolly laughed, sitting with Jeannette on the back stairs a few days later. There was a patch of ground behind their building with grass and mud puddles, and Dolly's girls were down there playing.

Jeannette had opened her eyes that dawn to Macon standing over her, shaking her by the shoulders. The covers were thrown back and he'd seen the blood before she did.

"I'm going to get a doctor," he'd said, but she shook her head and told him to go get Dolly, which he did, running out with a coat thrown over his bare chest. Mrs. James, Dolly's mother, had been a midwife in Mississippi and had taught

Dolly a thing or two about female business. Macon came back with Dolly and her two girls in tow and made them sit nice in the kitchen while she poked at Jeannette's belly and helped her clean up. Macon had gone to tell Jeannette's mother and then came back to the apartment, where Dolly assured him his wife wasn't dying and that he should go on to work. Mama arrived a couple of hours later, leaning heavily on her cane and carrying a sack of groceries she soon turned into a soup with a clear broth. Dolly prepared to go, saying Jeannette should rest and not worry, and that she'd be by to check on her again later. Mama helped Jeannette change out the soaked cotton rags for clean ones, patted her hand, and brought her the broth when it was ready.

"Are the pains lessening?" Mama asked.

"I think so." Jeannette closed her eyes, hoping the sadness that was rising in her heart wouldn't overflow. "You know what I wish?" she said, after a minute.

"What's that?"

"I wish I could hear you play *Moonlight Sonata*."

"Oh, yes." It was their favorite Beethoven, and Beethoven had always been Mama's favorite composer. "If only we had a piano here."

"Could you sing it for me?"

"Sing it?"

"Yes."

"You mean like… *ta da dee ta da dee…*" Mama sang. "Like that?"

"Yes, like that."

"I'll do the high notes, you do the low, we'll see if we can do it." She smiled, closed her eyes, and spread her fingers over her lap, as if on keyboard. "*Ta da dee ta da dee…*"

They knew the piece so well, they made it into sound with their voices, the notes weaving in and out of the air. The melody was indeed soothing, and soon Jeannette relaxed into the bed. It wasn't the crook of Papa's arm, but it was close.

Esther

The bleeding out of the pregnancy took a greater toll on Jeannette's heart than she would have expected. Sitting on the back stairs with Dolly while May and Iona played down below, one thing nagged at her at her especially.

"Did your momma ever say why miscarriages happen?" she asked Dolly.

"She always said it was nature's way."

"Is it maybe," Jeannette struggled, "that it happens because a baby feels unwanted?"

Dolly looked at her sharply. "Why? You didn't want it?"

"No," Jeannette said, her eyes starting to burn. "I mean like if anybody said something. By accident."

Dolly shook her head. "That ain't how it works. Babies get born whether they wanted or not." She said that her momma had helped a lot of girls get rid of their pregnancies, even more than she'd helped babies get born, because for one reason or another those girls were desperate.

Jeannette's body returned to how it was before, but her heart didn't. She believed what Dolly had said, but a part of her mind was still caught as if on a troublesome nail, on the idea that there had truly been a little Macon Charles who, because of his father's words or by fault of her own, didn't see fit to stay. Hadn't she, in the throes of nauseous misery, wished it to end? Had she strained herself getting that heavy highchair up the stairs? Dolly said, young as healthy as Jeannette was, she was sure to conceive again before she knew it, but the months rolled by and her menses kept coming, regular as clockwork.

Once he was over the shock of the miscarriage, Macon didn't dwell on it. He said they'd have a son before long anyway, and steered every suppertime conversation toward the new schemes he was thinking up with J.P., things to supplement the waning sales, like house painting and carpentry. Macon had worked in a number of jobs before becoming a salesman, he even knew a thing or two about auto mechanics.

"We've got to look ahead," he said. "Not get dragged down by the past."

✦ ✦ ✦ ✦ ✦

In the fall, on a crisp October day, Mama asked Jeannette to come with her to a show of paintings at a gallery co-owned by their friend Mr. Sanderson. So many galleries and clubs had closed in the past year, it was like a whole different Harlem. President Hoover, as it said in the papers, maintained that the general economy was unimpaired, but folks on the street knew better. Thankfully, Mr. Sanderson's gallery was surviving and there were still a few working artists.

Jeannette took Mama's arm as they walked through the little maze of paintings created by a series of partitions, the vibrant figures on the canvases so alive and inviting. How long it had been since Jeannette had looked at paintings, much less been to a concert or a poetry reading. Once, on one of their early walks, she had asked Macon if he liked to go to the Metropolitan Art Museum, a favorite place of hers, and he'd laughed, saying that he had much better things to do with his money.

"How about these?" Jeannette said to Mama, standing before a triptych of nudes painted in rich browns and reds, hung in sequence that made them look like they were dancing—one of them, a woman it looked like, with angular yet languid limbs arranged over a yellow sofa strewn with roses.

"Lovely," Mama sighed. "Sandy has a wonderful eye as ever. I do think Papa would have liked them too." She leaned forward to examine the artist's name card on the wall beside the paintings. "Braguine," she murmured. "That will be one to watch."

They moved on to the next series with a padded bench between the partitions. "I'll just contemplate these flowers," Mama said, in view of a large still-life. "You look some more and tell me what I shouldn't miss."

The place wasn't large, but Mama's pains kept her on a short leash. Jeannette entered a smaller room in the back with four large paintings of children playing, two girls just like Dolly's. Something soft caressed her heart when she looked at them, not exactly because she had grown to love May and Iona, though she had, but more because of a wish of her own. Two girls. How she would like that. She would take *them* to the art museum, teach them music. She would give them all the things she missed.

When Jeannette went back to the main room of the gallery, she found Mama still on the bench, now in lively conversation with Mr. Sanderson.

"Uncle Sandy!" Jeannette said, delighted to see him. "I didn't know you'd be here."

"Neither did I until the last minute." He jumped up to embrace her, his small frame not much bigger than Auntie Alma's. "My girl, my girl," he said, drawing back. "Let me have a look at you. It's been ages."

"How are things with you?"

"Not bad at all, I've been telling your mother." His silver mustache tilted to the side with his smile. "The paintings are selling well thanks to Mrs. Winters and her lot," he said, referring to the heiresses who once supported the Higgins Institute. "They haven't been affected one bit by the downturn, if anything they're richer than ever."

"Apparently, she's thrown a party at the Ritz," Mama said. "Competing with her rival, Miss Maxwell at the Waldorf-Astoria."

"Nora!" Mr. Sanderson sat down again, swatting her shoulder. "I didn't know you were one for celebrity gossip."

Mama rolled her eyes. "I got it by accident on the wireless."

"I don't like it at all," Jeannette said, "how they flaunt their wealth. People are starving right on the ground below them." She sighed. "But I'm glad they're buying your paintings, Uncle Sandy," she said, gazing around at the gallery. "It's wonderful to be surrounded by art."

✦ ✦ ✦ ✦

The vision of two little girls of her own returned to Jeannette in her quiet moments—washing dishes, walking on a side street—and brought warmth to the hollow places inside. Close to a year and a half after Papa had died, his death was no longer the calamity it had been at first, but the world was a vastly emptier place, and without her pupils and music to fill her days the little disappointments of married life ricocheted painfully through that shadowy interior. She didn't know if the miscarriage was a large or small thing, but Dolly had said it happened to a lot of women. Surely it was nothing compared to losing a born child.

Gerard had been in Paris four years now. When she wrote to tell him that Papa had died, and later that she was getting married, her letters were short. So strange how few words it took to say the things that wholly rearranged her life. Each time, she'd sat staring at the paper, the fountain pen hovering above it in her hand, searching for more words that never came.

Please tell me all about your days (she wrote to Gerard.) *You can't imagine how your letters cheer me, how your stories from Paris lift me up and carry me away from my troubles. These days I scarcely know whether I'm coming or going.*

I think of your dear father often, Jeannette (Gerard wrote back.) *As you know, he was a second father to me. Do look for the happy things in your days, even if they are small, I know they will be there. Find them and write about them so they can make me happy too, knowing you've lived them.*

Gerard's letters always included two or three colorful picture postcards, on which he wrote little anecdotes from the city. The stories and images were as alluring as fairytales, but better because she knew they were real, and she kept them in a carved, teak wood box her parents had given her when she'd graduated from high school. Every so often she took them out to reread them and absorb with her eyes the marvelous pictures.

✦ ✦ ✦ ✦ ✦

In April of 1931, nearly a year after the miscarriage, Jeannette's menses didn't come. It was easier this time, there was nausea in the mornings but not round the clock, and she was tired, but not extremely. She told Dolly first, who squeezed her hand and kissed her cheek with a big smile. "I told you," she said. "You just had to wait a little. Good thing I haven't needed those diapers back."

Macon was also pleased, though reservedly so. He smiled when she told him, and then rubbed his forehead the way he did when figuring how many tins of pomade to order for his sales, how many boxes of matches, what quantity of silk scarves and handkerchiefs. As Jeannette's belly grew Macon was more careful with her in bed, often leaving her alone entirely. She didn't know if it was because he was afraid of another miscarriage or because he desired her less, but she didn't ask. It was a relief to have more of the night to herself.

Jeannette had the first pains early on the morning of January first, New Year's Day, 1932. It was a Friday, still dark out, and Macon wasn't awake yet. She lay in bed, the tight cramp spreading from the small of her back around the front of her belly. It lasted only a few seconds and then passed. Carefully she got out of bed and went to the water closet, where she saw, in the dim electric light, a smear of something viscous and blood-tinged on her drawers. Dolly had told her, when she entered her ninth month of the pregnancy, to watch out for something like this as a sign of the labor coming on. She shook all over, it was really happening. But Dolly had also told her to stay calm and not beat it to the hospital first thing. "First babies especially," she'd said, "take their time."

Jeannette returned to bed and tried to rest. About half an hour later, the next pain came on, lasting slightly longer and leaving her catching her breath, but was still mild all things considered. She got up afterward, put on the woolen robe Mama had given her and went to start a pot of coffee. There were only enough grounds left for one cup, but she had some chicory root and added a few spoonfuls. The kitchen clock read five-twenty, when she picked it up to wind it, and five thirty-five when the next pain came. Then she woke Macon and asked him to go and get Dolly.

When Macon came back with Dolly, having left the girls with Dolly's mother, the sun was rising. Dolly determined that Macon should go to work, that she would go with Jeannette to the hospital in a few hours, and that he should come see them in the afternoon, saying that nothing would happen until then.

"I'll see you there," Macon called back up the stairs when he left. "Harlem Hospital. I'll see you right there."

"For a man who likes to be in charge, your husband sure gets nervous," Dolly said. She put an arm around Jeannette's shoulders. "Girl, you are going to be fine."

Calmly, they collected Jeannette's things and got her ready between pains. Dolly said they should call Mama from the hospital, and Jeannette nodded, happy to have Dolly's instructions. A great pull from deep inside her seemed to be sucking her mind down to her belly, the energy gathering there in what she imagined to be a giant ball of light. The whole rest of the morning they spent walking from one side of the apartment to the other, stopping so Jeannette could visit the toilet or lean on the furniture. Then, when the pains were stronger and closer together, they took the last of the housekeeping money and paid for a cab.

✦ ✦ ✦ ✦ ✦

The smell of disinfectant that assailed Jeannette's nostrils when she and Dolly entered the building brought memories of Papa's last hours back in a rush, and for a moment she had the desperate urge to run the other way. But Dolly gripped her arm, helped ease her into a wheelchair, and a colored nurse led them to the labor and delivery wing. Jeannette thought of both her parents and closed her eyes to invoke their presence in her mind. She herself had been born in that very place.

There were other women in the labor room, six of them. In her bed in one corner, Jeannette was scarcely three feet from a girl not more than eighteen, and who yelped like a puppy when her pains came on. The nurses told Dolly she had to go and so she reluctantly said goodbye, reassuring Jeannette once more that she would be fine, that nature would take its course, and that she would see her just as soon as she was able. Jeannette said that she had the urge to get up and walk, and Dolly told her to do it. "Do what you feel like doing," she said. "It will help the baby. Momma always says that."

Jeannette walked the length of the room between the beds, careful to keep her eyes on the floor and trying not to disturb the other women, though that seemed a flimsy conceit. A room with seven women in labor, moaning or gasping by turns, had no hope for actual privacy.

When the nurse finally came to bring her into the delivery room Jeannette was kneeling on the floor with her arms on the bed in a haze of pain. She was only aware of the sensations in her body, her heart beating, her heavy breathing, and the intense pains when they came, during which sounds came out of her that she hadn't known she could make. Under the bright lights of the delivery room they put her feet up in stirrups and told her to bear down, which she had no trouble doing, even though the position of her body frustrated her. She wanted to get up, and she said so, but the doctor said, "Oxygen," and they put a mask over her nose and mouth, and the loud hiss drowned out the voices. But she didn't need their instructions now, she didn't need anything outside herself. In her mind's eye, she saw again the giant inward ball of light, and she felt like a mountain issuing a rushing river.

The next thing she knew, the oxygen mask was off and one of the nurses was swabbing at a tiny, brown, squalling infant that she wrapped in a soft towel and placed in Jeannette's arms, telling her that she had a little girl.

Macon wanted to name her Esther, after his mother, and Jeannette thought that was a pretty name and agreed. They gave her the second name of Eleanor, after Mama. Jeannette had worried that Macon would be disappointed that she wasn't a son, but he never said a word about it. Instead, he crooned over her, carrying her around in his arms and singing a little song in a voice like a rusty swing.

"I didn't even know he could sing," Jeannette whispered to Mama, when she came home with them after the hospital.

"He can't," Mama said, just as low. "That hee-haw is a donkey voice if I ever heard one. But babies don't mind, as long as it's gentle."

Jeannette stifled a laugh, but she understood the magic spell that had come over her husband. The baby, Esther, from the very first moment, was the most entrancing thing she had ever laid eyes on—her tiny sleeping face, her little limbs that stretched when she was unwrapped, the mewling cry when she was hungry, her ability to suckle. Jeannette's pains of recovery from the birth, the breaking up of her sleep in the night, the extra washing, all of that was secondary to the new fact that she had in her life a treasure beyond compare.

Dolly and Mama came often in the coming weeks, with advice and warnings and pots of soup, but both agreed that Jeannette took to motherhood like a duck to water. Macon was still enraptured too, calling the baby Queen Esther, like from the Bible, the most beautiful of all, though if she cried or needed changing he handed her back to Jeannette, returning to his coffee or newspaper or dressing for work, or any other of the activities he considered befitting for a man.

One afternoon, when Esther was two weeks old, Mama sat with her in the rocker by the bedroom window. There was snow piled up on the sill and a bit of icy blue sky showed behind the buildings across the street. Jeannette had just finished taking a bath and had her hair wrapped up in a towel.

"She still sleeping?" Jeannette whispered. And when Mama nodded, she said, "I'll get the hot comb." She gently lifted the baby from Mama's arms, laid her on the bed, and tiptoed to the kitchen to fetch the hot comb where it was heating in her cast iron skillet. Back in the bedroom she settled down at Mama's feet.

"You got the hair lotion," asked Mama, still whispering.

"I already put it in."

They were quiet for a time, as Mama began dividing Jeannette's thick hair into sections and pinning them in place, then running the hot comb through them. Jeannette had always loved the feel of Mama's strong fingers in her hair, and was lulled by the hiss of the hot comb meeting the moisture; even the smell of the hair lotion was comforting.

"It took me a while to get used to you, I think," Mama mused. "When you were a baby."

"Who, me?" said Jeannette. "Was I difficult?"

"Not at all," Mama said. "But maybe I was."

Jeannette waited for her to say more.

"It just took time for me to get used to being a mother," Mama continued. "I guess it comes more naturally for certain women. Like you." She unpinned another section of Jeannette's hair and began running it through with the hot comb, the hiss quieter now as it had already begun to cool.

Jeannette wondered if what Mama said had anything to do with her having to give up Gerard when she was just eighteen, but she didn't ask it. Now that she had Esther the idea of giving up a baby seemed like torment one would scarcely survive. Instead she said, "I think she looks a little like you." It was true. When the baby knit her brow it was just like Mama's.

Mama laughed. "Don't curse the child like that. She's bound to be much prettier."

"Queen Esther," Jeannette said, thinking of Macon's declarations.

"The most beautiful of all," Mama said. "But she saved her people, and risked her own life to do it. You all picked a strong name for her, not just a pretty one."

"She'll be strong like her Grand Mama."

"And her mother."

Lions

As the weeks and months passed, Jeannette found herself fascinated by Esther's development, in a way that wasn't just motherly love. She recalled a course she'd taken at the teachers college on the learning stages in early childhood, and just how rapidly those progressed. But watching how Esther's hands found each other, found her mouth, how she began to smile and then grab at things and roll over, Jeannette guessed that the changes in infancy progressed at a much faster pace. And these changes weren't just physical.

Almost daily I see new expressions on her little face (Jeannette wrote to Gerard,) *expressions that belie her growing emotional landscape, which I swear changes daily, and all this before she's even begun crawling! I've been keeping a little diary with my observations, just like a scientist (surely you will see humor in this, as I do.)*

Esther must be a pure joy (Gerard wrote back) *another little niece for me to add to my collection (I am laughing here, with joy of course, and the thought of me with a collection of porcelain dolls on a shelf.) Sarai has two and Amelia has one, so that makes four for me, a happy uncle, but with my usual regrets at being so distant. I'm so glad for you, and have no doubt you are an exceptional mother, and scientist too.*

✦ ✦ ✦ ✦ ✦

On a humid day in September, the last of the summer's heat lying over the city like a damp wool blanket, Jeannette left Esther with Mama and took the streetcar down to the Central Library. Despite the swampish air, Jeannette felt a burgeoning excitement. There were a handful of names she remembered from her reading during her year at the teachers college, scholars and philosophers with theories in children's development—John Dewey, Jean Piaget, Lev Vygotsky, Elizabeth Peabody—and she wondered if they might also have written about infants and toddlers. It had been thrilling to read their works those years ago, and the prospect of reencountering their ideas made her impatient, as if she had already been waiting too long.

Walking up to the front entrance of the Central Library, she traversed the stairs to greet the two majestic stone lions on either side, old friends she hadn't seen in a long time. One of her earliest memories was when Papa and Mama brought her to see the ceremony when the statues were dedicated. She remembered the crowd and the fresh spring sunshine, and riding on Papa's shoulders. He said the two lions were called Leo Lenox and Leo Astor, and were there to show just how important books and knowledge were. *Once you've learned something*, Papa said, *nobody can ever take it away from you.*

Jeannette wandered the vast halls of the library and then roamed through the stacks, traversing the cool, shadowy aisles until she had an armload of books, and from these selected four to take out on loan. Running down the stairs with her books she felt again like she did in her days at the teachers college. Those were such hopeful times, shoulder to shoulder with her peers who were just as eager as she was, when there was everything to learn and nothing very sad had happened yet.

Once again on the main floor, she approached the long desk where the clerks and librarians registered all the loans. A tall, balding white man with spectacles and a silver nameplate pinned to his vest was marking a little stack of cards with a rubber stamp, and when Jeannette placed the books on the polished wood of the counter he did not return her smile. She handed him her library card.

"Harlem branch," he said, eyeing it. "That is the library for your use."

"Yes, sir, but I'm a schoolteacher," she said, omitting the fact that she'd been laid off almost two years ago, "and the Harlem branch doesn't have these books." She rummaged in her handbag for her teacher's certificate, which she'd brought in case of this kind of trouble. The librarian eyed the paper as he had the card, without touching it, then picked up the books and glanced at their spines.

"I'm sorry," he said, turning and depositing them on a cart behind him. "It would be against regulations for the library to loan these to you."

Jeannette flushed, anger clutched at her throat, but she calmed herself. "I'm sure it's not against any regulation for a New York resident—" she began, but he cut her off.

"I am certain that I know the regulations of this library better than you do."

Jeannette's hands shook as she collected her card and certificate and returned them to her handbag. She glanced at the silver nameplate, *E. Merrit*, and then at the clock that hung on the wall behind him. It was just after eleven thirty. Without another word she turned on her heel and walked down the long hall to the main entrance, her anger now tearing at her middle.

But she didn't leave. Instead, checking over her shoulder to see that the librarian wasn't watching, she ducked into a side hallway that led to a stairwell, where she paced slowly, calming herself. Countless times in her life, not least in high school and at the teachers college, an instructor or other person in authority had let her know in one way or another that her presence there, and that of her colored peers, was merely tolerated, and that she was not naturally entitled to the privileges of education that her white peers were. But her parents, time and again, told her to be strong and to reject those notions out of hand. Every person had the same right to knowledge, they said, and in fact this right must always be fought for. The stone statues at the library, the guardians of knowledge, these weren't lions for nothing.

As Jeannette's breathing slowly returned to normal, she kept an eye on another clock on the other side of the main hall, a new idea taking shape in her mind. Senior librarians were surely punctual about their lunch hours, and she kept up her slow pacing in time with the minutes ticking by. She wasn't wrong. At just past twelve noon, from her obscure position she saw the balding librarian striding stiffly toward the main door. He put a hand on his hat, keeping it down as a gust met him outside, and then strode down the stairs in a diagonal, no doubt headed to the park on the other side of the building.

Jeannette waited a few minutes and then made her way back to the front desk. Another clerk, a young woman with blond hair set in finger waves, stood behind the counter helping another patron. When her turn came, Jeannette approached the desk, again with a smile.

"Miss," she said, "I'm a schoolteacher and spoke with Mr. Merrit earlier this morning." She blinked and swallowed. When had she ever told such a bald-faced lie? "He put some books aside for me." She looked past the clerk at the cart. Her books were still there. "There they are," she said brightly, pointing toward the cart.

"Oh," the clerk said, uncertainly, her blond waves bouncing as she turned her head back and forth. "May I have your card please?"

"I'm a regular Mata Hari," Jeannette whispered to herself as she cracked open the first book, jostling in her seat as the streetcar ran over rut. Wouldn't Gerard get a laugh out of this. She'd write him all about it as soon as she got the chance.

That night, seeing the books stacked on her nightstand, Macon chided her. "What you want with those books?" he said while he undressed. "I think you worry too much. There ain't nothing wrong with the baby."

"I'm curious is all," Jeannette said. "About how children grow. It never hurts to learn something."

"Cockamamie ideas, I wouldn't doubt it. If there's one thing I know for sure it's how white men can jabber on."

After the next time he said that she was wasting her time with those books, she put them in the wardrobe under an extra shawl, because her husband—decidedly not a white man—could also jabber on just fine.

She read while Esther nursed, while Macon was out working, and now she included notes from her reading in her diary of Esther's activities. What she was doing it for she didn't know, but for the first time since getting married she felt as though she were waking up.

✦ ✦ ✦ ✦ ✦

A few months after Esther's first birthday she began to refuse the breast, clamoring instead for more potato, more mashed peas, sitting in the highchair Jeannette had found and that J.P. had repaired for them. Jeannette was alarmed at first, but Dolly said some babies weaned themselves and not to worry. When her milk dried up Jeannette's menses returned with regularity. But several months later they stopped abruptly, and soon after that the drain in the sink began to smell again. This time was different too, though the nausea was the same as it had been with Esther, she was more tired, and Macon grew more impatient. Times had grown yet harder. He was struggling to earn enough money to make ends meet and the thought of another baby only increased the pressure.

These days he put Jeannette's housekeeping money in the pantry mason jar, rather than handing her a stack of notes with a satisfied smile, and often the jar was all but empty. Jeannette and Dolly conspired to stretch their budgets to the limit. If one discovered a grocery item on sale at one of the stores, she bought extra to give to the other. They made soup out of whatever they could find, and mixed stale bread in with hamburger and lots of garlic, making a pound of meat feed the family for a whole week. And all the while Jeannette's belly grew, and Esther began walking and saying words, and understanding more and more all the time.

✦ ✦ ✦ ✦ ✦

As with Esther, Jeannette's labor began in the wee hours, but this time it came on quickly. In less than an hour the pains were so strong and close together that they took her breath away, and it was all she could do not to cry out. Only the thought of scaring Esther kept her quiet, but Macon heard her panting and muffled groans and didn't have to wait to be told to run and get Dolly.

Jeannette moved around the room, gripping the bedframe, fluid running down her legs. By the time Dolly and Macon ran up the back stairs, she was fighting the urge to bear down.

"Jesus, Lord," Dolly said, taking one look at Jeannette's sweat-bathed face. "You are having that baby right now."

"No, she ain't," Macon barked. "She's going to the hospital."

Dolly ignored him. "I'm going to wash my hands. Macon, get some towels down on the floor and get a pot of water boiling. We need to heat the sharpest knife y'all got. Now move, or so help me I'll use that knife for something else."

Macon's face turned a peculiar shade of yellowish gray, but he did what she said, and before the water even boiled in the kitchen Jeannette bore down with all her strength and Dolly caught the slippery child in her capable hands.

Another girl.

Macon helped Jeannette into the bed and Dolly laid the baby on her breast, cleaning the little face with damp cloth. When the knife was ready, having been sunk in the boiling water, Dolly tied a thread around the baby's navel and cut the cord. Somehow Esther slept through the whole thing, and by the time she woke up, just after seven, everyone else in the whole house was asleep.

✦ ✦ ✦ ✦ ✦

They named her Maude, after another of Macon's forbearers, and swiftly took to calling her Maudie. The name Maude was like a long heavy dress, Jeannette thought, an unsuitable garment for the tiny, beautiful thing that the newborn was, with her bright eyes and miniature limbs waving. She had a good appetite it turned out and could yell, and quickly grew into an active baby, intent on exploring her world and aggravating her older sister. Like the time Jeannette heard Esther scream from the bedroom, and, hurrying in, found her in the full throes of indignant tears. The little rag doll, whom she had put to bed so carefully in the corner under a folded dishtowel, was now on the other side of the room, clutched in Maudie's fists, with half her head in Maudie's mouth. The dishtowel lay in a twist in the middle of the floor. Jeannette had had to turn her back on the scene, to swallow down a giggle and set her expression to a serious calm. She picked up the baby and handed the doll back to Esther. "We'll get Maudie something else to play with," she said, petting Esther's cheek. "You go fix up Lily's bed again."

Columbus

With two children in the house and work scarcer all the time, Macon's dark moods all but took permanent hold, his temper shorter and his tongue sharper. It was a consolation that he was at home less, having to go farther afield for jobs, even upstate on occasion. The grocery money stretched thinner each week. There were days when, if not for Mama's contributions—which had to be taken in secret to preserve Macon's pride—they might eat nothing but porridge.

One night when Esther spilled her milk at supper, Macon slammed the table with his hand so hard the cutlery jumped into the air. For a timeless second dead silence reigned, and then Esther and the baby both began wailing. Jeannette gathered them up in her arms, trying to get them to hush and her own heart to beat regular. "Just an accident, a little old accident," she murmured to them.

"Damn noise," Macon said, rising. He threw on his coat and left, banging the door.

By the time he returned the children were in bed, asleep. He had a hangdog look and Jeannette knew not to reproach him. He sat at the table and rubbed his eyes with thumb and forefinger. Jeannette warmed the rest of his supper and he ate in silence.

Early the next morning Macon said that he would write to his cousin Darius who had a mechanics shop somewhere near Columbus, Ohio. Jeannette heard the baby crying, her breasts aching with milk, and with her head still groggy from sleep she missed part of what he said. After Macon had gone and she had fed and dressed the children, she recalled tenor of his voice, laced with both defeat and determination. The disturbing thought struck her that if he'd given up on finding enough work in New York that it might mean them moving away, though just as swiftly she stopped herself from thinking further. She had promised Dolly to help her with the window washing that day, and after that she was set to take the girls over to Mama's.

But four weeks later Macon had a reply, a letter from his cousin saying that business at his shop wasn't bad and that they could use another mechanic. It wouldn't pay much, but there was a room over the garage they could have that was big enough for a small family. Macon was visibly energized, if not jubilant. He shook the letter at the furniture, calculating what they might get for each piece and weighing it against the cost of train fare.

Fear clutched at Jeannette's throat, and her thoughts whirled. Leave New York?

"But, Mama," she started, when she found her voice. "I can't just leave her."

"Damn it, Jeannette." Anger flared in Macon's eyes. "We can't make it here. I'm broke. I'm dead broke. Your mama will get along."

Jeannette glanced over at the girls. Maudie was in the crib and had pulled herself up to standing, and Esther was busy poking an empty thread spool through the wooden slats. A pressure rose to her ears with a high-pitched whine, but she dared not say another word, fearing Macon would do something that would scare the children. She lowered herself onto a kitchen chair.

"I'll go on to Ohio first," Macon said, pacing the room. "Get things set up and then send for you." He continued, listing more details of his plan, but Jeannette barely heard him, as if he were already miles away.

✦ ✦ ✦ ✦ ✦

Jeannette watched helplessly, like a sandcastle in the waves, washing away bit by bit, as Macon set things in motion for the move. He sold the bedstead, a beautiful, heavy piece made of walnut wood, that was his wedding present to Jeannette, saying that she would have another just as nice in Ohio, and that it would only be a few weeks. The men who came to take it away also bought the wardrobe, leaving the mattress behind on the cold floor, and the clothes in two crates against the wall. With the proceeds, Macon bought his train ticket to Columbus and left Jeannette with enough money for a month's worth of rent and groceries. He packed what he could fit into the larger case he'd used for his sales and he left, kissing Jeannette and the girls each on the forehead. Jeannette said they'd go with him to the station but he didn't want it.

"I'll see you all soon," he said, his voice breaking. He swallowed and frowned. "I'll write you as soon as I get there."

Esther cried when he went out the door. "I wan' Daddy," she sobbed, and that set off the baby. She sat with them both in the rocker and said what Macon had: that they would see him very soon. What was more, she said, it was time to go see Grand Mama. And that they would go to Hammond's and Esther could have a piece of candy if she was good, and after that they'd go see Dolly and the girls. Esther hopped off her lap at that and ran to put her coat on.

"Let's go right now, Mama, I can' wait!" she said with such excitement that Jeannette laughed and Maudie blew spit with a happy *brrrrr*.

That evening Jeannette and the girls had a quiet supper. At one point, when Maudie dropped a lump of potato on the floor, Jeannette sensed her body tense, her shoulders rising to her ears. But Macon wasn't there to issue a reprimand, and she looked at the bit of potato with the new thought that she might even leave it there if she felt like it. She wouldn't, of course, she liked a clean house and hardly wanted to attract mice, but she took her time, first letting her shoulders relax.

In the next days a funny feeling came over Jeannette, for once not needing to worry that Esther might spill something or the baby would drop more food on the floor, or that one of them would screech. She didn't have to hurry back from Dolly's, and neither was she afraid that what she cooked would displease her husband. After she put the children to bed she lay down on the mattress on the floor with a sigh. It was a sad place to sleep without the bedstead, uncivilized, but she could stay up for a spell and read if she wanted, using a candle to save on the light bill. She could roll into the middle of the bed. And she was alone, without Macon there demanding anything of her body, whether she wanted to give it or not.

There was less washing to do now, less cooking, much less weighed on her mind save for the thought that one day soon there would be word from Macon, that things would be ready and then she would have to take the girls and go. The thought of leaving Mama was nothing short of ghastly. Ohio, as she conceived it, was a yawning, empty place. It would be everything New York was not, because it would be void of all the people and places she knew. Mama, Dolly and her family, and countless other folks who all held a vital key to herself.

After three weeks a letter came from Macon. He was working and that was good, but he figured it would be at least two months more before the apartment over the garage would be ready, because there were repairs needed and he was doing them himself. He told Jeannette she should look for a smaller place for herself and the girls. They needed to save on the rent and they didn't need so much space with him gone, and said they should stay with her mother. Jeannette, greatly relieved that the move wasn't imminent, knew that staying with Mama was out of the question. Mama had her boarders, and she needed that income, but Jeannette agreed that she and the girls could do with less room, and she wrote to Macon saying so.

Dolly had seen a for rent sign not far from her place and took Jeannette and the children to see the place while her girls were at school. Jeannette was excited at the prospect of living closer to Dolly but her heart fell when she saw the dilapidated state of the building. Dolly told her to look anyway. The landlady, an elderly woman in a torn chintz apron, met them in the foyer and took them up to the second floor. Jeannette ducked into the dark entryway of the apartment, holding Maudie in the crook of one arm and telling Esther to stay close, not that there was anywhere to run off to. Dolly went to check the taps in the water closet, and see that the toilet flushed, and Jeannette eyed the tiny kitchen. It needed cleaning—she scraped at the grime on the linoleum with her house key—but was bright enough, serviceable, with a small stove, a sink on the wall opposite the water closet, and a few small cupboards lined with paper. There wasn't any icebox, but Dolly said she wouldn't need one with the grocery store so close, and if she had to she could keep the milk out on the fire escape most of the year. Dolly said she should take it. The rent was only half what she was used to paying, so the price was right.

Jeannette poked her head into what the landlady called the "big bedroom" off the kitchen, which must have been a pantry before. The mattress would just fit. Then she heard Esther's voice. "Mama, I gonna sleep in here!" Jeannette hurried to find her, not realizing the child had wandered away and fearing an open window or unguarded mousetrap. She found Esther at the window of the little room at the end of the short, dark hallway, looking out with interest, though it was only an airshaft.

"Baby, watch your fingers," Jeannette said, in case anything sharp lay on the sill. Maudie squirmed and breathed heavily at her ear, wanting to get down. Jeannette knelt at Esther's side and they all looked out into the airshaft. They saw bricks walls and several other windows that might be illuminated at night, and if they pressed close they could see the sky above.

✦ ✦ ✦ ✦ ✦

The excitement of the move occupied Jeannette for the next few weeks. Dolly helped her clean, and J.P. borrowed a van and helped her take what was left of their belongings to the new place. One afternoon she pinned up all the picture postcards Gerard had sent from Paris. Maybe it was silly to do, but Macon would never see them and say they made the place look shabby or like a tollbooth.

Later that same day J.P. stopped in to say hello. Jeannette knew Macon had asked him to look in on her and the girls while he was away. He sat on a chair by the kitchen window with a cup of coffee and a sweet roll from the pan of them Jeannette had made. She had sold the old kitchen table and gotten a smaller one, and now had it covered with a flowered cloth.

"Miss Jeannette," J.P. said, wiping crumbs from his mouth, "I want to ask you your advice on something."

Jeannette laughed. "Advice? What could I advise you on? You must think I'm an old lady."

J.P. laughed too. "Naw, not at all. Not old. But you're a married woman, and I—" he cleared his throat, "I'm going to ask Winnie to marry me and I want you to tell me what to do to be a good husband."

Jeannette pressed a hand to her cheek because her heart had suddenly leapt up. "Oh, J.P." Tears came to her eyes.

"Is that a bad idea?"

"No," she shook her head. "Winnie's sure to say yes." They sat in silence a moment, and then Jeannette said, "I know you'll be happy together. I really believe it. I'm happy for you." And it was the truth, even though it made her so sad. Dolly and her husband argued a lot, but they were happy, she saw it in the playful way he grabbed Dolly around the waist and picked her up, and the way she relented, laying her head on his shoulder. And Jeannette's parents had certainly had a happy marriage. They had been equal partners in running their institute, that was no small thing, and Papa always said to Mama how, after all their years together, he was still *moony* over her, and Mama always shushed him, making a stern expression to cover her smile.

"So, how should I do it? How should I be a good husband?"

"I don't know I'm qualified to say," Jeannette said, quieting herself inside to think on it. "But I suppose it starts with showing her you love her. And not just at the beginning. I mean for always."

"Alright."

"And show her, tell her, you appreciate what she does for you."

"I see."

She sighed. "I don't know what all exactly. Be kind."

J.P. smiled again. "That gives me an idea."

"Just be as nice with her as you've always been with me."

"It's you that's always been nice, Miss Jeannette," he said. And then neither said anything more, until Esther came running into the room to say that Maudie had gotten ahold of the toilet roll again.

When Jeannette returned to the kitchen, J.P. drained his coffee cup and said he had better get going. Jeannette told him that once things were settled with Winnie to tell her she would be pleased to help her sew the wedding dress and he said he would, kissed her on the cheek, and was off out the door.

Jeannette stood a moment looking out the window. She thought of J.P. and Winnie making a home together, and for a moment looked down at her two feet standing on the linoleum alone, on the cheerful yellow and green checkerboard pattern that had emerged with scrubbing, and her children not far away—Maudie in the hall, slapping at the now latched door of the water closet, and Esther making her doll dance around the leg of the crib in the girls' bedroom. The sadness faded as she took a few deep breaths and her eyes wandered to the wall with the picture postcards. It felt good to have a home of her own, for however long she had it.

✦ ✦ ✦ ✦ ✦

In December, four months after Macon had gone to Ohio, he wrote to Jeannette to say things were finally ready for her and the girls to come. Jeannette wrote back to say that she couldn't leave Mama just yet, as she was recovering from the flu and had a cough that worried her, which was true. Another month later when Macon sent a bank draft for their train fare Jeannette, heart racing, ran downstairs and gave the money to the landlady instead, for another month and a half of rent. She wrote to Macon apologizing, they weren't able to come so soon, she had to wait until Mama had fully regained her strength. This time she knew it was a lie, but she didn't feel like any Mata Hari. Shame burned at the corners of her mind because the longer Macon was away the less convinced she was that she would follow him.

The arguments for why she should go came like hissing cats from those shameful corners, accusing her of being disloyal, of taking Macon's money without behaving as a wife should, of deceiving him, of keeping his children from him. But what got her most, the thought that most crippled her resistance, was the thought that she was denying her children their father.

What if Mama had ever done a thing like this? What if Jeannette had grown up far away from Papa? It was unthinkable. Jeannette loved her children more than anything in the world, and in fact in their presence she admired herself, taking a kind of deep pride in being their safe shelter, their intricate, colorful teacher, being a woman who was vast and grown-up, even wise. So how could she commit this crime, do them such wrong as to keep their father away?

For weeks Jeannette agonized, vacillating between possibilities. First, she would resolve to go to Columbus with the girls, telling herself that Mama would understand and that she would return to New York should Mama fall ill. Then, in the next hour, she would recoil from the impossible idea that she could fit herself back into a life with Macon—back under his roof and his rules, far away in Ohio. She dreamt at night of being stuck in the seam between two walls, paralyzed. Macon wrote back several times, and each time she put him off. And the time dragged forward, like a chain between them growing taut and strained.

When she spoke with Dolly about it, Dolly bit her nail.

"What does your Mama say," she asked.

"She says she'll understand if we go, that she'll be alright, but I'm afraid she won't be."

"How do you feel? In your heart of hearts?"

"On the fence, I guess."

"One hell of a fence."

Jeannette laughed, but then her throat closed. She looked over to where the four girls were playing in Dolly's sitting room. "He's their Daddy. I can't just…"

Dolly sighed. "One hell of a evil fence."

◆ ◆ ◆ ◆ ◆

Then, one evening in March the doorbell rang. Jeannette was feeding the children their supper, singing a little song she'd made up for them about the happy foods—the bright orange carrots, the sunny yellow eggs, the toasty brown bread—making them strong, and now she set down her spoon and told them to sit tight.

"That's probably Mr. J.P. come to say hello," she said. "I'll be right back."

But it wasn't J.P. downstairs on the creaky doorstep. It was Macon.

"Hello Jeannette."

"Macon!" She gasped a little, her breath taken away by surprise. "I didn't expect you." He looked the same, but different. He was unshaven and his hair had a shaggy look.

She wiped her hands nervously on her apron. "Come in, we're upstairs." Macon followed her, and Jeannette called up ahead to warn the children. "Babies, it's Daddy. Daddy is here from Ohio!"

The kitchen with Macon in it was very crowded all of a sudden. He smelled of the outdoors and the train, and a cold draft had come up from the street behind them. Esther and Maudie sat silent, their eyes wide and round as coins. Maudie had her fingers in her mouth and Esther's lower lip trembled. "That Daddy?" she said.

"Don't you recognize your Daddy?" Macon said a bit too loudly, smiling a hard smile.

"Give her a minute," Jeannette said. "Let me take your bag." She took the case he carried and put it inside her bedroom door. "Will you eat something?"

He accepted a plate with boiled eggs and carrots, and a thick piece of bread fried in lard, speaking in gentler tones to the children. When the girls had finished eating, Jeannette sent them to play in their bedroom. She washed up the dishes in silence, waiting for Macon to speak.

"I'm taking you all back with me," he said finally. "End of the week."

Jeannette dried her hands and sat down opposite him at the table, staring at its hard surface. In their six years together she had never defied him.

"I can't go just now," she said in a low voice. She didn't meet his eye.

"You can, and you will."

"No, I—"

He slammed the table with his open hand, so hard the legs jumped on the floor. Jeannette hunched forward as Macon staggered up. "Don't scare the children," she begged. "Don't scare them!"

"You still refuse? Your place is with your husband, Jeannette."

"Macon, don't—"

Macon squeezed his head in his hands, pacing the short length of the room, his face twisted into ugly gashes. "I'll take them with me," he roared. "I'll take them with me and then you'll come."

Jeannette heard crying from the other room but she dared not go, lest Macon follow her. She had to at least keep him in the kitchen. Heart pounding in her ears, her mind raced, trying to think what she would do if he did attempt to take the children. Scream for help? Wake the landlady and get her to call for the police?

But he kept pacing, then turned, first facing one wall and then the other, spinning like a kite in the wind. His broad shoulders crumpled forward and

Jeannette suddenly saw them there as if from above, two helpless people locked in a bitter struggle, with the children down the hall their fragile, mutual collateral.

"I'm sorry." Tears streamed down her face. She knew at last she would never go.

He collapsed onto the chair and buried his face in his hands, sobbing hoarsely.

"I'm sorry," she said again.

"You're breaking with me," he lifted his head to face her. "Ain't you."

"I don't know."

"Why?" His fists landed on the table. "What have I done but try to take care of you?"

"I don't know, I don't know," her voice broke like glass.

"You got somebody else?"

"No, no." She shook her head, wiping at her tears with her sleeve.

"Don't you love me at all?"

"It's not that," she said, shaking her head again. "I can't leave." But this wasn't the whole truth and they both knew it.

"Don't lie. You owe me that much. If you truly loved me, you'd stand by me."

They stayed quiet a long time. Finally, Jeannette rose and went to see about the children. When they had calmed and gone to sleep she returned to the kitchen.

"You must be tired," she whispered. "Go on and lie down. I'll sit with the children a while longer."

He didn't protest, just rubbed his face with his hands, went in her bedroom and closed the door. She heard the mattress springs creak.

Jeannette took her coat to the children's room and lay on the floor with her head on a pile of clean laundry she'd had stacked in the corner. For the longest time she listened to the children breathing, then she closed her eyes and slept.

Maudie

It was February of 1936, a few inches of snow covered the ground, shoveled off the sidewalks into uneven heaps splattered with bits of frozen mud. Jeannette walked hand in hand with the girls, bundled up in coats and scarves, on their way to Mama's with several books from the Harlem branch library. Mama had been ill with another winter flu and had a cough that made her wheeze, and Jeannette had checked out a biography of the composer Antonin Dvorak, who had served for a few years as head of the conservatory where both Mama and Gerard had studied. Jeannette thought reading it would help keep Mama content to rest more. She was busier now with planning the private concerts Auntie Alma had once suggested, but she was no longer the robust woman she once was. Every winter illness seemed to leave her weaker, and she was more plagued by the pains in her legs.

Over a year had passed since Macon's visit from Ohio. Every month Jeannette wrote to him, telling him the little daily details about the girls, hoping to maintain his link to them, but so far she'd had no reply. The money had stopped too. Macon was a man who needed a family, she knew. Most likely he'd find another woman and have other children, maybe he'd met someone already. Jeannette found work minding the toddlers of three different neighbors, taking them and her girls in a little gaggle to parks and other places, feeding them picnic-style on her kitchen floor, and teaching them the rhyming songs she'd used to sing with her students at the school so long ago. Between that and help from Mama, they got by.

"Mama," Esther's voice piped up. "Lookit me, I'n a lion." She scrunched her little face and held up her hands like claws, "Raahhrrr!"

"Me too!" Maudie said, attempting to copy her sister. "Ahhhh!"

Jeannette laughed. "Are you two as big as our library lions?"

Old Leo Lenox and Leo Astor. Mayor La Guardia had recently renamed them, Patience and Fortitude, the two qualities he said New Yorkers needed to weather the grueling consequences of the economic crisis.

When they arrived at Mama's house, Mama was reclined on the parlor sofa with a sheaf of papers and her old fountain pen. "Don't get up, Mama," Jeannette said, unbundling the girls. "I'll get them warmed up and then you can start their lesson." Mama had begun teaching the girls piano, sitting with them together on the bench, just as she had once learned with her brother Albert, from their grandmother in Montreal.

"Yes, alright." Mama set the papers down on her lap. "Girls, will you come and kiss Grand Mama?"

It was a Saturday and Mama's boarders were out, and during the piano lesson, Jeannette cleaned up a pile of dishes in the kitchen. Esther, four years old now, was taking well to playing, while little Maudie watched with a rapt expression. When Esther finished her exercises, Maudie would be allowed to press the keys and make her "music."

After the lesson they had lunch, soup and bread, and after that the girls played under the table and beside the sofa, with Grand Mama's collection of beaded necklaces and folding scraps of paper. Jeannette brought out the biography for Mama to see, and she inspected it with her reading glasses on, saying she'd be pleased to read it, how she remembered Mr. Dvorak from her first year at the Conservatory. She would have said more but she was seized by a fit of coughing that left her wheezing, her lips unnaturally pale. Jeannette hurried to get Mama her syrup and a glass of water, and when Mama had caught her breath, asked her if Doctor Kalman had been by that week.

"He has," Mama said. "But he didn't say much. Jeannette, I think I'd better lie down a while."

"Yes, do," Jeannette said. "The girls and I will go on home soon. I'll just do the stove first. We'll see you for church tomorrow."

"Alright," Mama said, beginning to move heavily down the hallway with her cane. "I'll be fine here, don't worry."

But Jeannette did worry. Usually she reassured herself after one of Mama's illnesses, going over in her mind all of the little signs of recovery and repeating what Auntie Alma once said, that Mama had always been strong. This time, though, her fretful state persisted.

Back at the apartment there were still a few hours of daylight left. Jeannette had housework to do and she put a chair up to the sink so Esther could do her "helping" as she was determined to, which amounted to dunking one fork repeatedly into the sudsy water. While Jeannette unpinned the laundry from a line she'd set up over the radiator, she caught the sound of Maudie's voice coming from down the hall. Curious, she set the laundry down and crept over to the bedroom door.

Maudie was sitting with her feet pointed toward the window, talking into the air. At two years old she had just enough hair for Jeannette to make three velvety little plaits that bounced when she nodded in earnest. Jeannette stood in the doorframe, watching as Maudie chattered on, saying something about Esther and a cat that visited outside, but the rest was unintelligible. Abruptly, Maudie stopped talking and looked intently in the direction of the window. After a long pause, she nodded and said, "Uh huh." And after another long pause, she shook her head and said, "Nuh uh."

It was curious how she carried on so. Esther hadn't ever behaved like that. At that age, Esther had babbled during her play, but had only seemed concerned with things right in front of her, and she'd only started pretending a year before. Jeannette remembered the moment that Esther had picked up an empty jar from the table and made like she was drinking from it.

"I drinkin' a cup of tea, Mama," she'd said, smiling.

Now Maudie was quiet for a good while, and Jeannette stepped into the room. "Who are you talking to, Baby?"

Maudie turned her head to look up at her, pointing her finger in the air.

"Who's that?"

Maudie struggled for a second. "Gan-papa."

"Who?" Jeannette knelt down beside her.

"*Gan*-papa," Maudie said again.

Jeannette's arms prickled. "Gan-papa?"

Maudie nodded, but seeing as her mother didn't understand, she said, "Mama-daddy."

Jeannette put a hand to her own chest, "Mama's daddy?"

Maudie nodded again, more vigorously. "Uh huh."

Jeannette felt faint. "What's he say, Baby?"

Maudie's wide eyes looked to the side, and her mouth hung open, listening.

"Say he love us," Maudie said.

Maudie crawled up to Jeannette's lap and put her arms around her neck. She touched Jeannette's cheek where the tears came down.

"Mama sad?"

Jeannette hugged her.

"Gan-papa say Mama no be sad."

Mama

By the next summer Mama no longer had her cough, which had lingered on through the spring, but was much weaker than before. She ventured out far less, even getting from the bedroom to the kitchen took her breath away.

I dread next winter (Jeannette wrote to Gerard) *as I am terrified of what another illness could do to her... On a happier note, the girls are coming along in their music. We listened to La Bohème on the wireless last Saturday and Esther tried to copy their singing, she loved it so. But not Maudie. She covered her ears and ran from the room!*

Jeannette asked about his work, as always, and said she wished they could see him again. This last, she thought she ought not to say, but she couldn't help it. She had longed to be able confide in him about her troubled marriage, and for him to advise her to do what she thought was right, even if it also seemed wrong, but she had never found the words for it. Gerard never spoke of any love interests, despite her occasional questions about romance in Paris, and she'd wondered if being so serious an artist left him without such desires.

When Mama was well enough to watch the girls again, she rode the streetcar to the Central Library and visited her lions. Patience and Fortitude, these words had new meaning for her now, though they offered up no answers. Her luck with the library clerks was intermittent, but regularly enough she was able to bring home several new books. Philosophy of education still held its old fascination for her, even if she had nowhere to apply it outside of her own home.

✦ ✦ ✦ ✦ ✦

In January of 1938, just after Maudie's fourth birthday, Mama became ill with influenza as Jeannette had long feared. The terrible cough returned, but worse than ever, and soon Dr. Kalman, clutching his white beard with one hand, declared it a grave case of pneumonia affecting both lungs. He had prescribed a sulfapyridine medicine, but it was not having the effect they had hoped.

"She may not have long left," he said in a whisper, as Jeannette saw him to the door, one morning. "I'm very sorry indeed." Jeannette nodded, cold shock meeting a colder knowing that invaded her to the core. "You must have a nurse here, round the clock. I'll have my office arrange it."

Mama's close friends were already coming in a steady rotation, including Mr. Sanderson, who spent hours by her side, holding her hand in both of his, recalling every humorous moment from their many years together at the Higgins Institute and beyond. Jeannette sent word to Aunt Melody in Montreal and Auntie Alma in Chicago, and she willed herself to be strong. Dolly took the girls as often as she was able, going off with them and her two with a wave of her hand, telling Jeannette not to worry and to focus on her mother.

Mr. Sanderson came one afternoon with armload of hothouse flowers, directing Jeannette to arrange them in vases around Mama's room.

"So expensive, Sandy," Mama struggled to say, but he shushed her.

"My dear," he said, holding her hand, his voice catching in his throat, "you deserve beautiful things."

Mama drew in a few labored breaths. "You always were the… expert on beauty."

"I won't deny it."

Mama smiled, wincing from the pain in her lungs, and Mr. Sanderson glanced over at Jeannette. "Shall we let her rest?" Then back to Mama, "Shall we let you rest, my dear?"

"Yes, I think so."

Mama closed her eyes but Mr. Sanderson stayed in the chair, laying Mama's hand down at her side and keeping his lightly on top of it.

By the time Auntie Alma arrived from Chicago, there wasn't much that could be done. Dr. Kalman arranged for an oxygen tent to be brought to the house so

Mama might breathe easier, but he explained to Jeannette that her mother's organs were failing and that it was only a matter of time. With a grave face he said that with Jeannette's permission he would give her mother higher doses of morphine, which would make her sleep and ease her pain, and to which Jeannette readily agreed. Watching Mama struggle to breathe and seeing the pain in her eyes was agony, and after the first injection, as Mama relaxed into sleep, Jeannette breathed far easier too.

Mama would not wake up again. Jeannette and Auntie Alma held her hands, Mr. Sanderson all but took up residence in the house with them and Dr. Kalman made his visits. And then one morning when the clock in the hall chimed ten and Jeannette had stepped into the kitchen for a moment for a cup of coffee, Mama slipped away.

Auntie Alma met Jeannette in the hallway and embraced her. "She's gone now, Honey." The clock's pendulum ticked back and forth as Jeannette wept and Auntie Alma held her and Mama's soul went to meet Papa's.

✦ ✦ ✦ ✦ ✦

Jeannette was grateful that Auntie Alma was there and grateful for Mr. Sanderson, their small frames and brisk movements as alike as an aged brother and sister pair. Despite their own broken hearts, they were everything solid that she needed.

Several days after the funeral, Jeannette sat with Auntie Alma in Mama's room sorting through a stack of papers. They heard Mr. Sanderson's voice in the hall.

"I've just stopped by with these canelés," he called out. He hadn't bothered with the bell.

Jeannette met him in the kitchen where he was fussing with the string on a pink bakery box. "Your mother always loved these," he said, then dropped into a chair and sobbed wildly into his handkerchief. Jeannette put her arms around him.

"Thank you," she said, when he was quiet.

He patted her arms. "Where are the children?" he asked, blowing his nose.

"With Dolly just now," she said. "Her girls are doing their hair in some special way they just learned about."

"Well, they can have these for their supper," he said, nudging the bakery box with one hand. "With milk."

Auntie Alma peeked around the corner. "Sandy," she said, "I'm glad you're here. Can you help us make sense of these?" She held up a wide ledger.

He stood up and dabbed at his eyes. "What would you two do without me?"

I can't believe we've said goodbye to her (Jeannette wrote to Gerard.) *I wonder if I ever will believe it. My heart is so broken it's like I carry one half of it in the left pocket of my coat, and the other in the right. Yet in the middle I'm still me and something sustains me. Being a mother myself is a great source of strength, as are my friends, and in quiet moments I sense both my parents with me. I'm glad she's no longer suffering, and I'm glad they are together again. I often look at the photograph of them on top of the piano, the one posed on a street in Brussels during one of their tours. They are so young and stylish, I am amazed every time.*

My brave Jeannette, (Gerard wrote back) *no one could be prouder of a daughter than your parents, or myself of a sister. I'm coming home, finally. I will see you very soon.*

Gerard

Gerard arrived just before noon on the appointed day. A cab pulled up in the street and Esther and Maudie, who happened to be pressing their noses against the glass of the bedroom window, saw him first, calling out "Mama, Mama!" And when she came to the window, she saw her brother paying the driver, with two suitcases at his feet and a guitar case on a strap over his shoulder.

She ran down to the street, a little girl again, despite all appearances.

His face was older, weary from travel, the same but seasoned, and embracing him she embraced both her brother and a stranger at the same time.

She looked up to the bedroom window where the girls were watching and waved, but by the time Gerard looked up they had disappeared.

"Come on inside," she said, taking one of the cases.

And he smiled, sighing, "My, oh my."

Later, when they sat together in the girls' bedroom, the face of the younger Gerard that Jeannette had had in her mind seemed slowly to fade into the new one before her, like two images on glass stacked together and held up to a window. His voice was a little different to, just a little hoarse, raspy edges gone gray like what was left of his hair.

"I hear you girls like music," Gerard said, opening the guitar case and pulling out a gorgeous, amber-colored guitar.

"I didn't know you played," Jeannette said. "You never mentioned it."

"I'm new to it," he said, beginning to tune the strings. "A good friend left this to me."

Jeannette rested her chin on her laced fingers, both girls leaning back on her knees.

"I know what that is," Esther said, importantly. "A ti-gar!"

Gerard laughed, "That's right."

"What will you play for us?" Jeannette asked.

"Would you all like to hear a song I made up myself," he said to the girls, "just for the two of you?"

Both girls nodded emphatically, Esther grabbing Maudie's little hands and preparing to dance.

"You'll need to help me sing it, it's called, 'Hello to the World', alright?" He played a few chords, filling the little room with their warm sound. "*Hello to the world, said the little girl,*" he sang, "*I'm but a little soul waiting to unfurl...*"

Gerard sang, and the girls danced, chiming in on the refrain. And Jeannette kept gazing at her brother's face, as it changed with the song.

✦ ✦ ✦ ✦

He stayed with them just a few days, until he'd found a room to let not far away, during which time Esther and Maudie slept with Jeannette, keeping her awake in the night with their active feet. Soon enough they'd be moving into her parents' house. She would keep the boarders upstairs and take the downstairs room that had been Mama's. It was spacious enough for two proper beds, one for her and one for the girls.

Usually shy with new people, the girls took quickly to their Uncle Gerard. In the morning after his first night with them, they walked the long blocks to the Higgins house, Esther and Maudie holding Gerard's hands and pointing out things of interest—storefront mannequins, the grates around trees—because they knew he had been on a boat and surely had never seen a city before. When they arrived and Jeannette opened the door with her key, Gerard took off his hat and held it at his side as he came in behind her.

"It's a little different than how you remember it," Jeannette said, hoping he wouldn't be disappointed. She'd been at work with extra cleaning, had done her best to repair a tear in the sofa, but she knew things weren't in the shape they once were, years ago when Gerard had last been there.

"It's lovely." He stepped over to the piano and peered at the photograph of Jeannette's parents, smiling sadly. The fallboard was open and he ran a hand lightly over the keys.

"Esther's eager to show you what she can do," Jeannette said.

"I'm ready when she is."

The girls had already scampered off to the bedroom, looking for the jewelry box with Grand Mama's beaded necklaces.

"What will you do next, Jeannette?" Gerard asked. "After you get things sorted with the house, and your husband?" Jeannette had told him that she'd recently had a letter from Macon, that he'd been to a lawyer about a divorce, and that there was another woman he intended to marry, though he'd said that he wanted to remain a father to the girls, as much as he was able. She'd written back to say that she was glad for him, and relieved for the girls, because she wanted nothing more than for them to still have a father.

"As a matter of fact, I do have an idea," Jeannette said. "I do have something I'm going to try."

◆ ◆ ◆ ◆ ◆

All that summer while Gerard met with club managers and old friends, looking to begin building his life again in New York, Jeannette and the girls collected bottles, jars, and tin cans. Jeannette carefully washed and dried each item, stacking them in boxes along with spoons, washboards, and her old washtub, all things that might be used for percussion. One set of jars she arranged on the sideboard in the parlor, with different amounts of water in them, so that struck with a butter knife they produced a range of notes. She bought a piece of board from a furniture shop, and a pot of white paint from Anson's Hardware, and, as she had always been good at lettering, created a sign that read:

The Higgins Institute for Children,
Music Lessons Daily,
Mrs. Jeannette Higgins Halvorsen, Certified Instructor
Pay what you can.

It would do for now.

For fifty cents she had a box of a hundred handbills made, with the same words as her sign, and also including her address and the schedule of her classes: three to five o'clock Sunday through Friday, and ten to one o'clock on Saturdays. She hung the sign on the front door where it was plain to see from the street, and together with the girls distributed the handbills all in one hot, sweaty afternoon, in a several-block radius around the house, securing them here and there in window grates and mailboxes and random nails on fences and telephone poles. At one point Esther got her thumb stuck in a grate around the corner from their house and getting it out caused a scratch that drew blood. Jeannette knew it couldn't hurt all that much, but she scooped up both children and flew home just to get things quiet again. Back on the street with the remainder of the handbills, Esther brandished her white-bandaged thumb like a proud soldier and frowning at the seriousness of their mission.

The first music class, the day after they put out the handbills, there were two children, Esther and Maudie, and the mason jar on the small table by the door stayed empty. Jeannette conducted the class anyhow, sitting at the piano and clapping out rhythms for the children to follow, just as if the room were full to capacity of eager students, and everyone had a grand time. But the next day there were three new children, a little brother and sister, who brought a penny, and an older boy of eleven or twelve, with a quarter-pound paper sack of oats. By the end of the week there were ten children in the three o'clock class, and twelve in the four o'clock, including Dolly's girls. Dolly brought a batch of soda biscuits she'd made, and they passed them around among the children at the end of the class.

Given her musical upbringing, and thirteen odd years as mother, teacher, and student of higher education, Jeannette had gathered vast repertoire of songs and rhymes to teach the children, and as far as she could tell they loved it all. Word spread rapidly through the neighborhood that music classes with Miss Jeannette at the Higgins Institute for Children lit the children up like birthday cakes. In only a few weeks parents were coming by to shake her hand and tell her that, thanks to the music classes, their sons and daughters were singing and smiling and staying out of trouble.

The mason jar collected coins and the table collected things like buttons and pins, and foodstuffs, including the occasional gory offerings of bloody soup bones and fish heads from a couple of the children whose father was an assistant to the butcher on the corner. These Jeannette gathered quickly and set to simmer in big pots in the kitchen where they turned into rich broths that she and the girls ate throughout the week, cooked with beans or rice, or handfuls of herbs and vegetables.

Once again, Jeannette had a roomful of music and children throughout the week. It brought back to her a sense of herself that had been missing for so long, and an energy that buoyed her as she learned, bit by bit, how to live without her parents and how to support her own children in their lack of a present father.

Patience and Fortitude

Since Macon had broken his silence, he and Jeannette had begun trading letters once a month. The way Gerard had used to send funny anecdotes of animals, Jeannette now wrote such things down for Macon about the girls, and included in the envelopes pictures they had drawn. Macon's letters were short but remained consistent. Every so often he sent a small sum of money with instructions for exactly how it was to be used—shoes for the girls, school supplies for Esther, mittens for winter.

One day in the fall a package arrived from Ohio, addressed to Misses Esther and Maude Halvorsen. Inside, below layers of tissue paper was a note that read, *Dear Girls, these are some late birthday presents. I'll be out to see you again as soon as I can. Be good for Mama. Love, Daddy.* Underneath more of the paper were two straight-faced, stiff-limbed brown teddy bears. Esther and Maudie peered into the box, eyes wide.

"These for us?" Esther asked.

"Yes, they are," Jeannette said, holding Macon's letter. "From Daddy. Aren't they pretty?" She dug her hands into the tissue paper and handed one bear first to Esther, and then the other to Maudie.

"This one mine?" said Maudie, unsure to be holding something so valuable. The girls had seen plush toys like these in shop windows full of things far too lavish to be seen in their home.

"I'n gonna call mine Sara Crew!" Esther said. Jeannette had lately been reading *A Little Princess* to the girls. "Maudie, you can call you yours Lottie."

"Mine's Lottie," Maudie said, smiling.

"Why don't you take them around their new home?" Jeannette said. "Be careful though, they're very special."

While Esther and Maudie took the bears to see all their play corners and their other dolls—the rag ones—Jeannette sat rereading Macon's brief words. He hadn't addressed her directly, and in that she saw his gesture of separation. But he'd said *Be good for Mama*, and she saw in that a gesture of peace. She would have the girls write thank you notes with homemade drawings on them. Maudie was particularly good with drawing and had a fascination for flying things—birds, balloons, angels.

A few months later, when the air was chill and all but the last leaves had dropped from the trees, another letter came from Macon saying that he would be in town soon, staying with J.P. and Winnie. He would see the girls, of course, but he wanted to see Jeannette first without them and talk things over. He said she should leave word with J.P. about a time and place to meet, and he would see her where she chose.

The appointed day of their meeting, Jeannette stepped from the streetcar at 40th Street and 5th Avenue, and made her way to the wide, magnificent stairs of the Central Library. She spotted Macon right away, sitting with his elbows on his knees, on a stone bench below one of the lions. It had been nearly two years since she'd last seen him, but she would have known his shape anywhere.

✦ ✦ ✦ ✦ ✦

She approached slowly, thinking he might look up and see her, alerted by the hard beating of her heart, but he didn't until she was only a few feet away. He wore a navy blue wool coat, a gray muffler, and a hat with a black brim, and when he did see her he just as quickly looked away, leaning back and rubbing his mouth with one hand. She touched the bench with one hand and sat down gingerly, resting her bag on the cold slats beside her.

"I hope you haven't been waiting."

He shook his head and cleared his throat. "You look different."

"I expect we've both changed."

He nodded. "How are you keeping?"

"We're getting along," she said, just as Mama had said they would. "The girls are looking forward to seeing you."

"They must be pretty big now."

They watched the people passing, the automobiles, the clouds in the sky, not finding much else to say. Jeannette looked at Macon, the squint of his eyes, angle of his jaw, those black brows against his ochre skin. Perhaps they should have been something other than a married couple, she thought, had a relationship that would have truly suited them, like teacher and school director, or a woman with a motor car and her trusted mechanic. But then she wouldn't have had Esther and Maudie, and she couldn't imagine her life without those two, not at all.

"So, you say Esther likes school, huh?" Macon asked, lifting his hat a moment to rub his hair.

"That's right." Jeannette had already told him how Esther doted on her teacher, and how she made friends easily.

"And Maudie, always drawing pictures."

"Morning, noon, and night."

He chuckled, shaking his head. "I'll take them to get their photograph taken tomorrow, nice big portraits in frames, that's how I'd like it. Right on the bureau next to my…" He trailed off a second. "I'm getting married next month."

"Congratulations." She meant it.

"Darius will be my best man. She wants a church wedding, so…"

"I'm glad. I'm very glad."

"Listen," he said, fishing around in his coat pocket. "I'd better get going. But I brought you this." He handed her what looked like a small notebook. She turned the flat, black book in her hands, its textured paper gave off a faint shine and was embossed with the words First National Bank. It was a passbook.

"I've opened an account for the girls," Macon said. "For their future. I'll make deposits and they'll have it when Esther is eighteen."

Esther eighteen, how far off and unimaginable that seemed.

"This is grand of you, truly, I—"

He waved her off, rising from the bench. "Between the two of us, we'll take care of them," he said, already starting to walk away. "Tell them I'll see them tomorrow, eight o'clock," he called over his shoulder. "Tell them I'll take them to the carousel at Sulzer's."

The first snow of November fell one day in gentle curtains. Saturday music classes were finished and Esther helped Jeannette straighten up the parlor, carting the boxes of instruments down the hall to the linen closet where they kept them stacked. Maudie had her face glued to the windowpane, entranced by the whirling white flakes outside.

The doorbell rang and Jeannette hurried to the door, expecting Gerard as he had promised to come for supper. Nowadays she looked forward to the moment he would sit on the sofa and let the girls climb over him, laughing and calling them his "tumble puppies." It was a new game they had—two little acrobats and one big uncle—a circus of three.

But it wasn't Gerard at the door, it was four women from St. Luke's African Methodist Episcopal, the church Jeannette's family had always gone to and where she now took the girls. Esther and Maudie enjoyed the music and the stories at Sunday School, and Jeannette found it comforting to sit among a collective in a worshipping mood—the familiarity of the hymns, the sermons, the community, the sturdy wood of the pews, the vault of sound made by the organ.

It was always good to be there, though being a divorced woman with children was uncomfortable inside the church. She had dreaded the awkward questions about her absent husband at first, but now Jeannette supposed her state of affairs was generally known. So many times in the past year the cold wind of doubt had blown through her, when she saw families intact, on the street after services, say, walking hand in hand, mother and father with the children.

"Good afternoon, Mrs. Halvorsen," said one of the ladies at the door. "We hoped we might bother you a spell."

"No bother at all," Jeannette said, ushering them inside. "Please do come in."

Though Jeannette knew them all by sight, the ladies—Mrs. Allard, Mrs. Locket, Mrs. Randall, and Miss Dennis—introduced themselves as the organizing committee for the Christmas program.

"Folks are saying marvelous things about your music school," said Mrs. Allard, the elder of the group. "And we wondered if you and your students might like to give a short concert, to help raise money for our neighborhood programs."

"You'll be compensated, of course," said Mrs. Randall. "Though modestly, since it is a benefit."

"A concert," Jeannette breathed. Already so many ideas were leaping to mind—which songs and what arrangements, which children would take the solos and carry the harmonies—that it took a moment for Jeannette to answer. "I would be delighted."

The ladies beamed. Miss Denis took a notebook and pencil from her bag.

✦ ✦ ✦ ✦ ✦

When their short meeting concluded, having made plans to regroup in another week, the ladies took their coats and bustled back out the door. Jeannette followed them out to the stoop, the freshness of the cold air hitting her face, watching as the ladies made their way down the snowy walk.

Always she had been careful, always she'd tried to do the right thing, until what was right felt wrong and what was wrong turned out to be her only option. But here she still was, behaving strangely perhaps, filling her parlor with bottles and tin cans and singing children every day, in a house of her own with no husband in sight. But instead of punishment, it surely looked as though her rebellion had been met with reward.

Jeannette turned her face upward toward the white sky, the snowfall laying its light touch on her lashes and against her cheeks, pricking her lips with pins of cold. Didn't everything come from the unexpected? From the unknown, after all? A sound came up from her chest and escaped her throat, a joyful laugh, and then another and another.

"What's funny, Mama?" Esther was by her side, and Maudie followed behind her. "What's funny?" The girls giggled, wanting to be in on the joke, and she held their hands, swinging their arms. They danced around her, and she was still laughing. "What's funny?"

"Oh, me," Jeannette said at last. "Me. Just me."

Part 3
Maudie

New York, 1949

It was Sunday morning, early in the fall, and Maudie stood between Mama and Esther with the backs of her knees pressing the edge of the wooden pew while the congregation poured its collective soul into a rendition of "Marching to Zion." Up behind the altar, the choir raised their hands over their heads during the chorus, and Mrs. Hannah at the organ played with her eyes closed. Maudie pressed and released the backs of her knees, pressed and released, the solid feeling of it was comforting somehow.

Maudie liked church fine, most of the time. The sermons were full of storybook characters and she did like the music, but the thing she liked most were the colored glass windows, the big one especially that hovered over the choir with its symmetrical radiant shards arranged in ornate rings all the colors of the rainbow. That window faced southeast so that on winter mornings, when the Sunday services were about midway through, the window was lit so bright you could hardly look at it, but you could see its colors fall over the faces of the people singing or praying, almost as if they'd already gotten into Heaven. Today, though, it was dim. The angle of the sun was such that it threw a shadow from the building adjacent over the glass, and the colors, though pretty, didn't shine.

When the service was over, the hellos and goodbyes began. Maudie followed at Mama's elbow in a slow progress to the church doors as the air filled with the rumble of people greeting one another, and Mama smiled and shook hands and embraced and enquired with many of the ladies. Two of Esther's friends bounded over and dragged her away into the crowd, already laughing, but Maudie stayed with Mama as usual. There was no one to drag her away like that. Nor did she engage too much in the ladies' conversation. She smiled and nodded when addressed, but otherwise watched for colors as they drifted in and out of her line of sight—the triangle of a man's red and white silk handkerchief peeking out from a gray suit-jacket pocket, a purple hat band edged in gold, a rhinestone broach like a glittering fish.

Finally, when they stepped outside and Esther rejoined them by the stairs, the three Halvorsens were released to the flow of the street. It was a fine fall day, the kind where summer, still brash, claims not to be beaten, and the chill of morning gives way to a sun hot enough to make folks sweat under their collars. Maudie wore the wool dress that Mama had suggested, and now, as the heat gathered up her spine and spread out in itchy prickles, she longed to get home and change into cooler clothes.

Maudie and Esther walked on either side of Mama, holding hands just as they always did, even though the girls were no longer children. Esther was as tall as Mama already, lithe and graceful, always drawing admirers, and Maudie hardly blamed them. She herself was a touch more solid, with a figure that took more after Mama's. But she knew it wasn't just her sister's physical attributes that made people like her. Esther always knew the right words to say. Her voice was musical and she laughed easily, she knew when to confide and when to hold confidence, and she naturally put folks at ease. This last, especially, was an ability Maudie knew she herself didn't have.

Maudie had overheard teachers and other adults call her "dreamy" or "far away," but in truth that was what Maudie thought about them. Marching to one's own drum might be good for some, but if there was a collective beat she just couldn't hear it. She had no choice but to remain out of step, and that was a lonely march. But there now, walking along with Mama and Esther, everything was well and just as it ought to be.

They didn't walk exactly like this every Sunday though. Sometimes Mr. Stokes was with them, Mama's gentleman friend of three years and he liked to have her on his arm while he told her about the prices of steel and titanium, or they walked together with Auntie Dolly and the girls, or Uncle Gerard, or any of various friends. But when they were just the three of them, for Maudie it was the most natural number. Just three, as far back as Maudie could remember, stable as a pyramid in Egypt. Maudie watched their joined shadows glide over the sidewalk, over and past any would-be obstacle. It was a sight as lovely as the windows in church.

Back at home, the girls helped Mama set things out for lunch, places for four, since Uncle would be by soon. He was rarely seen in church, only when Mama invited him for something special on the musical program. Maudie understood that most Saturday nights he was up late, playing piano at any of Harlem's fancier clubs, and Sundays he needed his sleep, though she suspected he had other reasons too. Uncle smiled proudly at them from the pew when they were on stage playing or singing, but she saw he stopped paying attention during the sermon and prayers and only mouthed an *Amen* once in a while to be polite. It couldn't be, though, that Uncle was one of those people the pastor called "non-believers" who were wild and strange and committed crimes large and small without even knowing it. Uncle wasn't like that at all, he was as solid and gentle as the biggest trees in the Park and, after Mama and Esther, her favorite person in the world.

After lunch, Mama would take her customary nap, one of the few indulgences she allowed herself, and Uncle would help her and Esther with the washing up, all the while telling them his marvelous stories—funny things that happened during the week, or from long ago when he lived in Paris, or even from the olden times when he was a child in Montreal. When he left, squeezing their shoulders and kissing the tops of their heads, Esther would go off to meet friends. Mama would be upstairs, snoring lightly, and not there in the parlor to tell Esther to bring Maudie along, as she had done in years past.

When Maudie was little it had been easy to play with other children, other little girls and occasionally boys too, who pretended that fallen leaves were boats going off on grand adventures or that the prickly balls that fell from certain trees held fairies inside. But as the years rolled on, one by one the other children left those fantastical worlds, preferring instead to chatter with each other about things that were real, while Maudie stayed behind and the empty distance between herself and them grew longer.

So Maudie watched Esther go those Sunday afternoons, equal parts relieved and sad, and turned to her quiet old desk upstairs by the window, rubbing her soft Crayolas over large sheets of creamy white paper that Uncle had given her on her last birthday. The desk was smooth and sturdy, with a wide, generous surface easy to spread out on. It had once belonged to Maudie's grandfather, Grand Papa Hig, who had died before she was born, though for as long as she could remember Maudie had always felt she knew him. She was almost certain she recalled his voice, and because of this took a special comfort from working at his desk. No one could be loved by a desk, she was old enough to know that, and yet this was a funny notion that stayed.

She spent hours there on her pictures, creating indoor or outdoor scenes, where furniture or nature were equal subjects to people, and where in the end not a speck of white paper was left uncovered. And it was peaceful, until the hands of the clock turned toward evening and the dreaded hour when schoolwork must be finished and the loom of Monday morning began to block out what was left of the sunshine.

Mama

Maudie was in the eighth grade now, fourteen years old, Esther was in tenth. Esther earned top marks as easily as she won friends but Maudie wasn't doing so well, and this was not new. A year or two ago her Arithmetic had begun to slide. It was as if the numbers themselves rolled off the pages and fell before Maudie could catch them. Then Composition became equally untenable, where how to structure an essay seemed about as useful as lining up dogs at a park. Why should they bark in a particular order when their true nature was to run free, chasing squirrels?

Mama sat patiently with Maudie night after night urging her to apply herself, explaining the rules of figuring and grammar, thinking that Maudie's lack of understanding was the problem, and Maudie didn't resist. She did try to do what Mama asked, but in the end her assignments went uncompleted. After supper, Mama would come into the bedroom and see her not studying but idle, outwardly, *Off gallivanting on the Moon*, as Mama put it, or worse, drawing again.

That evening it was the same.

"Why can't you apply yourself this way to your schoolwork?" Mama asked, real hurt in her voice, removing the drawings from Maudie's desk and carrying them down to her office where Esther was working on her own assignments. "You'll have these back when your homework is finished."

When she returned, she pulled the extra chair over to the desk beside Maudie's. They would start again. Maudie stared at the empty desktop, the desolate space empty now of color, soon to be encroached upon by her exercise book and the tight, sharp little black marks she was expected to crowd between the lines. It was the scratchiest of wool collars against hot, tender skin, but worse was the awful feeling in her heart because Mama was unhappy with her.

"Education is everything, Maudie," Mama said, scraping the chair closer. "A girl has no hope in this life without it." But with it, with a good education, Mama went on, she'd be able to do anything. "Look at Grand Mama," she said, "running the Higgins Institute with your Grand Papa all those years. And myself." Mama was a respected music teacher in their community. "It's because of your grandparents and the education that I've had that has allowed me to support you girls."

And while Mama spoke, impassioned, imploring, pleading, steadying, encouraging, tearing up or smiling, and often times both, for Maudie the words fell like rain. With her eyes she followed the lines of woodgrain under the shiny varnish, or she looked at Mama's face as it flowed between expressions, and she longed to be able to apply herself as Mama said because that would make Mama happy. But once again they got exactly nowhere.

✦ ✦ ✦ ✦ ✦

The last Wednesday in November was report card day. Maudie woke with a sickly sensation in her stomach, looked over at Esther still sleeping and wondered if there was any way she might skip school. But she knew it was hopeless. Esther always said you had to be at death's door for Mama to let you stay home from school.

As Maudie waited in her class line-up, her breath making white puffs that briefly obscured the braids of the girl in front of her, she felt as though she were headed down a long dark tunnel. One by one the teacher handed each student a folded paper, the report cards, as they entered the classroom, and when it was Maudie's turn she didn't meet the teacher's eye. She pushed the paper carelessly into her coat pocket for later. No reason to look now.

All day her coat hung on its hook near the door, the report card lying in the pocket like an ugly little tattletale ready to be handed over to Mama back at home. Esther would have her report card too and Maudie envied her, knowing she had nothing to fear. As the hours ticked forward, the only person who seemed to notice her was President Eisenhower who stared in her direction from his black and white portrait above the chalk board. Maudie always thought he looked like a big white baby who had skipped all the usual stages of life and gone directly into being an old man.

That evening Uncle came by for a visit after supper and Mama sent the girls upstairs because she wanted to speak with him alone. Esther and Maudie left without argument, but before long Maudie crept back downstairs under the pretext of getting Mama's pencil sharpener from her office. Tiptoeing across the parlor carpet she heard the adults speaking in low voices.

"I've been in so many times," Mama was saying. "They don't know what to tell me anymore. Her grades are barely enough to keep her in school. They'll have to hold her back if she can't improve." A cup clinked in a saucer.

"She's so young yet," Uncle Gerard said. "Let her grow up a little. She'll be alright."

"I'm a teacher myself." Maudie could almost hear Mama shaking her head. "I've taught so many children…"

"I know you have."

"How could I let my own child slip through my fingers?"

"Jeannette, she's got time…"

"I don't know. She doesn't bring friends home, she doesn't get invited places, I don't understand it. She's such a sweet girl."

Maudie's face burned. She sank slowly down onto the piano bench and poked her unsharpened pencil into her palm.

"You have to have people," Mama said. "And you have to have education."

"Maudie has people," Uncle said. "Hasn't she lots of people who love her? Is she so lonely after all?"

Chair legs scraped on the floor. Mama might be getting up and Maudie beat a silent retreat back upstairs. Esther didn't look up when she reentered their room, her gaze fixed inside the pool of lamplight over her homework, but she said, "Hear anything?"

Maudie sat down on her bed, fiddling with the edge of the quilt. "Nothing good."

Esther turned around in her chair. "We know she worries too much."

"Mm hm."

"You'll do better next time."

"Maybe." Maudie shrugged, biting her lower lip to keep it from shaking.

"No *may*be's," Esther said, jumping up. She grabbed the embroidered throw pillow from her bed and chucked it at Maudie's head. "I'm the biggie and I'm always right!"

"You say so, you *think* so, you mean," Maudie giggled, holding her arms up for protection. "I'm the only one that makes her look bad." She flung the pillow back at Esther.

"You make me look bad too, you know," Esther was laughing also and her words didn't sting. "So, you better shape up."

Maudie was throwing her old rag dolls at Esther now, and her pillows, though she left Lottie, her old teddy bear, out of the mix. Lottie was dignified and Maudie didn't want to hurt her feelings. "What kind of *shape* I'm going to be?"

"A fat old turnip!"

"Says you!"

Esther dodged all the dolls and plunked down on the bed beside Maudie. "Oh, shoosh," she said, looking at the mess on the floor. "Just don't fret, okay? Something good'll happen."

Maudie chewed a nail. "I heard Uncle say that."

"You did?"

"More or less."

"Okay, then." Esther pinched Maudie's arm. "It's settled."

✦ ✦ ✦ ✦ ✦

As the winter deepened into January, Mama's efforts with Maudie wore heavily on them both. One night, when Mama took her seat beside her at the desk and said, "Let's start with your English exercise," Maudie perceived such a strain in Mama's voice she felt herself go as flat inside as a popped balloon. Then as Mama began to go over the grammar, without meaning to Maudie began to drift away, as if someone pulled at that broken balloon's string. The more she tried to focus on Mama's voice, on the pencil and paper, the more her eyes traveled up the wall, to the shadow cast by the glass shade of the lamp. The fluted edge made a shadow that looked exactly like an engraving of the sea in a book of fairytales Uncle had given them one Christmas. A sea of dim light and dark shadow, with the round, smooth bumps of the waves rolling along like music. Up and down, rolling, all ease and no cares. If she were to cut out a little crescent of paper and hold it there, the shadow would make a little boat the same as the one the little boy in the story had used to search for his runaway hound...

"Maudie," Mama's voice was sharp, piercing Maudie's daydream and shocking her awake. Mama laid down her pencil. "I just don't know what to do," she said, pressing her fingertips to her temples. "I don't even think you are paying attention." She stood, the chair scratching backward over the floor. "I think I've had it for tonight."

Without another word, Mama turned and left the room. Maudie froze with a sudden fear. Never before had there been a rift between herself and her mother, and this felt as threatening as it was foreign. As Mama's footsteps faded down the stairs toward the parlor where Esther was practicing her scales, Maudie hunched her shoulders around her cold, cold middle, not daring to move for the longest time.

Uncle

The worst of it came in May, just when the colors of spring were bubbling up here and there in window flower boxes and budding trees, when things might otherwise have been at their most hopeful. Mama was called in to meet with the principal at the end of the school day, and when the final bell rang she was waiting in the courtyard for Esther and Maudie, the sight of her tense figure confirming what Maudie already knew.

Once back at home, Mama unpinned her hat and laid it with her gloves on the stand by the door, and then stood looking out the window at the street. Esther said she thought she'd get right to her homework, and when Maudie made to follow her upstairs, Mama said, "Stay here."

Maudie sat on the sofa looking at Mama's back, waiting for her to turn around. At last she did, and in a voice stiffened by dismay she relayed what the principal had told her in their meeting, that Maudie would have to be held back, would not go on to high school the next fall, and that if she didn't improve she would never go on at all. He had told Mama that she might do well to find training for Maudie in baking or cookery, or the applied arts, like tailoring.

"Is that what you want for yourself, Maudie?" Mama's usually gentle eyes were fierce and her voice was shrill. "No prospects other than cookery?"

A terrible quiet followed. Maudie couldn't answer.

"You know your Aunt Dolly has worked as a cook for years and what hardships she's had to deal with I can't even begin to tell you." Mama shook her head. "And at least she had finished high school. A black woman, a black girl, we're at the bottom of society's barrel, you know education is our only chance to get somewhere."

Maudie squirmed in her seat, and Mama took a breath as if to calm herself.

"Maudie, you clearly have talent as an artist, I see that and I appreciate that. From when you were tiny you made beautiful pictures. But Baby I don't know of one colored woman who makes her living as an artist, not one."

"Miz Molly..." Maudie ventured. Miz Molly was an elderly retired schoolteacher they knew from church who regularly painted portraits.

"Honey, she lives off her pension and the support of her children. I doubt she earns enough from her portraits to buy her paints." Mama lifted her fingertips to her cheek then, and turned abruptly away. She went into the kitchen and Maudie stayed on the sofa, too sunk down in despair to move.

No telling how long that awfulness would have lasted had not Uncle Gerard knocked at the door a few minutes later. He came in without waiting for an answer.

"Hey-ho!" he called, leaning his head and broad shoulders in the door, and then seeing Maudie's stricken face, said, "Oh, dear."

Mama came in, holding a dishtowel crumpled in her hands and waved Uncle back with her to the kitchen. Maudie heard the murmur of their voices and then Uncle reappeared alone, sitting down beside Maudie with a sigh. When he put his arm around her shoulders she collapsed in silent sobs.

Uncle fished around for his handkerchief. "*Ma petite*, is it all that bad?" he asked, dabbing at her face, wiping her nose like she was a tiny child. She calmed, breathing in his familiar smell, faint traces of aftershave lotion and tobacco.

"I'm being held back," she said, with a slight hiccup.

The idea of repeating the eighth grade would not have seemed so terrible if it wasn't for what it did to Mama and Mama's opinion of her.

"Well," Uncle said finally, "there's nothing we can do about it right this second, but I do have good news." Maudie looked up at him without raising her downcast face. "But I can't tell you when you're looking so puppy-dog."

A little laugh broke the surface of Maudie's sadness, and she scrubbed at her face with her hands for a second. "Okay, what's the good news?"

"Do you remember me telling you about my friend, Miz Paraibel?"

"The painter?" Maudie asked, still drying her eyes.

"And performer," Uncle said. "She's coming to New York soon, and she wants to see your pictures."

Uncle had told Esther and Maudie numerous stories over the years about Miz Anna Paraibel, one of the colorful characters he'd known in Paris. Miz Paraibel had left Paris shortly after he did, just before the war, and had gone to live in Mexico with other painters she knew. Uncle often read out passages from Miz

Paraibel's letters when the anecdotes were particularly amusing, translating from the French into a stylized English that especially delighted Esther. Now the thought of Miz Paraibel appearing, like a figure from a fairytale in the flesh in New York was shocking enough to momentarily make Maudie forget her troubles.

"When is she coming?"

"In a few weeks." Uncle smiled. Miz Paraibel would stay in New York until June, then she would be going up to the Catskills with a group to play a few of the resorts for the summer. "And I'll be joining the ensemble," Uncle said, rubbing at the back of his head where the hair was close-cropped and white. Maudie watched his long fingers as they moved over his nape. There was a small bakery down the street run by an elderly Russian couple that sold a dark pumpernickel roll encrusted in salt that always reminded her of the back of Uncle's head.

"The mountains are so beautiful, *ma petite*," he said. "In the distance, they look like great unmade beds covered in green and blue blankets. That's in summer. In autumn, the blankets are gold and red. Yellow. Orange."

Maudie's mind was still in the bakery, and now she imagined the mountains that Uncle described as the round tops of bread loaves lying against their slanted, wooden bakery shelves, disappearing into a shadowy distance. The country sunrise and sunset glowed like the coals in the baker's brick oven that she sometimes glimpsed from the front when she bought Mama's favorite raisin bread, with half a dollar in her pocket and a list of a few other groceries that she'd been sent out for.

Whenever Maudie returned home from such an errand, Mama'd ask where she'd been, what had taken so long, and Maudie thought that maybe she'd looked at something for longer than she'd realized—a neighbor's geraniums, a collection of brown bottles left in an alleyway, the nickel-plated shine on the bumper of an automobile.

"I think you'd like it up there," Uncle was saying. "In the mountains. How about you?"

"It sounds too pretty to be real," Maudie said.

"And you never smelled air so fresh." Uncle knew Maudie had almost never left the city, and not since two summers ago when she and Esther had gone to visit Daddy in Columbus, where the air was decidedly *not* fresh.

The doorbell rang.

Maudie looked around and saw the cloudy, stocky outline of Mr. Stokes, Mama's gentleman friend, through the parlor's side window.

Uncle stood, patting her hand. "I'd better hurry up and get going. I was only stopping in on my way to rehearsal."

Mama was already at the door. Uncle kissed her on the cheek and gave a nod to Mr. Stokes as he passed swiftly by on the stair. Uncle and Mr. Stokes were always plenty polite, even if they didn't have much to say to one another, music and machinery being such different trades.

Maudie remembered the Sunday three years before when Mr. Stokes had spoken to Mama after the church service, asking if he might take her and the girls to lunch. Mama had told them later that he was a widower with two grown children, his wife having passed several years before from a lung disease. He did some kind of work involving the sale of steel and other metals to factories, and Esther thought him a little dull. One Saturday when Uncle had taken Maudie and Esther to Central Park to walk around the Harlem Meer, they stopped to lean their elbows on the stone railing of a bridge and Uncle asked what their plans were for that night. Esther sighed and said, "Oh, Mr. Stokes is coming for dinner, and we'll have to be cheerful and listen all about his business. I get so bored with that I'd like to scream."

Uncle didn't laugh, as Maudie had thought he might. "Now," he said, "your mama enjoys his company. I'm sure you girls can stand to learn a little about business."

It was true that Mama enjoyed his company. Why else would she have him over for dinner or go to the pictures with him on an occasional Saturday. She even agreed to go away with him once to a country place for the weekend, but she had never said she'd marry him, though he had asked her. Mama said she didn't think she'd marry again, that once was likely enough.

Maudie didn't quite understand Esther's attitude toward Mr. Stokes—not that she thought her sister should be kinder or that she herself had such a different opinion. There were numerous people in their world she took little notice of, and Mr. Stokes was one. They were part of the scenery, the background, more like lampposts or hydrants—or wallpaper, if they were there inside your own house—than those few individuals who were truly vivid to her.

Uncle's gentle rebuke of Esther, Maudie could tell, was out of respect for Mama and her choices. Maudie thought her lamppost comparison might not be so far off from Uncle's own when it came to Mr. Stokes, but Uncle was fair, never mean about anyone, not even a little. If he had any outlying moods it was only that he sometimes seemed sad. Maudie had been to his modest apartment numerous times, a place with just enough room for his piano and other essentials including a few framed photographs that she knew he treasured. Maudie always lingered before the one of the two people named Claude and Miriam Cartier, whom she knew had been Uncle's friends in Paris. She'd noticed that sadness in Uncle, particularly keen, when she'd asked him about that picture.

"Were they very close friends, Uncle?"

"Oh, yes, *Petite*. Dearest of the dear."

Daddy

Unlike Mama, Daddy had remarried. He lived in Ohio, and when Esther and Maudie were still small he brought his new wife out to New York to meet them. Her name was Miss Constance, and she gave them two little headbands onto which she had stitched a few limp silk flowers. Pink for Esther and blue for Maudie. Now Miss Constance had a baby girl, and Daddy had sent a snapshot of Miss Constance holding a bundle of frilly blankets, inside of which they could just make out a tiny sleeping face.

Two years ago, way before the baby was born, Esther and Maudie visited Ohio for three weeks, traveling alone on the train, since Mama had agreed with Daddy that they were old enough so long as they found colored families to sit near. The northern trains weren't segregated like they were in the southern states, but it was safer to stick with your own kind.

The girls said they liked Columbus when Daddy asked them. Esther was always interested in seeing new things, but to Maudie Columbus was disturbingly strange. The air smelled of sulfur when the wind blew one way, and of coal when it blew the other, and of something dank rising from the big river, the Scioto. ("Sy-Oh-to," Daddy corrected Esther, when she pronounced it wrong.) Just as alien was the smell inside the house, infused as it was with Miss Constance's perfume and whatever it was she put in with the laundry. This scent evoked a sharp ache in Maudie's chest each night when she laid her face against the pillowcase, since bedtime was when she most longed for home.

Miss Constance was nice to them, no denying that, though when she complimented the girls on their manners and their help in the kitchen her words seemed designed more to please Daddy than themselves. Esther thought Miss Constance doted on Daddy a little too much, and she made Maudie giggle when they went to bed each night, imitating the way Miss Constance fussed over Daddy's clothes and meals, brushing lint off his coat with a special roller and placing the cutlery and salt and pepper shakers just so by his plate.

"Oh Macon," Esther said one night when they got into bed, throwing an arm across her forehead in mock distress, "there's a mote of dust sitting on top of your head. Do let me comb it out for you!"

Maudie crumpled the edge of the blanket over her mouth to keep quiet. Then, recalling the basket of clean laundry she'd seen stationed by the ironing board, said, "I think she irons his underwear."

At home Mama had them iron their school clothes and Sunday dresses every week, four outfits each, to be hung up on wooden hangers in the closet every Saturday. Linens and other things were simply folded when dry, since Mama didn't think anyone should get too carried away with the ironing when there was so much else to do.

Esther was giggling, her face jammed into the pillow. Maudie said, "Maybe she even has special hangers for it." Esther squeezed the edges of the pillow up around her ears to stifle a shriek. Finally, she lifted her head, gasping for air. "Darn it, I need the toilet now. Come with me," and the two of them crept together down the dark hallway.

A few days later it was Saturday and Daddy took them to a fair where they rode a Ferris wheel and ate candied popcorn and watched while he shot a little rifle at a line of cardboard ducks in the penny arcade. Otherwise they wandered the neighborhood on their own or read on the porch, books they'd brought with them in their suitcases. A couple of times they played hopscotch with girls down the street, though Esther thought she was too old for it. The girls asked them why they talked so funny. Maudie had wondered the same about them, but she didn't say so. Clearly, she and Esther were the strangers there.

When they wrote letters to Mama, Maudie didn't say much, though she missed her terribly. She didn't know how to put that into words without looking like a baby. Mama expected her to be the big girl of twelve that she was, but she didn't feel big. Maudie barely knew who she was at all in Columbus, and if not for the steady presence of her sister she might have gone so far as to forget her own name.

Daddy was given to little lectures at suppertime. One night when the slippery green smell of the Scioto was especially strong and stole through the window screens to do battle with Miss Constance's perfume, he began asking the girls about their schooling. Esther, as usual, answered for them both, but Daddy was more focused on his message than their answers. He seized on words and phrases like "dedication" and "take care of business," intent on imparting another of his hard-won lessons from life. Maudie didn't easily follow. Her ears filled up too fast with his forceful presence, which, though not threatening, was disquieting.

"You take my word for it," he said, gesturing with his knife and fork in the air, cutting shapes into it when he wasn't cutting his meat. "You've got to be prepared for living in this world."

"You girls are lucky to have a father who cares for you so much," Miss Constance said later, while they helped her with the dishes and Daddy was in the living room reading the paper. And Esther and Maudie said, "Yes, Ma'am," as Mama had instructed. Daddy was such a different sort of person from Mama. He was all angles and edges, while Mama was made of curves and curlicues. Maudie had no recollection of them married, couldn't imagine it, and hadn't much to compare against the idea other than Mr. Stokes, who had a softer, if somewhat impenetrable manner.

Maudie wondered how she would feel, if her father were to die. She'd wondered it before, one night in particular, at home in bed after Mama had seen to it that she and Esther answered his latest letter, because she wasn't always sure if she loved him like she was supposed to. He was half a stranger to her after all. But the thought of him dying made her so sad that tears came up and dripped down onto her pillow. She thought then that it must be she did love him, even if it was in a different way than with Mama and Esther and Uncle. About them she never had to wonder.

For Esther, in regard to Daddy, it was different, Maudie knew. Esther had been four years old when Daddy went away, and Maudie sensed a hurt lodged inside her sister, somewhere deep down. Once long ago, Iona Sutherfield, one of Aunt Dolly's daughters, had accidentally knelt down on a sewing needle that had been stuck in the floorboards. The needle had broken and half of it stuck inside Iona's knee, which, though terribly painful after Aunt Dolly had washed away the bit of blood, was invisible. For years afterward, Iona had a pain in her knee no one could find the source of, until one day the end of the needle made its way back up to the surface of Iona's skin and Aunt Dolly was able to pull it out with a tweezers. Esther's hurt was like that, Maudie thought. A thin spike of metal lodged in her sister's heart, invisible on the outside. It made Esther petulant with Daddy, because he couldn't see it and couldn't fix it, and it sometimes, every little once in a while, made her mean. At those times that stuck metal flickered in her eyes and she might call another girl—a classmate or someone from church—a name behind her back. *Odious, Odiferous, Superfluous,* long words she favored as insults. Even *Eponymous,* which happened once and made Maudie laugh, because it made no sense.

The night she imagined Daddy dying, she'd heard Esther yawn, still awake, and Maudie whispered, "Esther, do you love Daddy?"

Esther didn't answer right away, and Maudie sensed her tense. When she spoke, it was with a forced casualness. "Course I do."

Maudie sensed she shouldn't probe further, not right then at least, but she was suddenly desperate to know.

"Do you love him like you do Mama?"

The bedclothes rustled as Esther turned to face the wall.

"Don't be stupid."

✦ ✦ ✦ ✦ ✦

On the train home from Columbus that summer two years ago, Maudie and Esther filled the long hours rereading the books they'd brought with them. Esther read intently as she always did but Maudie looked up often to gaze out the window at nothing special. The vague dread she'd had on the way to Columbus was now replaced with a quiet exaltation. They were going home to Mama, to where Maudie felt safe and real and sparkly as drugstore fizzy water, and where she could sit at her desk in her own room and commune with her colors.

Miz Anna Paraibel

Two Saturdays after Mama's meeting with the school principal, Uncle came for dinner. He was supposed to bring the famous Miz Paraibel but he arrived at the door he with a tall, thin man, dressed in a light gray linen suit and matching felt hat. The hat had an audacious purple band, the same color as the silk cravat around his neck, and the brim hid his eyes until he was well indoors, greeting Mama and Esther with a bow. Mr. Stokes was there too, and he shook the stranger's hand, saying, "How do you do?"

Maudie saw it all occur as she slowly crossed the parlor, her bare feet silent on the carpet. Esther had already received a European-style kiss on both cheeks from Uncle's friend when she saw Maudie coming and grabbed her hand. Leaning close to her ear, Esther said, "You'll never guess who that is," then pulled her over to the cluster of people still hovering by the door.

"Maudie," Uncle Gerard said, "meet Miz Anna Paraibel."

The man doffed his hat, revealing hair just long enough to be knotted in a tight bun on the crown of the head, black but streaked with much silver, and the contours of what was, after all, a woman's face. And a striking face it was too—wide, slanting eyes with curled lashes, prominent, regal cheekbones, and full, curving lips that, when smiling, showed more white teeth than Maudie might have expected. Three or four of those teeth were capped in gold, and they shone against the deep darkness of the still taut skin.

"My little artist," Miz Paraibel said in a resonant voice with a French-sounding accent, and she kissed Maudie twice, as she had done with Esther.

Maudie, speechless, caught a look from Mama, prompting her to remember her manners, and she managed to whisper, "How do you do?"

Miz Paraibel nodded, her head askance. "I am well, thank you. Your Uncle Gerard has told me so much about all of you. I feel as though we are already good friends."

Mama said, "We feel the same, Miz Paraibel." Then she had Uncle and Mr. Stokes pull the table to the middle of the room and set the girls to laying out the dishes and cutlery, while Miz Paraibel drifted over to the piano to look over the framed photographs standing guard on its top.

Maudie sat entranced all through the meal, hardly tasting her food as Miz Paraibel recounted her train journey up from Florida, where she'd landed after the steamer from Veracruz. When Uncle interjected something—as he was always quick with a witty, mellow-toned comment—Miz Paraibel laughed loudly, her gold teeth flashing. She helped herself liberally to the butter in its dish in the center of the table, gesturing with the knife as it traveled back and forth between the many dinner rolls that disappeared between her words. Maudie grew less sure that Miz Paraibel really was a woman; she appeared so free, more like a man. The one most perplexed though was Mr. Stokes, whose facial expressions alternated between reluctant amusement and flat-out confusion.

When the meal concluded, with Miz Paraibel's many compliments to Mama on her roast and vegetables—she had not tasted glazed onions such as those since leaving Paris—their guest turned her penetrating eyes on Maudie.

"And so," she said, as if the subject had already been raised, "when will we see your pictures?"

Maudie sensed a funny sort of buzz strike her in the middle of her spine. She looked uncertainly at Mama, and then at Uncle—she hadn't expected this—but Mama nodded, and Uncle said, "I'll go along."

Upstairs in the girls' bedroom Maudie knelt by her bed, withdrawing from beneath it a large, haphazard, stack of colorful pictures and set them down on her desk. Uncle switched on the reading lamp, the light splaying over the surface, and Miz Paraibel stood beside him. She lingered over each drawing, making low sounds in her throat, and then, tracing her long fingers down an edge, moved on to the next one in the stack. Uncle Gerard stood beside her, answering Miz Paraibel's murmurs in French with simple *Oui*'s and *Non*'s. Maudie sat on the bed with her hands tucked under her thighs, the buzz in her spine making its way into the pit of her stomach.

Adults didn't normally see her pictures, in fact almost no one did. Esther saw them from time to time, as she came and went in their room while Maudie was drawing. And sometimes Mama, and she only said that Maudie ought to put them away and get to her schoolwork. Once Mr. Sanderson had seen her at work on a picture in the parlor and he'd nodded approvingly. "This child," he'd said to Mama, "might turn out to be a painter, after all."

Abruptly, Miz Paraibel turned to Maudie and said, "Tell me about this one, *Chérie*."

Most of the picture was soaked in the mauve and red tones of the plush parlor sofa from downstairs. A curious figure in ghostly blue hovered over it in a reclining position, and underneath the sofa, just visible between its short wooden legs, crouched the blurred, furry shape of an orange cat.

"Oh," Maudie searched for the right words. "It's sort of a dream I had. I fell asleep in the parlor once and I thought there was a cat under the sofa."

"So, is this you?" asked Miz Paraibel, pointing to the figure in blue.

"It's how I feel. Sleeping," said Maudie, knowing it would sound foolish.

But Miz Paraibel murmured, "*Magnifique...*" and Uncle Gerard looked over at Maudie and winked. Maudie smiled uncertainly, pleased with the attention but not knowing if Mama would approve.

Maudie had long known that there were artists and that art was publicly displayed, even bought and sold, even celebrated. Mama had always taken her and Esther to museums and to Uncle Sandy's gallery when there was an opening. The times Mama had taken her and Esther to the Metropolitan, Maudie read all the names—the great masters and the lesser known painters—on the little brass plaques by every painting they saw, and at the gallery she caught glimpses of the artists that hung their work, but never had she ever imagined herself among their number. As Mama said, it was the rare person who became a real artist, particularly if one were colored, and more so if you were female. The important thing was to get your education, that's what would keep you safe. Once you were fourteen and no longer a child, as Maudie was, you had to think about your future.

Mama was downstairs with Esther washing the dishes. Maudie heard the clinking. She knew Mr. Stokes would be drying the plates with a soft towel, lost still in his confusion over the apparition that was Miz Paraibel, and the thought made her swallow down a giggle.

When the viewing was finished, Miz Paraibel waved her hand, a signal for Uncle Gerard to put the drawings away. He hefted the unwieldy stack toward Maudie and together they stowed it all back underneath the bed.

Miz Paraibel spent a long moment gazing upward, her arms folded over the lapels of her suit. At last she said, "Maudie *chérie*, you have real talent." She swept her arms out in such a way that Maudie thought she might start dancing, but instead Miz Paraibel sat beside her on the bed and took her hand. "You must pursue this. Promise me you will."

Maudie didn't quite know what she meant. In fact, she had very little idea, but she was ready to accept whatever it was Miz Paraibel was advising.

"Yes, Ma'am."

✦ ✦ ✦ ✦

Downstairs, Mama had set out the coffee things in the parlor. Esther and Maudie were allowed their cup, mostly milk, at which these days Esther bristled, since she was sixteen and not a child. But Mama ignored her and Esther knew better than to complain in front of company.

Mama served Mr. Stokes first, then Uncle, and then Miz Paraibel, who took her cup—three sugars, no cream—and saucer, leaning back on the sofa with a contented sigh. She crossed one long leg over the other, so that one foot stuck out about a mile into the air, and Maudie noticed her shoes for the first time—wingtips—and hearing a rattle of china from the direction of Mr. Stokes, perceived that he had just noticed them too. Mr. Stokes dug a finger into his collar to loosen his tie, his cup clinking once more in its saucer.

Mama was telling Uncle how Esther now had two jobs for the summer, as she would be minding the children of the neighbors three doors down and helping out at Ansons' little hardware store on Saturdays.

"And the lessons," Esther put in. She was very proud of having gotten her first pupils. Teaching piano was a family tradition.

"Oh?" said Uncle, and Mama filled in the details.

"And what are *your* plans, *Chère?*" Miz Paraibel asked, turning back toward Maudie, whose face heated up like a skillet. She had no plans.

"Well," Mama said, stirring sugar into her own coffee, "we're working on that."

"Gerard," Miz Paraibel said, crossing her legs in the other direction, practically waving one shining wingtip under the nose of Mr. Stokes, "why don't we take her with us? It's only a month." She looked again at Maudie. "Child, have you ever been in the mountains?"

Maudie shook her head, struggling. A sip of coffee-milk had suddenly gone down the wrong way, but Mama cut in. "Oh, no. I don't think—"

"Jeannette, why not?" Uncle's eyes lit up and he leaned forward. "Yes, why not? We'll have our days mostly free, she'd be looked after."

Mama's eyes widened and her brows drew together. She glanced around among the adults, quickly at Maudie, her lips pinched, then looked down into her coffee. "I suppose we may discuss it later."

Maudie saw Mama was unsettled by the idea, and perhaps she felt similarly herself. She'd never been away for as long as a month. But Uncle seemed excited. His descriptions of the mountains made them seem so fresh compared with the heat she knew would come in the summer, like a heavy coat she could never take off. Green slopes and blue skies burgeoned up in her mind's eye.

"Landscapes!" Miz Paraibel proclaimed, shocking Maudie back to the reality of the parlor. "We'll paint the landscapes."

"Why should *she* get to go?" said Esther frowning, the pride of the previous minutes dissolving into envy.

"Esther!" Mama cut her a look, and Esther said nothing more. Her pout was visible though, and threatened to bring another giggle out of Maudie.

"Everyone could use a little vacation, I think," Uncle Gerard said, looking from Mama to Maudie and back. "What do you say, *Petite?*"

Maudie nodded and smiled. "Yes, maybe I would like to go."

She could already see Miz Paraibel's landscapes.

Longbrook

Except for the now distant journey to Columbus, this was Maudie's only time away from home. A caravan of three automobiles brought the troupe and their gear northward along the shores of the Hudson, green as emeralds, and then veered northwest through rolling farmland and small towns with funny names like Hurleyville and Neversink. After these came the little roads scrunched between forested bends and into the mountains. Maudie sat in the rear of the car that Uncle was driving, her flowered, tapestry carpet bag at her feet and Mama's lunch basket on her lap with her face pressed against the little triangular window. The two adults beside her dozed, while Uncle chatted with Miz Paraibel in French in the front seat, but Maudie barely took notice of them. Outside the triangle of bluish glass lay another world, one with so much space it made her dizzy just to look at it.

In the end, it hadn't taken too long to convince Mama to let her go. School was out anyway and when Uncle suggested that Mama allowing a little space between her and Maudie would ease the built-up tensions, she had to agree. Mama had put her arm around Maudie and given her a squeeze. "I'll sure miss you though."

"I'll miss you too," Maudie said. "But I'll write you a lot of letters. And postcards!" She thought suddenly of all the picture postcards they had from distant places. "Uncle, have they got postcards up in the Catskills?"

"Only in every shop in every village," he said, laughing. And so, it was decided.

✦ ✦ ✦ ✦ ✦

Longbrook Resort was built up around a sparkling blue lake, with two dozen or so scattered bungalows, acres of sweet-smelling pine forest, and a large central lodge where the troupe would be performing. When they finally arrived, parking the cars near the bungalows where they would sleep, and Maudie's shoes touched the gravel drive, the first thing she noticed was the quiet. She set her things on the ground, listening to it. A light wind moved through the tops of the pines in a gentle shush, softening the far-off tweeting of unseen birds and muffling the voices of the troupe. After all the movement of the long ride, stillness reigned.

That first evening they had supper in a wide screened-in porch at the back of the lodge where Mrs. Peebles, the colored woman who cooked for the thirty or so employees, served meals at four long tables with benches. Mrs. Peebles, who wore an apron and headscarf, was small in stature and soft-spoken, returning the friendly greetings from the staff with a soft-pedal kind of smile as she bustled in and out of the kitchen with large dishes of stewed chicken and vegetables, pans of cornbread, and pitchers of cold tea.

It was still light when they finished but Maudie was especially tired, and though she didn't look forward to sleeping in an unfamiliar place she did long to lie down. She would share the bedroom of one of the staff bungalows with Miz Paraibel and Uncle would sleep in the front room on the pullout sofa. Maudie had unpacked most of her things before dinner, setting the items from her tapestry bag onto a shelf at the foot of the bed, and she had put one of her half dozen books next to the pillow on the bed, *The Member of the Wedding*, one of Esther's. Maybe Maudie was terrible for arranging words into compositions for school, but like the rest of her family she loved to read. Just now, though, she was too tired even for that.

After saying goodnight to the adults Maudie lay down in the bed, the net of springs groaning beneath the mattress. Uncle and Miz Paraibel were talking in low voices, in French again, in the front room, and she saw the shapes of Miz Paraibel's many garments hung on hangers about the room. The pillowcase was stiff against her cheek and smelled faintly of detergent, but it didn't make her homesick as much as she remembered Miss Contance's pillowcases had in Columbus. She thought of Mama and Esther, and how they must be going to bed now too. As she began to drift off she thought of her Crayola box at the foot of the bed, sitting atop the fresh new pad of paper Uncle had bought for her, with all her colors lined up inside as if in their own little beds, eager to sleep so that morning would arrive that much quicker.

Jasper

Maudie's shoes crunched over a mat of fallen brown pine needles, sending up a sweet, fragrant dust. A path wound around from the staff bungalows, into the trees and toward a side of the lake unused by the Longbrook guests. There, the forest ended on the edge of a little grassy knoll from which Maudie saw the dusty trough of a smaller path that cut down swiftly to the water into a sort of cove. A short distance to the right, the forest took over again and curved around to where a pile of rocks jutted out into the water, not far from a little floating dock. A ways out to the left lay piles of thin logs bleached by the summer sun, and a waving bed of lush green water plants. Uncle and Miz Paraibel and the rest of the troupe were back at the lodge rehearsing and Maudie had until the dinner bell to explore.

Reaching the lake she hunkered down at its edge. It was about four in the afternoon and the sun glittered off the water, it touched her cheeks like warm hands and the fresh, lake-smelling breeze toyed with the wisps of hair that had escaped her plaits. A few white clouds decorated the sky, a hawk with a red belly fought with the wind to cross it and small black birds darted around the edges of the trees. Every now and then, the quiet rush of wind carried the faint sounds of distant voices, or the far-off clinking from the kitchens where cooking for supper was already underway. Maudie thought of opening up her bag for her sketch pad and Crayolas—perhaps she could weigh down the paper with rocks—but she didn't make a move to; for now just being there was enough.

All of a sudden, a prickling sensation on the back of her neck made her stiffen and she looked around, seeing no one. But then she spotted a thin figure in silhouette a distance away, standing on the pile of rocks that jutted out into the lake from the forest. She stood up again and almost waved, but the figure swung its arms forward and dove into the water, reappearing after a moment next to the floating dock. It looked like a boy about her age. He scrambled up onto the dock, streaming water onto the boards, and stood with his hands on his narrow hips, gleaming like a wet brown seal in the sun.

He waved now and she returned his wave, and then he lifted his arms in the air, threw himself forward into a handstand and flipped over into the water with a big splash. Maudie giggled, covering her mouth with her hand, wondering if this show was for her, and she laughed again when the boy's head reappeared on the water's surface with a big smile showing two rows of white teeth.

He swam toward the beach. When he reached shallow water he stood, several yards from her. "Hello."

"Hello," Maudie said.

He sloshed out of the water and sat on the damp sand, hugging his knees.

"I ain't seen you before," the boy said, starting to shiver, goosebumps rising over his long arms and legs. "I'm Jasper. Jasper Johnson."

"Maudie Halvorsen."

"Did you all come with them musicians?" he asked. "You all don't look old enough to be a performer."

"I came with my uncle. He's one of them," she said.

"From New York City?" Jasper asked.

"Yes."

"You live there?"

"Uh huh."

"Oh," he said. "Yeah, well I know all about New York City. I used to live there too."

"That so?" Already this was the longest conversation Maudie had had with a boy since she could remember.

"Yeah," said Jasper. "Right next to the Statue of Liberty."

Maudie frowned, perplexed. No one lived next to the Statue of Liberty, but she nodded. "I see."

"You live near there?" he asked.

"No, I live in Harlem," Maudie said. "Sugar Hill. Close anyway."

Jasper nodded thoughtfully. He said he lived up at Longbrook because his momma worked there, but he attended school in the village and he aimed to move back to the city when he was old enough. "I've got lots of plans," he said. "I'm a businessman."

A businessman, wet and skinny, in a pair of torn short pants. Maudie ducked her head to hide her smile.

"The City is the place to go," he said.

"What kind of business is it?" Maudie asked. "Your business."

"Aw, I'm still working that out, but one day I'll make a lot of money."

Maudie, not knowing what to say next, chewed a thumbnail. Probably he'd get bored with her in another second or two and leave, but instead he shook the water off his hair and said, "I'm good in school. I have ambitions. You go to school?"

"I go to school," she said, swallowing at a sudden tightness in her throat.

"Like it?"

She shrugged, hoping he wouldn't ask her any more about it. Thankfully she was spared, because right then a woman's voice came through the trees, calling a single word several times. Maudie couldn't make it out, but the voice grew closer and finally she heard, "Clarence...?"

Jasper stood, cupped his hands around his mouth and yelled out, "Yay-ah!" He looked at Maudie, "Aw, I gotta go."

"That your momma?" Maudie asked.

"Mm hmm."

"Mrs. Peebles?"

Jasper kicked at the mud with a heel.

"She call you Clarence?" Maudie looked in the direction of the voice and then back at him. "I thought you said your name was Jasper." Clarence Peebles. He must have made up the last name too.

"Well..." he said, smiling big like before, showing both rows of teeth. "Well, that's my *other* name." He leapt up the path to the grassy knoll. "Nice to meet you Miss Maudie," he shouted from the top, then dashed away.

Landscapes

The next day while Maudie spent the morning wandering the environs again Miz Paraibel snored away until noon. When she rose, she bathed in the bungalow's little shower room and took her coffee from the tray Uncle brought up from the lodge. She sipped slowly, sprawling languidly in one of the lawn chairs balanced on the narrow porch where Maudie sat reading, legs swinging over the edge. Uncle took something wrapped in a napkin from his tray and laid it at Maudie's side. Ham sandwich. At last, Miz Paraibel patted her cheeks, donned the beige fedora with the purple band, and told Maudie to go get her drawing things.

Out on the grassy knoll by the lake, Maudie watched as Miz Paraibel set up the folding easel she'd managed to cram into the bottom of her trunk, unroll a large sheet of paper and pinned it to the back of the easel with metal clips from her paint box. Then she drew out a tube of cerulean blue and a thin brush and began swiping at the paper.

"Don't you sketch with pencil first, Miz Paraibel?" Maudie asked. The painters she had seen from Mr. Sanderson's gallery always used pencil or a thin charcoal to start.

"No, Child," Miz Paraibel said. "No time for that." She laid a few more lines on the paper and then took a big breath and gazed around. "Just look at all of this," she said, spreading her arms and pointing out with the paintbrush. "Just *feel* it. An artist must paint her emotions, her sensations. She *feels* the world, do you see? And then she paints it."

Maudie had never thought of it like that. In fact, she hadn't *thought* about drawing or painting much at all, it was just what she did. The paper, the colors, were like magnets that drew her to them, her hands longed for them and her pictures grew from there like long, lovely exhales. But now that Miz Paraibel said this, about feeling the world, perhaps it was so.

Once, at Mr. Sanderson's gallery, Maudie had heard him talking with one of the artists about perspective and proportion and a number of other such technical things that, as she listened gave her the sensation of tasting something bitter, like a syrup Mama had once given her when she was a little girl and ill with a sore throat. Mama had promised that the syrup would taste like cherries but when the hard, sharp flavor hit her tongue she spat it right out, and ever after there was a red stain on the floor.

This was not at all how she felt listening to Miz Paraibel, just the opposite. Sitting in the grass near the easel, all her senses melted deliciously together as the paper before her awaited her hand. Now and then while she worked Maudie looked up to see how Miz Paraibel's painting was coming along. The blue lines grew denser a few red ones joined them, and so far Maudie couldn't see anything recognizable. It wasn't so windy today, the heady smell of the sun-heated grass enveloped her in a warm pocket, and inside that her own picture was taking shape—mountains, sky, and the lake, with spirals of heat rising on the air that must be pink, because that was the feeling of them.

When by and by the sun had changed its position, Maudie heard footsteps behind them, and turning, saw Uncle Gerard coming up the path.

"How are the artists?" he said, smiling.

"We are well, thank you," Miz Paraibel said, winking at Maudie.

"It really looks that way." He leaned over Maudie's shoulder to gaze at her picture. "*Sensationnel!*" Then he turned back to Miz Paraibel. "Anna, it's time to set up. We've got to run through all this evening's numbers. Maudie, *petite*, what do you prefer to do? You want to come back with us?"

"I think I'll stay a little longer."

When the older people had gone, she left her things, including her shoes and stockings, on the grass and meandered down to the edge of the lake. She didn't think of bathing, but she held up her skirt and waded into the water, her toes sinking into the warm muck, minnows darting around her ankles. Maudie began to sing quietly one of her and Esther's favorite songs, "Lord, Don't Move the Mountain." She had a fine singing voice, having grown up with so much music, but she was shy with it. Esther sang quite a few solos in meetings of the Young People's Choir, but Maudie preferred to blend in. Such was her feeling when the sense of being watched suddenly came upon her again and she cut off the song.

Turning around she saw the boy, Jasper, or Clarence or whatever his name was, standing atop the knoll.

"Afternoon, Miss Maudie," he said, grinning, waving.

"Afternoon," she said, her face turning hot. She hoped he hadn't heard her singing. A moment later he was at her side, dry and dressed this time, in black trousers with red suspenders, and a gray shirt with the tails tucked in.

"Is that your pictures up there?"

"Yes."

"You didn't say you were a artist."

She smiled. "I like to draw."

"Is that what you aim to be? When you're grown? A artist?"

"I don't know."

"Do they let you study that in school? Down in the City?"

"Not much," she said, biting her lip. The image came to her of Mama's disappointed, frustrated face.

"Oh, I see," Jasper said. "Your momma's like mine. No excuses for not doing homework. And chores."

"I guess you're good at school," she said. He'd told her as much the day before.

"I ain't bad, especially at figuring. I'm a crackshot at figuring. That's important for a businessman."

He wasn't shy, that was for sure.

"Well, I'm not," Maudie said, surprising herself by saying it out loud. "They're going to hold me back to repeat the eighth grade. I guess it's because I'm simple." Shame set her face on fire as she said it, but she looked at Jasper, challenging him almost. He didn't turn away.

"Aw," he said. He shook his head. He bent down, picked up a stone and hurled it far out into the water, then looked at her, appraising. "You ain't simple," he said. "I know people, I can tell, you ain't that."

Maudie stayed quiet. After a minute, Jasper spoke again.

"Hey," he said, "are you afraid of heights?"

✦ ✦ ✦ ✦ ✦

It was cooler in the forest, the dense spruces shading the path, springy under their feet with layers and layers of needles. The sparser areas of white pines let in a cold breeze from higher up the mountains, and by the time the path had all but disappeared and Maudie doubted whether she should be going so far, Jasper stopped at the base of a particularly tall pine. He laid a hand on the bark, and said, "This one here is mine."

Maudie looked up from the wide base of the tree's craggy bark. Several widths of old boards were nailed there, a few feet up from the bottom, and more of them nailed higher up going right up the side, forming a crooked ladder that ended where the branches began.

"You built this?" Maudie asked, amazed.

"Yessir," Jasper said, "and I've climbed clear to the top. Want to try?"

Maudie hesitated. "I don't know." She'd been up a ladder before, but she'd never so much as climbed even a little tree.

"It's solid," Jasper said. "You scared?" He grinned again, twisting back and forth at the waist, his hands on his hips. "Look," he said, "I'll go first."

He sprang up, grasping the board that constituted the second rung, got his feet against the trunk and hoisted himself upward until he was climbing steadily. "See?" he called down. "It ain't hard."

Maudie put her hands on the first board and pulled, struggled with her feet for a minute, but there was no way. "I can't," she said. "I'm not used to climbing."

Jasper jumped down and brushed his hands off on his pants. He looked at her and at the tree and back. "Okay," he said. "Well, let's go back before you get in trouble."

Maudie flushed again. Not good at school, not good at climbing. She wasn't seeming too smart in front of her new friend, but she couldn't think of anything to do about it. Surely he'd get tired of her soon.

✦ ✦ ✦ ✦ ✦

But the next afternoon when Jasper found her by the lake he said he had something to show her. When they returned to his tree Maudie saw he'd nailed on several more boards lower down, and this time she was able to climb up after him.

She climbed slowly, so slow that she could no longer see him by the time she reached the lower branches where the boards stopped.

His voice called down, "You still coming?"

Maudie swallowed, making the mistake of looking down. The ground was dizzyingly far below and she clutched at the boards, sensing her knees weaken. "Naw," she said. She wasn't going any higher.

The next day Jasper showed up to see if Maudie wanted to try the tree again. This time, her palms blackened with pitch and bark dust, she made it past the boards to where the climbing was easier, among the branches. Soon they were so high up they could see for miles, and Maudie, breathless and half-terrified, felt the sway of the tree. The other trees were swaying too, like hairy green giants slow dancing to a mysterious song.

Jasper pointed out a tree nearby with bare, charred branches on one side. The top of the trunk stuck up at the sky like a naked, blackened arrow.

"That one got struck by lightning last summer," he said.

Maudie didn't know whether to believe him, this Jasper-Clarence, who claimed to have lived next to the Statue of Liberty and said he was already a businessman. But the tree did look burned. It was taller than the rest, and the only one that seemed to show any signs of fire.

"I found me some roasted squirrels down below there, afterward," he said. "And I ate them with mustard."

Maudie burst out laughing, and Jasper did too.

"Don't believe me?"

"No." Maudie laughed more.

And Jasper said, "Aw."

♦ ♦ ♦ ♦ ♦

By the end of Maudie's first week at Longbrook, the days had taken on a pleasant rhythm. After waking, she tiptoed past Miz Paraibel—sunken inside her cascade of blankets, black silk sleeping mask, and vault of loud snoring—washed up in the shower room, dressed, and then took her book out to the porch to wait for Uncle. The new sun hit the tops of the trees at that hour, turning them gold against the blue sky and setting the birds chirping and flitting to and fro. Everything else lay still in a peaceful shadow.

Uncle woke around nine. The troupe was up each night into the wee hours, playing the Longbrook stage and visiting other nearby resorts whose guests had an appetite for jazz, but Uncle always said he didn't need much sleep. Plus, he'd promised Mama that Maudie would be well-looked after and so they went to breakfast together at the back of the lodge, filling their plates with Mrs. Peebles' soft boiled eggs, pancakes or grits, rashers of bacon, and fresh fruit from the bowl on the sideboard. Most of the Longbrook staff had already eaten and gone by then, and after Maudie and Uncle had finished they got out the checkerboard or backgammon.

While they played, he told her anything funny or amusing from the night before that Uncle considered suitable for the retelling: the trombone player, Miss Hornby, had put her mouth to her instrument, sensed something peculiar, and spit out a live spider; a man from Syracuse had brought a bouquet of yellow roses for Miz Paraibel; one of the pedals on the piano had gotten stuck in the middle of a set and they'd had to send for the custodian for a can of oil, and to disguise what was going on with the repair Uncle had the rest of the musicians file out among the tables with their instruments. It had gone over so well with the crowd, the troupe was considering making it part of the regular show.

"Do you like it up here in the mountains, Maudie?" Uncle asked one morning, as they contemplated the checkerboard.

She nodded and smiled, "I like it so much."

He rested his chin on his clasped fingers. "What do you like best?"

Maudie let her mind go soft and easy, it helped her think. "I like the birds singing. And smelling the air in the morning." There was no better smell in the world, she knew now, than the earth and plants waking up, so cool and green and eager to warm. "And I like how if crumbs from breakfast fall onto the floor, you can just kick them into the cracks between the boards for the squirrels."

Uncle laughed out loud. He took out his handkerchief and dabbed at his eyes.

After a moment, he said, "And your landscapes? Are you enjoying those?" Of course she did, so very much. Her afternoons with Miz Paraibel, drawing and painting, and these mornings with Uncle, it was more than she could put into words. Then Uncle said, "Mrs. Peebles told me that you and her boy are getting to be friends."

Flames licked at Maudie's cheeks. Perhaps more than anything else here at Longbrook, Maudie looked forward each day to seeing her new friend. All the things that back home she despaired of ever being—a pleasing daughter, a real artist, a person with a friend—all these were easily had here. It was natural almost.

There was something more to her sense of being in the mountains that she didn't say. It was a feeling she got from the ground itself, the waving forest, the expanse of the lake and the quiet wind, as if an unseen presence supported her. It was not unlike working at Grand Papa Hig's old desk, but now it was a feeling spread wide and seemed to arrive from all directions. It was calm and warm and kept her company when she was alone.

"You know, *ma petite*," Uncle said, stirring sugar into a second cup of coffee, "some of us don't fit in the way that other folks do." His tone was casual, but he leaned forward and looked intently into her face.

"Artists?" Maudie felt gooseflesh prickle her arms.

"Yes," Uncle took a sip of coffee. "And others. People who don't fit in for other reasons."

Did Uncle feel like that? Like he didn't fit in? It was shocking to think he might. He was a grown-up, after all. Esther always called grown-ups the *masters of the universe*. She didn't dare ask him though, children weren't supposed to ask grown-ups such things.

"But being an artist, being different," Uncle went on, "that can be wonderful, as long as you find other people who understand."

✦ ✦ ✦ ✦ ✦

Maudie and Jasper were up in the tree again. Jasper had a long pine needle between his teeth and, having kicked off his shoes, swung his bare feet in the breezy air. Maudie was getting more comfortable with the height but didn't have his ease. She sat on a lower branch and hugged the trunk with one arm.

"You ever been fishing?" Jasper asked. "I go fishing out on the lake pretty regular. Mr. Vimont lets me take his rowboat." Mr. Vimont was the caretaker; a taciturn, silver-haired man Maudie had seen at mealtimes.

"Once with my daddy," Maudie said. "In Ohio. He took me and my sister." Maudie remembered the bucket of slippery flathead catfish they'd brought home that Miss Constance had fried for supper.

"My daddy used to take me out too," Jasper said, "but he died."

"Oh," Maudie sucked in her breath. "Oh, I'm sorry." She'd wondered if there was a Mr. Peebles and now she had the saddest answer. She didn't doubt the truth of it. Jasper's face was shadowed, a cloud obscuring his usual sun.

"I don't remember him a lot," Jasper said, by way of consolation. "I was only three. He worked on the Susquehanna Railroad and there was a accident and that was it."

She knew what living without a daddy was like, though it was easier for her than for Esther. But Daddy was still alive, even if he was far away, and that was completely different. She didn't know what losing a father entirely would do to a person, to a family. She looked up at Jasper's face, the feathery shadows of pine needles dancing over him every time there was a breeze. She thought she sensed a line of tension prickle at the top of his shoulders, buzzing like electricity.

"Do you miss him?"

He shrugged. He said he and his momma got along alright and it seemed he didn't want to linger on the subject. "We should go fishing tomorrow," he said. "No offense to Miss *Constance*, but my momma fries fish better than anyone."

Maudie laughed at the way he'd said the name, like Miss Constance smelled bad, and not just from too much perfume. "Alright."

Jasper plucked a long green needle from over his head and stuck it in his mouth alongside the other one. He gave Maudie a sideways look. "You got a beau back in New York City?"

"Naw."

"Why not?"

"Just don't. Why should I?"

"Well, 'cause you're real pretty."

Maudie had no idea how to answer and instead stared at a line of little black ants marching along a crack in the tree bark. After a moment or two she looked back at Jasper. "What should we do now?" she asked. "Dig for worms?"

Lightning

It was indeed curious, here in these mountains, by the lake that seemed to smile at her approach. She missed home, missed Mama and Esther, but it was a relief to be away from Mama's disapproval, out from under the shadow cast by the bright light of her sister, far from the fog of invisibility in which she moved at school.

One morning after breakfast and backgammon with Uncle Maudie drifted back to the bungalow to get her drawing things, but instead of heading back outside with them she found herself studying Miz Paraibel's costumes. There was one long dress in peacock-blue sequins she particularly admired, and another made of brightly colored strips of cloth that formed a bodice with rectangle shapes, and a long matching skirt. Opening her pad of paper she began to make a sketch, quickly becoming absorbed in the drawing until suddenly she heard, "Are you making a picture of my little rags, *Chérie?*"

Maudie started, unused to Miz Paraibel waking so early. "Oh, no, did I wake you?"

Miz Paraibel pushed her silk sleeping mask up to her forehead and sat up in the bed, leaning with her back to the wall. "No, no, the birds did that ages ago. I think they must have seen a hawk." She shifted a little, tucking the edges of the blankets around her middle. "Let me see your picture, won't you?"

Maudie turned the pad to face her. "Not a landscape this time."

"Yes, I see. *Très jolie.* But would you like to draw one of these on the model?"

"Oh, yes please!"

Miz Paraibel rose from the bed, slipped the sequined gown over her silk nightdress, and held out her arms in a statuesque pose.

"Miz Paraibel," said Maudie as she began to draw on a fresh sheet of paper, "where do your costumes come from?"

"Oh, so many places. My wardrobe is like my personal history book." She shook her arms a moment and then resumed her pose. "This one I got in Paris, don't you know. I traded one of my paintings for it, to a singer I admired, Gabrielle. She had too many dresses anyway, she was glad to be rid of it."

"What about that one?" Maudie asked, indicating the one with the bright stripes and rectangular bodice.

"Ah, that is from Mexico. I had it made just for me by the most charming little tailor, Enrique Buzón. I don't know how he ended up with a last name like that. It means *mailbox*." Maudie laughed and Miz Paraibel fixed her with a mock frown. "Now, now," she said. "Respect!"

"Yes, Ma'am."

Miz Paraibel wagged a long finger. "'*Oui, Madame.*'"

"*Oui, Madame,*" Maudie smiled and continued her drawing, another question formulating in her mind. "Were you always… I mean, did you always earn your living as an artist?"

"Yes and no. I mean, performing yes, always, and painting too, starting in Paris. But early on I became a collector and a private art dealer. I've a good head for business, and that has been a good portion of my income for years. It helps to have a variety of skills." She shifted her position. "Of course, when I was very young I had to do some terrible things to earn my daily bread. Like waitressing. You never saw a worse waitress. I spilled the soup, I mixed up the drinks, all night long it was *Je m'excuse, Monsieur!* and *Je vous demande pardon, Madame!* I got fired so many times it became a joke among my friends. They took bets on how long I'd last at any new place."

Maudie, entranced by Miz Paraibel's words, had momentarily stopped drawing. Miz Paraibel stepped over to look at the paper. "Yes, I think you've captured her," she said. "Would you like to try the other one?"

While she changed dresses, Maudie flipped the paper over to start another fresh sheet. When she and Esther were little they had loved to make paper dolls with changeable paper clothes they cut and colored for hours. Maudie wondered what it would be like to make costumes like Miz Paraibel's. She had made an apron in school the previous winter in Home Economics class, but that had been a lifeless endeavor, nothing like these vibrant garments.

Just then footsteps sounded outside on the bungalow porch, and a moment later Uncle's knock at the bedroom door.

Miz Paraibel, in the Mexican gown now, opened up. "*Bonjour.*"

"*Bonjour, Mademoiselles.*"

"*Bonjour, mon oncle*," Maudie said.

"Hey," Uncle said, reaching into his coat pocket. "Look what came."

Maudie's heart leapt. A letter from Mama. Just seeing Mama's even handwriting on the familiar blue stationery was reassuring. She smoothed the folded paper flat and read it through. "Mama's coming to visit on Sunday!" she said to Uncle and Miz Paraibel. "With Esther and Mr. Stokes."

"Happy news," Uncle smiled.

"We'll show her our landscapes," said Miz Paraibel.

Maudie folded the letter and carefully replaced it in its envelope. Today was Wednesday, four more sleeps until she'd see Mama. The bubbly feeling that came over her reminded her of being on the train home from Columbus two years ago. The closer they'd gotten to New York, the more often she'd checked the train schedule, finding their current spot among all those names and numbers lined up on the columns of heavy folded paper. Each time they passed a station the countdown to Mama was another notch closer.

"You look like you're waiting on Christmas," Esther had chided her. But then she'd leaned in and asked, "How many more?"

There was a schedule now, only it was the sunrises and sunsets and all the hours in between.

✦ ✦ ✦ ✦ ✦

When Sunday at last arrived, Maudie waited anxiously on the porch of the bungalow, failing to read the book she had open in her lap. Uncle had brought coffee for Miz Paraibel, who had, for the occasion, roused and dressed early. Mr. Stokes would be driving his purple-blue Pontiac Streamliner, while Mama fanned herself on the passenger side and Esther sat tucked in the back with the picnic baskets.

Just after ten o'clock, the low growl of an engine and crunch of gravel announced the arrival, the sunlight bouncing harshly off the Streamliner's polished exterior, which to Maudie had always thought looked like a big old metal eggplant. She jumped up and waved her arm. She couldn't see faces through the windows yet, the glare was too much, but a moment later there they were.

Maudie stepped slowly down from the porch and across the grass. She wanted to run to Mama, now emerging from the car in her rose-colored skirt suit, but she held back, her heart beating wildly and longing to see love in Mama's eyes. But she needn't have worried. Mama and Esther embraced her together, Mr. Stokes shook hands with Uncle and, gazing around, took his hat off to Miz Paraibel.

They spent a pleasant hour strolling about the place. Looking over the lake, Mama held Maudie's hand. "If this isn't Heaven," she exclaimed over the beauty that lay before them. "A treasure of this world." And when Mama said how she hoped this lovely respite from the city made Maudie feel fresh and that a new beginning was possible, something like a knotted shoestring in Maudie's heart pulled loose and she relaxed, thinking then that things might really turn out alright.

But the notion was short lived. As they sat, back at the bungalow, on the porch with cups of tea from Mrs. Peebles' kitchen, Mama once again looked grave. Mr. Stokes took a sip of tea and then cleared his throat as if beginning to speak, though it was Mama who did so.

"I've been thinking constantly," she began. She turned her cup around in its saucer. "Maudie, you are almost fifteen and your welfare is all that I have on my mind, and as you know I've been very worried about your schooling." She gave the cup another half turn. "I've spoken with your father and we have reached a decision."

Maudie started. What had her father to do with this? She looked over at Esther, but her sister's eyes were glued to the braided rug on the floor.

"I think," Mama continued, "that a change of environment might be the best thing for you. A new start, with perhaps stricter supervision than what I have been able to give."

A dreadful second of silence passed, and then Mama said, "It seems right," she said, "for you to go to your father. To spend the next school year with him in Columbus."

A blow to the stomach. Columbus? She choked, as if the floor and ceiling were suddenly collapsing around her.

Mama was sending her away.

This was far worse than she might have imagined. Esther was still staring at the rug, the dark colors of which now sickened Maudie's senses. They mocked her. Everything and everyone in the room were nothing more than accomplices in her betrayal. Vaguely, Maudie sensed movement around her, rustling, quiet footsteps. When she next looked up, she was alone with Mama. There was no one to defend her, no judge or jury. Indeed, the sentence had been meted out with no trial at all.

"Baby, don't take it so hard, please." Softer tones crept back into Mama's voice. She said Maudie would come home for Christmas and they would write and that it would be no more than one school year, but Maudie was deaf to it. An overwhelming desire to lie down and sleep came over her. Her eyelids drooped.

"Maudie…" Mama spoke her name but the sound reached her as if she were way down in the dark bottom of a well. Somewhere distant, up in the sky, the wavy image of Mama's face hovered, but they were so far apart now that Maudie couldn't answer.

Next she knew, Mama was gone and Esther was by her side, tears in her eyes though Maudie's eyes were dry. "I told her not to," Esther was saying, "but she's made up her mind. I don't know—" Esther trailed off, desperate. "I even asked her to let me go with you," she said, "but she wouldn't have it."

At last Maudie spoke, in a voice flat and strange. "It'll be alright," she said, as if to console her sister. "It'll be alright."

Mama and Esther and Mr. Stokes left in the evening, bound back to the city. Maudie was still down near the bottom of that well, alone and quiet, and far away. When the Streamliner rolled out of sight, she lay down on her bed where a heavy sleep covered her. She thought she heard Uncle come to ask if she would take any supper. She thought there was concern in his voice, and Miz Paraibel's too, but it may have been a dream.

✦ ✦ ✦ ✦ ✦

All the next day, Maudie stayed in that quiet place. The hope and the warmth that had permeated the recent days was gone. Uncle made sure she ate breakfast, though swallowing made little sense to her, and Miz Paraibel took her out to the lake. But Maudie's hands wouldn't pick up the colors. They stayed empty, the paper blank. When the tiny head of a daisy landed in her lap, she looked up and saw Jasper's uncertain smile. He picked up another daisy, looped its short stem around the flower, and then popped it off with an abrupt little slide. "Daisy shooter," he said, and filled up the lap of her dress with pretty white and yellow decapitations.

Maudie knew he was trying to cheer her, as had Uncle and Miz Paraibel, but they too floated far away, at the lip of the well while she was down below. The wind was kicking up now, and a gust blew so that one side of her hem folded over the daisies. Far out over the lake, the sky began to darken with clouds. Jasper looked around. "Might get a storm tonight," he said, but Maudie didn't reply. She just wanted to sleep again.

◆ ◆ ◆ ◆ ◆

A sound like a handful of gravel hit the window and woke Maudie from her troubled dreams. She sat up in the bed. Hard rain rattled the glass panes and made the thin wooden walls of the bungalow vibrate. Uncle and Miz Paraibel would be out, up at the lodge performing and she was all alone. Vaguely she remembered Uncle asking her if she would like him to stay with her, and she'd shaken her head no, and now abruptly Mama's awful words came back. Maudie clutched at her throat where a sandpapery dryness rasped from the inside. She needed water.

Pitching back the blankets, Maudie's feet met the cold floorboards. Jasper was right, there was a storm, and now she realized it had been knocking all night wanting to come in, or else wanting her to go out.

Who's that knocking at your door?
Jump now, jump now, right off the floor!

Maudie opened the door and stepped outside, the wind whipping her nightgown tight around her, swirling from her bare feet on up to her cold face, taking her plaits like little skipping ropes in teasing hands. They were gleeful, these dancing winds, a hundred playmates, a chorus of windy wet voices that shouted and whispered for her to follow them because it was time for a game in the forest. Thunder rumbled in the distance playing call and response across the mountains and Maudie began to run, stumbling in the dark, pine needles springy underfoot and sticking to her bare legs.

The first flash of lightning overhead shocked Maudie wider awake, illuminating for a split second a thousand shining threads of water in the crevices of tree trunks. She caught a tree in a hug, breathing hard until the thunderclap boomed, and then ran on further down the path. Minutes later another flash lit up the sky, and this time she remembered to count, as Mama once taught her and Esther to do.

"One… two… three…" she counted up to seven before the thunder boomed, meaning the lightning was seven miles away. But it was coming closer, it wanted to join in the game, more determined even than the dancing wind that so carelessly flung around the rain. Maudie's feet grazed the edges of the path and she staggered with her arms out from tree to tree, and when the next flash came she knew exactly where to go—to the tree laddered with boards, Jasper's climbing tree.

Another flash of lightning lit up the forest, the thunder coming at the count of five. It was catching up, but she had to stay ahead—it was a race now and she had to get to the tree first, and she began running again. She fell once, tripping over a tree root, but she kept on, and in the next flash of light her hands touched the sodden boards of Jasper's tree. The thunder came at three counts—she was still ahead of it.

It seemed the wind and rain came from all directions at once, pelting her back, her eyes, filling her ears and even her nostrils, making the ladder-boards slippery as she hoisted herself upward. Below the high shriek of the wind came the low tones of the tree trunk creaking. Feet stinging on the edges of the boards, wet nightgown clinging and protesting against her bending knees, she climbed higher. All at once one of the boards under her feet cracked and gave way, both legs lost for a moment in midair, her hands gripping mightily at two slick boards, lungs gasping for breath. She kept climbing, all the way to the lower branches of the tree. It was louder up there, with the rush of countless flailing branches shedding needles and twigs in the wet wind. She felt the sway of the trunk now, a dizzying back and forth, and the branches lashing to and fro as if trying to escape her hands.

Another lightning flash.

Maudie saw the fork of it crack the sky, and the thunder, right on its heels, broke so loud the sound penetrated her bones. But she kept climbing further, higher, she had to get up to the heart of the storm, right up into the sky. That was the way out, because if she got up there she'd never have to go to Ohio, never have the unbearable pain of leaving Mama.

The ladder-boards were far below and forgotten now, she was higher than she'd ever gone, past the thicker branches and into the thin ones that snapped and bent in her fingers. Flying needles stung her face, her eyes, cutting the air, hissing like angry cats.

An explosion of light erased the tree, erased the whole forest, the sound so loud it erased all sound. A scream tore her throat. A smell like hot metal seared into her brain. And then she knew she was falling.

An endless fall in silence, and everything was peace. It was a river of peace and she floated in it, sleeping.

She was all alone, and the she wasn't. She sensed a pair of arms, strong, warm, loving, taking her into an embrace she had known before. There was a shoulder and she laid her head down on it.

"Who are you?" Maudie asked.

And the voice said, "Don't you know me?"

"Grand Papa?"

"Yes, Baby."

Maudie felt her eyes close. She hummed a little song, a lullaby she used to know, and fell asleep again.

✦ ✦ ✦ ✦ ✦

Something jagged and hard struck her hip, tearing the skin. Wind hissed loud in her ears. She struggled back toward sleep, but she wet things whipping her from every side. There was no light anymore, just blackness and blinding rain.

She heard a voice, ragged, saying, "I've gotcha, I've gotcha," and then sobbing. It was Uncle's voice. Maudie wondered what had put so much pain in it.

Water struck her eyes, and the arms enfolded her, and Uncle said again, "I've gotcha," as if fulfilling a promise.

✦ ✦ ✦ ✦ ✦

There was darkness and sleep, and then voices, Uncle and Miz Paraibel and maybe Mrs. Peebles, but she couldn't rouse herself enough to open her eyes. She slept again, until she dreamt there was a bitter taste at her lips and a cat pawing at her arm, and then she woke enough to realize that someone had ahold of her wrist. With great effort she managed to open her eyes enough to see a dark-haired white man smelling of pomade sitting beside her in a chair studying a watch. Further back, two or three blurred figures stood in the doorway. She turned her face against the pillow and slept once again.

When Maudie next opened her eyes, the darkened windows had paled and all was quiet. A figure dozed in the chair that was now back against the wall. Or was it a pile of coats? She wasn't sure, but drifted off again, and then in the earliest light of the sun she saw it was Uncle.

Then Uncle was gone and the windows shone bright and blue, and another figure moved into the room, carrying a glass of water.

Mama.

Maudie turned her head slightly, preparing to speak, but as she did so a sharp pain seized her neck and shoulder, making her dizzy. And when she did whimper Mama's name, her tongue was heavy and slow. She tried to move again, but Mama came forward and said, "Hush, Baby," hurrying to set the glass on the night table.

"Don't try to talk now," Mama said. "The doctor's given you some medicine, and I'm here now. I'm—" But her voice broke off and she drew her hand back, covering her eyes.

✦ ✦ ✦ ✦ ✦

Maudie woke again. The thin rafters of the bungalow ceiling were there, dotted with their now-familiar knot holes. Miz Paraibel's long garments hung on the opposite wall, the late afternoon sun making the sequins glitter. She remembered seeing Mama and called out her name.

Mama appeared in the doorway. She sat on the bed with Maudie and put her cool, sweet-smelling hand to Maudie's forehead.

"Am I sick?" Maudie was waking more fully, but shreds of her dream still floating in her consciousness confused her. Grand Papa, a storm. She wanted to sit up, but everywhere was stiff and sore.

Mama told her to be still. "You had an accident," she said gently. And she said Maudie would have to rest for a while. The doctor had come and nothing was broken or burned, thank God.

Nothing burned. The storm and her running in the forest came rushing back. She'd wanted to touch the lightning and it hadn't reached her. Shame that she'd run off and relief that she was back flooded her equally, making a further mess of her face. She whispered, "I'm sorry."

"No," Mama wiped Maudie's tears and nose with a soft cloth, shaking her head. "No, Baby," she said. "I'm the one to be sorry." She touched Maudie's hand. "I'm the one to apologize. I pushed you too hard. I was wrong to do it."

Maudie wasn't sure she understood, but she heard the pain in Mama's voice and her own words rose up with great urgency. "Please, don't send me away."

"Maudie, I won't," Mama said. "I'm not letting you out of my sight for a good long time."

✦ ✦ ✦ ✦ ✦

The next days passed, filled with Mama's reassuring presence, more sleep, medicine, pots of warm soup in covered crockery, the pain lessening. Soon enough she was able to sit up in bed, then get to the toilet without help. One afternoon in the bungalow bedroom Miz Paraibel helped Maudie lay out her pictures to show

Mama. Mama gazed at one picture and then another, folding her arms and pinching her chin like she did at the art museum.

"They are beautiful, Maudie," she said. "And unique." She kissed the top of Maudie's head. "Like you, my rare flower."

Just then, Uncle tapped his knuckles on the doorframe.

"Maudie, the Peebles boy is outside. He's been asking after you every day, just as worried as the rest of us. You want to go say hello?"

Maudie looked at Mama. "Are my eyes puffy?"

Mama held Maudie's chin. "Not at all."

When Maudie went out to the porch, Jasper was several paces away pitching pine cones into the trees, and when he saw her he didn't smile as he usually did.

"You all feeling better now?" He kicked at another cone on the ground.

"Yeah, I'm a lot better." Embarrassed was what she mostly was.

"Well, I'm glad."

Something else occurred to Maudie now. "Did you—" she bit at her lip. "Did you get in trouble because of me? Because I climbed up your tree?"

Jasper shrugged and shook his head, which Maudie understood to mean that yes he had, but no he didn't mind. A little stab of shame got her in the chest and she was about to apologize when he said, "It don't matter. I shoulda taken it all down a while ago anyhow."

"I'll make it up to you," Maudie said, not knowing how that might be. But then she had an idea. "Wait one second."

She ducked inside and scooped up one of the drawings. It was one she'd done out by the lake, of a rowboat with an open bottom like a window into the depths of the water where a school of fish swam, and among them the dark purple figure of a boy.

When she gave it to Jasper he studied with a half-frown, half-smile. "That me?"

She nodded.

He laughed. "Aw."

Gnossiennes

"Maudie, hurry up before my arms go to sleep!" Esther called up the stairs from the parlor.

"Coming!"

It was autumn. Mama had taken Maudie back home with her and had written to Daddy telling him that plans had changed. She kept a watchful eye on Maudie but allowed her to come and go as she usually did, and even let her go with Miz Paraibel to Central Park to create more landscapes. When school started up Miz Paraibel returned to Mexico for the winter season, but not before gifting Maudie a watercolor set of her own.

Just now Maudie had gone upstairs to fetch her pin box, having run out of them downstairs. Picking up the tin from her desk, her eyes had lingered on Jasper's latest letter. She hadn't answered it yet, but she would as soon as she made a picture to go with it, with Miz Paraibel's watercolors.

Pin box in hand, she hurried back down to the parlor to where Esther was waiting, arms outstretched, as if preparing to fly. Uncle was at the piano playing Satie, the *Gnossiennes*, and it might have looked like Esther was frozen in the middle of a dance if not for the carefully cut swaths of fabric pinned together over her in a loose drape. This was the beginning of a Simple A-Line dress, Maudie's first assignment in the tailoring course she was taking after school.

It was October now, a Saturday afternoon, and the late sun slanted golden into the room, lighting each little pin on fire, and Maudie's nimble fingers drew them from the box and pressed them into the fabric in accordance with the notes from the piano. Mama was at the kitchen table marking a stack of her students' papers, no longer worried about Maudie's studies, or if she was she didn't let it show. They had agreed Maudie would repeat the eighth grade, which made her subjects a little easier, and this year Mama let her decide how much time to spend on her homework, only asking to see Maudie's assignments when she had them completed. For now, it was enough to get along.

When Maudie had finished with the pinning, Esther rushed off to Mama's room to look in the full-length mirror on the closet door, excited because if the dress turned out well she'd wear it to Iona Sutherfield's birthday party the following week. Maudie had had the wonderful idea to use the scraps to make a cloth flower for the lapel that Esther thought would make all the girls jealous.

Maudie stood still and closed her eyes a moment. The warm sun pooled around her feet in their spot on the carpet, notes of music alighting in her ears like little white butterflies. Each time their wings fluttered a new color showed itself. She opened her eyes. Uncle was looking at her over his shoulder. He'd promised to take Maudie and Esther to a matinee the next afternoon after church, a play written by his friend Mr. Edmonds. Mr. Edmonds was even going to meet them afterward at a bakery, to talk about the show.

Uncle winked, smiled, then turned back to the keyboard where his fingers played out the music of the composer he loved most. Maudie closed her eyes again, listening. Music was the color of time, that's what it was. Time's color. Pink morning, blue night, golden afternoon. Green, green forever.

Acknowledgments

Heartfelt thanks to Chris O'Connor, Asa O'Connor-Jaeckel, Leora Hoshall, Jo-ann Rosen, Louis Jaeckel, and Patricia Kidd for their generous support and keen editorial feedback; to Chris Wolfe and Josie Varda for their expertise in writing about music; to Holland Gidney for sharing her superpowers in grant-writing; to fellow authors Lisa Maas, Vanessa Winn, and Michelle Mulder, for offering guidance, support, and for sharing the journey; to Erika Lunder for professional guidance and myriad supports; and to Reagan Rothe and the team at Black Rose Writing for bringing this book into the world.

Utmost thanks to Nadine Ijaz and Philip Fitzgerald, for their crucial insight and guidance in regard to writing about race, culture, sexuality, and experience of oppression. Greatest thanks of all goes to the magnificent Neesa Sonoquie, my editorial Kung Fu master. This is our third book together, and I hope it's not the last.

About the Author

Jenny Jaeckel is the award-winning author and illustrator of several books including her novel *House of Rougeaux*—a companion book to *Boy, Falling*, a collection of illustrated short fiction entitled *For the Love of Meat*, and the graphic novel memoir *Spot 12: Five Months in the Neonatal ICU*. When not writing, Jaeckel works as an editor and translator. She lives in Victoria, British Columbia, with her family.

Note from the Author

Word-of-mouth is crucial for any author to succeed. If you enjoyed *Boy, Falling*, please leave a review online—anywhere you are able. Even if it's just a sentence or two. It would make all the difference and would be very much appreciated.

Thanks!
Jenny Jaeckel

Thank you so much for reading one of Jenny Jaeckel's novels. If you enjoyed the experience, please check out our recommended title for your next great read!

House of Rougeaux by Jenny Jaeckel

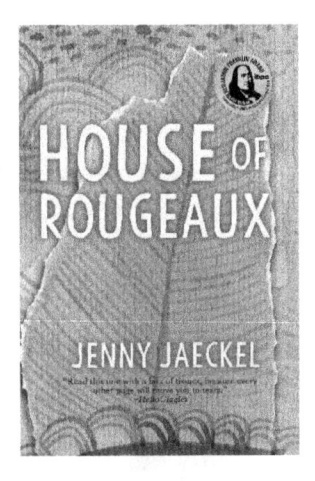

"Read this one with a box of tissues, because every other page will move you to tears."
-HelloGiggles

View other Black Rose Writing titles at www.blackrosewriting.com/books and use promo code **PRINT** to receive a **20% discount** when purchasing.

BLACK ROSE writing™

CPSIA information can be obtained
at www.ICGtesting.com
Printed in the USA
BVHW071351170621
609399BV00001B/14

9 781684 337194